CLOSE
MY
EYES

BOOKS BY BEVERLEY HARVEY

The Perfect Liar

CLOSE MY EYES

BEVERLEY HARVEY

bookouture

Published by Bookouture in 2021

An imprint of Storyfire Ltd.
Carmelite House
50 Victoria Embankment
London EC4Y 0DZ

www.bookouture.com

ISBN: 978-1-83888-959-3
eBook ISBN: 978-1-83888-958-6

THEN

Sweat from dancing combines with late-night mist, cooling her skin and causing the dress to stick to her thighs as she walks into the dark recesses of the garden, far from the music and laughter. Wary now and placing her feet carefully, she calls out, softly at first, then again –louder this time – her senses on high alert for signs of life. She pauses and holds her breath. Behind her, there's the crack of a twig under foot, a scuffle of movement, a sudden impact. Then, the feel of dew on the palms of her hands as she falls to the cool, damp earth.

CHAPTER ONE

Beth

The sweet scent of leylandii, like pine mixed with nutmeg, catches Beth's breath. Feeling her throat constrict, she wonders if she is allergic to its dense foliage as she brushes past on her way to the compost pile, cradling the plastic bowl filled with veg peelings.

It surprises her that the neighbours haven't complained. Mr and Mrs Henderson next door are almost as old as Beth's father, yet their garden is a vision of manicured perfection – due in no small part to a local firm who buzz, clip and hoe noisily once a month. The way her dad's hedge eclipses their dahlia patch must be a source of great irritation to them.

Braced against the October chill, she prods the rotting debris with a stick, adds the peelings to the mound and watches as steam curls into the fading light.

She looks back at the house, where her father's silhouette waves from the back door and her heart contracts. When she'd arrived at noon, there were wet trousers in the laundry basket. Another accident. Not that it matters – a spill of coffee, a dribble of wee, what difference does it make, once discreetly loaded into his old but reliable washing machine? How long though before Tim is unable to look after himself? Moving him to a care home is not an option.

Beth considers her own flat in Sydenham, opposite the park and the bus stop, with its year-round whiff of grass mixed with diesel. As modest as her home is, it is her sanctuary and the thought of selling it to live with her father for the rest of his days is not a happy one.

She walks back towards the house she was born in thirty-nine years ago and marvels that it's been in the family for so long. Detached houses in this leafy avenue are changing hands for unseemly sums these days. This one would too, despite its frayed condition and dated fixtures and fittings. Estate agents would call it a 'doer-upper', hoping to attract middle-class families with an eye for a bargain, fleeing inner London for a new life in the suburbs, perhaps to start or grow a family, just as her own parents had done all those years ago.

With an unexpected shiver, Beth looks back at the garden's gathering shadows and hurries inside.

At home, the odour of last night's fish and chips greets her – the result of leaving greasy paper and congealed scraps of batter in the kitchen bin overnight. Beth goes around turning on lamps and opening windows, letting the cold air rush in. After hauling the rubbish outside, she makes tea and settles in front of the television, a familiar crime drama flickering on the screen.

When her mobile phone buzzes from the coffee table, Beth realises that she's missed two texts. The first is from Alex. With a groan, she reaches for her reading glasses.

Beth, thinking of you and missing you terribly. Sending you all my love, always. Ax

Ignoring the nub of guilt forming in her chest, Beth sets the phone aside for a moment before remembering the second text. It's from Gemma, chatty and upbeat as always.

B, hope all ok at your dad's today? Don't forget Miya's Halloween play on Weds, then dinner at ours. Guy is making pumpkin soup! xx

Beth smiles at her friend's customary stream of emojis – on this occasion an entire line of pumpkins, ghosts and laughing faces.

After replying how much she's looking forward to seeing Miya as a witch's cat, Beth takes an open bottle of pinot grigio from the fridge and pours some into a glass. Shivering, she quickly closes the windows and sits down to focus on the frustrations of Detective Inspector Mellish, before realising that she's seen the episode. Reaching for her phone, she re-reads Alex's message.

She'd meant for things to be different this time. Alex is a good man, whom she liked. A lot. Certainly enough to sleep with him for the last six months. But recently, she'd seen the confusion and disappointment in his eyes… he could tell. Just like the others.

Beth reflects on the men in her life. Excluding playground crushes, there have been five boyfriends during her entire adult-hood. Proper grownup relationships, where there had been an expectation that things would 'go somewhere'. Yeah, she thinks wryly, like to the estate agents, to find a flat; then to Ikea, to load up with cheap, fashionable furniture; and finally, to church, to make solemn vows… It's enough to make her head spin.

Poor Alex. She hadn't meant to hurt him.

But the words he'd needed to hear had stuck in Beth's throat; words that came so easily to others. To her sister, Laura, who said *I love you* to her husband several times a day; to her best friends, Guy and Gemma, who said it all the time, and right in front of her. Sometimes, she'd hear teenagers in school uniform calling out *love ya* to each other as they got off the bus, before wending in opposite directions. And yet…

Once, when she and Alex had enjoyed a wonderful day out – a Saturday afternoon spent wandering around the Royal Academy, followed by a walk in Hyde Park eating warm, sticky crepes from waxed paper – in a moment of pure happiness, she'd almost said it then. Almost.

The acidity of the wine smacks the roof of her mouth. She considers opening another bottle, then thinks better of it. She'll need a clear head tomorrow for the Monday morning status meeting run by Nessa, who no doubt will be wearing the close-lipped smile she adopts during the frequent and sycophantic interjections by Ray. Creepy Ray, who smells of mints and carries a leather-bound notebook he never opens. Beth lives in hope that one day he'll leave and take his polos, his retro Filofax and his sanctimonious air to another charity.

*

'You're late,' Nessa snaps before Beth has even removed her coat.

She's about to explain how her train was delayed by some idiot roaming the line near Brockley when she catches the inappropriateness of it, given she's the press officer of a small mental health charity. She looks around and notes she is last to arrive. Not the best start to Monday morning. 'I'm sorry, Nessa. My train was a bit late. I'll make a point of getting in early tomorrow.'

Nessa nods, then hovers, her blonde eyebrows raised half-moons.

Beth does her best to look attentive, aware that she's probably missed something.

But Ray is on his feet, looking pleased with himself. 'Don't worry, Beth, I've just sent five copies to the printer.' He flashes her a smile that does not reach his small, mud-coloured eyes.

And then it dawns on her: it is her turn to print copies of the status report, ready for the 9.30 a.m. meeting. One glance at Ray tells Beth that her own fuzziness has made his day. She throws him a look, knowing that he'll revel in making her appear small and stupid until at least lunchtime.

Eventually, with the whole team of five huddled around two desks pushed together, which passes for a meeting area, the conversation gets underway as projects are updated, next steps decided, and tasks are assigned for the week ahead.

Beth looks round at the earnest, committed faces of her colleagues as they sit clutching mugs of instant coffee, some furiously scribbling notes. It is a quiet source of pleasure that apart from Ray, she genuinely enjoys the company of her workmates and would be content to sit in a bar and drink with any one of them. The accommodation could be better: two dusty rooms – one with a kettle and scant tea-making facilities in the corner – and a unisex loo, above a dry cleaner's in New Cross Gate is hardly the stuff of corporate dreams. Wages have been frozen for three years running and the hours can feel ceaseless in the winter, walking through South East London streets hollow with grime and shadows during her weekday commute of barely five miles. Nevertheless, there are days when the office is buzzing with life and energy, even triumph.

Beth rarely tells strangers that she works for a charity – and even less so that she works in mental health. It embarrasses her, the way people's expressions change, heads to one side with a barely perceptible nod, before gushing about 'giving back' or 'doing one's bit', as if she'd fished for their approval.

At the end of the meeting, Nessa steers her to one side. 'Beth, fancy popping out at lunchtime? I'd like to talk through this month's key messages on social media,' she says, her round eyes challenging Beth to refuse.

Hattie's Wholefoods is alive with hipsters and yummy mummies so slender they look as though they've never given birth. Nessa points out a quiet corner table and after a perfunctory glance at the familiar menu, they order quiche and salad from a teenager with pale green hair and a pierced eyebrow that looks perilously inflamed.

'God, poor thing. She should get that checked out for infection,' Nessa says, setting down her tablet and a handful of typed pages.

When their food arrives, Nessa puts her pen down and studies her colleague's face. 'Beth, are you all right? You look tired – and if I'm being honest, a bit sad,' she says, a furrow appearing between her brows.

Beth weighs up whether to invent something or to level with her boss. She opts for the latter, which seems easier, given that Nessa is big on honesty and that she's known her for years.

Beth nods. 'Yes, I'm fine. Alex and I have split up, but I'm okay. It was the right decision. He wanted things to move forward and I wasn't ready for anything more serious.' She takes a sip of apple juice and waits for Nessa's response.

'Oh no! Beth, that's awful. I'm so sorry... I thought you two were good together. I only met Alex a couple of times in the pub, but any fool could see he worships you. I'm guessing you don't feel the same?'

'No, I don't, and I can't imagine that changing any day soon. So, that's it, it's over.'

They eat in silence for a moment but thinking about Alex has wiped out Beth's appetite and the pie crust of her quiche turns to cardboard in her mouth.

'Look, tell me to mind my own business,' Nessa says, 'but haven't we been here before? Isn't this exactly what happened with you and Andy?'

Beth shakes her head. 'Andy was different. He wanted to get married and have kids, he was always putting pressure on me. It's just not for me...'

Nessa holds up a hand. 'You've got intimacy issues if you ask me,' she cuts in.

Beth checks herself. 'Maybe I have. Look, can we talk about something else, please?'

'Of course.' Nessa nods, firing up her iPad and getting down to business.

CHAPTER TWO

Gemma

Gemma removes three pins from between full, rose-pink lips. 'Miya, please, keep still – unless you want me to fix this tail to your actual bum.'

Miya giggles and continues shifting her weight from one foot to the other.

'Okay, take the whole thing off and I'll sew it up properly. While I do that you can watch TV in the sitting room, just until Daddy gets home, okay?'

Gemma helps Miya back into her jeans and stripey jumper and resumes sewing; tiny, neat stitches that soon transform a shop-bought catsuit into a bespoke, glittering Halloween costume. She's just tying off the last stitch when she hears Guy's car mount the drive, swiftly followed by his keys in the front door.

'Daddy!' shrieks Miya, skidding back into the kitchen in socks with Guy at her heels.

He dumps his briefcase on the kitchen floor. 'God, it's been a long day. Meeting after meeting, after bloody meeting!' He rakes back dark, collar-length curls, kisses Gemma and bends to hug Miya.

'What's for dinner, sexy?' Guy's hand grazes Gemma's behind.

'Fishcakes and salad – something quick because you're making soup.'

Guy's eyes widen. 'Am I?'

Incredulous, Gemma shakes her head. 'Yes. You promised Miya you'd carve a Jack-o'-lantern with her and make soup from the filling. We're supposed to be having it after the play. Did you forget?'

'I did, didn't I?' Guy grimaces. 'Sorry, love. I'm knackered, to be honest. Tell you what, I'll make something nice at the weekend, give you a night off.' He loosens his tie and goes out to the hall, returning shoeless. 'Have you heard from Beth? Is she still coming tomorrow?'

'Of course,' Gemma says, taking a bottle of sauvignon blanc from the fridge door, filling two glasses and handing one to her husband.

He takes a sip. 'Cheers, Gem. How was your day?'

'It was fine. I did an hour of Pilates at the gym, then I had a wash and blow-dry at the salon this afternoon.' Gemma swings a cascade of pearl-blonde waves for Guy's approval.

'Gorgeous,' he purrs.

'And since then,' Gemma continues, 'I've been trying to fix Miya's costume, but sewing's not exactly my thing.'

Gemma reaches for her handiwork and passes it to Guy. He smiles his approval. 'Looks really good to me, must have taken ages to stitch these sequins on.' He pulls his daughter to him. 'Hey, stinker, are you excited about the play tomorrow?'

'Yes, yes!' Miya wriggles free and begins to pogo up and down.

Huddled at one end of a dining table made for eight, Guy and Gemma swap news over Miya's head as the TV on the wall burbles in the background. It's almost eight o'clock by the time Gemma kisses her daughter goodnight. As she loads the dishwasher, she can hear Guy growling and play-fighting as he chases Miya upstairs.

He soon reappears. 'I didn't even get to the end of the chapter tonight. Bless her, she's exhausted.' He tops up their wine glasses.

'No wonder, she had rehearsals all afternoon,' Gemma says, scanning the kitchen with a critical eye for missed spills or crockery out of its correct place.

Guy steers Gemma out of the kitchen and towards the sofa. 'Come on, hon, let's relax a while, see if we can find something on the telly for an hour,' he says, grabbing the remote as he settles back against silk cushions with a sigh.

Gemma listens, alert to the snuffles and whinnies coming from her daughter's room, while the light click in Guy's breathing tells her that he too is asleep. Her hands travel over her toned body, pausing at her midriff. With a sense of satisfaction, she feels the hardness of her stomach, through buffed, silky smooth skin. Pleased that her gym sessions are paying off, her thoughts turn to the following evening.

Gemma pictures herself at the school, wedged between Guy and Beth, inhaling the dry odour of chalk and polish mixed with the sweetness of Pan Stik and hairspray as they wait, wired with anticipation for Miya's moment in the spotlight.

It pleases Gemma that Beth will be there. She imagines seeing her friend's serious face light up as Miya takes to the stage and performs her feline dance; the intensity of her dark-eyed gaze as she leans forward and absently tucks thick brown hair behind her ears for a clearer view.

Gemma wonders whether Alex will be there. Alex is rarely invited. To anything. Kept at arm's length in an awkward vacuum, somewhere between friend and lover, he is grudgingly wheeled out for kitchen suppers, pub quizzes and cinema dates – any occasion where it's necessary to even up the numbers. Poor Alex, destined only to be a plus-one.

Gemma stiffens as Guy – who has no time for Beth's would-be boyfriends – murmurs something in his sleep before turning over with a faint snore.

Guy has his own theories about the state of Beth's love life. 'Alex is a nice bloke, but he's all wrong for her. Beth can be a bit serious, can't she? Probably from hanging out with the do-gooders at work. What she needs is a good shag – someone to get all caveman on her, loosen her up a bit. It's funny, even when we were kids, all the boys fancied her – not that Beth noticed. It's because she's got that sexy librarian thing going on,' had been Guy's armchair analysis.

To Gemma's relief, Guy at least kept his opinions to himself. To her shame, his warm, easy friendship with Beth had bothered her once upon a time. Because even though Gemma was five years Beth's junior and would be considered beautiful in any context, the fact that Guy and Beth had grown up on the same suburban street, and that their parents had been close – their fathers spending hours on the golf course together, while their mums shopped for clothes and cooked elaborate suppers in matching spotless homes – had made her uncomfortable.

Guy had only scoffed. 'Oh, you needn't worry about Beth. I think the world of her but we're like brother and sister. I'm two years older than her and that's a chasm when you're a kid. We never so much as kissed behind the bike sheds. And anyway, she's not my type,' he'd concluded with a shake of his head as if the very idea were preposterous.

'Well, what about her sister, Laura?'

'What *about* Laura?' Guy had shrugged. 'She was in my year at school, but we were all just friends – and that was mostly because it suited our parents. Anyway, that was before I went off to do my exams at private school and got involved with a whole different crowd.'

Her curiosity satisfied, Gemma had let the subject drop and Beth had become an ally; a surrogate aunt and unofficial godmother to Miya and gradually a confidante to Gemma herself, despite being Guy's friend first.

Sleepless, Gemma reaches for her mobile on the bedside table and steals a look at the time: 01:20. She'll need a ton of concealer under her eyes tomorrow. In five hours, she and Guy will rise, shower and have coffee together before waking Miya at seven fifteen; a well-oiled routine.

Swinging long, tanned legs out of bed, Gemma pads to the bathroom. Goosebumps rise on her arms, a reminder that the heating went off hours ago. She pauses in front of the mirrored cabinet with its touch-sensitive light, then, feeling behind a clutch of jars and tubes, pulls out a slim box. Inside, three foil blister packs of tiny pills rustle. She considers liberating and swallowing one, recalling the warm, cossetted feeling that the Zammertil gives her on the brink of deep dreamless sleep.

She thinks back to how she'd weaned herself off them the minute Miya had started school and she'd begun to feel like herself again. She'd meant to throw them away or return them to the pharmacy. Yet something had prevented her. Because having a supply on hand 'just in case' felt like having her own secret safety net. And anyway, what harm could a mild tranquiliser do in the grand scheme of things?

Not that Guy would see it that way. He abhorred drugs of any description, regarding them as a sign of weakness.

'You're better off without that rubbish,' he'd said once Gemma had announced her intention to quit. 'I can't bear it when you're bombed out on pills – and anyway, you already drink too much. Not a good combination.'

Gemma considers the bottle of wine they'd drunk with dinner. In a few hours she'll be on the school run and, as fabulous as it is, her new white Range Rover will not drive itself.

She tucks the pills back into their hidey-hole and creeps back to bed.

CHAPTER THREE

Beth

Beth spots Guy and Gemma Ward before they see her. Under the harsh glare of the fluorescent lights and against the draining palette of the school corridor, the shadows under Gemma's eyes tell her she is tired. Nevertheless, the Wards shine like celebrities attending a red-carpet event; a golden couple out to get papped.

Guy sees her first and waves. Beth smiles, and starts threading her way through the throng of animated parents. Drawing closer, she can see that Gemma's smile is tight and wonders if they've argued in the car.

'Hi! Great to see you. Where is she?' Beth asks after kissing them both.

'Probably backstage wetting her little knickers,' Guy's voice booms to Gemma's obvious embarrassment. '*What?*' His wide brown eyes are innocent. 'She's nervous, isn't she?'

Gemma's expression softens. 'Oh Beth, you should have seen her this morning. She was up early, trying on her costume and practising her dance routine. Even with my crap sewing, she looked amazing.'

Beth smiles. 'Gemma, I hope you don't mind, I got Miya a little present – as it's her first proper school play.'

Guy rolls his eyes. 'Beth, you shouldn't spoil her. I don't want her getting a princess complex,' he admonishes, 'I get enough of that from her mother.' He cringes against a playful slap from Gemma.

Then a bell rings and a voice over the tannoy instructs everyone to enter the auditorium – the assembly hall on any other day – and the parents file into rows, the scraping of metal chair legs masked by the play's overture.

When the lights go down there's a ripple of throat-clearing and a flutter of programmes as the narrator takes to the stage: a witch-cum-fairy, dressed in voluminous layers of earth-coloured tulle, flanked by small goblins and something unfathomable which looks like a marrow.

'Or an anaemic butternut squash?' Gemma sniggers to Beth behind a cupped hand, her warm breath tickling Beth's ear.

Twenty minutes into the story, Miya pirouettes onto the stage when the witch-cum-fairy summons her familiar. Guy slams his hands together in a thunderclap. 'Go on, Miya,' he roars. Beth steals a look at Gemma's profile. Her blue eyes shine with tears.

At eight thirty, flushed and petulant with exhaustion, Miya is put to bed.

'I'll go – give you ladies a chance to catch up,' Guy says, half carrying his bleary-eyed daughter to her room.

Beth scans the kitchen. A hand-carved Jack-o'-lantern burns cheerfully on the granite-topped island and creepy candles, burned almost to stumps, form shadows that leap and dance on taupe walls.

'Guy's so good with her, Gem. You're the perfect family, you know that?'

Gemma doesn't answer, just strokes the stem of her glass and gives a funny little wobble of her head which Beth can't translate. 'Are you okay?' she adds.

Gemma's smile is a stretched grimace. 'Tired,' she sighs, 'I hardly slept last night. Think I got a bit stressed and excited for Miya. Bless her, she was so nervous… but it went okay, didn't it?'

'*Okay*? It was bloody fantastic – fabulous, in fact. Miya was the cutest kid on that stage by a country mile and her dance was flawless. I had a massive proud auntie moment. Dinner was wonderful, too. Guy's pumpkin soup was delicious.'

Gemma hoots with laughter. 'Yeah? That's probably because I made it after Guy forgot… which was fine.' She takes another sip of wine. 'You know, it was really kind of you to finish work early and make such a fuss of Miya.'

'I wouldn't miss it for the world. You three are as much family to me as Laura and the boys. Especially now.' Beth stops talking, realising that she hasn't told either Guy or Gemma about Alex.

'What? Tell me… what have I missed?' Gemma leans forward, her eyes sparkling in the candlelight.

'I didn't mention it because… no, honestly it's fine—'

'What is?' Gemma places her hand on Beth's forearm, her face a mask of concern.

'Alex and I have split up. It was overdue… he'd started talking about it being time we moved in together.'

'Oh, God, that's awful. I really thought you two might… might actually *go* somewhere,' Gemma says, looking cut-up.

'And that's just the problem, isn't it? I don't *want* things to go *anywhere*. Why can't couples just go out together, you know? Have nice meals and see great films and go to galleries and… and do cool stuff?'

Guy creeps in and looks from Gemma to Beth. 'Why do I get the feeling I've interrupted something?'

'Tell him,' Gemma urges.

'Oh, it's no big deal. It didn't work out with Alex and me, that's all.'

Guy purses his lips. 'Well, I can't say I'm surprised. The guy's a door-mat.'

'Guy!' Gemma cries, startled by her husband's candour.

Beth shrugs. 'It's fine, Guy's right. It's done now, and I feel good about my decision.'

Feeling suddenly tired, Beth gets up and starts casting around for her handbag. 'I need to get going. Thank you for a lovely evening, but we've all got to get up early in the morning.'

'Which reminds me, mind if I watch *Newsnight*?' Guy says, picking up the TV remote control and angling a stool towards the screen. 'Only I've got lunch with some eco journo tomorrow, to talk about how our company has almost eliminated plastic from our range of disposable coffee shop supplies. Then on Friday, I've got a radio interview in Tunbridge Wells; you'd be amazed by how often *Newsnight* is an icebreaker at these PR things.'

Gemma catches Beth's eye and winks. 'He laps up media attention, of course,' she says, loading the coffee machine with foil pods. 'Beth, are you sure I can't tempt you with coffee?'

'Of course, she'll stay for coffee,' Guy insists, before tuning out of the conversation and into the day's current affairs.

Beth returns the wink. 'Okay, just a small one,' she says, sitting down again.

CHAPTER FOUR

Gemma

Gemma checks her watch and sees that she is running late for Caleb, her new personal trainer. Today will be their first session together and arriving fifteen minutes late is, in Gemma's book, an inauspicious start. Regrettable as it is, it couldn't be helped – neither is it her fault.

At 9.15 a.m., the executive car booked for Guy's radio interview in Tunbridge Wells had failed to turn up. He'd been apoplectic, phoning his PA and calling her a moron, although he'd called back to apologise once the onus on the car company had been established, given that Martha was no more to blame for the car's no-show than Guy himself.

'Gemma, you'll just have to take me.' It had been an order, not a request.

'What? Can't you take the train?'

'There's no direct route from here and if one leg of the journey breaks down, I'll be late. I can't risk it,' Guy had answered hotly.

'But, darling, it's a three-hour round trip and I've got stuff to do.'

'Such as? Gemma, just once, I ask for your support. Just one fucking time. This interview is important. I'll be pitched against some bloody hemp-chewing, tree-hugging eco-type as well as the MP for Tunbridge Wells, who also happens to be Secretary of State for Business and Energy. I've done hours of research ahead of this thing and I simply will not cancel.'

'So why not just take your car? Why do you need me?' Gemma's voice had sounded small.

'For God's sake, Gemma! Because I'm up against it and I haven't got time to trawl around looking for a parking space when I get there. Look, the longer we stand here arguing the toss…'

So, Guy had driven in fractious semi-silence, station-surfing the radio and making hands-free calls to colleagues, and all the while driving just above the speed limit. Parking askew right outside the studio entrance, he'd leapt from the SUV with barely a wave, never mind a kiss or a *safe journey home, darling,* before passing through a revolving glass door.

Then Gemma had parked nearby and gone into a coffee shop to gather herself before getting back on the road.

At the recreation ground where they'd arranged to meet, Gemma spots Caleb in the car park, loading fitness equipment into the back of a Golf. He strides over, hand outstretched, smile on full beam.

'Hi. I thought you weren't coming,' he says, hauling weights and a balance ball back out of the car's boot.

Embarrassed, Gemma gives Caleb an edited summary of her morning.

'Don't worry, these things happen,' he says, pushing aside her apologies. 'Okay, let's get to work.'

Caleb is better looking than his website photo suggests, with Mediterranean colouring and thick lashes framing sea-green eyes that shine with good nutrition and vitality.

At first Gemma is shy and self-conscious, but before long, on a foam mat that buffers her from the damp November chill, Caleb is putting her through a tough, bootcamp routine of squats, lunges and burpees.

An hour later, cheeks flushed from exertion, and hair frizzed from the weather, Gemma feels energised and powerful.

'Well done, Gemma! Good work – you needed that, I can tell,' Caleb says, high-fiving her.

Gemma's breath is ragged. 'Thank you, that was hard work, but fabulous.' She pushes back damp hair, then leans into a stretch, breaking eye contact with Caleb and conceding that most women would find him attractive.

'Well… Okay, thanks again,' Gemma says, glancing at her watch. 'I need to pick my daughter up from school and I'm a bit tight for time. I'll sort out a bank transfer for you as soon as I get home.' She waves, striding towards her Range Rover. Glancing in her rear-view mirror as she pulls away, she can see Caleb still watching, his stance robust, arms crossed over his broad chest.

'Daddy's here!' Miya squeals, delighted to find her father sitting up at the breakfast island, drinking tea and munching toast.

'I didn't have time for lunch,' Guy grins, wiping a smear of butter from his chin.

Gemma leans in to kiss him. 'How'd the interview go? Were you happy with it?'

'It went well. Got my key messages across and a couple of good B2B plugs for our products. The car home arrived on time, and the driver was deeply apologetic about this morning. Sorry I was a bit crabby, Gem – and thanks for bailing me out. How was your day?'

Gemma watches Miya loading chocolate biscuits onto a saucer, her tongue protruding from the corner of her mouth.

'Okay, three is more than enough – seriously, Miya, I don't want you spoiling your dinner later. You can put the TV on if you want.' She turns back to Guy. 'It was fine. The traffic was light coming back from Tunbridge Wells and then I went straight to my new bootcamp.'

Guy makes a face. 'Bootcamp? Don't you think you do enough exercise already, what with the gym and running around after Miya?'

'I'm just trying something— I'm getting a bit low on motivation.'

'*Motivation?*' Guy echoes. 'Gemma, you're far too thin as it is, so either eat more food or take less exercise. It's a simple equation. Darling, you're fading away…' He walks across the room, scoops an arm around Gemma's waist and kisses her. 'Mmm. I like it when you're all sweaty,' he breathes into her ear, pinning her tight against him.

'I didn't know what time you'd be back. I was going to shower…'

'Well, not on my account,' Guy says, wiggling his eyebrows suggestively. 'Follow me upstairs – Miya will be fine for ten minutes,' he whispers, before sweeping out of the room and taking the stairs, two at a time.

Gemma chews her lip. Miya does indeed seem caught up with her programme. With a sinking feeling, she takes a deep breath and moves towards the stairs.

CHAPTER FIVE

Beth

Her dad's old Jaguar slumbers under a duvet of dust, tree sap and fallen leaves. By stark contrast, her sister's car – shiny and new – is parked across the drive. Beth makes a mental note to call a gardening firm; the last thing any of them needs is for her father to slip and fall on his way to the shops.

Laura opens the peeling front door before Beth can even insert her key. The boys' laughter bubbles out, followed by a gruff, jocular shout from their grandfather.

Beth hugs her sister, surprised she is first to arrive and wondering what condition Laura found the place in. 'Hello, love, you're early.'

'Beth. How are you? You look tired.'

Beth removes her padded jacket and drapes it over the newel post in the hallway.

She shrugs off Laura's concern. 'I'm fine. How are you? How are the boys?'

Laura rolls her eyes. 'Overstimulated after squash and dough-nuts – as you can hear.'

Beth follows her into the sitting room, where their father is perched on the edge of his armchair, watching Jack and Alfie ramming a chaotic stack of trucks and engines into each other on the olive carpet, their wet sugary lips mimicking explosions.

'Hey, Auntie Beth.' Alfie speaks first, but it is his older brother Jack who jumps up to kiss her hello. At eleven he looks embarrassed to be caught playing with toy vehicles; he rubs his left cheek, tells her sheepishly that Granddad wanted to see Alfie's new stuff.

Beth hugs her nephews, then bends to kiss her father whose eyes are full of merriment.

'Coffee?' Laura asks. 'I've brought lunch for us all, too – it's definitely my turn.'

Beth smiles. 'Thanks, love, that's great. I'll just pop upstairs, grab a few bits and put a wash on.'

Then she and Laura swarm their father's house, restoring warmth, order and a degree of cleanliness while the boys keep his rapt attention, boasting about their antics.

'I wish he'd sell this house and move somewhere bright and modern – not to mention easier to clean. It's ridiculous Dad living here all alone,' Laura says, slathering chicken joints with herbs, butter and olive oil before slamming them into the oven.

Beth sighs. It is the same conversation they've been having since their mum died five years earlier and their father's response is always the same: 'Why on earth would I move into a modern box? This is my home, all your mother's things are here – all our memories and treasures. You girls were born in this house.'

Despite several bin-bag laden trips to the Sue Ryder shop by Beth and Laura in the weeks following Jeanette's death, the master bedroom still harbours some of her clothes. In the wardrobe, their mum's best wool coat hangs beside a selection of evening wear – beaded dresses that shimmer and whisper to the touch, and an elegant velvet catsuit that neither Laura nor Beth can squeeze into. There are toiletries, too. Un-opened bottles of salon-brand shampoo and conditioner, scented body lotions and pots of face cream, and a half-used bottle of Guerlain's Shalimar which has darkened with age.

'Your mother was a very stylish woman – and always *so* feminine,' Tim remarks wistfully, whenever Beth or Laura deign to broach the subject. 'You girls could take a leaf out of her book, but it's all jeans and those ugly fleece things these days.'

Beth tries to picture her parents as others saw them. *A handsome couple* was how friends and neighbours would have described Timothy and Jeanette Harding in their heyday. Timothy – Tim to most – well-read, smart and in-the-know, was a successful photographer, a revered artform before the digital age robbed photography of its myths and mysteries. Jeanette: proud stay-at-home housewife and mother. Pillars of the community, the Hardings had been active in the local Rotary Club, had always given generously to charity and had supported friends and neighbours during illness or bereavement.

And yet, beneath Jeanette's decorously feminine exterior lurked something hard; peanut brittle beneath the cherry cup. Even now, Beth cannot remember her mother ever having said a single kind word to or about her, as if her younger daughter's very presence irritated her.

'Why *must* your hair be so *thick*?' she'd say, battling it into bobble-tied braids for school or roughly winding Beth's stubborn locks around heated curlers for special occasions. Meanwhile, Laura's hair, blonder, finer – and best of all in Jeanette's opinion, *cooperative* – was held up as a paragon of perfection.

At age twelve, Beth had asked for dance classes. Some of the girls in her year were doing modern jazz on Wednesday evenings in the Methodist church hall around the corner and for some reason it appealed far more than compulsory sports at school.

But her mother had scorned the idea. 'What, with your figure?' she had said, with a giddy little laugh, her eyes flicking to Beth's burgeoning breasts. 'I doubt the other girls have got *those* bouncing in the way.' And the subject had never come up again, not only because it was pointless trying to appeal to Jeanette once her mind was made up, but moreover because the following year, Beth suffered a bout of glandular fever that rendered her horizontal for weeks on end and physical exertion of any description became unthinkable.

The insistent bleep of the oven timer snaps Beth back to the present and she helps Laura ferry steaming Pyrex dishes to their childhood oak dining table.

It's only three thirty but already the light is fading and shadows loom.

'I'll wash, you dry,' Laura says, tossing a tea towel in Beth's direction. They stand, hip to hip, speaking in hushed tones. In the next room, subdued by food, Jack and Alfie are watching a programme about bats with Tim, who has an arm curled loosely around each of their shoulders.

Beth takes a deep breath. 'Laura, you might as well know. Alex and I have split up,' she says, bracing herself for her sister's reaction.

Laura's head snaps round, surprise registering on her face. 'Oh no. When?'

'A week ago. And it's fine, really. Look, please don't worry. I mean, it's not as though we were married or living together, is it?'

'I know, but you'd been together a while and we all liked him. Alex is lovely. So, what happened? Whose idea was it?'

'To end things?' Beth purses her lips. 'Mine, I suppose… Alex wanted more, I didn't. Honestly, I made the right decision and—'

She's interrupted by Jack skidding into the kitchen, demanding a cold drink.

'We need to talk properly about this,' Laura says, running the cold tap into a tumbler and dispatching her son back to the sitting room. 'Why don't we go for a drink later, just us?' Laura dries her hands carefully, rubs cream into them. 'But before that, I thought we could have a few fireworks as it's Bonfire Night in a couple of days!'

Beth's eyebrows shoot up. 'Really? Have you got it all organised? How are the two of us and Dad going to cope with lighting explosives in the back garden?' she says, shaking her head.

'All sorted,' Laura beams, 'Mike's on his way.'

*

The bonfire crackles in the darkness, a shower of sparks erupting from the blaze. Beth watches Michael, jabbing at the flames with a gnarly old rake of her dad's while Jack and Alfie look on in awe and delight from behind the cordon Laura has created with outstretched arms, her face a picture of pride and pleasure as she surveys her husband and sons.

Laura walks around to where Beth is standing, an arm linked through Tim's as he studies the leaping fire, wrapped up well against the cold.

'You're both very quiet,' Laura says, nudging Beth with her shoulder.

'We're mesmerised; it's impossible to look away,' Beth answers, gazing into the flames.

'We had wonderful firework parties when you girls were children,' Tim says, his face breaking into a faraway smile. 'All the neighbours would come, and school friends. We often had a house full of people. This garden has seen some life…' His eyes are glassy with emotion.

Beth and Laura exchange sad little smiles. 'That's right, Dad. You and Mum gave the best parties – you were known for it!' Laura says as Beth nods in agreement.

'Right, one more whirly thing, then we'll send the rockets up, okay kids?' Michael calls out above the spitting bonfire and walks over to where a Catherine wheel is nailed to the trunk of a bare cherry tree.

'Too close, boys,' Laura warns. 'Mike! Tell them to stand back a bit, we don't want any accidents.'

Beth squeezes her father's hand. 'Are you cold, Dad? I can go and fetch another layer if you like, although I think we're coming up to the finale.'

The smell of gunpowder hangs heavy now and the bonfire has lost some of its ferocity. Jack and Alfie are bickering, boasting about who can stand the loudest bangers.

'Well if it's *bangers* you want…' Mike plays to the gallery, swaggering to where three rockets are cued up. 'Ready lads?' Arm outstretched, taper in hand, he bends to light them. One, two, three: they fly up in quick succession as the boys shriek with excitement.

And just for a second, the children's delighted shouts, the glow of the flames and the smell of leylandii pull Beth back to another time, to something that happened long ago. Something dark and ugly, that causes an unexpected twist in her gut as it flickers at the edge of her memory before being snatched away at the speed of Mike's rockets.

CHAPTER SIX

Beth

It's over twenty years since Beth and Laura last set foot in the Ship Inn, but only the price of the drinks and the wallpaper have changed. The yellowing, faux-Edwardian chandelier still hangs in the centre of the lounge bar, there are dusty nylon flowers on the sills of the leaded windows, and through an arch, Beth can see a dartboard on the wall as men in trainers and denim jackets drink pints and jostle for their turn. Even the music seems dated as retro nineties pop and American rock anthems burst from the speakers.

Laura sighs. 'This place hasn't got any better, has it? Let's sit over there, away from the speakers so we can chat.'

They'd walked to the Ship from their father's house. Mike had offered to bundle the boys into the car in their PJs, pick the girls up when they were ready and deliver Beth to her own car, before going on home.

At the bar, Laura orders a Diet Coke for her sister and a gin and tonic for herself. 'Sorry, it's a bummer you're driving. Mike would have happily taken you home too,' she says.

Beth shakes her head. 'Thanks, Laur, but then I'd be without my car all week. I'm fine with this.' She raises her glass. 'Cheers.'

'Well?' Laura says, turning her blue eyes on her sister once they are seated in an area of relative privacy.

'Well what? Laura, I'm fine… I don't need to *talk* about anything,' Beth says, drawing air quotes with her index fingers.

'Darling, I'm worried about you. Do you think there's any chance you could patch things up with Alex? I mean, he's kind, reliable, good-looking and—'

'Laura, please… I know all that. Alex is great. But I don't love him. And yes, we could have gone on pleasantly enough for another six months, just going through the motions, but he wanted more. I don't. It wouldn't be fair to lead him on.'

Laura takes a sip of her drink. 'Sorry. It's only because I care about you. I'm your big sister, it's my job.'

Beth smiles and squeezes her sister's arm. 'I know, and I love you for that, but you honestly don't need to worry.'

'Good!' Laura grins and clinks Beth's glass, adding, 'Christ, what a dump this is. Why ever did we come here?'

Beth scans the room. 'Because they didn't ask for ID and it was so close we could stagger home and sneak in the back door once Mum and Dad had gone to bed. Plus it was easily the cheapest boozer in Beckenham.'

'Yeah, well, no wonder!' Laura laughs.

Beth is about to reply when the street door opens and two wirily built, sandy-haired men walk in, silencing her words and freezing her thoughts.

'You look like you've seen a—' Laura follows her gaze, lighting on the two men, who are identical in appearance except for the small variation in their clothes; they waste no time in ordering drinks from the smiling barmaid. There's a fumble with change as one of the men hunts through his jeans' pockets, and an exchange of banter and laughter before they move in the direction of the dartboard, where a volley of 'all rights' and 'hiya mates' ricochet around the room.

Laura speaks from the corner of her mouth. 'I don't believe it. That's Kevin Binks and his brother, isn't it?'

Beth nods, her mouth inexplicably dry. 'The Binks twins… of course. I recognised them straight away, but I'd never have remembered their names. Where are they from?'

'Seriously, you don't remember? They used to live at the far end of our road, on that estate where all the dodgy cars were parked, you know, the brown block of flats? Bloody hell, they look exactly the same, just older. And harder,' Laura says. 'I can't believe I actually went out with Kevin a couple of times.'

Beth only nods, unable to speak for the thumping of her heart and a sudden, urgent desire to escape.

She can see Laura watching her. 'What's the matter? Your colour has completely drained. Are you all right?'

Beth grips her glass, notices the tremor of her right hand.

Laura begins gathering up coats and handbags. 'Come on,' she says, 'I can see you're feeling rough. I hope I didn't poison everybody with the chicken earlier.'

Beth numbly gets to her feet, barely registering that Laura has draped her coat around her shoulders and threaded her handbag onto her arm before steering Beth out onto the street.

Beth takes a long, ragged breath as if surfacing from deep, icy water.

'I'll ring Mike,' Laura says, concern etched on her face.

Beth shakes her head. 'No, no need… the fresh air's good. Let's walk round to Dad's,' she wheezes, still breathless. 'You can call Mike en route, explain we're on our way back.'

They walk half a block in silence as Beth sucks cold air into her lungs until her breathing begins to return to its natural rhythm. 'Sorry we left so abruptly. I just felt really *odd* in there,' she says, her voice hoarse.

'Are you sure you're okay? You're still very pale. I hope you're not going down with something. Bloody norovirus usually hits about this time of year,' Laura says with a shudder.

'Well it's not that. Honestly, I feel okay… just a bit wobbly. Hey, when we get to Dad's, let's not disturb him, we can just go straight home.'

Laura nods, tucking her arm into her sister's. 'I don't need to call Mike – my car's still at Dad's, too. I only had one G&T and didn't finish that.'

By the time they reach number eight Fairlawns Way, the house is in darkness.

'Looks like Dad's gone to bed early, it's only quarter to nine,' Laura says as she and Beth stand looking up at the detached Edwardian house they were born in.

Beth smiles. 'Probably reading in bed. You know how Dad loves his books. Laur, I'm sorry about my funny turn and cutting the evening short.'

'Don't be. It'll do us good to get an early night,' Laura says, holding her arms out. As they say goodnight, Beth feels the fervour of her sister's hug.

With no traffic on the roads, Beth is home within fifteen minutes. A cup of tea and two bourbon biscuits later, she wearily gets into bed, expecting tiredness to overwhelm her. Instead, her thoughts keep returning to Kevin and Billy Binks, to the sight of them as they'd walked into the pub, like spectres from another dimension, still sporting identical haircuts and similar clothes. Just as they had done as teenagers, when they'd lived in the estate where men had tinkered with battered vehicles and dogs had barked night and day, only metres away from the other neat suburban homes, with their manicured gardens and shiny cars parked on well-swept driveways. Metres and yet a million miles, the Binks' world so far from the Hardings'; why then had their sudden appearance unnerved her so much?

CHAPTER SEVEN

Gemma

Gemma finds a lone pink sock at the bottom of the stairs. 'There's always one,' she mutters, picking it up and going to the utility room where the washing machine whirs with the second load of the day.

It's noon and already she has vacuumed the ground floor, dusted the sitting room and hallway, made the beds and cleaned two out of three bathrooms. The day yawns ahead of her.

In three hours, she'll be back behind the wheel and on the school run. Miya will do the funny little shimmy she always does when she first spots her mum at the school gates. There, Gemma will chat to Katya, Rosie and Lucy – beautiful but interchangeable women, all gym-honed, with expensively highlighted hair like her own and dressed in high-heeled boots and designer jeans, topped off with faux-fur-trimmed jackets, or cosy wool coats, their style more uniform than that of the children they are meeting.

She boils the kettle, makes herself a cup of lemon and ginger tea and carries it to the sitting room where she surfs the television for a while.

Her mobile phone shudders from the coffee table. Guy's name pulses on the screen.

'Hey, Gem. What are you up to?' Guy bellows before covering the mouthpiece and speaking to someone else.

'Hi, darling. Oh, you know… just the usual. Where are you? Sounds like you're outside.'

'I'm in Westminster with a couple of colleagues.' More muffled dialogue and a volley of car horns. 'Darling, I'll be late tonight… I should be back around ten, maybe later. I'll grab something on the hoof, so don't worry about supper. Kiss Miya for me… I've got to go, love you.'

'Okay, hon. Be careful out there,' Gemma says to the sound of the dialling tone.

At seven fifteen, the doorbell rings. Beth stands there, clutching a bottle of wine.

'Hi, Gemma. Are you okay, love? You sounded so flat on the phone.' Beth says, unwinding her woolly scarf and shedding her boots in the hallway. She follows Gemma into the kitchen where Miya is sitting up at the island, legs swinging from a high stool. She squeals at the sight of Beth and instantly launches into a story about one of her classmates getting a puppy.

Beth turns to Gemma and lowers her voice. 'Uh-oh. Do I hear the patter of tiny paws?'

Gemma shakes her head. 'Shh, don't give her ideas.' She turns to her daughter who has yet to draw breath. 'Miya, less talking, you need to *eat*. Come on, two more sticks of chicken, please.'

'Okay, but, Mummy, they're called goujons.'

The women exchange looks and stifle giggles.

Beth's expression grows serious. 'So why the SOS text? I mean, I wasn't doing anything else and you know I always love coming over…' She pauses and looks across at Miya who is plainly eavesdropping.

A furrow rumples Gemma's brow. 'Oh, I've just had one of those days, you know? Maybe I always feel a bit gloomy at this time of year.'

Gemma takes white wine from the fridge door and twists off the cap. 'This one's already cold,' she says, adding, 'ahh, my favourite sound,' as the wine glugs into two large glasses.

'Hey, that's plenty for me, I'm driving home, remember. Cheers!' Beth says, touching her glass to Gemma's.

Cosy in the kitchen on squashy sofas, Gemma can see Beth scrutinising her face.

'So, are you going to tell me what's up, or do I have to guess?' Beth says, right on cue.

Gemma shrugs. 'Nothing's *up*, I just can't seem to *grip* anything. I mean, I'm so lucky. Most women would kill for what I have… beautiful house, adorable child,' Gemma pauses, listening intently for sounds overhead, adding, 'Miya will sleep until morning – we won't hear a peep out of her,' before taking a long swallow of wine and refilling her glass.

'You left out handsome, successful husband,' Beth says.

Gemma scoffs. 'Who's often conspicuous by his absence and when he *is* here—' She bites her lip. 'Oh, God, listen to me… moan, moan, moan. Sorry, I just feel a bit… discombobulated, and sometimes I think, *is this it?* Is this what my life amounts to? The school run, shopping and cooking, going to the gym… Hey, did I tell you I've got a new personal trainer? He's called Caleb, and he's hardcore, but bloody brilliant. One of the mums at school recommended him.' Again, Gemma stops talking abruptly. 'I sound really spoilt, don't I?' She paces to the fridge and returns with another bottle. 'Okay, that's enough about me – I just need to get out more. What's your news, darling?'

Beth shakes her head. 'I don't have much. Work is… work, you know? Ray's been getting on my wick recently, but that's standard. Alex has left me a couple of mournful messages, guilt-tripping me, but I'm not at home to his passive-aggressive nonsense so

I haven't replied.' She pauses, swallows the last of her wine and studies Gemma's embroidered silk cushions. 'I saw Dad at the weekend as per. My sister and the boys were there. Mike joined us with some fireworks – which was lovely actually – and then I had a drink with Laura in one of our teenage haunts, but we left because I had a funny turn.'

Gemma frowns. 'What kind of funny turn?'

Beth shrugs. 'I don't know. It was so sudden. One minute we were chatting away and then the next, I felt dreadful. My heart was pounding, I felt sick, sweaty… It was scary to be honest.'

'Poor you, that sounds horrible. It could have been food poisoning. What had you eaten?'

'That's what Laura said… she made chicken for everyone at Dad's. But it wasn't that because it passed as soon as we left the pub.'

'Well, maybe it was just hot and airless in there. It's easy to get overwhelmed in bars and restaurants, especially in the winter. You walk in, all snug in a big coat and then the heating practically knocks you out! I wouldn't worry too much if I were you.'

The women look up as they hear the distinctive ticking sound of a taxi arriving.

Gemma jumps up, rakes back her hair, and finishes her wine in one swallow. 'Guy's back early,' she says before intercepting him in the hallway and putting a finger to her lips. 'Miya's asleep,' she mouths, offering her cheek and adding, 'and Beth's here.'

'Hello, lovely,' Guy says, mooching through to the kitchen and giving Beth a hug.

'I thought you said you'd be late.' Gemma watches Guy as he prowls the room, before opening the fridge and peering at its contents.

'I know, but we covered what we needed to so there was no need to stick around. I'm starving… I've only had a few nuts and olives. Have you girls eaten? Shall we get some takeaway? How are you, Beth?' Guy butterflies from one subject to the next, not waiting for answers.

'Darling, you said not to worry about supper. I can do you a cheese omelette or something…' Gemma opens a pan drawer, takes out a skillet.

Beth gathers up her handbag and car keys. 'I'll leave you to it,' she says with a wink, 'give you chance to catch up properly.' She hugs Gemma and pecks Guy on the cheek before heading to the front door.

Gemma walks Beth to her car. 'What a beautiful moon,' she says, looking up at the sky. 'Thanks for coming over tonight – and I'm sorry about the pity party. I've no right to complain, especially when *you're* the one going home to an empty house and getting up early for work tomorrow.' Gemma rolls her eyes. 'Hey, at least you won't have to start cooking when you get in!'

Beth shakes her head. 'Tell Guy to make his own sodding omelette.' She grins, unlocks her car and slides behind the wheel.

Gemma makes a face. 'What, and have him use every utensil in the house?' She waves until Beth is out of sight then turns back to the house, tension knotting her stomach.

CHAPTER EIGHT

Beth

It's almost ten when Beth arrives home. Ignoring the three items of junk mail that one of her neighbours has propped against her front door, she goes straight to the kitchen where she downs a glass of water standing at the sink.

She considers her visit to Guy and Gemma's. Why does she have the distinct impression that Gemma is keeping something from her? Something is clearly awry, because despite the picture-perfect image that Gemma so carefully cultivates, not for the first time, real sadness clouded her friend's eyes.

Watching her down at least a bottle of sauvignon blanc had been disconcerting and uncomfortable. Beth had had the distinct impression that Gemma had something to say – until Guy had bounced in demanding to be fed.

With a yawn that seems to ricochet around her whole body, Beth pushes away her nagging doubts and gets into bed.

In the morning, it's still dark when Beth leaves for the station. Following the vapour trail of her own breath, she cuts through the park where a handful of dog walkers wander silently, some of them dressed for the office and impatient for their pets to perform. She passes a couple of local drinkers, regulars she's begun to recognise, beer cans held to cracked, sore-covered lips, reserves protruding from ripped, stained pockets. She looks away, suffused with a vague sense of guilt.

Her train journey to the office is uneventful and when she arrives, the familiar smell of dry-cleaning fluid stings her sinuses as she takes the stairs to the first floor.

Ray is there already. 'Good morning, Beth,' he trills, insincerity leaking from his smile.

'Hi, Ray. Are we the only ones here?' Beth replies, glancing over at him.

'Yes, indeedy. *You* look nice today.'

Beth is taken aback. 'Thanks, Ray. Er… you too.'

She is spared having to make further small talk by the arrival of Nessa, Dominic and Claire, who appear to have all been on the same bus.

The day flies by, taken up mainly with the writing and distribution of two press releases in quick succession, part of a new project which Nessa has tasked Beth with leading and which she finds engrossing and enjoyable. The second of the two news releases, which is based on research linking chronic disability with mental illness, gains instant traction on social media, winning Nessa's approval at once.

'Well done, good work,' she calls through her open door, beaming in Beth's direction. 'I've just had a call from Sonya White, features editor at *Mind, Body & Spirit Journal*. We're getting a mention in the January issue. Can you knock up a full press pack and email it over as a PDF, please?'

A murmur of approval ripples around the room, bringing a flush to Beth's cheeks. Ray tries to hide his irritation but isn't quick enough. He says something to Claire from the corner of his mouth, but she frowns, moves away from him and towards the kettle.

'I'm making tea. Anyone else?' Claire pipes up pleasantly to a rousing chorus of 'yes please'. Then there's a groan of disappointment at the discovery they've run out of milk.

'I'll go to Benny's,' Beth offers, keen to take a breather and stretch her legs. She shrugs on her coat, feels the blast of cold air on the stairs and strides out onto pavements stained amber by streetlamps in the gathering dusk. A few youths in school uniform straggle along the high road, disappearing into shops for sweets and snacks. Opposite, Beth can see a short queue of people holding wire baskets at Benny's, the grocer's. To its right is the brightly lit betting shop, the cheerful array of sporting posters in its windows falsely alluding to something wholesome inside. To the left, draped dustsheets and stark plasterboard signal a shop refit as rap music vibrates within. Beth is about to dart across the road, when two men wearing work clothes and carrying tools emerge from the empty shop. Even under the streetlamps, Beth recognises Kevin and Billy Binks, their matching sunken, angular faces giving them away at once. Saliva pools in her mouth; she tries to swallow but her throat spasms and for a second, she is gasping, choking – not helped by the dry, musty smell which suddenly envelops her.

Lightheaded and trembling, she grips the dry cleaner's A-board for support, then watches in grim fascination as the twins begin loading tools into a van parked two doors down, before it disappears into the traffic.

Corrina from the dry cleaner's appears then, searching Beth's face and asking her if she is okay.

Beth tries to smile. 'I'm a bit dizzy,' she says, looking into the kind eyes of the young woman. 'Thanks though… I'm probably just hungry. I was going to Benny's for milk anyway – I'll get some chocolate while I'm there.'

Somehow, Beth had pulled herself together sufficiently to buy milk in Benny's, then back at the office, still shaking, she'd surprised Claire by heaping sugar into her mug, saying she felt tired and in need of a boost.

Now, sipping sweet tea, she is relieved to be back at her desk when Nessa wanders over.

'Beth, did that press pack go?' she asks.

'Yes – about half an hour ago. Is there anything else I can do for you?'

Nessa shakes her head. 'Cheers, but no. All under control.' She frowns and fixes her gaze on Beth. 'Hey, are you all right? Only you're terribly pale. I mean, I know it's November, but you look like you've seen a ghost.'

Beth hesitates, unsure how to answer. 'Actually, I'm not feeling great. Hope I'm not getting a bug.'

'Talk to me,' Nessa says with a look of consternation. She marches back to her office, signalling for Beth to follow. Once inside, Nessa shuts the door. 'Beth, go home. No offence, but you look bloody awful and I can't afford to have everyone off with flu,' she finishes with her usual customary honesty.

Beth tries to laugh off Nessa's concern. 'What? Well, none taken! Honestly, I'm okay. I might be a bit run down, though. I've had a couple of dizzy spells over the last few days. I might just get my blood pressure checked. Is it okay if I make a doctors' appointment?'

'Of course, Good idea. Better to be safe than sorry.'

Beth's usual ten-minute train ride home is almost doubled, thanks to a power outage at Forest Hill where her journey is halted. Standing on the platform, the cold bites through her padded jacket and despite woollen gloves, her fingers feel frozen and bloodless.

Eventually, Beth's train rattles in and she is back on the move. She distracts herself from the cold by focussing on something ordinary, comforting, like what she can heat up for dinner. Suddenly, all she can think about is devouring a steaming plate of winter stodge, like cottage pie or sausage and mash. Getting off at her usual station, she makes a short detour to her local Tesco Express.

Darting inside, she makes a beeline for the Ready Meals aisle, choosing cottage pie and grabbing a head of broccoli as an afterthought with the vague notion that anaemia could be her problem. Then she hurriedly pays at the self-checkout and briskly walks the couple of blocks home.

Once inside the flat, she cranks the heating up and turns on all her lamps to make the place more cheerful. Then she switches the TV on, nukes the cottage pie in the microwave and takes a tray to the sofa where she gratefully sinks back against the cushions.

The cottage pie is warm and comforting. She reflects on the day, which overall had gone well, winning Nessa's approval by gaining excellent online media coverage. And it had felt good, having everyone clap her on the back – until she'd gone out for milk and had clocked the Binks twins, working as shopfitters. Is *that* what they did these days; how the twins made their living?

And as soon as she'd seen the twins, instantly, something had shifted in her. A feeling of utter panic, which had almost knocked Beth off her feet as she'd fought for breath. And that *smell*. Dry and musty, like the motheaten fur stoles she and Laura had often seen in the junk shops and flea markets they'd trawled together during their brief vintage phase in their early twenties.

Had the smell been real or imagined? Spooked now, Beth carries her tray to the kitchen and boils the kettle for tea, keen to feel the comfort of her duvet around her.

CHAPTER NINE

Gemma

At the school gates, the usual suspects vie for pole position, keen to see and be seen. Today, Gemma is unwilling to stick around and chat about who has succumbed to Botox, lost five kilos or blown a stack on the latest must-have handbag.

Spotting Miya, she cuts through the other mums with a wave and a smile, grabs her daughter's hand and steers her back to the gleaming SUV.

'Sorry to rush you, sweet pea, but we've got people coming to the house tonight and Mummy has a lot to do.'

Miya pouts. 'What people?'

'Daddy's invited some business contacts round – important people. I've spent all day cooking and cleaning, pumpkin; please don't make a mess.'

In the rear-view mirror, Gemma watches Miya roll her eyes. 'Does that mean I'm going to bed early?'

'No, usual time, but you can watch TV in your room before then if you like, while Mummy makes dessert.'

By seven thirty, the kitchen resembles the set of *MasterChef*: blanched asparagus awaits a hot griddle, Gemma's homemade hollandaise is chilled to perfection and the warming scent of slow-cooked lamb wafts from the oven. Six portions of lovingly whipped chocolate mousse occupy the top shelf of the fridge, served in Gemma's best martini glasses. The champagne is on ice, and a fine bottle of Barolo is breathing in the decanter.

Candles flicker prettily and Guy's preferred chillout music pipes from the concealed speakers.

Shattered but with the satisfaction of a job well done, Gemma removes her apron, and checks her appearance in the hall mirror, smoothing down her black jersey dress and stepping into the high-heeled ankle boots that Guy likes to see her in.

Upstairs, a well-fed and watered Miya has brushed her hair and changed into PJs, ready to say goodnight and vanish for the evening.

Everything is perfect; Guy and his guests are due. Now she can only wait.

Gemma paces a worn circuit of oven to fridge to window and back again. Her scented candles are burning away, the lamb is beginning to dry out and the champagne no longer sits on ice, but bobs in chilled water.

Where the hell is Guy? Gemma dials his mobile number for the umpteenth time; her call goes straight to voicemail.

At nine fifteen the landline warbles. Finally.

Gemma runs to the phone. 'Hello?'

A rattling soundtrack of crockery, glassware, music and conversation greets her.

'Gem, darling! How are you?' Guy slurs.

'How *am* I? Guy, where the hell *are* you? Dinner is ruined!'

'Shit. I'm sorry, hon. We had a last-minute change of venue; it was just one of those things. We're still in the City, at the Shard—'

'Guy, if you knew how long I'd spent cooking and cleaning today—'

'*And?* You've got bugger all else to do, surely?'

'Well… what am I supposed to do with all the food? Jesus, what a waste!' Gemma fumes.

'For heaven's sake, Gemma! *I* don't know… bung it in the freezer? We'll eat it tomorrow instead. Trust you to make such a big deal out of things. I've got to go,' Guy says, ending the call.

All her effort, her attention to detail; all the money wasted in Waitrose and the smart delicatessen on Lordship Lane. Guy hadn't even sounded contrite. If anything, he'd been defensive and dismissive.

Heels clacking on the tiled floor, Gemma stalks over to the fridge and opens a bottle of sauvignon blanc. Still furious, she fills a large glass and drinks half of it without taking a breath.

'Screw you, Guy,' she says to no one, topping up her glass, mindless of her personal training session in the morning.

How dare Guy dismiss her efforts? When was the last time he'd made so much as a cup of *tea*, let alone cooked three courses from scratch, *after* spring-cleaning the house? Between gulps of wine, Gemma sets about rescuing as much of the food as possible, blows out the candles and disassembles her stylish table.

By the end of the bottle, she is like a toddler spent from a tantrum. She collapses on the sofa, still in her dress and tights, then picks up her mobile and sends a text to Caleb.

Looking forward to training tomorrow at 10.30. Bring it on. Gemma xx.

She presses send, then with a flash of horror, realises she has added kisses. It was automatic; she puts kisses on all her friends' texts. But Caleb is not a friend. He is someone Gemma pays, to challenge – no, *torture* – her body into the best shape she can be, and a young, good-looking and, as far as Gemma knows, *single* man at that.

When no reply arrives, Gemma begins to ruminate. Has Caleb blanked her, thinking her over-familiar? Has he in fact got a girlfriend, who has seen her text and misunderstood? Or is he merely tucked up in bed on a weeknight?

Realising that she's consumed nothing except an entire bottle of wine, Gemma fuzzily scrambles to her feet and goes to the fridge where she grabs a handful of asparagus spears before nuking them in the microwave and adding a glob of Hollandaise sauce.

Appetite well and truly stimulated, she tears off a chunk of black rye bread, then devours one perfect portion of chocolate mousse. After scraping the glass clean, she quickly consumes another, wiping her index finger round the rim.

'Mummy?' Miya is standing in the doorway, her face puffy with sleep. 'I need a drink…' She yawns, rubbing her eyes.

'Okay, sweet pea – but just water. You should be asleep. Come on, let's get you back to bed.'

Miya cocks her head to one side. 'Mummy, your hair's all fluffy, and why is your face red?'

'I fell asleep, pumpkin. Come on… it's late. Let's both go up to bed.'

'Where's Daddy?'

'You might well ask. He went out to dinner instead of bringing his work friends back here. It's okay, we can all have a nice lamb stew tomorrow night – Daddy, too.'

Gemma lies awake, heart-pounding, listening. If she concentrates, she can just hear the thrum of traffic from Lordship Lane and the occasional alarm bark of a fox. She is alert to every taxi that drives by within a mile radius. Where the hell is Guy?

Wine, sugar and rage ferment in Gemma's gut. She feels sick. Why did she drink so much? And eat two – *two* – desserts. She'll need to train doubly hard tomorrow morning with Caleb.

Jesus, Caleb! She'd signed her text with a kiss, without giving it a second thought. She signs all her texts that way. She plans to say as much in the morning – if she even makes it to their session. Perhaps her hangover will be too severe, in which case, she'll make an excuse: food poisoning, or car trouble, or—

For God's sake, go to sleep!

Gemma's bladder throbs. She sits up, reaches for her phone: almost two o'clock.

In the bathroom, alarmed by her deranged reflection, she splashes cool water on her face and reaches for the pot of so-called miracle night cream she's partial to. Her fingertips graze the pack of Zammertil.

'Avoid alcohol,' states the box in bold type. Would half a tablet be so bad, just to help her sleep?

Gemma stiffens. Through the open en suite door, she hears a car approach as headlights sweep the room.

Finally.

As angry as Gemma is, the last thing she needs is a confrontation. She slides the tablets back into place and creeps back to bed, ready to feign sleep until she hears Guy's soft, telltale snores.

Pale winter sunshine hits Gemma like a slap. Her eyelids feel scalded and stuck, her mouth is dry and from her chin down, nothing will move.

'Wow, this is some hangover.' She forms the words silently, unsure whether Guy is beside her or not. Swallowing the cotton wool in her mouth, she manages to sit up, noting the open drapes and the hot drink on the bedside table. Hands shaking, Gemma grips the steaming mug, raises it to her lips and takes a tiny sip. Nausea swishes in her stomach.

'Oh, so you've finally surfaced.' Guy peers round the door, his face a mask of disapproval. 'Jesus, Gem – I thought *I* was the one who had the late night.'

'What time is it? Where's Miya?'

'In registration by now, I imagine.' Guy's tone is imperious.

Gemma winces. 'No, no! How…? Guy – why didn't you wake me? Did you drive her?' Adrenaline finally propels Gemma out of bed.

'*Wake* you? I tried, Gemma, but it was like trying to raise the dead. I thought *I'd* be the one with a stinker of a hangover today. You should be more careful, mixing wine and pills like that. What if—'

Guy's words penetrate the fog. 'What? Why would you say that? I admit I had a few glasses of wine – I was upset after working so hard all day – but pills? I didn't take any.'

Guy's expression is glacial. 'Gemma, come on. You were out cold… The packet was still by the sink when I got home. I don't want drugs left around for Miya to find.'

'Guy, I didn't—'

Head and heart pounding, Gemma pulls on her dressing gown and heads into the bathroom where she peers into the cabinet. The Zammertil are in their rightful place but when she checks the blister pack, three are missing.

Stunned, Gemma dredges her memory. She remembers being furious with Guy for leaving her high and dry after more than a day spent cooking and cleaning; she remembers getting stuck into the white wine, then with a lurch of her stomach, recalls shovelling down two portions of dessert. But then Miya had come downstairs wanting a drink and at that point, they'd both gone to bed. Yes, it was all coming back to her… She'd tucked Miya in, then lain awake ruminating crossly and had *considered* taking half a Zammertil but then decided against it. Hadn't she? Yet three pills were missing. Three! She'd only ever taken one at a time and had always been careful not to mix them with alcohol.

She also remembers tucking the pack out of sight – mindful of a conversation like this. Only recently, she'd noted the foil card was almost full. Now three had gone and were unaccounted for.

With rising panic, Gemma turns the shower on, twists her hair into a loose knot and steps under the hot needles. Could she really have been so drunk as to mindlessly swallow three Zammertil? She breathes deeply in the steam, trying to slow her heart rate. Either she, or Guy, had made a mistake… a simple misunderstanding.

Showered and dressed in faded jeans and a taupe cashmere sweater, Gemma finds Guy sitting up at the breakfast island, sipping espresso.

'Are we going to talk about this?' he says.

Gemma fumes silently. 'Yes, let's. Guy, have you any idea how hard I worked yesterday? In the last couple of days, I've spent goodness knows how many hours shopping, cooking and cleaning and then you and your contacts just go AWOL. And all you seem bothered about is whether I took a sleeping pill or not.'

Guy purses his lips. 'Okay. You're right. But I didn't want to break the flow of the evening while it was all going so well. In fact, I think I got a very lucrative contract out of last night – I just need to get a couple of signatures. Gemma, surely even you can understand that all this,' he sweeps an arm around their kitchen, 'comes at a price.'

Gemma bites her lip, determined not to rise to his dig.

She shrugs and attempts a smile.

'Look, I'm sorry, I'll make it up to you,' Guy says, his face softening. 'In fact, why don't we go out for brunch? I can be late for once. We can catch up properly at Margo's on the high street and maybe talk about why you still feel the need for those bloody pills. I worry about you, Gemma – I really do.'

Gemma agrees, relieved to at least escape the house, if not another lecture. An hour later, sipping her second Americano, and queasily toying with smashed avocado on rye, Gemma realises she has missed her training session with Caleb.

CHAPTER TEN

Beth

One evening, two days after her sighting of the Binks brothers in New Cross, it had happened again. Beth had been ironing a work blouse with the TV on in the background, half listening to the cliched dialogue of a soap when she'd felt a sudden change in her heartbeat.

It had come out of nowhere and she'd been practically winded by the sensation of a weight pressing down on her. Oh, and that *smell*! The dry, musty odour of mangey fur that was becoming all too familiar – where *had* it come from?

Queasy and shaking, she'd collapsed on the sofa, and waited for the episode to pass. And it had, eventually. Just like the time in the pub with Laura, and again outside her office as she'd gone to buy milk, but this time, the toll of physical exhaustion had been harder to shake off, leaving Beth barely enough energy to unplug the iron before almost crawling to bed.

What the hell was happening to her? She'd heard how people who suffered from seizures sometimes experienced smells, sights and sounds that warned them of an impending attack. Was that what was happening to her?

Three strikes could not be ignored. Three instances where frightening physical changes had stopped Beth in her tracks. So far, she'd managed to keep herself safe, but what if her symptoms escalated? What if an episode occurred in public, while she was crossing the street, or while she was alone and vulnerable, taking a bath? It wasn't a massive leap to imagine herself falling and hitting her head.

At work she'd already mentioned seeing her GP after Nessa had remarked how pale and sickly she looked. But then feeling foolish and flaky, she'd pushed it to the back of her mind, until fear had driven her to book an appointment at the group practice around the corner from her flat.

When Beth enters the room, Dr Linda Johnson is scrolling through her medical history. She pushes square-rimmed glasses up through a thick auburn fringe and smiles.

'Hi, sit down, please. Have I seen you before? I don't think so… No, you last saw my colleague, Dr Nazir. What can I do for you today?' She crosses slim legs wrapped in opaque tights and looks at Beth intently.

Beth is unexpectedly emotional, a lump rising in her throat. 'I don't know why I'm here,' she says, her voice small.

'Take your time.'

Beth takes a deep breath and tries again. 'I think I may be suffering from anxiety.'

After a thorough examination, the fact that Dr Johnson had found no physical anomalies had offered no reassurance. Instead, she'd gently suggested that Beth might benefit from one of the *talking therapies* on offer by the local NHS Trust: specifically, CBT.

Beth had felt the room tilt and the rug slide beneath her feet. 'Cognitive behavioural therapy, yes, I know what it is.'

Then the doctor had explained how CBT could be useful in providing the tools to manage anxiety.

'I understand – I work for a mental health charity – but why now? I'm thirty-nine years old. Why would I suddenly turn into a quaking jelly?' *And why am I picking up phantom smells?* she'd wanted to add, keeping her thoughts to herself for fear of sounding unhinged.

Dr Johnson had nodded. 'Often there are triggers; underlying factors that you might not even be aware of. Beth, I'm not a psychiatrist – which is why I'm recommending you try counselling. Please, try to keep an open mind.'

Not feeling remotely soothed, Beth had left the surgery with a clutch of leaflets, and the promise of more information by post.

Now on pavements slick with rain, she walks the three blocks to her flat, wondering whether to tell her sister or not. It doesn't feel like a choice, given how close they are and the fact that Laura is her next of kin.

As she reaches her building, through the glass panel of the street door, Beth sees two of her neighbours chatting. Smile fixed in place, she breezes past and takes the stairs up to her flat, where despite the heating being on a timer, the air feels chilled. She turns up the thermostat and goes into the kitchen in search of supper.

There's little in the fridge except for a block of cheddar, some out-of-date salad and a low-fat chocolate mousse. With a jolt, Beth realises how poorly she's been looking after herself recently – certainly since the weird episodes started.

Well, it has to stop. Something terrifying and unpredictable is happening to her. A problem – a puzzle – that needs solving.

'*Keep an open mind*,' Dr Johnson had said. Beth goes to her handbag where the leaflets on CBT are stuffed into a side pocket. She takes them out, smooths down the paper and places them beside the kettle where they cannot be ignored.

The following morning, by eight o'clock the pavements are still wet, but the rain has stopped, and the sky is sliced with silver as daylight peaks through the clouds. Cutting through the park,

Beth feels a renewed sense of hope. These attacks are a blip that she needs to take charge of.

'Well? How did you get on last night?' Nessa hisses later, as the two of them stand beside the photocopier. Beth gives her a warning look and mouths *not here* as they move towards Nessa's glass partition.

Once inside, looking outwards, she can see Ray staring, his expression slack with curiosity, desperate to know what Beth and Nessa are talking about.

'So, I take it you saw your GP?' Nessa says. 'How did it go?'

'Blood pressure normal, urine normal, ears and eyes poked, stomach prodded – and I'm still none the wiser,' Beth shrugs, attempting to make light of the situation and wondering how much to spill.

'And…?'

'Okay, the thing is, everything points to the sudden onset of panic attacks and the doc recommends a course of CBT to break the cycle of whatever's going on with me. But, Nessa, I don't know… I mean, it probably won't even happen again, and the NHS is short enough on resources, without me—'

'Beth, stop it.' Nessa glares. 'Don't you dare. You've every right to use this service. Bloody hell, we all pay enough tax. Okay, so there's no quick fix, but you'll get there. The thing about anxiety is, one minute you're gliding along and everything's fine and then *bam*, something flips in your head and you're flat on your backside. Just do what you need to do. I worry about you and I want you back to your old self again.'

CHAPTER ELEVEN

Beth

Beth regards the bird-like woman standing before her; wide green eyes gaze back, framed by a thatch of ash-blonde hair.

'I'm Zara. Great to meet you, Beth. Please, sit down,' she says, her voice warmed by soft northern inflections. 'Do you mind if I record our sessions? I can assure you nobody will hear them except for me and my manager.'

Beth shakes her head, wondering what on earth she is doing here at five o'clock on a Thursday afternoon. She scans the magnolia walls; there's little to see, apart from a calendar depicting a snowy scene, a *Stop Smoking* poster and a dusty aspidistra in an ikat-painted pot, the room's most attractive feature apart from Zara herself.

There's form filling to be done, including a questionnaire containing a section on Beth's propensity to take her own life.

'Look, Zara, I'm really grateful and everything but I'm not sure your questionnaire applies to me. I'm not depressed… I've been having anxiety attacks and to be honest, each one is becoming more frightening.'

'Depression is a spectrum, Beth. The feelings of anxiety you've had recently are a symptom of something else, and it's my job to help you figure out what. Now, why don't we start with you telling me a bit about yourself.'

Beth rattles through the bones of her life, giving a textbook version of where she was born and bred, that she is currently single, and where she now lives and works – dry facts that sound dull even to her own ears.

Zara nods and writes something down. 'All right, are you able to share a bit about your family? Are your parents still alive?'

'My dad is. He still lives in Beckenham in the house I grew up in. We're close. I help him as much as I can. My mum died a few years ago from pancreatic cancer. It was very quick.'

'That must have been difficult for you, Beth. How did it make you feel?' Zara asks, holding her gaze.

Beth is surprised when her throat constricts, and tears spring into her eyes. 'It was worse for my sister, Laura. She was closer to Mum than me.'

'Don't underestimate your own grief, Beth – it is no less valid than your sister's. Tell me about Laura.'

Beth pictures two little girls in matching gingham sundresses and flip-flops, holding hands on the seafront at Broadstairs, and is flooded by a palpable sense of loss. Tears slide down her cheeks.

'I'm sorry. I don't know why I'm crying,' Beth takes a tissue from the box on Zara's desk and blots her eyes. 'Laura's great. I mean, we've always been close and I see her most weekends when we visit Dad. He's suddenly aged and can be a bit forgetful. We both worry… he rattles around that big house, flatly refusing to move somewhere more manageable.' The words tumble out as Zara listens intently, saying little but somehow conveying encouragement, before an alarm bleeps and Beth's first session is over.

When Beth arrives home to a ringing landline, she knows it is Laura before she even lifts the handset.

'How did the counselling go, love?' Laura says, getting straight to the point.

Beth starts to speak but then Laura is covering the mouthpiece with her hand and telling Alfie he's being 'too rough'. Beth sighs, waits for the kerfuffle to pass.

'Sorry. I'm back. Tell me what happened.'

'Nothing much, really. We just talked. Well, I talked. Zara, the therapist, hardly said a word. The weird thing is, Laur, I got upset talking about Mum and Dad… and you. I walked in there feeling okay, mouthing off about how I wasn't even depressed, but by the end of the session, I was in bits. I'm not sure counselling – or CBT when we come to it – is for me.' Beth shrugs her coat off, goes through to the kitchen and tucks the phone against her shoulder, leaving her hands free to put the kettle on.

'What did she say about the anxiety attacks?' Laura asks.

Beth drops a teabag into a mug and pours on boiling water. 'That's just it… nothing. She didn't even ask me about them. To be honest, it felt like a total waste of time.'

Laura scoffs. 'Beth, you've waited weeks to see this woman: the least you can do is to give her a chance! Some people are in therapy for years, trying to figure out their issues.'

'I haven't got issues!' Beth can hear the defensive edge to her voice. She goes to the fridge, finds milk and adds it to her mug, before taking a breath. 'Sorry, I know you're only looking out for me.'

A pause yawns across the line; Beth pictures her sister frowning and nibbling her thumbnail while she considers what to say next.

'What are you up to this weekend?' Laura says, changing the subject.

'I'll probably go to the pub after work tomorrow – just for a couple of drinks.' Beth blows on her tea. 'Then on Saturday I've got the Wards' Christmas party – which is always lovely and festive. I need to find something to wear… maybe I'll trawl the charity shops, see what I can find.'

Laura grunts. 'Oh, sod that. Treat yourself to something new. Beth, the Wards are well-connected, you never know who you'll meet there.'

Beth laughs. 'Maybe. Anyway, Laur, I'll be at Dad's on Sunday as usual. Might see you there, but don't worry if you can't make it; I know you've got the kids to sort. Speak soon, bye.'

*

It's almost six when Beth and Nessa join Claire, Ray and Dominic in the Bricklayers Arms, or the Brickie as it's known locally. In the fug of beer and sweat, the usual suspects crowd the bar: a blend of office staff, people from the housing estate nearby and construction workers passing through, keen to satisfy their thirst before heading home for the weekend. Multi-coloured fairy lights twinkle above the bar area and an artificial tree glitters, reminding Beth why the pub is extra crowded.

Earlier, as the others had begun packing up and tugging on jackets and scarves, Nessa had taken Beth aside, eager to know how her first counselling session had gone. Not for the first time, Beth had felt like a moth impaled on a pin. Other people's newfound interest in her wellbeing: it was exhausting! They meant to be kind of course, but sometimes caring seemed an awful lot like prying, and concern like curiosity.

'It was interesting,' Beth had said, unsure how to answer. 'I liked Zara the therapist... so you know, I'll stick with it.'

Nessa had attempted to dig deeper, but Beth had diverted the conversation elsewhere, hoping Nessa would get the message.

Now, sipping rhubarb and ginger gin and tonic, Beth soaks up the banter between Claire, Dominic and Ray, glad of their frivolity, and by their fourth round of drinks, even Nessa is giggly.

Beth peers around the packed pub and feels her head swim. 'Whoa, if I have one more drink, I'll need an escort to the loo,' she says standing carefully and mentally mapping her route.

Shouldering her bag, she weaves her way to the rear of the bar, which tonight seems thick with testosterone as mostly men crowd the area. Someone has put Thin Lizzy on the jukebox; it's a song Beth recognises despite it being released before she was born, and two or three men are good naturedly yelling along with the lyrics. Focussing ahead, she gingerly swerves the dartboard, wondering at its appeal and fascination.

In the ladies' room's tarnished mirror, Beth studies her reflection. The woman looking back at her is flushed with alcohol, her eyes shining. She musses her hair and rummages in her bag for lip gloss. Feeling uncharacteristically light-hearted, Beth pushes the door to re-enter the bar, but her path is blocked.

A sandy-haired man excuses himself, stepping out of her way. Beth moves past him and starts towards her friends, then looks up, straight into the pale eyes of one of the Binks brothers. Feeling her insides curdle, she tries to smile. At once she can see that he recognises her, too.

'Well, fuck me. I know you, don't I? Yeah, that's right… I used to live round the corner from you and your sister. You were in one of the posh houses – me and my brother were on the estate.' He bites his lower lip, drums two fingers on his forehead. 'No, don't tell me… it'll come to me. Laura!' Binks says, with a snap of his fingers and a look of triumph.

Beth's heart is hammering so loudly, she can only just hear Binks's banter. Feeling sweat trickle between her shoulder blades, she grips the jukebox for support.

'Yes, Laura's my sister,' she manages, her tongue feeling thick in her mouth.

'It's me. Kevin! Don't you remember? What's your name?' He shakes his head in frustration. 'Wait – I'll get it in a minute,' he says tapping his forehead again.

'Beth,' whispers a faraway voice that doesn't seem to belong to her.

'Yeah, of course,' Binks says, 'I remember now. Me and Billy gatecrashed your sister's fancy dress party once. Your folks were all right about it, nobody said nothing. Do you live this way? Me and Billy are still in Beckenham – not together, that'd be weird. We're shop-fitting on the high street, a few doors up,' he says, inclining his head. 'Good money, so it'll do.' Kevin's grin becomes wolfish. 'I see you turned out all right then… Yeah, nice – very nice indeed.'

Beth shudders as Binks's eyes drift over her body, lingering on her breasts before travelling the length of her legs which are tonight encased in tight-fitting jeans. Then it hits her: the same sour, musty odour that's been dogging her for weeks, and the shadow of a memory – vague, dreamlike and just beyond her grasp – slides into her mind but is gone just as quickly. Gripped by an ice-cold fear, for one terrible moment, she feels she could actually be sick—

'Well, say hello to your sister for me, yeah? I always fancied her, but we only went out a couple of times… She was way out of my league.' He laughs, a smoker's rattle born of a thirty-a-day habit. He continues to stare. 'Well, Beth,' he enunciates her name, as if to help him remember it, 'hope I'll see you around, yeah?'

Heart throbbing wildly and legs gelatinous, Beth teeters back to her colleagues. Claire looks up, frowns and asks if she's okay; she doesn't reply, just downs the last of her drink.

Then Nessa stands and threatens to leave, despite calls for one last round. Seeing her chance to escape, Beth shakily gets to her feet, and is vaguely aware of being hugged goodbye.

Outside the chilled December air hits her. She takes a long steadying breath.

Nessa's expression is a blend of amusement and concern. 'You okay? I hope they weren't doubles or we'll all have stinking hangovers tomorrow. Fancy sharing an Uber? I practically go past your place.'

Gliding through deserted south London streets, Beth barely registers the smell of fried food in the back of the cab – or Nessa's ramblings about her weekend plans. Instead, she replays the conversation with Kevin Binks, her tipsiness in the bar replaced now by a laser focus.

What the hell had gone on back there? Binks had been chatty – friendly, even – and yet, from the moment she'd seen him, his lean frame barring her route back to her friends, she'd felt utterly repelled. And not with the irritation or embarrassment she associated with running into an ex-boyfriend, or an old mate with whom she had nothing in common, but with something far more potent. Beth feels her pulse quicken and her mouth dry as a blast of adrenaline grips her: a feeling she recognises now as pure cold terror.

CHAPTER TWELVE

Gemma

By the first weekend in December, all eight houses in Darwin Drive were sparkling with Christmas decorations. Fairy lights twinkled from trees and window displays glittered seductively, hinting at the lavish celebrations within.

Gemma prides herself that her house – one of only two detached homes in a horseshoe of contemporary semis – is the most attractive of all. The centrepiece to Gemma's winter wonderland is the magnolia tree which sits squarely in the middle of the Wards' plot, and which every year is beaded with tiny white lights; Guy's sole physical contribution to the family's Christmas preparations. The lighting up of Guy and Gemma's magnolia tree is the cue for the neighbours to launch their own festivities.

Lighting-up weekend is also the precursor to another of Darwin Drive's traditions that takes place on the second Saturday of December: The Wards' Christmas Drinks Party.

Gemma takes a slow, steadying breath. Tomorrow her home will be filled with not only the residents of Darwin Drive, but at least a dozen acquaintances whom Guy deems it necessary to impress.

Gemma had challenged Guy the morning after a laborious trip to Waitrose that had taken almost twice as long as the weekly shop. 'Darling, I understand inviting all the neighbours, but why must we ask local business owners? Surely, they've got better things to do than hobnob over drinks.'

'Gemma, don't be so dense,' Guy had snapped. 'These people are useful contacts – not just in business but in *life*.'

Gemma had winced, wishing he'd stop alluding to how dim she is, which has become something of a mantra. 'I don't think you realise how much work goes into planning a party – even a small one – not to mention all the expense. Surely it should just be for friends, no?' she had sighed, wishing she could just run the vacuum round and offer the neighbours crisps and prosecco, and be done with it.

'Well, get some help then. Get a cleaner… whatever. Stop whining and just sort it!' Guy had barked, before leaving for work and slamming the front door behind him.

As if Gemma could have found a reliable cleaner at the drop of a hat! And anyway, she could never justify hiring one. After all, she doesn't work – not in the traditional sense of getting paid to be somewhere other than home – and Miya is hardly high maintenance.

Regardless, by Friday lunchtime, it's all coming together. The house is fragrant and picture-perfect as, except for a punishing hour spent in the local recreation ground courtesy of Caleb, Gemma had spent most of Thursday cleaning like a demon.

The festive decorations are up, the fridges are well stocked, the champagne, wine and gin are chilled, and this afternoon and early evening can be dedicated to baking two extravagantly decorated cakes and a couple of vegetarian quiches thanks to Katya, one of the school mums, who took Miya home for tea with her daughter Sophia, with the promise of running her home at seven o'clock.

Gemma texts Beth, asking if she can bear to come over on Saturday lunchtime – partly to help with the food and drink, but mainly to boost her own flagging morale. To Gemma's relief, Beth replies saying she'd love to.

By three o'clock, relieved of the school run, with the first sponge rising in the oven and the batter mixed for cake number two, Gemma rewards herself with a glass of prosecco. Surely she's earned a little treat after slaving away for days on end?

Dancing around the kitchen, listening to Christmas songs on her smart speaker, and inhaling the cosy scent of vanilla and cinnamon, Gemma is soon enjoying herself. So much so that she doesn't notice she's drunk almost a bottle of prosecco, or that the second cake is left smouldering in the oven long past its prescribed cooking time. And it is thanks to Mariah Carey's Christmas album that Gemma jumps when Guy strides into the room, demanding to know why he can smell burning and bellowing at the smart speaker to 'STOP!'.

Gemma sniffs the air. 'Oh my God, the cake!' she cries, putting on oven mitts and hauling the charred sponge out of the oven, conscious that all her meticulous planning of the last few days has gone up in smoke. Literally.

Guy's stare is contemptuous. 'Well,' he says after a pause, 'you can imagine how delighted I am to come home early and find the kitchen on fire and that my drunk wife has shit herself.'

Following his gaze, she looks down at her jeans and spots the offending smear of chocolate frosting on the crotch. 'Oh! That's just icing. Sorry, I'll clean it up. And Guy, please don't worry about the cake, the first one's perfect and I can always bob round to the patisserie for another in the morning.'

'Oh, well, that's all right then,' Guy says, his voice icily calm. 'I notice you've nothing to say about why you're off your face?'

'What? Darling, I'm not. I just got a bit hot and it was all lovely and festive in here, so I opened a nice cold bottle. Don't be cross… I've worked really hard for this party and it's going to be perfect, I promise you.'

Guy shakes his head, then spins on his heel. 'Where's Miya?'

'At her friend Sophia's. Her mum Katya said she'd drive Miya home.'

'Well, that's something I suppose. At least Miya didn't see her mother pissed.'

Gemma is stung. 'Guy, what the hell has got into you? You've been in a foul mood for weeks. It's not fair and I don't deserve it.'

'No, I don't suppose you do – anymore than *I* deserve to have a wife with a drinking problem.' He throws up his hands. 'Gemma, you have no idea how stressed I am at work and frankly, you only add to my problems. Look, I haven't got time to stand here arguing. I'm going for a shower.'

Moments later Katya's car pulls into the drive and Gemma can hear her chatting to Miya as they approach the front door together. After a brief mums' exchange about who has eaten what and a shrill 'thank you' from Miya, they return to the kitchen.

Miya wrinkles her nose. 'Pooh, what's that awful smell?'

'Sweet pea, don't be silly, it's just burnt cake. Hey, did you have fun at Sophia's?'

'Yes, Mummy, it was lovely…'

Gemma listens with one ear while Miya chats happily about her play date, the other ear cocked for Guy's footfall on the stairs as she prays the hot shower will have sweetened his temper.

CHAPTER THIRTEEN

Beth

It's still dark when Beth wakes up to a fuzzy head and a raging thirst. She reaches for her mobile: 06.10. So much for her usual Saturday lie-in.

Thoughts of the night before judder into place.

Binks. She'd seen him again. This time they'd actually had a conversation; superficially at least, a pleasant one. And yet, her body had betrayed her. It was uncanny. Three sightings, three panic attacks – four, if she counted the time she'd been home alone, ironing. And last night, she'd been aware of something else: a half-formed memory, or the fragment of a dream. Something just out of reach…

Sitting up carefully so as not to anger her headache, Beth goes to the kitchen, the tiles icy beneath her bare feet. Longing for another two hours' sleep, she rummages in a drawer for paracetamol and downs a tumbler of water. A pit stop in the bathroom confirms she looks as rough as she feels. Shivering, she heads back to bed and pulls the duvet up to her chin, cursing herself for drinking so much and skipping dinner again.

Craving sleep, Beth tries to push Binks from her mind, but his face is there, grinning gormlessly, leering at her, the memory of last night as sharp as the angles of his face. Abandoning the idea of sleep, she props herself up on pillows and allows her mind to roam.

Why the adverse physical reaction to someone she hasn't seen in twenty-odd years? Her anxiety is fast growing into phobic proportions, the way her heart races and her mouth pools with nausea, not to mention the way her legs practically give way beneath her. And yet, until the night she'd walked into the Ship with Laura, she had not remembered Kevin or Billy; neither one had crossed her mind in decades.

He'd mentioned a fancy dress bash at her parents' house. And it was entirely plausible; the Hardings had been known for their parties after all. Beth closes her eyes and pictures her parents' garden filled with music and the laughter of friends and neighbours. But a fancy dress party? She remembers no such thing – nor can she imagine Kevin or Billy at her family home. And what had he meant about Laura? How he'd always fancied her – even dated her a couple of times – but that she was out of his league.

A thought occurs to her: Had the Binks boys been friends of hers and Laura's at some point? It seemed unlikely that their mother would allow either Laura or Beth to spend time with them; even by her own admission, Jeanette had always been snobbish and selective about who her family socialised with. Yet only a month ago, huddled in the Ship Inn, when they'd seen the Binks brothers for the first time, Laura had admitted to going out with Kevin.

Despite her ruminations, Beth realises she has been asleep. Her mobile is saying eight forty-five and now the weak December sunshine peeks through the curtains.

Oh, God, Gemma's party. She stretches her arms over her head, relieved that at least her hangover is abating.

For a moment, her thoughts return to Binks and their conversation in the pub, but she bats them away and steps into the shower, where the steamy water and peony-scented gel revive her.

After cocooning herself in jeans and an oversized sweater, craving sugar and carbs, Beth ventures outside where the air is unusually crisp and the sky overhead a wash of pale blue. She cuts through the park opposite where a couple of dog walkers say hello, and a young mum pushing a lurid pink buggy smiles at her. The contact with regular, cheerful people lifts her mood and puts a spring in her step.

But as Beth approaches the high street, she sees a man in overalls unloading boxes from a white van. Uninvited, Kevin Binks's leering face makes a sudden appearance in her mind.

'Okay, this has to stop,' she mutters through gritted teeth. Seeing Binks three times in a matter of weeks may be unusual but it is not freakish. After all, South East London is only a collection of villages and clearly his stomping ground. It should be no surprise that a guy like Kevin still drinks in his teenage watering hole, neither should it be a giant leap that as a builder, he's currently shop-fitting across the street from her office in New Cross.

And what of it, anyway? Binks in no way figures in her life, past or present. This ridiculous nervous obsession must end.

Beth's tour of the supermarket is purposeful as she fills her basket with plum jam, crusty bread, croissants and a carton of orange juice; enough to set her up for Guy and Gemma's Christmas party in the company of their well-heeled friends, she reasons.

Guy answers the door. 'Hurray, reinforcements! Hello, lovely – you look well,' he says, hugging Beth and ushering her inside.

A high-pitched, whistling cacophony assaults her ears as Miya, her expression solemn with concentration, walks towards her playing 'Jingle Bells' on the recorder.

'Give it a rest, Miya,' Guy says, shaking his head. 'How about we listen to some carols now that Beth's here.'

'Good idea,' Beth mouths over Miya's head, going through to the kitchen in search of Gemma.

'Oh my God. You're a lifesaver,' Gemma cries, pecking Beth on the cheek and thrusting a glass into her hand. 'Thought we'd start as we mean to go on,' she says, filling it with prosecco. Gemma lowers her voice. 'I need to pace myself though. I'm in the doghouse after last night...' Her eyes flick towards Guy, who is bringing in beer from the garage.

'What's that?' he says, his eyebrows shooting up.

'Nothing,' Gemma says with a wink, 'just girl talk.'

Beth gazes in awe at the festive tableau before her: a six-foot Nordmann fir, elegantly decorated in white, ivory and nude ornaments and lights fills the window. Frosted tea light holders are dotted around ready to light up when guests arrive, and the marble-topped island has been transformed into a well-stocked bar.

'You've been busy,' Beth says, stating the obvious. 'Gem, it looks gorgeous in here. How can I help?'

'Most of the food's done, but maybe help me make some canapés to hand round when people arrive? Look, all the ingredients are ready to assemble over there.' Gemma glides from one area of the kitchen to another, directing the operation.

'So,' Gemma begins as they stand working hip to hip while Guy and Miya are out of earshot, 'how's it going?'

Beth hesitates, wondering whether to mention the counselling. She laughs softly. 'It's going, that's for sure.'

Gemma's eyes widen; she turns to Beth. 'Why, what has happened?'

Beth looks over her shoulder, lowers her voice. 'You remember I went to the doc's because I was having panic attacks, and that she suggested counselling? Well, I had my first session on Thursday. It was... interesting. At least Zara, my therapist, is nice.'

'Okay, well that's positive, isn't it? Here, eat this.' Gemma posts a smoked salmon blini into Beth's mouth. 'So why the hesitation?'

Beth chews carefully. 'This isn't a very festive conversation, is it? Your guests will be here soon.' She takes a sip of prosecco, adding, 'Gem, I'm just not sure it's for me. To be honest, we didn't actually talk about what's really bothering me.' *That I'm obsessing about some bloke I knew as a teenager, even though I can hardly remember him,* she finishes in her head.

'Give it chance – you've only had one meeting. What did Zara say about the panic attacks?'

Beth shakes her head. 'Nothing. We didn't talk about them… that's what I mean; she said we'd come to them later… Guess she wants to find out what kind of basket case she's dealing with first.'

Guy steals up on them, reaches over and helps himself to a canapé. 'Mmm, bloody gorgeous. What else can I eat? Gem, have we got enough ice?'

'There's plenty of ice in the garage and darling, please don't eat those, can't you wait?' Gemma says, pulling cling film across the food she and Beth have plated up.

'But I'm hungry,' Guy moans, looking to Beth for sympathy. 'See what I have to put up with?' He goes away again, muttering over his shoulder that he's got a Christmas playlist to sort.

'Guy can be such a child,' Beth says, her smile indulgent.

'You could say that.' Gemma loads a handful of items into the dishwasher. 'He certainly likes his own way. Was he like that when you were growing up?'

'Not from a little kid's perspective. You don't think about that stuff, do you?'

Gemma grips Beth's arm, her eyes glittering with mischief. 'Okay, so I've done two stupid things in the last twenty-four hours,' she giggles, 'actually three, if you count burning one of the cakes.'

'What are you talking about?'

'So yesterday afternoon, I was here by myself, getting this lot ready. I'd already cleaned the house from top to bottom earlier in the week – anyway, the kitchen looked so cosy, and I was baking and singing along to the music… and somehow I drank nearly a bottle of prosecco!'

Beth purses her lips. 'Right… is that the punchline? You had a little Christmas tipple?'

'Guy was fuming. He was so rude to me; he said I have a drink problem. Do you think he's right?'

Beth scowls. 'No! I bloody don't. Yes, you like a drink, but so does he! So do most people – especially over the holidays. Jesus, the hypocrisy of it. What was the other so-called stupid thing?'

Gemma covers her eyes, pink spots appear high on her cheeks. 'I texted Caleb, my personal trainer, and invited him here.'

'So?'

'Beth, Guy will go batshit. Because apart from the neighbours – and you, of course – it's just *his* people… local business contacts and so on. He'll be furious when a nobody like Caleb rocks up. Beth, what have I done?'

'Absolutely nothing wrong, Gemma, and it's ridiculous that you feel that way. For goodness' sake, you've done all the work. Of course, you should invite people.'

Gemma chews her lip. 'Let's hope Guy sees it that way…'

CHAPTER FOURTEEN

Gemma

Arm in arm, Gemma and Beth weave their way across the kitchen, now thronging with some thirty people.

'Cheers for that; you're a star,' Gemma whispers, leaning against her friend.

'Anytime. I could see you needed rescuing from that boring little man.' Beth pauses to refill Gemma's glass. 'Well done, you. Everyone's having a great time. Cheers.'

'Thanks. The neighbours are no trouble, they entertain themselves. Even the kids are behaving, bless them.' Her eyes alight on Miya, who is playing with two older children from next door; all three are giggling and bouncing up and down in time to the music. Gemma takes a sip of her prosecco. 'We're lucky – everyone in the close is lovely,' she says, eyeing Jonty from next-door-but-one as he delivers the punchline of a funny story, to the uproarious laughter of his audience.

She looks for Guy and finds him chatting to Lucille Goff, sixty years old if she's a day, and loving his attentions. Gemma can see that Guy is flirting with her, leaning close, holding eye contact. A pang of pride catches her unawares. She nudges Beth. 'He's still got it.'

Miya runs up to her, pink-cheeked and sweaty. 'Mummy, there's a man at the door – can you come?'

'Well done for finding me, sweet pea,' Gemma says, following Miya and mouthing, 'we don't talk to strangers' to Beth over her daughter's head.

And there is Caleb, barely recognisable in black jeans and a good wool jacket, a red scarf tied loosely around his neck. Against the flare of a streetlamp, Gemma can see a light drizzle is falling; it sparkles on his hair and shoulders. He hesitates, then hands Gemma a bottle of sparkling rosé.

'Caleb! Come in.' Gemma accepts the wine. 'Thanks, you didn't need to bring anything,' she says, hanging his jacket in the hall closet and ushering him towards the action.

'So, you found us okay; where did you park?'

Caleb grins. 'Oh, I took the train so I can relax and have a couple of drinks.'

'Good idea… well, come and meet some people. My husband's somewhere around,' Gemma says, in no hurry to introduce the two of them.

The volume of laughter and conversation has crept up in direct proportion to guests' alcohol consumption, and the room is a sea of white teeth and shining eyes. Somebody has swapped Michael Bublé's Christmas album for dance music and people are beginning to twitch and gyrate where they stand.

Guy is working the room, scattering wit and compliments, making sure that all his guests feel important.

She watches him, charming Alan and Anya King who live in Darwin Drive's only other detached house.

'Did I see you on TV last week, Guy? I just caught the tail end of *Business Tonight*,' Anya is saying, her voice straining above the music.

Guy affects modesty and confusion. 'Er, probably. Actually, I need to ease back on the media commitments,' he says, 'it can take over your life if you let it. Excuse me, will you.'

Gemma watches Guy stride over, his brow furrowed, his eyes dark.

'Who the bloody hell is that?' he says, jerking his head in Caleb's direction.

Gemma raises her eyebrows. 'Who?'

Guy scowls. 'Him. The gigolo in the corner.'

'Oh! Sorry, you mean Caleb, my fitness coach? I asked him at the last minute. I felt a bit awkward, banging on about the party and how stressful it was – so I ended up inviting him, not thinking for one moment that he'd come along.' Gemma cringes inwardly; she can hear herself babbling.

'I'd better say hello, then,' Guy says, squeezing between a couple of neighbours.

'Hi, I'm Guy, Gemma's husband.' He thrusts his hand out, totally disregarding the fact that Caleb is already in conversation with a young couple. 'So, *you're* the one responsible for my wife looking like a sack of sticks.' He pauses and grins. 'Relax, I'm only joking.'

Gemma watches, heat creeping into her cheeks. But Caleb is holding his own. 'Good to meet you, Guy. And I agree, Gemma needs to eat more carbs and protein. She knows my view. I try to focus on strength, not weight loss,' he says evenly. 'You're in excellent shape yourself. Do you work out much?'

Gemma exhales and goes in search of Beth, hoping that Guy won't antagonise the younger man.

'Wow! *He's* easy on the eye,' Beth giggles, staring in Caleb's direction.

'Is he? Oh, I hadn't noticed,' Gemma says, her face a picture of innocence.

At around ten thirty people begin to drift off, complimenting Gemma on her delicious food and congratulating Guy on another fabulous Christmas bash.

Caleb is last to leave, kissing Beth on the cheek and shaking Guy's hand warmly.

'Great party – thank you so much for including me,' he turns to Gemma. 'Can you help me find my coat, please?'

Gemma takes Caleb's jacket from the closet and holds it out for him to slide into. He hugs her, catching her off balance.

'Thanks again, Gemma,' he says, 'see you on Thursday – last session this year.'

'Goodnight, Caleb,' Guy calls from the kitchen doorway, 'be careful out there.'

Abandoning her plan to take a cab home, Beth had crashed in the guest room.

Guy had waved Beth's polite objections away. 'Don't be daft. You'll only end up forking out for another cab when you collect your car tomorrow. Stay. Relax.'

Gemma had agreed, offering Beth a spare toothbrush and a T-shirt to sleep in.

Now, perched at the kitchen island, nibbling wholemeal toast and drinking their second coffees of the day, Gemma and Beth dissect the highlights of the party, while Guy bangs and crashes his way through the recycling in the garage.

'Is it me, or is Guy in a filthy mood?' Beth asks, her voice low.

'No, it's not you. He's sulking. I knew he'd have a problem with me inviting Caleb, I bloody knew it,' Gemma hisses, blotting crumbs from her lips with a napkin.

'He's jealous.' Beth folds her arms across her chest. 'Guy's used to being the best-looking bloke in the room and he can't stand the competition.'

'Maybe,' Gemma whispers, 'he gave me such a hard time last night, accusing me of flirting. I told him he was being paranoid.

I mean, I hope I made Caleb feel welcome, but it's not like I was all over him.'

Guy appears in the connecting doorway to the garage, his expression martyred. 'Right, I've sorted all the rubbish and recycling. You just relax, Gemma – everything's under control.'

Beth makes a face. 'Well done, Guy. Good of you to help clear up, after Gemma has spent three entire days cooking, cleaning and organising.' She dusts crumbs from her fingers, takes a last swallow of coffee. 'I need to go. I'm at Dad's this afternoon and he'll only start fretting if I'm late. Meanwhile, you two play nicely. And that means you.' Beth waggles her finger in Guy's direction, before hugging them both and letting herself out.

As the sound of Beth's hatchback dies away, Gemma braces herself for Round Two. She doesn't have to wait long.

'Are you intending to shower and dress today at all? Only it's almost noon, so it's not too much to ask, is it? I bet Caleb doesn't see you looking whey-faced and sullen – I'm quite sure you're all smiles for him.' Guy flounces, loading Beth and Gemma's breakfast things into the dishwasher.

Gemma's tone is patient. 'Guy. Stop it. You're not being fair. I'm sorry if I made the wrong call inviting Caleb. I really didn't give it much thought. But it's done now and it's not like we'll be socialising with him again, is it? Can't we do something with Miya today? Maybe go for a walk in Dulwich Park, the forecast said—'

'I don't care what the fucking weather is doing,' Guy yells, making Gemma jump. 'Anyway,' he adds, lowering his voice, 'I might go into the office for a few hours. I'm not in the mood to sit around here bickering all day.'

'Neither am I,' Gemma says wearily.

CHAPTER FIFTEEN

Beth

It takes Beth three trips to her father's attic to retrieve her parents' artificial tree and two dusty, dank-smelling boxes of Christmas ornaments.

She drags everything downstairs and into the sitting room; a treasure trove of fairy lights and once jewel-bright baubles, their lustre dimmed by age.

From his armchair, Tim exclaims over each ornament as one by one Beth liberates them from tissue wrappings. 'That robin was always Jeanette's favourite,' he says, his expression wistful.

Beth keeps her surprise to herself, unable to picture her mother being sentimental about anything, let alone a tree decoration.

'Dad, I don't know why you keep all this stuff,' she sighs. 'I wish you'd let me take you shopping, there are some gorgeous trees and decorations around.'

'There's nothing wrong with these. Some of them are older than you,' Tim answers, his mouth set and stubborn.

'Then I rest my case.'

After hanging the last ornament, Beth switches on fairy lights shaped like icicles and goes into the kitchen to prepare lunch.

'You're a good girl, Beth,' her father says once they are seated at his oak dining table, their plates steaming with poached salmon and hot buttery vegetables.

'Don't be daft, Dad. You act as though I'm doing you a favour, which is ridiculous – I love seeing you,' Beth says, piling extra potatoes onto his plate.

After hugging her father goodbye, feeling flat, Beth calls round at Laura's house.

Laura answers the door in PJs and a face pack. 'I'm on my own,' she explains, steering Beth through to the kitchen. 'Michael and the boys are next door but one, playing some new *Star Wars* game thingy,' she says, filling and switching on the kettle. 'Anyway, how was Dad today?'

'He was a bit forlorn. I put the tree up for him. Laur, it looked so old and sad, like some nineties relic. Dad mentioned Mum about ten times today. I guess he misses her more than ever at this time of year.'

Laura hands Beth a mug of tea. 'I'll pop round mid-week, take Jack and Alfie with me, they always cheer him up. We'll just have to make a big fuss of him on Christmas Day, won't we?'

Beth pictures Laura's chaotic Christmas Day. Eight of them, including Mike's parents, squashed around the table until none of them can eat another mouthful, followed by charades and boardgames in the evening; a winning formula that Laura and Mike have rolled out every year since Jeanette's passing.

Laura excuses herself, and returns minus the face pack, her skin pink and shiny. 'Anyway,' she says, 'what's going on with you?'

Beth shrugs. 'Oh, you know – the usual stuff. Saying that, I went to Guy and Gemma's party last night. It was mostly the neighbours and a few of Guy's contacts. I tell you what, though, Laur – Guy can be a bad-tempered sod. Honestly, the way he speaks to Gemma sometimes… it makes me cringe.'

Laura makes a face. 'What, *our* Guy? He's normally such a teddy bear. Maybe he's under a lot of pressure at work. I heard him on the radio the other day – spouting about how his company has halved the plastic content in the packaging they supply to coffee shops and cafés. It's a shame other firms don't take a leaf out of Guy's book.'

Beth frowns. 'Doesn't give him the right to be rude to Gemma, though. Anyway, listen to this for a coincidence. So, you remember when we saw the Binks brothers a few weeks ago in the Ship Inn?'

'How could I forget?' Laura says dryly.

'Well, I spoke to Kevin on Friday night, or rather he spoke to me.'

Laura's eyebrows shoot up. '*No*, really? I can't wait to hear this.'

Then Beth recounts discovering Kevin and Billy working as shop-fitters across the street from her office, and how Kevin had recognised and approached her in the Bricklayers Arms.

'I can't believe he remembered me,' Beth says, aware that her pulse has elevated during the course of the story, that her mouth has become dry and her hands are prickling with sweat.

'Well, that is a surprise. We were all just teenagers. Kevin's obviously got a good memory. The thing is, Beth, you don't look much different now than you did back then.'

Beth recalls Kevin's unwelcome take on her appearance: *I see you turned out all right then… very nice indeed.*

An involuntary shudder ripples through her. Binks had almost certainly said it to flatter her, but it had felt inappropriate at best and sleazy, even predatory, at worst, threatening and unwanted. Beth takes a deep breath and squares her shoulders. 'Look, I have to ask, Laura, what *did* happen between you?'

Laura covers her already pink face with her hands, a cackle of laughter escapes her.

'Oh, my God.' Beth's heart is racing now. 'You slept with him, didn't you?'

'Actually, no, he asked me out – whatever that meant back in the day – and I kissed him once or twice and it did get a bit touchy feely, but that's all. I had standards, you know, even then! The Binks brothers were trouble, with their scary dogs and shitty bikes. I used to see police cars parked outside the flats they lived in all the time when we were kids. Mum and Dad would have had a fit if I'd gone out with Kevin properly.'

Beth shakes her head. 'I wish I could remember him. It's weird. I do and I don't. I knew Kevin and Billy's faces the minute they walked into the Ship, but I can't remember a single other thing about them. It's just a feeling of… oh, I don't know. Something.' Beth catches sight of the kitchen wall clock, it's already a quarter to eight. 'Anyway, love, I'm off. The boys will be back soon. Give them a kiss from me and I'll see you on Christmas Day, if not before,' she says, shrugging on her jacket and hugging Laura goodbye.

Once in her car, Beth takes several deep breaths, turns the radio on and sets the aircon to warm.

Shit. It had happened again. The same feeling that seemed to engulf her whenever she saw, thought about or spoke of Kevin Binks. She can no longer ignore the connection. Just talking about him to her sister had chilled her and given her a sickening rush of vertigo.

Fifteen minutes later, Beth pulls straight into her reserved space, relief washing over her as she hurries inside, triggering the hall light as she passes. The only sounds are of her feet on the stairwell and the distant, almost comforting thrum of traffic.

Once inside her flat, she closes the curtains shutting out the night. It cheers her to find a cosy mystery is just starting on TV: it's all she has the energy for these days. In the kitchen she finds a heel of crusty bread perfect for toasting, and some left-over wine in the fridge door. Humming to herself, Beth settles in front of the television, pulling a rug across her lap as she munches toast and sips the chilled wine.

She wakes with a start and rubs her eyes. How long has she been asleep? It's colder now; the heating must have gone off for the night. The cosy drama has finished, gentle Cotswold lanes replaced by something hard and aggressive – a reality police show set somewhere bleak and urban; it's the last thing she wants to see.

Moving stiffly, she turns the TV and the lights off and goes to bed.

CHAPTER SIXTEEN

Gemma

Under a white chiffon sky that threatened rain, the morning school run had included a mercy dash to collect Sophia, thanks to her mum Katya's burgeoning migraine.

'Thanks so much, Gemma, I'm really grateful,' Katya had said at the front door as she'd handed over Sophia's Mr Tickle rucksack and lunchbox. 'It goes without saying, I'll do the same for you sometime.'

'Fortunately I don't suffer from migraines and anyway, this one's no trouble – are you, sweetheart?' Gemma had answered, running a hand over Sophia's silky blonde curls. Then Miya and Sophia had sung all the way to school, doing some hand-clappy thing on the back seat that had reminded Gemma of her own childhood, growing up on the Sussex coast, visiting her aunt Marina and playing out with her cousin Cindy.

School run sorted, Gemma had driven home and put a wash on before heading out to the recreation ground for her last personal training session of the year.

As usual, Caleb is there already, unloading weights and other fitness props from the boot of his Golf.

'Good morning, Gemma,' he calls, a broad grin on his handsome face.

'Hi.' Gemma is suddenly shy as she remembers Guy's waspish welcome at the party and is embarrassed by it.

'Thank you for Saturday night,' he says, straight off the bat, before Gemma can dwell on any awkwardness. 'I had a great time. Your friends are nice, too. Maybe you could recommend me to them sometime,' he says with a wink and a knowing look.

Gemma smiles. 'Of course – if any of them are looking to get fitter next year, I'll be sure to put in a good word.'

A pause yawns between them until Caleb claps his hands, all business again. 'Okay, Gemma, let's stretch, then we're going straight into a circuit of squats, lunges and burpees – give me fifteen reps, three sets. Go!'

And whether it's the thought of Christmas overindulgence, or the fact that she'll be unable to train for a fortnight, or an increased sense of wanting to please Caleb, Gemma is a machine, flying through her routine with a grim determination that surprises them both.

'Brilliant! Well done, that was amazing!' Caleb says, allowing Gemma to get her breath back and sip some water.

Moments later, they set off at a steady pace, jogging in sync towards the copse at the back of the rec.

'Keep going. You're doing great,' Caleb encourages as they run towards the trees and are soon weaving through the patch of urban woodland, emerging out onto the rec again, before sprinting for the home straight.

'Gemma, you nailed it today! Well done. Fancy a victory lap?' He laughs. 'Only joking. That's it. We're done until New Year. Give me five!' But as Gemma raises her hand, Caleb clasps it, lacing his fingers through hers and holding eye contact. Confused, she pulls away.

Caleb steps back, with a small shake of his head. 'Sorry… Take care of yourself, Gemma. Call me if you need anything. Seriously, I mean it.' His tone is no longer hearty, but earnest and sincere.

Gemma nods and turns away, wondering at the significance of his words as she walks back to her car.

The hours between bootcamp and the school run are a blur of housework carried out on autopilot as Gemma replays her time with Caleb in the park. What *was* that? Flirting? Or friendship and concern? The man could be under no illusion, Gemma was married with a small child. What had he expected? That she would respond by falling into his arms? The very idea seemed ridiculous, almost as though she'd imagined it. And what exactly had he meant by his 'call me if you need anything,' remark? What on earth could Gemma possibly need?

A text arrives from Katya.

Migraine a little better but not up to driving. Would you mind collecting Sophia, please, Gemma? Thanks so much. X

Happy to help, Gemma replies, adding as an afterthought that she'll feed Sophia and keep her for a few hours, giving Katya longer to recover.

A row of hearts and flowers emojis ping back to her.

Gemma listens with great amusement to the happy chatter between the girls as they pick their way through pizza and salad. Then with much giggling and negotiation, they take out their tablets to play an online game concerning the care and training of dolphins, before Katya arrives, sheepish and apologetic.

'Bless you, I'm glad you're feeling okay now,' Gemma says kindly, taking in her friend's pallor. 'And anyway, you're welcome, they're so sweet together.' She bends to give Sophia a hug. 'Got everything, sweet pea?' She turns back to Katya. 'Well, see you in the morning for the girls' last day. Can you believe it's Christmas in a week?'

An hour later, with no word from Guy, Gemma puts Miya to bed and pours herself a large glass of wine before sinking into the sofa, TV remote in hand. Moments later, she hears the distinctive throb of Guy's car pulling onto the drive.

At once the volume of his voice and the floppiness of his limbs tells her he has been drinking.

Concerned, she jumps off the sofa and puts a finger to her lips. 'Shh, please don't wake Miya,' she begs. 'Darling, have you been drinking?'

'I may have had one or two,' Guy says, his expression innocent.

'And you've just driven home?! What the hell are you doing? There are police *everywhere*, it's the week before Christmas. Don't you realise—'

'Get off my case, Gemma, for fuck's sake,' Guy talks over her. 'How dare you, of all people, lecture me on drinking?' He indicates her glass. 'What's that? Your first or second? *Bottle*, I mean,' he adds nastily. 'Never mind, I'm sure you'll find a way to justify yourself. You must have had a very trying day, what with your Adonis of a personal trainer and your yummy-mummy mates at school.'

Gemma's heart sinks. She hasn't the energy for a fight and there's no talking to Guy when he's in this mood. 'This is my first drink – check the bottle if you don't believe me,' she says, wondering why the hell she needs to defend one glass of wine. 'And not that you asked,' she adds, 'but my day was fine. Why don't I make you a coffee and you can tell me about yours. Are you hungry?'

Guy sags visibly, then follows her into the kitchen. 'No, I had a big lunch but apart from that I haven't stopped all day. Drinks were with the marketing team. It was Heather's last day before Christmas – you know, the one with frizzy hair? She and her husband are taking the kids to Lapland.'

'Oh, wow! They'll be blown away. Must be an incredible experience for children. We should take Miya next year, while she's still young enough to believe.'

Guy scoffs. 'I doubt she believes now – it's alarming the rate at which she's growing up.' He takes his 'World's Best Dad' mug from Gemma and sits up at the marble-topped island.

'Have we got anything I can eat?' he says, finishing his coffee.

Gemma sighs. 'Guy, I just offered you… yes, of course. Poached eggs on toast? It's a bit late for anything else.'

Later, they slump side by side in front of the ten o'clock news.

'I don't know how these retailers survive,' Guy says, shaking his head, following a report about reduced footfall in the high street pre-Christmas that mentions several high-profile stores.

'Nor me,' Gemma stifles a yawn.

Once in bed, Gemma turns away from Guy, hoping he'll be in the mood for sleep, but to her surprise, he reaches for her, roughly kissing her lips and nibbling her neck and shoulders before moving down to her breasts.

'Gently,' she cries out, as he nips her with his teeth. Ten minutes later, Gemma is relieved when he rolls away from her and is soon breathing rhythmically.

By midnight, craving sleep that will not come, Gemma pads to the bathroom and opens the mirrored cupboard. She eyes the pack of Zammertil and considers the wine she's already drunk; one and a half glasses at most. What harm can half a tablet do? Guy is snoring drunkenly and will be none the wiser…

Before she can overthink things, Gemma releases one of the tiny blue pills and presses its middle seam with her fingernail; at once it snaps in two. Then, cupping her hand under the cold tap, she gulps it down and creeps back to bed.

CHAPTER SEVENTEEN

Beth

Beth's heart falters to see her father, overcoat on and clutching a leather holdall, already waiting by the front door.

How long has he been standing there? Is the waiting some new eccentricity, perhaps? Thank God she is on time.

'Hi Dad, Happy Christmas!' Her tone is brisk as she leans forward to hug him – an awkward manoeuvre because of the bag he's holding.

'Thank you, darling – and to you. Shall we go?'

Beth walks Tim to the car, and they set off for Laura's five minutes down the road.

'So many Christmases spent in this house,' he says, looking back at his home as Beth pulls away.

Your mother loved Christmas, Beth hears before the words are even spoken – and sure enough, it is her dad's next wistful comment.

'Dad, I know you really miss Mum and everything, but Laura's excited about doing Christmas and it'll be lovely, all of us together just like last year. Anyway, it's brilliant that you're staying overnight. I hate the thought of you waking up alone on Boxing Day.'

She can see Tim is trying to smile but there's a tremor to his chin.

There is no welcoming committee at Laura's. Mike opens the door of their Edwardian semi, looking frazzled, before sweeping

Beth and his father-in-law inside and hugging them both, as though he's suddenly remembered what day it is.

Laura calls out from the kitchen, 'In here! Having a bit of a— Oh, shit!' A crash erupts, followed by a metallic reverberation as Beth imagines something wheeling across the kitchen floor.

Beth winces. 'Do we need hard hats?' she quips, as the three of them head towards the din.

'Hi!' Laura grins, putting out her arms to hug her father and sister. 'Happy Christmas.' She lets out a semi-hysterical cackle. 'It's all under control in here as you can see… Not!'

Then she grabs a bottle of bubbly from the fridge door, hands it to Mike to open and lines up four glasses. 'Let's start as we mean to go on,' she says, flushed and shiny-eyed. 'Merry Christmas. Cheers!'

Apart from a brief interruption with the arrival of Mike's parents, John and Sue, Beth and Laura crack through their *To Do* list and by three o'clock, the twinkling festive dining table they've created is groaning under the weight of roast turkey and seven veg.

There's a collective gasp of appreciation as everyone comes to the table, taking in the mouth-watering dishes, Laura's careful flower arrangements and the display of sparkling tea-light holders dotted around to cast an intimate golden glow.

Beaming, Mike looks around and raises his glass. 'Let's have a toast. To our chefs, Laura and Beth,' he says, holding his wife's gaze at the other end of the table.

And then there's a frantic scrabbling and weaving of arms as everybody piles their plate, ravenous now at the sight of it all.

Beth catches her sister's eye. *Good job*, she mouths, raising her glass in a silent toast.

Barely an hour later, only a few greasy scraps remain.

'Bloody hell, our family can eat,' Laura says, surveying the decimated table.

'Which is kind of the idea,' Mike says, starting to collect up dirty plates. 'Right, no arguments, you and Beth go grab a space on the sofa while I start the clearing up.'

Drowsy with food and wine, all three elderly parents are soon snoring gently, Sue and John filling one sofa, while Tim, his head lolling awkwardly, sits in Laura's best armchair. Even Jack and Alfie are rendered silent by a tear-jerking animation about a reindeer who has become detached from the herd and is desperate to find his family.

'Oh, for goodness' sake, look at me!' Laura says, impatiently wiping her eyes and getting to her feet. 'Can't believe I'm sobbing at a cartoon. Why don't you and I sit in the snug with a little tot of toffee vodka?'

'Now you're talking,' Beth says, following her sister to a tiny room at the back of the house.

Laura shivers. 'Shall we light the fire, warm things up a bit?' she says, closing the curtains on the night sky.

Beth nods, unscrews the cap of the sweet vodka and pours out two shots. 'Chin-chin, Laura.'

Soon the fire is burning well, its faux gas flames glowing with heat. Laura raises her glass. 'Ah, the relief. So now it's just us and we can catch our breath, what's been going on with you? How is the counselling going? Is it making any difference?'

Beth sighs. 'Not yet, although to be fair I've only had two sessions.' She falls silent, gazes into the fire. 'There's something though, Laura, I can feel it. A dream, a memory... I don't know. It's like, I catch a glimpse, then I blink and it's gone.' She leans closer, and takes a sip of the warming liqueur. 'The thing is, Laur, there's a common theme… and I can't believe I'm telling you this, because once I do, I will sound like a mad woman.'

Laura shrugs. 'Not to me,' she says gently.

'All right. You remember when we saw Kevin and Billy Binks in the pub? And I felt all sick and giddy?'

A furrow appears in Laura's brow as she leans in. 'Yes, of course. Go on.'

'And you know that I saw them again, while I was at work and they were fitting out an empty shop opposite. And most recently, I saw Kevin in the Bricklayers. Well, that time, we chatted… or rather he did; I was paralysed with fear, too focussed on not throwing up to say much. But the thing is, whenever I see, or even *think*, about the twins – especially Kevin – I feel absolutely terrified, as though something truly awful is about to happen.'

Frowning, Laura nods slowly. 'Beth, there'll be a reason. Some weird association thing, to do with that first time. You saw them in the Ship, felt rough because of something you'd eaten probably, and now the Binks brothers are a trigger, making you feel ill over and over. It happens. Like me with boats. Remember when Mum and Dad took us to France on the ferry, and I was seasick all the way? Well, since then, I've only got to look at a boat on TV and my stomach starts lurching. It's that,' Laura finishes, sounding decisive.

Beth shakes her head. 'Maybe. I don't think so.'

Just then, Alfie charges in, holding up his brand-new remote-controlled car. 'Mummy, it's broken,' he says, his face puckered with disappointment.

'We're talking. Take it to Daddy. It probably needs new batteries already,' she says, turning back to Beth.

Beth chews her lip, watches her nephew as he stomps off with a theatrical sigh.

'Wait here.' Laura gets up and returns moments later, her laptop tucked under her arm. She switches on, stabs a few keys.

'What are you doing?' Beth asks.

Laura's eyes gleam with intrigue. 'What do you think? I'm googling the Binks twins.'

Beth sits up straight, rigid with apprehension. 'Wait. Is this such a good idea?'

Laura purses her lips. 'Sure, why not? We can sneak a look at Kevin and Billy's Facebook pages and maybe their work website – if they have one – or find them on one of those hubs where builders advertise their services. There's bound to be something.'

Beth swallows hard as she watches Laura's fingers fly over the keys. Then her breath is coming in short painful gasps, a mounting blend of suspense and horror restricting her chest as news links begin to roll before her eyes and the words jump out at her.

Laura clicks on a headline near the top of the page – a short news piece from the *South London Press,* dated April 2007.

'Listen to this,' Laura says, pushing the snug door closed with her foot before reading aloud.

'PC Yvonne Walker, 29, was one of several Police officers who were honoured yesterday in a special ceremony in recognition of those who have saved lives, secured significant jail sentences for sex offenders, and who have gone above and beyond the call of duty in making South East London's streets safer.

PC Walker was praised for her role in the arrest and subsequent conviction of Kevin Binks, of the Holmbush Estate, Penge, SE20, now serving seven years for the serious sexual assault of an unnamed woman...'

Laura's voice trails off. She looks up from the screen, her eyes searching her sister's, and for the first time, Beth sees her own fear reflecting back at her in Laura's face.

CHAPTER EIGHTEEN

Beth

'Oh, God,' Laura's voice is hoarse with shock. 'I don't think I can read the rest.'

Hearing footfall in the hallway, she slams her laptop shut as Michael shambles into the room demanding turkey sandwiches and a game of charades.

'Okay, just coming,' Laura gasps. Mike eyes them suspiciously before returning to the living room, which by the sound of things, has burst back into life now that the adults have woken up.

Beth pushes down the swirl of nausea, the quickening pulse and crawling skin sensation that has become all too familiar in recent weeks.

Only this time, it makes sense and seems justified.

Suddenly it has a point and a focus. Kevin Binks is a convicted sex offender. And the answer is staring her in the face. Clearly, on some unconscious level, Beth had seen – then buried and forgotten – the news story before, possibly as far back as 2007, and it has left a festering sore. A wound which had re-opened the night she and Laura had seen the Binks twins in the Ship.

Now it all made perfect, horrible sense.

'Come on, Beth. We can't talk about this now. Everyone's waiting for us,' Laura hisses, turning off the fire.

Then as if nothing out of the ordinary has happened, they play a boisterous game of charades, letting the boys win. The volume rises and laughter rattles through the house as three generations mug and mime their way through *Downton Abbey*, *The Minions* and *Coronation Street*.

On Boxing Day morning, after a late breakfast of tea, bacon sandwiches and mince pies, Beth and Laura hug their father goodbye before Mike drives him home.

On Mike's return, they tog up against the chill and walk in Beckenham Place Park, meandering through the woods and around the golf course, enjoying the crisp, clean air. Regardless of the festive mood, Beth is distracted, replaying the grim discovery she and Laura made the night before about Binks, but with Mike and the boys constantly in earshot, she keeps her thoughts to herself.

'Listen, don't think about that… *thing* we found,' Laura whispers later, as Beth sets off for Guy and Gemma's at dusk. 'Let's meet for coffee next week. I'll be desperate for a break from my lot by then anyway. Call me if you need anything. And Beth: it'll be okay. Love you.'

It's dark by the time Beth arrives at Darwin Drive and the magnolia tree in the Ward's front garden sparkles with a festive spirit she no longer feels.

Pushing her discovery about Binks from her mind, Beth pastes on a bright smile and marches up the drive, noting the absence of Guy's car.

Gemma answers the door in loose tracksuit bottoms and a hoodie, her long hair unbrushed. Stifling a yawn, she beckons Beth inside, hugging her with real warmth.

'It's just us,' Gemma says with evident relief, as they move through to the kitchen. 'Miya's gone to bed early after all the excitement and Guy's dropping his mum home.' She glances at the digits on the oven clock. 'He'll be about halfway by now and he's staying over. So, what can I get you? Tea, coffee, wine?'

Beth accepts the offer of tea and her expression softens. 'Gosh, Gemma, no wonder you're tired. I forgot you had Pam here for a couple of nights. She's um… difficult, if I remember rightly.' She makes a face. 'Ha! No wonder she and my mother were as thick as thieves back in the day.'

Gemma fills the kettle, turns back to Beth. 'It's not her fault. I feel for Pam. she's lonely. It's been three years since Guy's dad died.' She smiles. 'I quite liked old Alastair. He was much more down to earth than Pam and he adored Miya as a toddler.' She hands Beth a mug of tea. 'Cake? There's loads left.'

Beth shakes her head. 'No thanks. One thing I remember about Alastair is that he and my dad used to smoke cigars together – especially when the scotch came out. Ugh, the smell! Mum and Pam always had a fit. Anyway, that's enough ancient history. Other than placating Pam, how was your Christmas? Did Miya have a good time?'

Hunkered down on the sofa, Beth listens to Gemma's talk of presents, festive food and films they've watched over the holiday.

'Did you have fun at Laura's?' Gemma asks, tucking her legs beneath her.

'It was lovely, thank you. My sister puts on a fab Christmas.' She hesitates. 'But then I found out something… interesting.'

Gemma raises her eyebrows. 'Oh? Interesting how?'

'It was something that Laura and I read online about an old boyfriend of hers. Well, they weren't exactly *going out,* we were only kids at the time.' Beth pauses, unsure whether to go on.

She takes a deep breath, feels emotion welling, then pushes it aside. 'Gemma, Laura and I used to know two brothers, twins actually, Kevin and Billy Binks. Well, they were bad lads, you know? Always getting into scrapes – so our parents said. Anyway, recently I ran into Kevin – the ringleader of the two – and he gave me the creeps. I mean, he seriously freaked me out… and I've started to think that the anxiety attacks I've been having are connected to this man.'

'How?' Gemma frowns, absently twiddling a lock of hair. 'What did you read online?'

Beth inhales sharply, blows out her cheeks. 'That Kevin Binks got put away for serious sexual assault. Gemma, the guy went to prison.'

Gemma's eyes widen in shock. 'And your sister actually went out with this guy? God, that's horrible. It's so creepy. I'd be mortified to think I'd been friends with a… a sex offender.' A furrow appears between her brows. 'Thing is, Beth, I'm not trying to freak you out here, but you started having panic attacks well before you read about this bloke online. I mean, maybe something about him has always scared you; something from way back. Kids are very intuitive, aren't they?'

Beth chews her lip, not trusting herself to speak.

'Hon, I can see you're worried.' Gemma gives Beth's hand a squeeze and leans closer. 'Maybe you should mention this at your next counselling session.'

In no mood for mindless radio, Beth drives home through the deserted streets in silence. Gemma had seemed limp and tired at first, her energy no doubt drained by forty-eight hours spent in her mother-in-law's acidic company. But then she'd come to life, her interest piqued by their conversation about Binks.

Maybe something about him has always scared you; something from way back. Kids are very intuitive, aren't they?

Hearing Gemma say the words had made the idea real and tangible. Perhaps this wasn't some confused, befuddled association after reading a news article that had put ideas into Beth's head years ago. Maybe Gemma had a point and it was connected to something real that had actually happened; an incident she'd seen or heard.

That seed sown, Beth had left Gemma's earlier than expected, suddenly exhausted, and now all she wants is to curl up in bed with a good book – anything to take her mind off the unwelcome thoughts that are circling.

By nine thirty, wrapped in her cosiest PJs, a mug of strong tea on the bedside cabinet, Beth is struggling to focus on her new book. By one of her favourite authors, it has all the ingredients to entertain her, but to her annoyance, the words won't stick as she re-reads the same page for the third time.

Giving up on her novel, Beth pads into the sitting room, feeling the chilled floor beneath her bare feet, and collects her laptop from the coffee table. She dives back under the duvet, feeling her heartbeat quicken as she switches it on and opens her default search engine.

She hesitates, as if typing the words will somehow invite darkness into her home. 'Oh, for God's sake,' she says aloud before entering the words *Kevin Binks sexual assault* and pressing enter. Then through narrowed eyes, Beth stares at the screen and re-reads the article from the *South London Press*. According to the cutting, Kevin Binks had been sentenced to seven years, meaning that even in the unlikely event he'd served his full term, his release date would have been several years ago. Long enough for Binks to have buried or shaken off the stigma of being a convicted sex offender, enabling him to crack on with his life and to set himself up as a builder no less; a potentially lucrative career with his brother and sidekick, Billy, that on some jobs would surely necessitate him being alone with female householders. It was unthinkable.

She considers Binks's victim. Or should that be victims, plural? The article referred to an 'unnamed woman', but perhaps there had been others, too terrified to come forward.

Binks's taut, angular face swims into Beth's mind: *say hello to your sister for me, yeah? I always fancied her, but we only went out a couple of times…*

A couple of times? Well, that was two too many! Jesus, poor Laura, what must she be thinking now?

The thought that she and her sister had grown up five minutes' walk from a future sexual predator was horrific enough. How much worse for poor Laura then, who had, at the very least, enjoyed a flirtation with Binks – and possibly more than she was admitting to. How sickening for her to make such a grim discovery years later.

Beth considers Gemma's advice about getting Zara's take on Binks's deviant past and whether it could be connected to her panic attacks.

Her thoughts are whirring now, vacillating between her own (preferred) theory: that she'd read about Kevin's conviction years ago, filed it away and the memory had resurfaced after her first chance encounter in the Ship Inn, and Gemma's suggestion that her anxiety was linked to something insidious concerning Binks from far back in her past. Beth massages her temples where the first signs of a headache threaten. She drains the last of her now lukewarm tea, snaps her laptop shut and puts out the light. She will speak to her therapist at the earliest opportunity; confide in her about Binks. Because something has to give. And the sooner, the better.

CHAPTER NINETEEN

Beth

In January, on Beth's first day back at work, Nessa seems edgy and out of sorts.

'Okay, listen, everyone,' she begins, one hand wrapped around her first coffee of the day, the other clutching her mobile phone.

'Happy New Year, all. Hope you've had good Christmases and managed to relax, because the next few months are going to be tough.'

She then rattles through a series of updates, including the sudden loss of a major sponsor and the fact that the rent on the building was under review. There's a collective groan at this point: this is not a good start to the new year.

'Obviously, like every other mental health charity, our overheads are already trimmed to the bone, so we need to pull something out of the bag quickly, team. That means booting up our visibility on social media, in the trade press and, of course, pushing harder than ever for corporate sponsorship…'

At the end of her address, looking pinched and harassed, Nessa retreats to her office, leaving everyone else to swap disgruntled looks before getting back to work.

'Shit,' Ray mutters under his breath. 'So I'm guessing no pay rises – again,' he adds with a roll of his eyes.

At noon, Beth knocks on Nessa's door.

'Do you have a moment, please? I'm sorry, I know my timing is off and we're all hands to the pump, but I'm due to have another counselling session today and it means leaving work half an hour early. Obviously, I'll make my time up in the next day or two.'

'Obviously,' Nessa snaps. She winces and sags in her chair, 'Beth, sorry. I'm just stressed. Not least because I had some grisly flu virus all over the holidays... the whole thing was crap to be honest.' Her smile is forced. 'Press on with your counselling – it's important.'

'Thanks, Nessa – that's good of you,' Beth says, meaning it.

It's already dark by the time Beth backs out of the office with a brisk wave. Nobody asks where she's going, or why she is leaving early, although she can see by the way he's trying to catch her eye that Ray is itching to say something.

She boards the train in the direction of home, getting off a stop before her usual one, relieved that going home afterwards will be a cinch. The last two sessions had ended in tears and self-pity. Well, not tonight. She has new information to share with Zara. An important nugget which Beth feels in her bones has a bearing on her anxiety attacks.

By the time Beth arrives at the clinic her therapist shares with an osteopath and a chiropodist, the receptionist has left for the day and Zara herself is hovering by the entrance.

Her greeting is warm. 'Hi, Beth. Happy New Year. Everyone else has gone home. Please, come on up.' Beth follows Zara up half a flight of stairs to the same bland room at the back; even the aspidistra has gone, leaving the room barer than before.

Zara looks different, too – older and less robust; she pulls a tissue from her sleeve and wipes her nose. 'Sorry,' she explains, 'tail end of a cold.'

As soon as they're seated, Beth is eager to start the conversation.

'Look, I think I've worked out what, or rather *who*, is responsible for the panic attacks I've been experiencing. And in a way I feel better just for knowing that, so I think after today—'

'Beth, slow down.' Zara's voice is soft, patient. 'Instead of planning ahead, try to stay in the moment. Okay, can you share your thoughts with me? Take your time.'

Beth nods. 'So, you remember how I was experiencing anxiety symptoms – you know, nausea, racing heart and an almost irrational fear? Well, I've thought about it, a lot, and I can't ignore the fact that these feelings started after I bumped into someone from my childhood.'

Zara tucks her hair behind one ear and leans forward. 'Can you be more specific?'

'A boy, a teenager, who lived near us… He had a twin brother. He wasn't in our circle really… my sister remembers him more than I do. Anyway, the thing is, I've seen him around a few times and my reaction is always the same – it's the whole panic attack thing every time.'

Zara laces her fingers together. 'So you feel this boy is somehow connected to your current state of mind?'

Beth nods and shifts in her seat. 'I read something,' she begins, 'my sister and I googled this person. What we found was distressing… horrible. He… this man ended up going to prison for sexual assault.'

As the words leave her lips, Beth feels the familiar tingle in her hands and a liquifying sensation in her stomach. So much for being in control. She tries to swallow but her throat spasms and she almost gags. 'May I have a drink, please?' she manages.

'Of course.' Zara leaves the room and returns with a glass of water.

Beth takes rapid sips and waits for her mouth to unstick sufficiently to go on.

'Do you need a break?' Zara whispers, concern etched on her face.

But Beth shakes her head. Something is building, a whooshing sensation, then a feeling of pressure, a shortness of breath, followed by the same dry smell of musty fur that seems to follow her these days. She breathes deeply, her nails digging into her palms.

Zara has crossed to Beth's side of the desk and is bending beside her now.

'Beth, you're okay, you're safe. Look at me, it's just us. Let the feelings wash over you, like a wave... it's leaving you now. Slow your breathing. You feel safe and calm... that's better, breathe in... and out...'

'What's wrong with me?' Beth asks, her speech thick and slurred. She tries to stand, but her legs are numb. 'Am I going mad?' she whispers, as tears blur her vision.

'No, of course not. Anxiety can be powerful. We need to focus on this one issue, explore *why* it's happening before we look at coping strategies.'

The even pitch of Zara's voice is having a calming effect. Beth gulps the rest of the water, blows her nose and attempts a smile.

'I'm sorry about that. What I was trying to say, is that I must have read about this man in the past, about him being a sex offender, and then forgotten all about it – until I bumped into him recently.' Recovering now and feeling foolish, Beth sits up straighter. 'Zara, do you think I could have filed that information at the back of my mind, and somehow turned him into a monster... all because of something I read in the local news years ago?'

Zara is nodding slowly. 'It's possible. But perhaps your fear is less about something you've read, and more about something you've experienced.'

Gemma's words ping into Beth's mind: *maybe something about him has always scared you; something from way back...*

Her heartbeat begins to accelerate again; she grips the chair with her fingertips as though she might fall otherwise. 'What are you saying?'

'Do you know what a flashback is?' Zara asks quietly.

'Yes, of course, but—'

'Beth, flashbacks can be very vivid. People can experience sounds, smells and sensations connected with a traumatic event from the past, reliving them as though they are happening in the present.'

'Are you talking about PTSD?' Beth's voice is hoarse.

'Yes. Flashbacks are a common symptom of post-traumatic stress disorder. Another is emotional detachment... being unable to express affection, a subject we've touched on before, particularly in the context of your relationships with men.'

Beth shakes her head. 'No, that's not it. It's obvious that I haven't got PTSD, because nothing traumatic has ever happened to me – life hasn't been that exciting. I'd tell you if it had. Zara, I don't mean to be rude, but this is our third session and I'm not sure it's helping much. Perhaps now I've made the connection about this boy, I should try figuring things out on my own. Maybe my doctor can prescribe beta blockers or something... just until this thing passes.'

To Beth's immense relief, the alarm on Zara's desk bleeps. She gets up, reaches for her bag and shrugs on her coat. 'Thank you. You've been brilliant and today's been really... interesting but I'm not sure I'm ready to... What I mean is, I don't think I need these sessions anymore.'

Zara is on her feet. 'I disagree. Beth, I understand your apprehension, but I'd urge you to reconsider. I'll email you tomorrow – is that okay?'

Beth's expression is a frozen grimace as she marches from Zara's room and out onto the street where the stench of traffic, rain and dust hits her. She takes a deep breath, filling her lungs with damp polluted air before swerving the tube and power-walking all the way home.

CHAPTER TWENTY

Beth

The following day, it's almost noon when an email arrives from Zara. Still unsettled by the night before, Beth scans the words once before filing it away. But not before she's got the gist: that Zara is qualified in age regression therapy, a technique used to unlock memories linked to significant past events.

Which would be okay – all very laudable, even – were it not for the fact that Beth has no past issues to unlock.

So after checking that nobody is around to read her screen over her shoulder, Beth sends Zara a brief – and she hopes, upbeat – reply, assuring her that she is feeling much more positive and able to cope, and confirming that she's taking a break from therapy to think things through on her own.

Relief coursing through her, Beth strides over to Nessa's office. 'Can I interrupt?' she asks, poking her head round the door.

'Sure. You okay?'

'Yes, thank you.' She smiles. 'I just wanted to let you know, I won't be leaving early again. I've cancelled my therapy sessions.' Without waiting for a reply, she returns to her desk.

But Nessa is on her feet, arms crossed against her narrow body as she walks towards Beth. She frowns and purses her lips. 'Right… well, I don't know why you've decided not to go back – and honestly, I wouldn't pry, it's none of my business. But Beth, you've not given your therapist a chance in my opinion. Something must have really touched a nerve in that room for you to—'

'Nothing happened,' Beth says, more sharply than intended. 'Zara just has some funny ideas. Look, Nessa, it's sweet of you to worry, but I'm fine. The whole thing was a mistake…' Beth trails off and feigns an interest in an email that has just dropped into her inbox.

It has the desired effect. With an irritated shrug, Nessa returns to her room and closes the door.

There's clomping footfall on the stairs and the buzz of conversation as her colleagues return from the lunch run. Claire approaches, sets down a brown paper bag and a cola can, misted with condensation. 'On me. You got me a sarnie last week.'

Beth smiles, thanks Claire, and takes a bite of her lunch. But her tuna and sweetcorn wrap might as well be wallpaper paste on paper for all the pleasure it gives her. She sets it aside and sips the cold drink instead.

Claire mooches over, a look of concern in her hazel eyes. 'Sorry Beth, did I get the wrong thing? Is it not nice?'

Beth sighs. 'It's fine. I'm just not very hungry today.'

Claire's lips form a thin line and she hesitates. 'You don't seem your usual self… I'm a good listener if you fancy a chat?' She waits, head cocked, for a sign of encouragement.

Then Ray is on his feet, half walking, half sliding across the carpet tiles, his expression full of intrigue.

'What's the matter, what's happened?' he gushes.

Beth wheels back her chair. 'Nothing. I'm fine – or I *would* be if everyone just stopped bloody fussing,' she snaps, getting up and marching to the washroom. Once inside, she takes several deep breaths and studies her reflection. Why is she so angry?

In one of two stalls, a frosted window overlooks the street. Beth throws it open, embracing the blast of cold air that rushes in as she stares out at the empty shop diagonally opposite. Today there are no builders at work; in fact, the shop looks ready for occupation. She wonders idly what it will be.

Hearing the soft moan of the washroom's outer door, Beth shuts the window, tucks stray windblown hairs behind her ears, and finds Nessa waiting.

'Beth, I'm sorry you're at a low ebb, but this can't go on – snapping at the team like that! They're only trying to help.'

'Or being nosey,' Beth counters, regretting it at once. 'Sorry, not Claire – she's a sweetheart. I'll apologise to her.'

'You should,' Nessa says. 'Look, I can't believe I'm saying this, but take the afternoon off. I'll say you're not feeling well, and I'll see you on Monday.'

It's two thirty by the time Beth exits her local station and starts for home but the thought of being cooped up in her flat until morning drives her into the park. She's dismayed to see two familiar drinkers sitting on a bench, huddled under a filthy duvet.

Christ, and I think I've got problems, Beth thinks as she draws closer, plunging her hands in her coat pockets and hurrying past. Realising that it's too cold for walking aimlessly, she heads for home.

She'd meant to clean the flat and put a wash on, but her good intentions have faded with the light.

Instead, nursing a cup of tea while staring out at the park and trying to pierce the gloom, Beth reflects on the last twenty-four hours in which she's sacked off her counsellor and upset her boss and all her colleagues. *Way to go.*

She reaches for her mobile. 'Laura. It's me. Can I come over?' she says, without preamble.

'Of course, love. You all right? You sound funny. You're home early… why aren't you at work?'

'Oh, just one of those days,' Beth says, ignoring her sister's questions and forcing a smile into her voice. 'I'm just fed up, January blues, maybe.'

Then without so much as dragging a comb through her hair, Beth slides her coat on and goes out to the car park, relieved that there are no neighbours around to delay her. Because suddenly, she *needs* to see her sister, to look into Laura's eyes, to feel loved, cared about – and like she matters.

More than that, she needs answers: about what happened during the summer she was thirteen and Laura turned sixteen. In the pub, Binks himself had crowed about being at a party. What was it he'd said? *Me and Billy gatecrashed your sister's fancy dress party once.* Surely between them, she and Laura can join the dots – without putting herself through any more upsetting therapy sessions that to date have done more harm than good.

Creeping along in second gear, hypnotised by drivers' stop lights, Beth barely registers the drive to Beckenham as she tries to shape the conversation with her sister in her mind.

She'll hold it together – keep it light. Explain to Laura that there are gaps – gaping holes – in her childhood memories, specifically the summer she had contracted glandular fever and had spent the school holidays in bed, in a hazy nightmarish world of fever and sickness, recovering just in time for school in September. Then she'll steer the conversation around to the Binks twins, because right now, all her instincts point to there being a connection.

Right on cue, Beth feels her palms prickle and the hairs on the back of her neck rise. With a shudder, she clutches the wheel tightly, eyes trained on the road ahead.

Whatever there is to know about Kevin Binks, she will uncover it herself, in her own time, and without the help of any new age gimmicks by Zara or any other so-called therapist.

Beth winces, remembering the abrupt way she'd marched out of Zara's office. What if – deep breath – Zara had a point? And her panic attacks were flashbacks after all?

Parking two doors' down from Laura's and walking briskly, Beth arranges her features to resemble a cheerfulness she does not feel. Alfie opens the front door as Laura appears behind him. 'Well, let Auntie in then,' she says, moving her son aside. 'So, how are things?'

'Er… not bad, thanks,' Beth's voice cracks with emotion as she shrugs off her coat, dumps it on the newel post, and follows her sister through to the kitchen.

Laura sweeps a magazine and a handful of Lego off the Carver chair Beth has sat in so many times before. 'Come on, sit. I don't believe you. What's happened? You look terrible.'

'Oh, thanks!' Beth tries to smile despite the tears leaking down her face. 'God knows, Laur. I feel like I'm losing my mind, but that's no excuse for rocking up here feeling sorry for myself.'

'You did the right thing,' Laura says, starting to fill the kettle then changing her mind. 'Sod that. You need a drink.' She opens the fridge, takes a bottle of white wine from the door and fills two glasses.

'It's a bit early,' Beth says, blotting her face with a tissue, but taking a grateful gulp, nonetheless.

There's a drumming of feet as Jack appears in the kitchen. 'Mum. Can I get—'

'Out!' Laura shoos him away and shuts the door, refocussing on her sister.

Beth shakes her head. So much for keeping it together. She'd meant to swap news, speak to Laura about her part-time job at the call centre, ask after Jack and Alfie.

Instead she takes a gulp of sauvignon blanc and blows her nose. 'Laura, tell me everything you can remember about the summer I was thirteen and contracted glandular fever.' She takes another mouthful of the wine. 'And about Kevin Binks.'

CHAPTER TWENTY-ONE

Beth

May 1994

Ants are biting the back of Beth's legs. She sits up, her outline still visible on the flattened lawn.

Laura is already on her feet, brushing down polka dot shorts, unaware there are bits of grass in her fine blonde hair. 'Why is that boy staring at us? What does he want?' she says, squinting against the sun.

Beth shrugs, stands beside her sister in an instinctive act of solidarity. 'I don't know – don't look at him. Anyway, I've been bitten to buggery – look.'

Laura grimaces. 'That'll be you covered in calamine tonight then. And don't say buggery.'

From the vantage point of their front garden, Beth peers up the avenue. Garlands of fallen blossom and grit swirl on a stiff breeze – the same wind that is causing clouds to scud at a dizzying rate across the blue wash above. The boy who had snailed past them on his bike is nowhere to be seen now.

'Laur, are we going for a bike ride, then?'

Laura huffs. 'In a minute, keep your wig on. What's the rush?'

'Nothing. But we always go on Saturday mornings.' Beth's eyes widen. 'Look, he's coming back – with another one.'

Laura frowns. 'Another what?'

'Another boy. See? They're twins.' Beth steps closer to the low Box hedge that separates their garden from the pavement.

'All right?' Says one of the boys, as both slow to a crawl, passing three metres from where the sisters stand.

Beth wrinkles her nose, tucks her hair behind her ears.

Laura smiles, shifts her weight onto one hip. 'Yeah, you?' she says.

Encouraged, the boys cease their leisurely freewheeling up and down the traffic-free street, lining up on the pavement, their front wheels almost touching the Hardings' neatly clipped hedge.

Struck by how identical the boys are, Beth's gaze roams to one lightly tanned, bony face framed by spiked hair the colour of white sand, then to the other, looking for differences and finding none. Four ice-blue eyes look back at her.

One of the boys grins. 'How old are you?' he asks Laura.

'Fifteen. Sixteen next month. You?' She giggles, rakes a hand through her hair.

But the girls are left hanging as Jeanette opens the front door and strides down the path towards them.

'What have I told you about playing out here?' she barks, glancing at the boys without acknowledging them.

'Mum, we're not playing at anything,' Laura's tone is haughty, 'we were about to go cycling.'

'Well, not right now, you're not,' Jeanette snaps, crossing her arms and taking a second look at the twins. 'You can both sit out back for now. All that lovely garden to play in and you want to hang around the street like urchins,' she huffs, turning back towards the house.

Laura hesitates, smiles shyly at the twins. 'Bye then. See you around.' She gives an awkward flap of her hand.

The boys look at each other, and with a machine gun volley of laughter, cycle back up the avenue as fast as their feet will pedal.

Taking the side gate, the girls walk around the back, where the lawn is in full sunshine. The kitchen door is open, and the radio is playing Take That, accompanied by Jeanette's de-de-de-deeing along.

'I need a drink,' Beth says, passing through the back door.

'*Feet!* I've just swept in here,' Jeanette bellows.

'Mum, why can't we cycle? We go every Saturday morning,' Beth says, dribbling squash into two tumblers and running the cold tap.

'I'm not having you two out there, while those… lads are sniffing round. You know where they live, don't you, hmm? In the brown flats on the estate, that's where,' Jeanette blusters.

'So?' Laura says, sidling in and taking a glass from her sister.

'Have you any idea what that place is like? Broken-down cars parked all over and dogs barking day and night… You two don't know how lucky you are.'

Laura pulls a face. 'Mother, how come you know so much about it?'

Beth wipes away an orange moustache with the back of her hand. 'Yeah, when have you been there, Mum?'

'Through the Rotary Club,' Jeanette snaps, 'not that it's either of your business but I've taken food donations there at Christmas. One has to do one's duty.'

Beth and Laura exchange glances. 'Well, what about your duty to us, then?' Laura remarks. 'It's a boiling hot day and we're not even allowed out.'

'It's not boiling, it's pleasant. Now go on, you can play out the back like civilised children,' Jeanette chides, chasing the girls' glass-shaped water marks off the worktop with a dish cloth.

'Like civilised children,' Laura mimics, dragging a canvas chair into the sun. 'Children! I'm sixteen in three weeks, but you wouldn't bloody know it.'

'Even *I'm* a teenager,' Beth says with a nod of empathy. 'Jesus, this is boring.'

'Don't say Jesus, either – or God will smite you.'

'Bollocks,' Beth smirks.

*

Lying on her bed watching *Blind Date*, Beth can hear the clatter of pans and crockery as her parents bump around each other in the kitchen.

'No, not like that. For goodness' sake, Tim!' Jeanette's irritation reverberates through the house.

Beth sighs, pictures her father's default apologetic expression and goes next door to Laura's room.

'What are you wearing?' she says, poking her head around the door and finding her sister painting her nails a lurid shade of purple.

'What do you mean?' Laura asks, without looking up.

'Are you changing for dinner?'

'Of course not. It's only the bloody Wards, and they're always here.' Laura reasons, admiring her manicure.

Beth disappears to her own room: if grass-stained shorts are good enough for her sister, then they're good enough for her. No doubt Guy will be made to wear a jacket and shirt. Poor Guy – always so stiff and old-fashioned!

She goes downstairs, leans in the kitchen doorway. 'What are we having?'

'Coq au vin – everybody loves my coq.' Jeanette smiles serenely, oblivious to her daughters' sniggers behind her. Her expression turns to horror as she looks round at Beth.

'Do you deliberately set out to shame me? Go and change at once; the Wards will be here any minute. I'm not having you show me up in front of Pam – especially as Guy is always so immaculate.'

'Resistance is futile,' her father whispers, with a wink.

Beth winks back. Knowing better than to argue with her mother, she obeys and scampers upstairs.

'And tell your sister to put something decent on while you're about it,' Jeanette bawls from the hallway.

Moments later, Beth hears the doorbell, and the predictable, instant change in her mother's voice, from shrill to warm and well-modulated.

She and Laura converge on the stairs, having heeded their mother's advice on changing and each sporting clean, ironed jeans and spriggy cotton tops.

Guy eyes them both through a thick fringe of lashes, the wispy shadow of a moustache darkening his top lip.

'Hi,' he says, lifting his gaze briefly before shuffling through to the Hardings' formal sitting room, which is pungent with air freshener.

'Do go through,' Jeanette beams after handshakes and pecks on the cheek have been swapped. 'Tim's on bar duty, and as always, we have everything.' She bats mascaraed lashes and bows out of the room leaving Tim to take drinks orders.

'You two, don't just stand there in the way – give me a hand setting the table. I've done absolutely everything else,' Jeanette says, ladling on the guilt.

Beth makes a face as she and Laura go about laying the table with Jeanette's best linen cloth and the good cutlery. She hears the clatter of ice cubes as her father passes by, wielding a tray of gin and tonics, and a tall glass of cola for Guy.

Dinner is the usual tedious affair: Jeanette's coq au vin is indeed a success, but the conversation is mundane and Beth cringes inwardly to see her parents and Pam and Alastair Ward getting louder with every drink that passes their lips. Apart from humouring the adults when asked a direct question, Guy says little.

'Mum, can we be excused?' Laura begs, after the last mouthful of tiramisu – Jeanette's signature dessert – has been swallowed, and *the children* are released to watch television in the den.

There's the usual scramble for the best TV viewing position on the large L-shaped sofa and, predictably, Beth winds up on the floor at her sister's feet.

'Why do I always have to sit on the floor when *he's* here?' She scowls, looking from Guy to Laura.

'Is that a real question?' Laura asks, 'Guy is a guest and I am older than you. End of story.'

Guy undoes the top button of his shirt, settles back to the point of almost lying down. He burps loudly, looking round for the girls' approval. 'Bet they're getting drunk in there,' he says, adding, 'it's ridiculous that I'm only allowed coke when we come around here. You should see what I have at home: beer, cider, vodka – the lot.' This portion of the conversation is directed at Laura, who rolls her eyes, either in irritation or disbelief – Beth isn't sure which.

Laura ignores Guy's boasting and changes the subject. 'So, how did you do?'

'In my exams? Okay, I think – except chemistry. I'm pretty sure I fucked that up. What about you?'

Laura shrugs, 'All right – apart from maths, which was the pits, but it's always been my worst subject. Anyway, we'll see, won't we? They're done now until next year. Shit, I'm dreading my A Levels.'

'Me too,' Guy says, 'but at least you've got a choice about whether to take them or not. I'll need them if I'm going to get a business degree.'

Beth rolls onto her back with an ostentatious yawn. 'Can we talk about something else? This is nearly as boring as dinner with our parents,' she moans, picking up the remote control and surfing through the channels.

Laura and Guy trade sympathetic glances. 'That's because you're just a kid,' her sister says. 'Just you wait, Beth Harding – you've got it all to come.'

CHAPTER TWENTY-TWO

Gemma

Gemma forces her eyes open, aware that a necklace of razor blades has somehow attached itself to her throat during the night. She sneezes, three times in quick succession. Sitting up carefully, she can hear the shower running in Guy's bathroom. It's still dark outside but a glance at her mobile tells Gemma that Miya needs to get up for school. *Just five more minutes…*

But another twenty have passed by the time Guy wakes her with tea, his manner unusually sympathetic. Gemma groans, sits up a second time and sips the hot strong liquid in her favourite mug. Great. Only two weeks into the year, and already she's poleaxed by a streaming cold.

It's a relief when Guy takes control. 'I can sort Miya out and drop her off at school, you concentrate on getting well,' he says, already dressed for the office.

'Thanks, hon. I'm so sorry you're having to do my job on top of your own,' Gemma apologises, her voice muffled by congestion. 'Don't worry about Miya getting home. Katya can fetch her for me – she'll be pleased to help.'

*

By the third day of surfing between bed and sofa, Gemma is beginning to feel like herself again – not to mention stir crazy.

Reaching for her mobile, she sends a text to her personal trainer.

Hi Caleb. Recovering from heavy cold. Should I work out tomorrow or not? Gemma.

Almost at once, his reply arrives.

Sorry to hear that. I recommend GENTLE exercise. See you usual time and place. C.

Pleased to have a modest goal to aim for, Gemma peers at her reflection, wishing her eyes and skin looked less dull and her nose less florid. She goes to her bathroom cabinet, takes out an array of jars and tubes, and sets about an emergency repair job.

'Christ, you look like a different woman,' Guy says baldly, arriving home from work to find Miya watching TV having already eaten, the house clean and tidy, and Gemma with shiny, blown-out hair and make-up on her face.

Gemma smiles. 'Yes, thank God I'm over it. I just hope you don't succumb at some point. Thanks for looking after us all,' she says, putting her arms around Guy's neck and nuzzling into his shirt, a warm muddle of citrus and sweat. 'How was your day, darling?'

He drops a kiss on her hair. 'Oh, you know… same old, same old. What's for dinner?'

'Shepherd's pie,' Gemma says, putting on padded gloves and removing the cheese-topped bubbling dish from the oven.

'My favourite,' Guy beams, 'am I a lucky man or what?' And he goes off to wash his hands.

*

On Thursday morning, shivering, Gemma turns the heating up high in the car and sits watching the rain as Caleb's Golf swings into the car park. He flashes his headlights, pulls into a space nearby and walks towards her car.

'Morning, Gemma,' he says, a huge grin lighting his handsome face.

'Hi,' Gemma says, getting out of the SUV. She points to the sky. 'What do you think?'

'I think as you're just getting over a cold, we should do a light jog through the trees, some squats and lunges and then call it a day. It's fine – I won't even charge you.'

'Oh no, you must, I don't want you out of pocket on my account,' Gemma says, secretly relieved that she's not about to undertake a full-blown bootcamp session.

They set off at a light jog; a lap of the rec, followed by a circuit through the woods and then back towards the car. But now, as well as shivering, Gemma has started to sneeze.

'Right, that's it. I'm calling it. Training suspended,' Caleb says. 'I've got a flask of tea in my car and a couple of energy bars. Come on, get in.'

Faces misted by sweat and drizzle, the interior of Caleb's car feels too close, too intimate, bringing a slight flush to Gemma's cheeks. But if Caleb notices, he hides it well, opening the flask and handing her a hot cup of tea, before reaching across her and fishing a couple of cereal bars from the glove compartment.

'My bad,' he says, 'I should have checked the weather forecast. The last thing you needed was to get soaked to the skin.'

Gemma smiles. 'No harm done. I was desperate to get out of the house, to be honest.'

Caleb nods. 'How's Guy?'

'Fine, busy as ever. Bless him, he was doing the morning school run while I was laid up.'

Caleb purses his lips. 'Good of him,' he says, sarcasm in his voice.

'It was. That's my department – Guy has enough to do, running the business.'

Caleb shrugs. 'Miya's his daughter, too – just saying.'

Gemma reaches for the door handle, keen to get off the subject. 'I need to get back. Thanks for today, and for the tea.'

'Wait.' Caleb touches her forearm lightly. 'Sorry, I shouldn't have said that. Of course, Guy was happy to take his daughter to school – any father would be and it was rude of me to suggest otherwise. Okay, madam,' he says, mock sternly, 'straight home for a long hot bath. I'll see you next week.'

'Thanks again,' Gemma says before jogging back to her car with relief.

It's turned nine o'clock when Guy's car mounts the drive.

'How're you feeling now?' he says, discarding his shoes and kissing Gemma's cheek.

'Better, almost normal, thanks. I made chilli. You never mentioned you'd be late tonight.'

'Didn't I? Sorry, I thought I'd sent you a text. Chilli sounds good. I'm starving, didn't even have time for lunch today because of back-to-back meetings.' With a yawn, Guy loosens his tie and flops on the kitchen sofa. 'I'm knackered.'

'Bless you, hon. You work too hard. Oh, Miya wanted me to give you this,' Gemma says, handing Guy a crayoned masterpiece.

He laughs, shakes his head. 'I've no idea what that's meant to be.'

Gemma giggles, before admitting that she too has no idea what Miya has drawn this time.

They sit up at the island together, swapping news while Guy devours two bowls of chilli in quick succession. But when Gemma tells him about her training session, his face darkens.

'*What?* You mean to tell me that you were exercising in the pissing rain today? When you've just got over a bad cold?'

'It was only drizzle and I was desperate for a change of scene.'

'*Really?* Or were you desperate to see your boyfriend?'

Gemma laughs nervously.

'You think this is funny?' Guy's tone is suddenly low, menacing. 'Only, why else would you meet him in such lousy fucking weather, when you've been sick in bed for a week, while I've been charging around like a lunatic doing everything?'

'Guy, how can you say that? You're being ridiculous. Anyway, I was only ill in bed for two days. I thought I'd shaken it off pretty quickly, considering how rotten I felt.'

Guy pushes his bowl away, ramming it too hard into his water glass which then shatters on the tiled floor.

'But not too rotten to go chasing after your gigolo mate, clearly. Anyone would think you'd faked being ill, just to earn yourself a nice little rest,' he hisses between clenched teeth.

Fighting back tears, Gemma squats at his feet and begins raking up the broken glass with a dustpan and brush. She reaches for one large shard with her fingertips, then is crying out in shock and pain as Guy stands and brings a socked foot down on her hand, jabbing her thumb in the process. Blood oozes freely from the cut, adding to the mess on the floor.

'Oh my God! Look what you've done!' Gemma shrieks, grasping for a tea towel and stemming the scarlet flow. Holding her swaddled thumb to her chest, she uses her good hand to reach for the first aid kit where she frantically hunts for plasters.

'Guy! Don't just stand there. Help me… please!' she cries, her voice quaking.

Guy eyes her with contempt. 'For Christ's sake, Gemma, it was an accident. For once in your life, stop fucking whining, or you'll wake Miya,' he snarls, stalking from the room and leaving Gemma alone to dress her injury and clear up the mess he's made.

CHAPTER TWENTY-THREE

Beth

May 1994

Mrs Mahoney's poodle, Pepé, is on loan for the week. More accurately the poor dog has been dumped on the Hardings while neighbours Evelyn Mahoney and her husband Derek are sunning themselves in the Algarve.

'He's no trouble,' Evelyn had assured Jeanette, setting down his bed and bowls in the kitchen, along with a bag that contained his rhinestone-studded harness and lead, and a selection of colourful toys. 'Just two walks a day, a meal after each, and lots of cuddles for my baby,' she'd said, nuzzling his sweet, pointy face and escaping before the tears that threatened spilled over.

'As if I didn't have enough to do,' Jeanette had huffed, eyeing Pepé with suspicion.

Tim's take on his arrival had been warmer. 'Well, I think he's a nice little chap and it's only for a week. But if it's going to be a hassle for you, he can come to the studio with me every day. He might make a good prop. People relax around animals, don't they, and the best photos are always the most natural.'

Jeanette had adopted a martyred expression. 'Oh, don't bother. I'll walk him in the mornings and the girls can take him out after school.'

*

'Where are we taking him?' Beth clutches Pepé's lead, her face flushed and sweaty, thanks to a combination of double netball earlier and a temperature of twenty-two degrees.

Laura shrugs, eyes hidden by faux Chanel sunglasses bought at the weekend from Miss Selfridge with her own pocket money.

Beth had wanted a pair, too, but Jeanette's response had been scornful. 'They wouldn't look right on you. Not with *that* face shape!'

Her mother's reaction had left Beth not only disappointed about the shades, but also baffled and newly self-conscious about the dimensions of her face, something she'd never given a second thought to – until now.

Laura looks at the little dog; a tremor has started up in one of his back legs. 'Aww, bless him. He's excited. Aren't you, boy? Are you coming for a walk? Walkies! Yes?'

Giggling at the way his ears swivel whenever the *W* word is mentioned, Beth and Laura start dawdling in the direction of the park, stopping for Pepé to sniff and wee against posts and hedges as they go.

Nearing the park gates, the girls are stopped in their tracks as two boys fly past them on their bikes, make a trick jump turn, and bounce to an abrupt halt only inches from poor startled Pepé.

'Hey! Mind the dog, idiots,' Laura cries, stepping back.

Two identical grinning faces split even wider.

'Is it yours?' says the boy wearing a T-shirt emblazoned with the words *Screw You*. He continues to jerk the bike back and forth, perilously close to poor quivering Pepé.

'No. Now sod off,' Laura says.

'Oh, that's nice. That's fucking charming, that is. There's me thinking you were a posh bird.' Yelps of seal-like laughter follow.

'What's your name?' T-shirt boy says, running his hand over spiked upright hair.

Beth smiles gamely. 'She's Laura and I'm Beth. And this is Pepé. His family are on holiday. He's sweet, isn't he?'

Laura is indignant. 'Beth! For God's sake. Don't talk to them.'

'Nice to meet you, Beth.' The other boy's voice is softer, his smile hesitant. 'I'm Billy, this is Kevin. He's oldest. By seven minutes.'

'What's it like being a twin?' Beth asks, shielding her eyes from the low sun.

Kevin grins at his brother. 'Fucking great.'

'Sorry about all the swearing, he always does that,' Billy scratches his chin, embarrassed by Kevin's potty mouth.

During a beat's silence, Beth is aware of Kevin and her sister sizing each other up.

'We've got to go,' Laura says, skirting around Kevin's bike. Billy rolls back allowing her to pass, but Kevin blocks her, his eyes fixed on hers. 'Not until you give me the password.'

'The password is dickhead.' Laura says, her cheeks flushing. She yanks the dog's lead from Beth, turns back towards home and begins marching up the avenue.

'But what about the park – aren't we taking Pepé?' Beth asks, watching as Kevin and Billy tear away on their bikes, their shouted remarks unintelligible.

'He's had enough,' Laura snaps, adding, 'and so have I.'

*

'Your dad's a perv.' Kevin Binks spits the cigarette butt from his mouth, crushes it beneath a grubby trainer and waits for a reaction.

It's almost a week since Beth and Laura last saw the Binks twins, during which time Pepé the poodle has been reunited with his family, relieving the girls of their dog-walking duties. Now, they are on a mission to buy strawberries and cream from the grocer's on the parade.

Laura tosses her hair and sizes up her opponent. 'A perv, eh? How do you work that one out?'

Beth screws her face up. 'What's a perv, Laur?'

The twins' laughter is raucous and high-pitched, reminding Beth of a programme she'd seen about hyenas.

'So?' Laura's eyes blaze with defiance. 'Well, go on.'

'He takes photos. I've seen his shop on the high street. He does porno out the back – my mate Joey told me. Bet he don't put *them* in the window like all that fucking wedding shit.'

Beth looks from Kevin Binks to her sister. Billy, meanwhile, is stripping bark from a young tree, and shredding it nervously with his fingers. 'We need to go, Kev,' he says, bored by his brother's attempt to wind the girls up.

'Your mate Joey is obviously a half-wit then,' Laura smirks at her own bravado and cleverness, 'which explains why he hangs around with you.' She folds her arms and marches towards the shops as Beth scuttles to keep up with her.

'Wait. I was only joking. Laura! I'm winding you up, mate.' Kevin calls, starting forward, as though he can't decide whether to run after her or not. But as Beth turns, it is Billy who jogs towards them.

'Wait,' he says, falling in step. 'He don't mean nothing by it. He only acts like that cos he likes you, Laura.' His cheeks flush. 'Will you go out with him?'

'Of course not,' Laura snaps, studying the pavement beneath her feet.

'I think you fancy him, too,' Beth mumbles, after Billy has sheepishly returned to his brother.

'And what would you know about it? You're just a silly little girl,' Laura says, her face hot.

'You should go out with him. Then he'd be nicer to us. You could kiss him and everything. Like this,' Beth wheels round to face her sister, blocking her path. She sucks the back of her hand.

Laura's expression is one of horror. 'What the hell are you doing? Stop it, Beth. Don't be stupid.'

That evening, huddled in front of *Poirot* after dinner has been eaten and cleared away, Beth hears the metallic clang of the letter box.

Jeanette tuts, mutters something about 'rubbish takeaway fliers coming at all times of the day and night', while their father snores softly in his favourite armchair.

Beth stands, tugs up the waistband on her jeans. 'Toilet,' she announces, swiftly passing the TV screen before her mother can complain.

On her way back, she detours to the front door area. Indeed, three yet-to-be-thrown-away junk food menus litter Jeanette's polished console table, with its push button phone and display of silk orchids. And something else. A small brown envelope, the kind bills arrive in, sits on the bristle doormat. In capital letters, it says:

TO LAURA, PRIVAT.

Beth giggles, understanding at once who the sender is. *He can't even spell private,* she murmurs under her breath, pocketing the note before creeping upstairs and into Laura's bedroom, which smells of antiperspirant spray and nail polish. Her eyes roam her sister's domain before planting the note on Laura's pillow, beneath the floral duvet.

'Well?' Beth hisses during their breakfast of cereal and orange juice.

Laura shrugs. 'Well, what?'

'You know, the note. It was *me* who bloody left it for you so that Mum wouldn't find it, least you can do is tell me what it said.'

Jeanette appears, already dressed and made-up, demanding to know what they are whispering about.

'Homework,' they reply in unison.

Once out of the house, Laura rolls the waistband of her skirt over, transforming her modest uniform into a mini.

Beth makes a face. 'You're not allowed to do that – it means you're a tart.'

'Which means what, exactly?' Laura teases.

As they pass the Wards' house, the front door opens and they snigger to see Guy wrestle away from his mother's kisses.

'Wait!' he calls, hurrying towards them. Then, shouldering school bags, the three of them straggle up the avenue. But after an initial greeting and a summation of who watched what on television the night before, Beth can bear the suspense no longer.

'So, what did the note say, Laur?'

'What note?' Guy's interest is piqued at once.

'It's nothing. She's talking crap as usual,' Laura says with a wave of dismissal.

Guy winks at Beth. 'Which means it's obviously *something*.'

Encouraged, Beth spills what she knows – which on reflection isn't much.

'Oh, for goodness' sake! I can't imagine what's so interesting,' Laura flounces, unable to stop herself smiling. 'I'll tell you both if you swear not to tell anyone else. Especially Mum and Dad.'

'Absolutely no one,' Guy says, crossing his heart with his index finger.

'I swear,' Beth says, her expression grave.

'Right, well last night, Kevin Binks stuck a note through our letter box, which Beth intercepted – cheers for that, sis – and it was kind of a love letter. I mean, the writing was rubbish, but he said some really nice things and he wants to take me to the cinema this weekend.'

'You can't go,' Guy says, curls bobbing as he shakes his head. 'He's kind of an oik. Not like us at all.'

Laura gasps. 'Jesus, Guy. You're such a snob. You're worse than our parents! Just because someone's poor doesn't make them a complete loser. I think he's interesting, and very cool. He and Billy look like Bros, don't you think, Beth?'

Guy smacks his forehead in disbelief. 'Bloody *Bros*? And that's a good thing, is it? They're not even together now and their music is shit. Christ, Laura, you've really let yourself down.' He pauses in his stride, face serious. 'Those two are trouble, who knows what they're into. Just be careful. See you, Beth.' Guy peels off in the direction of his own school without further comment.

Laura scowls at Guy's back as he marches ahead. 'None of his bloody beeswax,' she pouts, 'I can see who I like.'

'Laura fancies Ke-vin,' Beth chants, wiggling her hips and dodging a slap from her sister.

CHAPTER TWENTY-FOUR

Beth

Beth had listened intently, really concentrated while Laura had talked about their childhood in the spring and summer of 1994. Then she'd called round at her dad's and had surprised him by asking to borrow the family photo albums from that era, before poring over them in the comfort and privacy of her flat. Still nothing resonated.

Why is she categorically unable to remember that part of her childhood? Laura, on the other hand, is a mine of information, remembering songs they'd danced to at school discos, picnics they'd been on with their parents, other children they'd played with, special outfits they'd worn and treasured. She'd even mentioned a neighbour's poodle – whom Laura claimed they'd looked after while the dog's family had been on holiday. All of it, every single detail, had been news to Beth.

Baffled, Laura had shaken her head. 'It doesn't make sense. It's as if you have total amnesia for that whole year… it must be connected to your illness.'

'I don't remember that, either. Well, not really. I know I was ill because you, Mum and Dad always talked about it. But I don't remember how it actually felt.'

'Probably just as well,' Laura had mused, 'best not to dwell on spending weeks puking into a bucket, lying there sweating and delirious. I've always thought it was a miracle that I didn't catch it, too.'

'Must have been awful for Mum and Dad,' Beth had conceded. 'Maybe Mum was kinder than I remember. It would have taken a lot of strength and patience to nurse me through that. Must be horrid dealing with a sick child twenty-four seven.'

'Trust me, it's not much fun,' Laura had agreed. 'Anyway, that's almost certainly your culprit: glandular fever, so vile you blocked it all out.'

They'd talked about the Binks brothers of course: two chippy kids from the estate, who'd been up to mischief, but no more than scores of other children in the neighbourhood, once outside the leafy avenues Beth and Laura's relatively privileged background had afforded them.

'If you ask me,' Laura had said, taking her sister's hand, 'you need to move on now. That thing we read on Christmas Day evening about Kevin Binks getting banged up for sexual assault… That information was in the public domain for years and although it makes me sick to think of him being around when we were kids, he was just a gobby little boy then, not some terrifying sex pest. It's obvious what has happened: you read that article years ago, forgot all about it and filed it away under irrelevant, but then got a shock when we bumped into the twins that night in the Ship. The fact that you saw him afterwards – out and about working – only made it creepier. But that's all it was, a set of odd coincidences, and you know that deep down. Please, Beth, try to forget it.'

And she *is* trying – even picturing Binks in a compassionate way: as someone who has done his time, paid back his debt to society and is now working hard, rehabilitated by his years in jail. And yet. He is never far from her thoughts, buzzing like a dozy bluebottle on an autumn day, refusing to die, making her tense and jumpy, creeping into her dreams and disturbing her sleep.

Beth hadn't intended to tell her sister about Zara's insinuations; about her theory that the panic attacks could be flashbacks, but somehow over the last few days, as Beth continued to pick at a sore that wouldn't heal, it bubbled out on a tide of emotion and self-pity. Always the voice of reason, Laura's view had been pragmatic.

'Beth, you're my little sister. I'd know if something bad had ever happened to you. To either of us. We were inseparable as kids. You might not be able to remember our childhood very well, but I can. Sometimes I wish you'd never met that bloody counsellor. She was supposed to help with your anxiety, but so far, all she's done is scare you by opening up a whole new can of worms.'

CHAPTER TWENTY-FIVE

Gemma

Gemma is awake before the late January sunshine has had time to show itself.

Mindful of giving Guy a Saturday lie-in, she creeps along the landing, past her daughter's room and into the guest suite, where she uses the bathroom and pulls on sweats and trainers from an overspill wardrobe.

Once dressed, Gemma flexes her hand and rotates her thumb carefully, marvelling at how well it has healed since her fight with Guy and the broken glass accident.

Accident.

It seems simpler to remember it that way. After all, Guy hadn't *planned* to inflict a painful cut on her thumb, that had throbbed for two days afterwards. Nevertheless, it frightens her the way he loses his rag over small, irrelevant and often imagined situations. Gemma gives herself a little shake, unwilling to ruin the positive mood she's woken up to, and quietly lets herself out through the front door.

Five minutes later, she is cracking a lively pace through the streets, hair hidden beneath a beanie, a chill wind reddening her nose and cheeks.

Except for a handful of open-all-hours shopkeepers, a few van drivers and a couple of dog walkers, the world around her slumbers. Somehow, the fifteen-minute sprint she'd intended becomes forty-five, and an hour later, exhilarated and glowing with sweat, Gemma arrives home to find Guy frantically pacing, phone in hand while Miya eats Coco Pops in front of kids' TV.

'Where the hell have you been?' Guy bellows, shattering Gemma's bubble of tranquillity and oneness with the world.

She gestures to her running attire. 'Where do you think? Darling, I didn't want to wake you, so I just slipped out. It's such a gorgeous day. I ran as far as the rec and then along—'

'I was worried sick – anything could have happened,' Guy cuts in. He looks across at Miya and throws his hands up. 'Am *I* taking our daughter to dance class this morning then?'

At the mention of dance, Miya clatters her spoon into her bowl. 'Are we going now, Daddy?'

Gemma's heartbeat quickens; instinctively she takes a step back.

'Guy, I can take her, there's plenty of time,' she says, choosing her words carefully. 'Her class is at eleven o'clock and then I'm meeting Beth for brunch straight after. Had you forgotten?'

'Yes. No!' Guy snaps. 'Are you planning to spend *any* time with your family this weekend?'

'Of course, the rest of it. Guy, honestly, I only went for a jog – and I'm meeting a friend for brunch. You act like I'm jetting off on holiday or something.'

'*My* friend,' Guy says, sounding petulant, 'I might join you.'

Gemma moves to the coffee maker, fills its jug from the filtered water tap. 'Yes, your friend first,' she says, humouring him. 'You should come, I'm sure Beth would love to see you.'

She can see the stress ebbing away, his body becoming slack and docile.

'You know what, I'll pick Miya up after her class. You and Beth have your girly… thing, and we'll both be here when you get back.'

Gemma smiles. 'Great,' she says, relief washing over her.

*

By the time Gemma arrives at Café Nine – all exposed brickwork and hanging lightbulbs – Beth is already there, scrolling through her phone. Seeing Gemma, she gets to her feet wearing a smile that looks forced.

Instantly, Gemma is struck by Beth's appearance. Looking thin and pale, there are shadows under her eyes that Gemma has never noticed before. What has happened? Has she been ill recently, too?

'Lovely to see you,' Gemma beams, 'It's been a while.'

Beth nods. 'Yes, the last time we met was Boxing Day evening.' She frowns, her eyes darting to Gemma's plastered thumb. 'Ooh, that looks nasty. What happened?'

Gemma hesitates. 'Oh, just me being clumsy. I dropped a glass and managed to cut myself while I was clearing it up. Duh!' she adds goofily, pushing away an image of Guy's expression that night, seething and hateful. She changes the subject. 'Hey, we're lucky it's just the two of us; Guy almost gatecrashed.'

Beth shrugs. 'That would have been okay. How is he?'

Gemma pauses, unwilling to launch into her shocking story or to make their brunch all about *him*.

'Stressed,' she manages eventually, picking up the menu and scanning the specials. 'I'm starving. I've earned my food today. I was out running by seven thirty – not that Guy was impressed,' she adds, catching the waitresses' eye and ordering poached eggs and avocado on toast for both of them, along with two flat whites.

Beth, who has her coat draped around her shoulders as if in readiness for a quick getaway, has volunteered little so far and Gemma can hear herself babbling to compensate. She takes a deep breath. 'Hon, are you all right? You look a bit tired – and I can tell you've lost weight.'

Beth seems surprised. 'Have I?' she looks away. 'I suppose I am a bit low. January blues, probably.'

Gemma nods in sympathy. 'A lot of people suffer, don't they? Are you sure that's all it is? Hey, how's the counselling going?'

Beth puts her knife and fork down and needlessly stirs her coffee. 'Oh, it's on hold for now.'

Gemma's eyebrows shoot up. 'Oh, okay. I thought you were going to give it a chance, see if it helped to—'

'Zara couldn't help me.'

It's a bald statement of fact, with no room for doubt or second chances.

Gemma lowers her voice. 'Hey, you know you can tell me anything, don't you? That's what close friends are for.'

Beth hesitates, as if on the brink of confiding in her. 'Nothing much to tell,' she says eventually. Her expression softens. 'How's Miya?'

Realising that Beth isn't ready to spill whatever is bothering her, Gemma runs through their recent family news – minus the fact that life with Guy is currently an exercise in walking on eggshells and avoiding confrontation.

Beth's eyes glint wickedly. 'Are you still seeing your hot personal trainer?' she asks, sounding more like herself again.

Gemma laughs. 'Yes, he still tortures me once a week. Not sure how long I'll keep him on though; it all seems a bit self-indulgent.'

Beth purses her lips. 'Don't be daft. It's up to you what you spend your money on.'

They sit a while longer, chatting about Beth's work, Laura's family news and how on a day like today, spring seems just around the corner.

Outside on the street, it's with real affection that they hug goodbye. 'So glad we met today,' Beth says, as they part company under a crisp blue sky.

'Don't be a stranger,' Gemma calls over her shoulder, but Beth doesn't turn around and just keeps walking.

When Gemma arrives home, dumping her coat, bag and boots in the hallway, her heart swells to see Guy and Miya baking messily at the kitchen island. One of her daughter's favourite Disney soundtracks pipes from the speakers and Guy is singing along with the chorus but getting the lyrics all wrong, much to Miya's amusement.

'No, Daddy, that's not it!' she chuckles, smearing flour across her cheeks as her hands fly to her mouth.

'Any room for me?' Gemma says, putting an arm around each of them, the warmth of love flooding through her.

'Look, Mummy, we're making red velvet cake.' Miya's shout is triumphant as she stirs the gloopy mixture.

Gemma feigns surprise. 'Wow! Red velvet, eh? Gosh, that's very ambitious.'

Miya and Guy exchange looks, enjoying a secret.

'What?' Guy says, his face the picture of innocence.

Gemma crosses to the recycling bin, peers in and reaches for a flattened box close to the surface.

'So that cake you're making… it didn't come in a *K.I.T.*, did it?' She says, brandishing the packet with a hoot of laughter as Miya and Guy also erupt into giggles.

It is a moment of pure joy and happiness, when everything is right with the world; for now, nothing else matters and everything Gemma needs is right there in the room.

CHAPTER TWENTY-SIX

Beth

The Saturday of Beth's brunch with Gemma had felt like a brief respite from the worst of winter, but by Sunday, after another night's fitful and broken sleep, she pulls back the curtains to find a white sky and sleet striking her window.

Shivering, she puts on her dressing gown and goes to make tea. Then, wrapping both hands round the mug and enjoying the warmth, she stands at her living room window, gazing out at the park. Nobody is there today, not even the most seasoned dog walker wanders the paths, and the hardened drinkers have vacated their favourite bench.

Beth picks up her mobile, hears her father's faltering voice recite the same telephone number she'd memorised as a child.

'Dad, it's me,' she says, enunciating clearly as she always does when speaking to Tim on the phone these days. 'Just to say, I'll be with you by one o'clock. Do you fancy a roast dinner today? Might be nice while the weather's so grotty.'

'Oh yes, darling – if it's not too much trouble. I'll switch the oven on, shall I?'

Beth smiles. 'Maybe wait until I get there, Dad. See you later then. Bye.' She hangs up, pleased to have a focus for the day.

Beth's tour of her local supermarket is brisk, then she's back at the car, dumping carrier bags laden with fruit, vegetables, half a leg of lamb and a copy of her dad's beloved *Sunday Telegraph* in the boot. She sets off for Beckenham, relieved that the sleet has given way to fine rain.

As usual, before she's even out of the car, the front door opens and Tim stands waving. Dressed in his favourite maroon cardigan and beige slacks, it's as though he's been waiting for hours.

They hug hello, hindered by Beth's shopping bags before she pulls away and lumbers through to the kitchen. At once, she picks up the stale smell of neglect, despite it being only a week since her last visit. She longs to throw the windows open, but it's much too cold.

As usual, she parks her dad with a cup of strong tea before flying round gathering up towels and the few clothes he's worn during the week for washing. Not for the first time, she finds damp underwear in the laundry basket. She pauses, bites her lip, tells herself it doesn't matter; it's just a tiny accident.

With the washing machine whirring, Beth gets to work, peeling and chopping, filling the house with the tempting aroma of roast lamb.

Seated opposite one another in the drab dining room that had once been the height of fashion, Beth does her best to be upbeat and lively, but today the effort is draining.

After trading family news, with Laura and the boys as the main topic of conversation, Tim lays down his knife and fork with a satisfied sigh. 'Thank you, Beth. You're so good to your old dad,' he says, a note of sadness in his voice.

'Don't be daft, Dad, it's my pleasure and I wouldn't have it any other way.' She gets up, goes to the kitchen and returns with two microwaved portions of shop-bought rhubarb crumble.

'Oh, don't let me forget,' she says, thinking aloud, 'I've got all your photo albums in the car. I'll go and get them when we're done here.'

Her father smiles absently. 'There was no rush to return them. Those albums are a drop in the ocean. There are hundreds more photos in the loft. I'm afraid you and Laura will end up sorting them out one day…'

Beth shakes her head, unwilling to have the 'after I've gone' conversation with him.

A thought occurs. 'Dad, apart from the photos in the album, are there any from the summer I was ill?'

Tim nods. 'Of course, your sister's sixteenth birthday springs to mind. There are so many from that night… all the lovely young people in fancy dress. I took dozens, hundreds probably.'

An image of Kevin Binks standing by the dartboard at the Bricklayers Arms flashes in her head: *Me and Billy gatecrashed your sister's fancy dress party.*

Beth frowns. 'I wish I could remember. I mean, I know Laura *had* a party, but only because other people have mentioned it. In fact, almost everything from that summer is a blur.'

'The illness, I expect,' Tim says, his expression resigned.

After retrieving the photo albums from her car and depositing them on the coffee table, Beth cleans the kitchen thoroughly, knowing that her father has become blind to the spills, crumbs and dust that gather all week. Then she does a quick audit of the fridge, binning any out-of-date food, or dubious looking leftovers covered by clingfilm. Lastly, she picks up the plastic bowl used to collect all the veg peelings. 'Just going out to the compost,' she calls, unlocking the back door.

Outside, the light is fading and the once-cherished garden, now a tangle of weeds and overgrown shrubs, is full of shadows. Treading carefully so as not to slip, Beth shudders as she catches the scent of the leylandii, which seems to close round her, oppressive and choking. Her throat tightens and something lurches in her stomach. Reaching the compost heap at the end of the garden, she feels her heartbeat quicken and her breath come in ragged gasps.

No. No way. Not now. She cannot have an anxiety attack in her father's garden. Leaden-limbed, Beth presses on with the task at hand: to simply empty the bowl of its contents, before hurrying back inside. With great resolve and determination, she dispatches the peelings, prodding them with the same gnarled stick she has always used.

With a shudder, she turns back to the house but is overwhelmed by a sensation of being shoved to the ground. She staggers, losing her balance and landing on the chilled damp earth, an icy feeling of fear and dread pinning her there. With mounting terror, Beth shuts her eyes, willing it all to stop. And then it hits her: the same unwelcome stench that has followed her for weeks, that is so often present these days, without any visible cause.

Hearing the distant whimpering of a child, Beth tries to pierce the shadows, her eyes failing in the gathering darkness. And then she realises. The cries are her own.

CHAPTER TWENTY-SEVEN

Beth

Jeans damp and muddied, hands streaked with dirt, Beth had made a Herculean effort in front of her dad, even joking about her clumsiness as she'd explained how she'd slipped on her way to the compost pile, before making her excuses and escaping.

'Are you sure you're all right, darling?' Tim had said, studying Beth before hugging her goodbye at the door.

'I'm fine. But I went down like a sack of spuds and I feel a bit winded to be honest. I'll be okay tomorrow, good as new. Night, Dad. Don't forget to lock up properly. I'll ring you in the week. Love you.'

Once in the car, Beth grips the wheel, aware of her hands shaking. There's mud in her nails from where she'd grabbed at the earth as she'd fallen, before lying there, beached on the cold damp ground, pinned there by a profound sense of terror. The rain on her windscreen mingles with her tears as Beth realises she has never felt more confused and alone.

Back at her flat, she lights the lamps, puts the TV on for the buzz of reassuring background noise and makes herself a cup of tea. Huddled on the sofa wrapped in a throw, she waits to feel better, or to stop trembling at least. When a text arrives, she expects it to be from her dad, checking she's home safe. But it's from Laura, asking after Tim.

Beth replies that their father is safe and well, and that they'd eaten a roast dinner together. She hesitates then sends a second message.

Me? Not so much. Had panic attack in garden. V. embarrassing!!

At once, the phone vibrates in Beth's hands and Laura is on the line, demanding to know what has happened.

'Laura, calm down. I'm fine, I just went a bit wobbly for a while, that's all. It was weird… I mean, it felt like somebody physically shoved me on the ground and kept me there. Sounds so stupid saying it out loud… you must think I'm going mad.'

'Beth, of course I don't. But I'm worried, obviously.'

There's a pause in the conversation. Beth can picture her sister thinking things through, sifting the facts. She inhales sharply. 'Laura, what if Zara's right? And that I *am* suffering from PTSD? And the panic attacks *are* flashbacks, just as she suggested. The thing is, she's already right about one thing. There *are* gaps in my memory. Huge gaps from that summer I was thirteen. And then there's the stuff with Binks. My mind doesn't even remember him but ever since we ran into him in the pub, my body tells a whole different story.'

'I'm so sorry you're going through this. I wish I understood it better,' Laura says, sounding flat and resigned. 'Maybe I haven't been as supportive as I could have been—'

'That's not true. You're always there for me, Laur. And anyway, there's not much you or anyone else can do to help, is there?'

'There must be,' Laura replies. 'Another counsellor? Someone with – I don't know – different skills?'

Beth bites her lip, remembering. 'Actually, Zara is qualified in helping people to overcome PTSD. She mentioned it in an email, but I'm afraid I wasn't very receptive at the time.'

'Well, that's a start, isn't it?' Laura says, sounding more upbeat. 'Beth, you need to know what is haunting you. And the sooner the better. Get back in contact with Zara. Tell her you're ready to sort this out once and for all.'

Beth sighs. 'I'm not sure it's as simple as that. I doubt I'll just be able to pick up where I left off. She'll have closed the file on me and contacted my GP to let them know I declined the service.'

Frustration leaks into Laura's tone. 'Then go private. Mike and I will pay. Beth, stop making obstacles where there are none. Look, I know I said you needed to move on, but that was before you collapsed in Dad's garden. This is scary shit and it's escalating fast. Email Zara tomorrow. Please, love. For me. Now, do we have a deal?'

Still clutching her mobile, Beth goes to the window, pulls back the curtain. A man walking a rotund Staffie is passing under a streetlamp; two young women stagger by, giggling and leaning into each other on their high heels, evidently on their way home from a drinking spree. It's just a regular, typical Sunday night, when most people are safe and warm in their homes, eking out the last few hours of the weekend before Monday morning brings work, school, the routine of normal everyday commitments. Only for Beth, nothing feels normal – not even work – now that she is trapped in her own private hell.

'Beth? Are you still there?'

'Yes, Laura. I am. And yes, we have a deal.'

CHAPTER TWENTY-EIGHT

Gemma

The following Saturday, despite February's relentless dark skies, the mood at Darwin Drive is upbeat.

'This is a major coup, Gem – don't you understand? *At Home With…* magazine isn't just read by finance geeks, it's currently *the* lifestyle must-read of the chattering classes. Better still, it's a well-known fact that everyone goes straight to the last page and reads "How They Made It" first. I've got to hand it to the PR agency, they've excelled themselves this time.'

At first Gemma had struggled to see how a magazine that mainly featured clothes, cars and interiors could possibly benefit a business that supplied catering products to coffee shops, and her naivety had frustrated her husband. Now the penny has dropped – thanks to Guy's infectious enthusiasm.

'It's all about awareness, Gem. Association. That's why I made sure we were ahead of the whole eco-friendly, sustainability curve, and why I've been banging the PR drum about it for years. Positive association builds brands. Hon, I know I get stressed and you think I put work before everything else, but I'm doing it for the three of us. For our future.'

'I know, darling. It's brilliant about the profile piece and if you're happy, I'm happy.' Gemma puts her arms around Guy's neck and smiles up into his eyes. 'Anyway, I like having a famous husband – it's sexy.'

Guy's grin is wolfish. 'Oh, is it now? Want to show me how that works?' He cups her face and brushes her lips with his.

'Oh, yeah,' Gemma murmurs, surprised to feel genuine desire coursing through her for the first time in weeks. 'We've got a whole hour before Katya drops Miya back from her play date,' she whispers, allowing Guy to lead her upstairs.

'Hi, Mummy!' Miya gives Gemma a hug, then makes a beeline for the kitchen.

Katya smiles. 'She's such a little joy, Sophia adores her. At home it's Miya this and Miya that…' She scrutinises Gemma's face. 'Gosh, you look disgustingly healthy. Have you just had a facial?'

Gemma giggles. 'No. It's just… make-up,' she lies, realising that she must be glowing from her impromptu hour of passion.

Katya's expression becomes knowing. 'Ah, got it… Sorry, didn't mean to pry. Anyway, I must run, Sophia is in the car.' She backs away, wearing a tight smile.

With a grimace, Gemma shuts the front door and moves through to the kitchen where Miya is describing her play date to Guy in minute detail.

He looks up, eyebrows raised. 'Katya didn't want to come in?'

'No, she had to dash. Another time,' Gemma says, going to the fridge and removing a bottle of wine. 'Okay, let's get this Saturday night started,' she cries, suffused with a sudden rush of happiness.

She pours two glasses of wine and hands one to Guy, before putting Nina Simone on the smart speaker. Then, holding Miya's outstretched arms, the two of them begin dancing to 'My Baby Just Cares for Me', stalking up and down catwalk style, posing, twirling and pointing their toes, while Guy claps in appreciation, a huge grin lighting his face. 'More, more!' he roars as the two of them take a bow, flushed with pleasure.

Gemma holds Guy's gaze, feels that something has shifted. Whatever has made him cruel and ill-tempered for the last few months has run its course. Relief and hope flood through her.

'Your turn, Daddy!' Miya jumps up and down. 'Your turn to dance with Mummy.'

Every surface, mirror and object gleams with cleanliness. In the sitting room, every cushion is plumped to perfection and lavish displays of blue and white hyacinths scent the air.

Guy completes his inspection of the ground floor. 'Well done, hon. Everything's immaculate, you've worked really hard.'

Gemma smiles. 'I had help this time,' she admits. 'Mrs Vickery who cleans for Alan and Anya King was a complete godsend, bless her.' She appraises Guy's appearance, nodding her approval. 'You look perfect; your eyes are like molten chocolate against that shirt. In fact, you look every inch the handsome, stylish entrepreneur. Right, well, I suppose I'd better put something decent on, just in case they want me in the background somewhere.'

Gemma jogs upstairs, changes into a cornflower cashmere sweater, her favourite designer jeans and cream suede ankle boots. Then she brushes her hair, glosses her lips and joins Guy who is pacing nervously in the kitchen.

'She's late,' he says, his voice gruff, after midday has ticked by and Carolyn Gow from *At Home With…* is a no-show.

'Well maybe she's stuck in traffic?' Gemma volunteers. 'Or perhaps we've got the time wrong?'

Guy takes out his mobile, scans his emails. 'No. Look, I've got it here – definitely midday.'

With the phone still in his hand, it begins to vibrate. He receives the call, signals to Gemma.

'Hello? Yes, this is Guy Ward speaking. What? Oh, I'm sorry to hear that… Well, does she— Oh, I see. All right. We're ready and waiting. See you shortly… Yes, you can park right outside. Great. Bye.'

'Who was that?' Gemma asks.

Guy's expression is one of barely concealed pride. 'That was Paul Mundy, the features editor at the mag. Carolyn is dealing with a family crisis – a sick child, apparently – but rather than cancel, Paul wants to interview me himself. He's on his way… reckons another forty minutes.'

'Oh, darling – that's wonderful. I mean, not for Carolyn, obviously – but they must really want you if they're prepared to shuffle everything around at short notice.'

Guy shrugs. 'It would seem so.'

Gemma observes Paul Mundy as he briefs Guy about the magazine's readership, its demographic and its online presence. Estimating him to be in his late thirties and with the perma-tan of the well-travelled, she can't help but notice how he'd look at ease modelling Armani on the lifestyle pages, rather than editing or writing for them.

'Can I get you a drink, Paul? Tea, coffee, something cold perhaps?' Gemma's smile is warm, accommodating, as she hovers, torn between supporting Guy and giving him space and privacy.

'Nothing, thanks, I always carry my own water.' He pauses, really looking at Gemma for the first time. 'Look, will you be around for this— sorry, I've forgotten your name…'

'It's Gemma. Just give me a shout if you need anything.' She smiles before escaping to the study and leaving the door slightly ajar.

She can hear Guy, trotting out the usual key facts about his business, as if Paul were a potential client, talking up the company's eco-friendly philosophies, its ethical values.

'And yet,' Paul interrupts, 'one wouldn't necessarily get that from looking at this house and the cars on the drive. I mean, it's just an observation, but you see where I'm coming from.'

Gemma stiffens. Comments like that will not go down well with Guy. And anyway, how dare this man judge him?

Guy's reply is smooth, unruffled. 'I keep my business and private life very separate. At home we keep our carbon footprint relatively low by flying rarely, recycling practically everything and using ethically sourced and organic products where possible. I'm sure you're aware, Paul, *real* change happens at a corporate level.'

There's a shift in subject, a hushed exchange as Gemma hears her own name mentioned. Guy peers round the study door. 'Gem, can you come, love? He wants to give you a mention, maybe take a couple of pics, too.'

Gemma gets to her feet, momentarily flustered. 'Really?' she checks the time, mindful of collecting Miya from school within the hour. 'Okay. Do I look all right?'

Guy smiles. 'No, you look bloody gorgeous – now get in there.'

CHAPTER TWENTY-NINE

Gemma

At the school gates, after watching Miya skip to her classroom with Sophia, Gemma chats to Katya and a handful of mums before driving to Waitrose and heading straight to the magazine aisle.

Moments later, clutching an Americano and three copies of *At Home With…* magazine, she dials up the temperature on the Range Rover's aircon and flips straight to the last page, eager to read all about Guy in the 'How They Made It' section.

Only it isn't about Guy. The subject is Gustav Clark, a young designer with wet-look eyebrows and teal-coloured hair, whose aspirational accessories are made exclusively from recycled plastics.

Disappointed, Gemma finishes her coffee and crawls home in second gear, caught up in the last knockings of school run traffic.

Deciding against phoning Guy and risking his wrath at the piece being postponed, Gemma swings into Darwin Drive at nine forty to find Alan and Anya King chatting to Lucille Goff, who gives her a vivacious wave as she approaches. Surprised, Gemma stops the car, and lowers her window. It is then she notices that both Lucille and Anya are clutching copies of *At Home With…* magazine.

What a coincidence, Gemma muses, realising that both households must be subscribers. 'Hi, Lucille, morning, Anya, Alan. How is everyone?' Gemma's tone is warm and pleasant, although she can feel her bladder throbbing from the coffee and anyway, she has no desire to get sucked into drive-side gossip with the neighbours this morning.

'One half of our celebrity couple returns,' Lucille gushes.

'Cracking piece, Gemma. Love the photos,' Alan calls, earning him a sharp glance from his wife.

A tiny furrow appears between Gemma's brows. 'I'm sorry... what?'

Anya steps towards the car holding the magazine up like a stop sign. 'Oh, haven't you seen it yet? Pages seventy-two and seventy-three. Fabulous! You look incredible, quite the film star.'

Confused, Gemma puts the handbrake on, reaches across to the passenger seat, grabs a copy and rifles the pages. 'Oh my God!' she exclaims, unable to conceal her shock.

And there it is, about two-thirds of the way through the mag: a glossy double page spread, by-lined by Paul Mundy, Features Editor, depicting some barely recognisable, airbrushed power couple in their *sumptuous London villa*. She scans the photographs, totting up seven (seven!). One depicting Guy, alone, looking moody and rakish, two photographs of Guy and Gemma in a tender, cheek to cheek pose, and four large prints of Gemma alone, posing in the various outfits Paul Mundy had asked her to wear.

'Gosh. Well, this is unexpected,' Gemma manages, her smile freezing on her face. 'Sorry, I must go, I've got to— Nice to see everyone,' she says, rolling forward onto her own drive and practically scuttling inside the house, keen to get away from the admiring – even envious – glances of the neighbours.

'Oh, no! Guy will go batshit,' she says aloud as she legs it to the cloakroom.

After cutting through the morning's chores like a woman possessed, Gemma is on time for her training session with Caleb. As usual, he is already there, leaning against his car, a huge grin on his face.

'You know I charge extra for celebrity clients,' he teases, as Gemma jogs towards him.

The magazine. Has the whole of bloody south London seen it?

'Ha! Funny,' she says, feeling the warmth creep into her cheeks.

'Seriously, Gemma – you look amazing. I should put that picture of you in the black and gold dress on my website as a case study!' He laughs. 'Hey, I'm only joking. You look fabulous. Own it, woman.'

Gemma's flush deepens. 'I don't even know what happened. They came to the house to interview Guy for a business profile, and somehow it turned into… *that*!'

Caleb's expression changes. 'Ah, okay. I think I see the problem. Gemma, it's hardly your fault, is it? You should call the journalist when you get home, find out what happened.'

By the end of the session, despite the damp and the mud, Gemma drives home feeling cautiously hopeful. Caleb is right, it's not her fault the article is not as expected. Perhaps Guy will be proud of being the last in a run of celebrity spreads that includes European royalty, an A-list racing driver, and a Premiership footballer with his bride to be. On the other hand, it wouldn't hurt to know the circumstances, forewarned being forearmed.

Gemma goes to the study and straight to Paul Mundy's business card. On the second ring, the phone is answered by a cheerful female voice.

Gemma clears her throat, and asks for the features editor, wondering what an earth she's going to say next.

'Paul, hi. It's Gemma Ward. How are you?' she begins, nervously. 'Look, I'm really sorry to ask you this, but I've seen the mag and I was surprised. I mean, it's not what I thought and I just wondered—'

'Gemma, I understand,' Mundy cuts in. 'You're quite right; we don't usually put, um, real people in that section of the mag so I'm sure you'll appreciate what a fantastic opportunity it is. It was a twist of fate. The celeb couple earmarked for those pages had a death in the family the night before we went to press – it was a case of filling the space at short notice. The photographs of you – and your husband of course – were fabulous, so we ran with them. As for the profile section, we bank those weeks in advance, so we just grabbed another one. No need to thank me.' Gemma is aware of him covering the mouthpiece and speaking to someone else; she has lost his attention. 'I must get on,' Paul adds. 'Ciao.'

And she's left listening to a dial tone. Queasy with the realisation that the whole thing is out of her hands, Gemma takes a long hot shower. Then she dresses in clean sweats and heats some soup which she eats sitting at the kitchen island while re-reading the magazine with mounting horror. For the first time all day, she wonders why she has heard nothing from Guy and feels a stab of dread for his homecoming.

By early evening, anxiety has made Gemma unusually waspish with Miya.

'*Please* stop messing me around and eat up. I'm not in the mood for your silliness,' she snaps, watching her daughter paste ketchup around her plate whilst managing to eat almost nothing.

'Not hungry and I *hate* sausages.' Miya pouts, flinging down her fork.

Gemma takes a deep, steadying breath. 'Since when? Oh, you know what, Miya? Eat or don't. It doesn't matter to me.'

With a stab of guilt, Gemma sees a look of hurt cross her daughter's face as she meekly picks up her cutlery and begins to eat in silence.

By the time Guy arrives home, food has been played with, eaten and cleared away and Gemma feels sick with dread at the prospect of his reaction to the magazine spread.

As usual, Guy puts Miya to bed, returning after only ten minutes, his face softened by love.

'We're so lucky, Gem,' he says, pulling a stool up to the island where Gemma is dishing up shepherd's pie. 'Ooh, hello. What have I done to deserve my favourite?' he rubs his hands in anticipation.

Gemma waits until Guy is enjoying his meal before she opens the magazine and lays the spread before him.

'This came out today,' she says, not quite believing he's gone all day without mentioning it.

Unable to eat for butterflies the size of bats in her churning stomach, Gemma watches Guy scan the photos, nodding slowly while reading the copy in silence.

'Wow. Well, they certainly liked you,' he says eventually, his eyes fixed on Gemma's. 'I mean, for fuck's sake: "former model" Gemma Ward? Christ. It beggars belief,' he says icily, getting up and dumping his plate in the sink. 'When exactly were you a model?'

'I wasn't, you know that – and so does Paul Mundy. He asked me whether I'd ever modelled, and I said, "Only at a friend's charity fashion show at college". Guy, I said that. You heard me. Don't you remember?' Gemma gabbles, aware that panic is making her stutter.

Guy shakes his head. 'What *I* heard was you flirting shamelessly with Paul fucking Mundy the whole time he was here. Honestly, Gemma, the clothes he had you put on… mutton dressed as lamb or what? I mean, just look at this one – the black and gold job. Christ, you look like a hooker.'

Gemma is stung. 'Guy, you bought me that dress, you used to like it.' She sniffs as the tears that have threatened all day spill down her cheeks. 'For what it's worth, I don't like the article either. The whole thing was supposed to be about you. But I can explain – I rang him and he—'

'You *rang* him? Bloody hell, Gemma. What the actual fuck?' Gemma steps back, the low rumble in Guy's tone a warning shot.

'I… I phoned to ask him what had happened to your profile page. He said he'd run it at a later date,' Gemma lies, her voice shaking, 'but that he had to pull another spread because someone died and that it was us or blank pages.'

She watches him weigh up her explanation.

'Oh, I *see*. Okay…' He gets up, paces the room. 'Well, thanks for making me look a total twat, Gemma. And for making this all about *you*. Cheers for that.' He starts for the door, then looks back, his eyes narrowed and hard. 'How am I supposed to face people now, hmm? Now that my wife has been emblazoned across the pages of a magazine, looking like a cheap glamour model? What exactly does that say about *me*, Gemma? About our family? You *disgust* me,' he all but spits the word.

Gemma gasps. 'I disgust you? Guy, how can you say that? I'm your wife… and Miya's mum.'

'Then act like it. Anyway, I can't stand here arguing with you. I've got an early start tomorrow – some of us actually work for a living – so I'm going up. To the spare room,' he adds with contempt.

'Guy, I'm sorry, but how is it my fault?' Realising she is wasting her breath, Gemma sinks onto the kitchen sofa and gathers herself before loading the dishwasher and finally taking the stairs to bed.

The face that looks back at her from the bathroom mirror is not that of a model, or a celebrity housewife, but of a deeply unhappy and stressed woman. A woman who – *admit it, Gemma* – is afraid of her own husband. She winces, remembering his stinging words: *You look like a hooker… You disgust me…*

What kind of man can feel, let alone *say* those things to his own wife? Even a year ago, the idea of Guy speaking to her that way would have been unthinkable. Now, she finds herself cringing in anticipation of what he'll do next. What does that say about the future of their marriage?

Desperate to shut down her racing thoughts, Gemma reaches behind the jars and bottles and pulls out the box of Zammertil.

Piercing the foil, she removes one tablet, pops it into her mouth and scoops a handful of water from the cold tap.

How could Guy possibly believe she'd flirted with Paul Mundy, or that she'd *enjoyed* posing for his photographs in the eveningwear he'd picked from her wardrobe? She'd felt like an idiot, trying on clothes for his approval, her discomfort obvious at the time.

Wired but exhausted, Gemma gets into bed, curls up on her side, small and still, and waits for the Zammertil to take effect.

CHAPTER THIRTY

Beth

There's a new addition to the room: a print of a Mondrian, its primary colours stark against the magnolia walls.

Zara smiles. 'Eye catching, isn't it? I've ordered another one. I thought the pair of them would inject some life,' she says, gesturing for Beth to sit.

Zara herself has undergone somewhat of a makeover. Her hair is shorter, blonder, and there's a rosy hue to her cheeks that Beth has never seen before, making her wide green eyes even brighter.

Beth takes a deep breath, holds her therapist's gaze. 'I owe you an apology. I'm sorry for the way I acted the last time I was here. I appreciate you seeing me after I was so rude and awkward.'

'You weren't rude or awkward, Beth. You were fearful. Believe me when I say I've seen every emotion in this room. You have nothing to apologise for. Do you mind me asking, what changed your mind about continuing with our sessions?'

Beth sighs. 'Knowing that it won't stop. It'll get worse, won't it? I was at my dad's recently and something happened in the garden. A sort of collapse, a paralysis. Dad was in the house, none the wiser – I kept it from him – but it made me realise that it'll keep happening until I get to the root cause.'

'That must have been very frightening. And very noble of you to protect your dad. You obviously love him very much.'

'Of course,' Beth whispers, 'I can't bear that the day will come when he won't be around anymore.' She swallows the lump blocking her throat. 'Anyway, I spoke to my sister that evening and she was very supportive. We both agree that I need to get to the bottom of this thing, however stressful it is.'

Zara nods slowly. 'And your sister is planning to help you throughout the process?'

'Yes…' Beth hesitates. 'The man I've mentioned to you… he's called Kevin Binks. He was sort of a friend of Laura's. I've tried speaking to her about him, and it's like watching an old film I've seen before. Bits come back to me as she's talking, but there's something else, just out of reach.' Beth shudders. 'Zara, I need your help to remember. Because if I don't, I'll never move forward. I know that now.' Her chin wobbles. *Keep it together.*

Zara pushes a box of tissues towards her.

Beth shakes her head. 'Thanks, but I'm okay.'

'All right,' Zara says, 'let's start by talking about something you *do* remember. Beth, I want you to close your eyes and think back to the year you were thirteen; now I'd like you to describe whatever comes into your head.'

*

May Bank Holiday, 1994

Beth sniffs the air: bacon. Its unmistakeable smell entices her downstairs and into the kitchen where her mum, in housecoat and slippers, is standing at the stove. Visible through the connecting arch, their father sits at the table, engrossed in the *Daily Telegraph*.

Tim looks up, smiles and enquires whether her sister is awake yet.

Beth shrugs. 'How would I know? I'm not psychic,' she says, hovering beside Jeanette, her mouth watering as she gazes into the spitting frying pan.

'Mind, or you'll get splashed. Go on, out of my way!' Jeanette barks, basting golden yolks with a spatula.

Beth sighs heavily then moves towards the table, sits opposite her father and helps herself to orange juice.

'Morning,' Laura says, joining Beth at the table and helping herself to tea from the pot.

'Can someone give me a hand?' Jeanette calls, her back still turned.

At once, Beth is on her feet and carefully carrying two plates of full English which she sets down in front of her dad and sister, before returning for her own and devouring every scrap.

'Look at the state of you,' Jeanette admonishes, 'bloody egg yolk all over your chin!'

Beth grins and scrubs at her face with a napkin.

A satisfied silence descends, punctuated only by the clatter of cutlery.

Tim looks up from his empty plate and smiles at Jeanette. 'That was absolutely delicious, darling. I could eat it every day.'

Laura shakes her head. 'Then it wouldn't be a treat, would it? Dad, can we go out today? It is a holiday after all.'

Tim sighs. 'Not for me, I'm afraid. I've got far too much work to do. I'll be in my darkroom most of the day, developing.'

Beth's eyes light up. 'Can I come? Please, Dad, can I?' She reaches for the last piece of toast in the rack. 'Might as well go to work with you. There's nothing else to do around here,' she says, earning an eye-roll from Jeanette.

Beckenham High Street is all but deserted. Some of the smaller shops have opened, but the traffic is light and there are fewer parked cars than usual. Gleeful at finding a space right outside the studio, Tim whistles as he jangles a bunch of keys, turns off the alarm and bends to pick up a small mound of post. Bypassing the shop floor, they make their way through to the back. Without the benefit of natural light streaming through the windows, it seems dark and oppressive, until Tim flicks a switch, illuminating a cramped office area with a desk and swivel chair, two metal filing cabinets and shelves heaving with books, old magazines and all manner of reference material. Two closed doors tantalise: on the left, her father's darkroom, with its pungent smell and dim red lighting. But it is the other room that fascinates Beth, her hand hovering over the door handle.

'Can I look inside, Dad?'

Tim nods. 'Of course, but don't touch anything.'

'I won't,' she calls, opening the right door, and it's as if she has entered another world. Crisp and white, a blank canvas of new paint, the studio houses two telescopic frames holding giant rolls of paper that serve as backdrops, one as white as the walls, the other a deep caramel brown. A third roll, blue – dappled like a summer sky – lies flat on the linoleum floor. Against one wall, there's a wooden stepladder and a trestle table festooned with props: hats and scarves, a metallic wig, a feather boa and huge plastic sunglasses. Beth imagines herself, halfway up the step ladder, posing like a model in a magazine.

Turning off the lights, she backs out of the room and goes straight to her father's desk, where she sits in his chair and begins twirling back and forth. 'What shall I do?' she asks.

'You can give me a hand if you like, while I'm in my darkroom. I've got a wedding to process and I don't want you in there, inhaling all those nasty chemicals.'

Beth nods. Keen to be useful, she is soon put to work sorting piles of contact sheets on her father's desk, matching them to their corresponding 10x8 prints and inserting both into large brown envelopes – or Job Bags, as he calls them.

She scrutinises each contact sheet, marvelling at the rows of tiny pictures, each minutely different from the one before, like the miniature components of a movie. Most of them are of weddings; brides in beautiful gowns with flowing veils and shining eyes, standing beside grinning, surprised-looking men in dark suits. Beth's eyes are drawn to the bridesmaids. How long before Laura gets married and she can wear a silk dress with matching slippers and flowers in her hair?

There are baby photos: tiny tots, toothless and smiling, plonked on rugs and furs. Older children, too; boys in bow-ties, little girls with hair ribbons and smock dresses, cheeks dimpled by uncertain smiles.

Near the end of the pile, there are pictures of a couple at a grownups' party, where the guests have crinkled faces and browning teeth, champagne glasses raised in a toast.

And right at the bottom, photographs that give Beth an odd fizzing in her stomach. A woman, with long, untidy blonde hair in an array of outfits: a red bikini; a tiny silver dress that barely hides her black lace knickers; and a scarf with butterflies on it, draped around her otherwise naked body. Beth stares. Why would anybody want these? The others all look like special, happy occasions, but these look like a dressing-up box gone wrong. Is this unsmiling woman a model, perhaps? Thickly lashed round eyes gaze back at her—

Beth jumps as the dark room door opens, casting its warm amber glow.

'All right, darling? How are you getting on?'

'Nearly finished, Dad.' She smiles, still holding a 10x8 of the woman wrapped in the butterfly scarf, the contours of her body clearly visible beneath.

Tim's eyes rest on the print.

'Dad, is this lady a model?' Beth asks, curiosity getting the better of her.

'Yes. In a way.'

Beth frowns. 'Then she could have worn something nicer. Like in the magazines.'

Tim hesitates. 'Well, some people like that kind of thing… it was what she wanted to wear.'

'I think she looks awful – she's not even smiling. Does Mum like these?' Beth asks, somehow knowing the answer but testing the water anyway.

Tim clears his throat. 'Oh, we don't need to mention these to your mother, do we? Weddings and babies are much more her style,' he says, smiling in a way Beth doesn't recognise. 'Not that there's anything wrong with this type of thing, you understand. In fact, some people call it art. Even so, Beth, there's no need to mention this at home.' Tim rests a hand on her shoulder. 'It can be our secret.'

*

Beth takes a deep, slow breath, her eyes meeting Zara's over the narrow desk between them.

'Gosh, I have no idea where that came from. I haven't thought about that day for years. It was the first time I realised Dad wasn't perfect. Because there he was, lying to Mum. Just as Laura and I lied to our parents when we were naughty.'

'And how did that make you feel?' Zara asks.

'I liked that we had a secret from Mum. It made me feel special.'

She jumps as the alarm on the desk sounds.

Zara pushes her seat back. 'You did really well, Beth. So much detail and clarity; see how much you can remember when you focus and still the mind?'

Outside, startled and pleased by how light it is, she looks for Laura's car and finds it parked under a budding cherry tree, its blossom ready to pop.

Laura sits reading a magazine, setting it aside when Beth opens the passenger door and gets in beside her.

'Hi. Thanks again, Laura.' Beth smiles gratefully. 'It's good of you to come with me, I don't deserve it.'

Laura frowns and purses her lips. 'Nonsense. Of course, you do – and I wouldn't have it any other way. Let's go get a drink and you can tell me all about it,' she says, pulling smoothly into the traffic.

CHAPTER THIRTY-ONE

Gemma

On the Friday morning, Gemma had fought her way through sleep, her tongue thick and her eyes slow to focus as she remembered the bitter row about the magazine spread the night before.

Miya had bounced on the bed. 'Don't be a sleepy-head, Mummy. Daddy's downstairs and he says you've *got* to come.'

'I bet,' Gemma had murmured, swinging her legs out of bed and staggering to the bathroom.

Downstairs, with a martyred expression, Guy had made a big deal of making coffee for her, and giving Miya her cereal, hissing about her 'pill-popping addiction' as soon as Miya was out of earshot.

Then he'd left for work. 'I won't have it, Gemma. Look at the bloody state of you. Sort yourself out, for fuck's sake,' had been his parting shot.

Somehow, she'd held it together during the school run, desperately hoping that none of the mums would mention how tired she looked, or reference the magazine from the day before. Nobody did – it was already old news. If only Guy could forget as quickly.

Once home from school, grateful to be alone, Gemma takes the stairs to her bathroom and reaches for the Zammertil with the intention of throwing them away. Not that Guy has a point; no *way* is she addicted to her pills. The only reason she's resorted to the odd one recently is because of the stress that Guy himself has been putting her under. And even then, there have only been five or six instances in as many months, surely?

Hands shaking slightly, she slides the foil packs from their box, then stares in disbelief.

One of the three blister packs is missing, another is half empty.

Think, Gemma, *think*. She'd taken one last night. Of course, she had, knowing that she'd never get to sleep with Guy's cruel words ringing in her ears. Similarly, in the last few weeks, she'd taken half a pill on the nights when he'd let her down, shouted at her and made her feel worthless. Even then, Gemma can only summon a handful of occasions.

So where exactly are the rest?

Soon the ground floor has been vacuumed and dusted, the washing machine whirs with its second load of the day and Gemma is on her third cup of coffee and feeling more robust.

Guy's vicious words had been spoken in anger and disappointment. Firstly because of the magazine article, which in fairness to him, had been a million miles from the profile piece he'd expected. And secondly, because he was phobic about drugs of any kind – even ones prescribed by the doctor.

And he'd only lashed out and been so vile to her because he was worried about where it was all going. Could it be possible, then, that Guy himself had removed the pills – to stop Gemma from taking too many?

She hugs herself as a shudder rips through her. What if she has been so stressed lately – so cowed and distracted by Guy's unpredictable behaviour – that she's been doing odd things on autopilot? Things she wouldn't consciously do at all. Losing her memory. Losing – *don't go there, Gemma* – her mind?

She shakes herself. *Okay, stop it now with the catastrophising.* The row with Guy had been horrible and his treatment of her shocking, but no doubt he'd come home from work this evening, contrite and sheepish, with flowers, or some little trinket he'd hurriedly bought at lunchtime.

I must try harder, make more of an effort, Gemma reasons, looking around her stylish home and reminding herself how lucky she is.

With a pang of guilt, she pictures Beth in her dowdy, soulless flat, rotating her wardrobe of tired, cheap clothing. Beth, who asks for nothing – and receives as much.

On impulse, Gemma sends her a text.

Fancy Sunday lunch? It's been too long… we miss you! xx

Hoping that Beth will be free and that they can all get round the table as a family and fill the house with conversation and laughter like they used to, Gemma presses on with stripping the beds and vacuuming the first floor. Fleetingly, she wonders if perhaps she should have asked Guy's permission, rather than issuing invitations off her own bat.

But an hour or so later, when Beth is presumably grabbing a sandwich at her desk, a reply arrives.

Sounds lovely but will be at Dad's. Another time though? Hope all well. Miss you too, X

Feeling idiotic for forgetting Beth's weekly visit home, Gemma resolves to organise something else – and soon.

Exhausted but satisfied following a top-to-bottom house clean and a trip to the organic butcher's for steak, Gemma waits for Guy's return, ETA seven fifteen.

By seven forty-five, Gemma is ravenous after her industrious day and Miya is becoming cranky with tiredness.

'When will Daddy be home,' she whines, 'I want my story.'

'I don't know, sweet pea, he should be back by now. Maybe he's stuck in traffic, or perhaps he had to work late. Shall we call him?'

Gemma dials Guy's mobile, but after three rings it goes to voicemail. Ten minutes later, she tries again but this time the phone is switched off.

With a growing unease, she re-wraps the steak, returns the salad to the fridge and pours herself a glass of sauvignon blanc, wondering if Guy has been unavoidably delayed, or whether he is still punishing her for last night.

By nine thirty, Gemma knows the answer. Running late is one thing, but total radio silence smacks of meanness. Blurred by wine and self-pity, she rings Beth and is surprised when her call is answered on the second ring.

'Beth! How are you, hon? Is it too late for a chat?' Gemma can hear the slight slur in her words. So what? No way will a close friend like Beth judge her for having a glass of wine.

'Of course not, it's been ages,' Beth says, sounding regretful. 'How are things? And how come you're ringing me on a Friday night? Where's Guy?'

'Fuck knows.' Gemma giggles. 'Sorry – excuse my French. We've had a row and right now, I haven't a clue when – or even *if* – he'll be home.' She hiccups into the handset.

'Gem, that's not good. Look, are you okay? Have you had a drink tonight?' Beth asks gently.

'Jesus, don't you start! Guy thinks I'm a pill-popping alcoholic as it is.'

'Sorry, I honestly didn't mean it like that. And Guy can be such an idiot sometimes. Even when we were kids, he could be so bloody self-righteous.'

Gemma groans. 'He's hard work. Beth, I can't take much more of this. Everything I do is wrong these days. Guy used to be so loving and easy-going – well, maybe not easy-going exactly, but the little things never rattled him. But now, I spend my life wondering when he'll next blow a gasket.'

'Are you serious? Gemma, that's horrible. I'm so sorry. I've been such a rubbish friend recently, too wrapped up in my own… stuff. What set him off this time?' Beth asks, real concern in her voice.

It's a relief to talk and Gemma finds herself explaining about the magazine and Guy's bizarre overreaction to it. Beth's indignant cries feel like a warm, comforting blanket across the line.

'He takes you for granted, Gemma,' Beth says. 'He's so used to being the big cheese at work that it's gone to his head. How dare he treat you like this? It's Easter in two weeks so Miya will be off school. You should get away for a few days. Give him a chance to miss you. That'll teach him.'

Gemma laughs, enjoying the camaraderie and realising how much she's missed it. 'But where would I go? I don't fancy sticking Miya on a plane and going to see Mum in Spain – although I probably should. Lord knows when she'll come over next.'

'I'd offer to have you both, but my flat is so small and there's no garden for Miya if the weather's nice. Haven't you got an auntie in Sussex?'

'Yes, my aunt Marina, near Eastbourne. God, I haven't seen her since Miya was a toddler.'

Gemma pictures her aunt: gentle china-blue eyes that shine out from a weathered face, her fine ash-blonde hair escaping its claw clip. And the house, with its garden full of lavender, hydrangeas and hollyhocks, and on a clear day, a view of the wide, sandy bay.

'Beth, come with me.' The words are out, before Gemma can think them through.

'What? I can't do that. I mean, a few days at the seaside would be dreamy, but I can't just tag along, can I?'

'Why not?' Gemma says, warming to the idea. 'Auntie is very chilled, and she loves meeting new people.' Then reality hits like a slap. 'God, Beth. Guy will have a fit. I can't take Miya away without his permission. It won't be a lesson. It'll be the end of my marriage.'

'Gemma, promise me you'll at least think about it. I can't stand the way he treats you recently. It's just plain weird.'

Gemma sighs. 'Guess I need to grow a pair and stand up for myself. Okay, enough about me. How are you doing?' She listens as Beth bolts through the headlines of her life: her work, her dad's health and that she is giving counselling another chance.

'Gemma, I just feel… stuck, somehow. There's stuff I'm working through, to do with my childhood – you and I have talked about it before – and my therapist is convinced that I'm having flashbacks, rather than panic attacks. I dismissed it at first – flashbacks to *what*? I had a happy childhood. But recently there is something, like the snatches of a dream, just as you wake up… And now I'm thinking if I don't sort this out, then nothing will ever change for me. Gem, please don't mention it to Guy, will you? It's too close to home, too private. Does that sound silly?'

'No, I totally understand.' She pauses, suddenly on high alert as Guy's car swings onto the drive. 'I'm sorry, but I've got to go. He's home.' And then she can hardly end the call quick enough as Guy walks into the room, his expression tight and closed.

'Hey,' he says, dumping his briefcase and helping himself to a glass of water as though they are casual acquaintances.

Gemma straightens up, smooths her hair. 'You're late. Is everything okay? I didn't know what to do about dinner.'

'I got engrossed in something at work and ended up going for a drink with a couple of guys. And before you say it, Gemma, I had *one*. One drink, so I was fine to drive.'

'Of course,' Gemma is meek, deflated, realising that this time, there are no flowers, no quirky little gifts – and absolutely no sign of an apology.

CHAPTER THIRTY-TWO

Beth

June 1994

'Swear to me you won't tell Mum and Dad?' Laura lies on her back, hands laced behind her head, while Beth sits upright, one foot perpetuating the gentle motion of the swing seat which is almost in shadow now.

Indignant, Beth wrinkles her nose. ''Course not! What do you take me for? On one condition: you tell me all about it when you get home. *Everything*.' Beth says, wiggling her eyebrows.

Laura studies her fluorescent orange nails. 'I don't know what you mean. We're only going for a drink. At the Ship Inn, probably. Kevin says they never ask for ID in there.'

Beth frowns. 'I'm not bothered about the pub, Laur. I want to know if you *kiss* him. Or if you let him, you know… touch you.'

'For God's sake, Beth. You're so bloody weird. You're as bad as Guy; he keeps obsessing about me and Kevin.' Laura sits up, hugs her knees. 'Not that it's anyone's beeswax but mine. I'll be sixteen in three weeks, so it's up to me, isn't it?'

'All right, keep your wig on – just asking,' Beth says, crossing her arms. 'Anyway, I thought he was taking you to the pictures.'

Laura shrugs. 'Nothing on that I want to see.'

Later, while Saturday night TV blares from the sitting room, Beth watches Laura pick at Jeanette's spag bol, eventually pushing it aside.

'Sorry, Mum – it's lovely, I'm just not hungry.'

Beth shoots her sister a look, knowing she's too excited to eat. 'Shame to waste it. I'll eat hers,' she offers, slurping the last of her own spaghetti.

'You will not! Another dinner is the last thing you need, young lady – just look at those hips,' Jeanette snaps.

Beth's eyes fall to the offending part of her anatomy. 'What's wrong with them?'

'Nothing at all, darling,' her dad's smile is kind, 'you're a growing girl, that's all.'

Laura excuses herself and goes upstairs, returning twenty minutes later in her best jeans, red sandals that match her lips, and a white broderie anglaise top straining over her chest.

'You look nice, Laur,' Beth says.

Jeanette shakes her head in disapproval. 'Although God alone knows why you need all that make-up for listening to music round at Kerry's.'

Laura and Beth's eyes meet. 'Just fancied a change. Right, I'm off then. I'll be back by eleven – Kerry's dad'll drop me home. Bye!'

The front door slams and Beth is left alone with her parents. Another Saturday night yawns ahead.

In Beth's experience, Jeanette is at her most receptive whilst engaged in a task, so she waits until they are side by side at the kitchen sink before voicing her idea.

'Mum, can Laura have a party this year? I mean, sixteen's kind of a big deal, isn't it?'

Jeanette purses her lips. 'As a matter of fact, your father and I have been having the same conversation.'

'Oh!' Beth's eyes widen. 'How about fancy dress? And a proper DJ? Mum, we'd need decent music. And a barbeque… with maybe a—'

'Hold your horses. Daddy and I haven't decided yet.'

Beth smiles to herself as she dries the cutlery, polishing it with extra care. At last, something to look forward to.

Beth had planned to lie awake and listen for Laura coming home, before grilling her for every detail. Nevertheless, she'd fallen asleep sometime after ten and now dust motes dance between a gap in the curtains, heralding Sunday morning.

She gets up, puts on her gingham dressing gown and pads down to the kitchen, where Tim is waiting for the kettle to boil.

'Good morning, darling. Did you sleep all right?'

'Morning, Dad. Yes, thanks. Seen Laura?'

Tim pours boiling water into two mugs and starts prodding the teabags with a spoon. 'Still in bed, I think.' He smiles. 'Right, I'll just take your mum a cuppa. Get yourself some juice, won't you?'

Standing on tiptoes, Beth takes two tumblers from a high shelf and carefully fills them with orange juice. Then she takes the stairs, knocks once and enters Laura's room.

She gazes at her sister. Fine blonde hair spilled across the pillow, reminding her of Sleeping Beauty. Laura's lips are a blurred stain from the night before. Beth gasps. On her neck, just below her right ear, an angry purplish bruise marks her otherwise flawless skin.

'Oh my God,' Beth whispers, then louder 'Laura! Wake up. I brought you some juice. It's practically lunchtime,' she lies. Laura's digital clock glows 08.40.

Laura flings an arm across her face, shielding her eyes from the sun. 'Hmm? Sod off, it's Sunday!' She sits up, last night's mascara still clinging to her eyelashes. 'Shit, you're annoying, Beth. Thanks for the juice, though.'

Beth waits until Laura has drained the glass. 'No need to ask if you had a good time.'

'What? Yes, it was okay.' She turns away, a lazy smile curving her lips.

'So, you kissed him then?' Beth persists.

'Why on earth do you want to know, weirdo?'

'I know you did, so don't bother to lie,' Beth points to Laura's love bite. 'Mum will have a fit.'

Laura scoffs. 'Only if you tell her. I'll hide it with makeup or a scarf. Anyway, if you're desperate to know, we went to the Ship – which was quite crowded actually – and I had two Bacardi Breezers, and Kev drank cider. Then we walked to the Rec and sat in the little shelter thingy and—'

'And that's when he kissed you!' Beth's eyes gleam with intrigue.

'Maybe. Beth, it's private. I'm not saying another word.'

'You don't have to.' A thought occurs to her. 'Do you think Billy fancies me? We could all go out together, sort of double dating.'

Laura shakes her head in disbelief. 'Honestly, what planet are you on? No, of course Billy doesn't fancy you, Beth. You're a *child*. The twins are my age. Look, stop all this silliness or—'

'Or what? You'll tell Mum?' Beth frowns. 'I don't think so, not with what I've got on you, Laura Harding.'

She marches from her sister's room and straight to her own, hurriedly dressing in yesterday's clothes. How dare her sister call her a child?

CHAPTER THIRTY-THREE

Beth

With the sun beating down from a cloudless sky, the temperature is more June than April.

Eyes hidden by sunglasses, Beth watches in amusement as Laura corrals her family to the trestle table erected by Michael that morning.

'How lucky are we?' Laura says. 'I never thought for a minute we'd be having our Easter dinner in the garden. Where's Dad, is he still washing his hands?'

'I'm here,' Tim calls, stepping stiffly onto the patio area before wedging himself between Jack and Alfie. He beams, surveying Laura's festive table, bedecked with spring flowers and tiny fluffy chicks.

Beth dives back into the kitchen and helps ferry steaming dishes of vegetables to the table before Laura sets down her centrepiece: a beautifully carved leg of lamb. At the sight of it, she is suddenly ravenous. 'You really are a total domestic goddess, Laur. I'm practically drooling here.'

'Well, don't stand on ceremony, dig in, everyone.'

Beth observes the well-oiled machine that is her sister and brother-in-law's marriage. The clearly defined roles: Laura, hostess, chef, magic-weaver, while Mike, who has spent the morning cutting the lawn, putting up the table, chairs and a huge parasol, is now keeping glasses topped up with ice-cold French rosé.

'Mum, did you and Auntie Beth have Easter eggs when you were children?' Alfie asks, squinting into the sun.

Grinning, Laura and Beth exchange glances. 'Of course, it wasn't the stone age, you know, chocolate had been invented.'

By four o'clock the heat has left the sun and the adults drift inside, leaving the boys bug hunting in the garden.

Tim is soon dozing, his slack jaw emitting soft snores. Michael gets up. 'Mind if I check my emails?' he says, excusing himself.

'So, how's it going?' Laura asks, waiting until her husband is out of earshot and speaking softly so as not to wake their father.

'How's what going?'

'You know, the counselling. Do you feel you're getting any-where?'

Beth shrugs. 'Maybe. I've only been once more since you took me, and it's just me talking – like I'm thinking out loud. But it's funny the way things are coming back to me. I'm remembering a lot more about Mum and Dad.'

'That's great, Beth. I hope it helps, honestly, I do. Have you talked much about Kevin… and about that summer?'

'Not so far—'

Tim comes to with a start. 'Goodness, have I been asleep again?'

'Relax, Dad,' Laura says, getting up and arching her back into a stretch. 'Anyone fancy a drink?'

The conversation dries as Laura and Beth make a pot of tea for the adults and orange squash for the boys, who come in tired and bedraggled. By seven o'clock, everyone is growing restless.

'I should go. I'll take Dad home on my way,' Beth says, shrug-ging on her jacket. 'I only had one glass of wine and enough food to feed an army. Thank you, Laura. It's been a gorgeous day.'

'My pleasure, love – thanks for coming. I'll ring you in the week, shall I?'

In the car, Tim gazes out of the window. 'You can talk to me, you know, Beth,' he says during their five-minute journey together.

'I know, Dad. But I'm fine, honestly. Here we are. Isn't it a relief to see the lighter evenings again?' Beth parks at the foot of Tim's drive and helps him from the car while he grumbles about her changing the subject. Ignoring his comments, Beth minesweeps the house for any horrors before hugging him and saying goodnight.

'I heard you and your sister talking, you know,' Tim says, his eyes pink-rimmed and hooded as they stand by the front door, 'about the counselling. Don't dig too deep, my darling. Sometimes the past is best left there. Goodnight.'

CHAPTER THIRTY-FOUR

Gemma

In her quiet, throwaway style, Beth had sown a seed. Now, the idea of getting away for a few days, to escape arguments and point-scoring, the relief to walk on a beach, to taste sea spray on her lips and feel the wind whip her hair, seemed beyond blissful.

Then, the morning after their conversation, Gemma had taken the kitchen rubbish outside and opened the wheelie bin to find her black and gold dress – the one she'd been photographed in for *At Home With…* – slashed to ribbons and wedged in among the plastic sacks, and that had clinched it.

How could Guy do such a thing? The meanness, the pure, boiling rage he must have felt while destroying her dress scared her. For her own sanity, Gemma had to get away.

Fearful of his reaction if she confronted him, she'd said nothing about the dress. Instead, she'd waited until Miya was on school holidays and Guy was in a positive frame of mind, before marshalling her courage and tackling the subject of visiting her aunt.

'The thing is, Marina's not getting any younger and I don't want to have regrets after she's gone. Auntie was so good to me when I was a child. I've got lovely memories of playing with my cousin on the beach during the school holidays – memories and experiences I'd like to share with Miya. It would be good for her, don't you think, darling?'

Guy had only sagged, his expression beleaguered. 'Gemma, I get it. But right now, I can barely take weekends off work, never mind jaunting off for a bloody mini-break. You've no idea how stressed I am. Anyway,' he'd added sulkily, 'I've only met Marina once, and that was at our wedding. There's only so much old-lady twaddle I can stomach, you know.'

Despite Guy's uncharitable remark, Gemma had seen a chink of light appear – slim, but bright.

'In that case,' she'd said, emboldened by hope, 'why don't Miya and I visit Auntie alone over Easter? It'll take the pressure off you for a few days and you needn't feel guilty if you want to work through the holidays. Seriously Guy, it could be ideal for all of us.'

Guy had narrowed his eyes. 'Ideal how?'

Careful, Gemma, don't blow it.

'Miya gets to play on the beach all day, I get to spend some quality time with Auntie, and you get to focus entirely on work, without having to worry about us.'

Guy had smiled then, an open, genuine smile that had reached his eyes and for a second Gemma had ached to put her arms around him and ask where he'd been.

*

Miya has stopped singing now and is firing Gemma with questions from her booster seat in the back.

'And Mummy, does your auntie have any pets? Will I have anyone to play with? Where will I sleep?'

Gemma smiles, regards her daughter in the rear-view mirror. 'Miya, you'll see when we get there. Trust me, you'll love it.'

'But will Daddy come another day? I miss him.'

A pang of guilt prickles in Gemma's chest. 'Not this time, sweet pea. He has to work. Anyway, we only left home two hours ago: how can you be missing him already?'

And then, ahead, their first view of the sea; a valley of sparkling blue glimpsed between a white Edwardian hotel and a brown sixties office block.

'Look Mummy, I can see it! I can see the sea.' Miya shrieks, and the decades drop away as Gemma remembers being driven in her parents' car during the summer holidays.

Miya's excitement is infectious. 'I know, isn't it brilliant? We'll be at Auntie's in a few minutes. You were only two the last time I brought you, so it'll be like meeting her for the first time. And remember, best behaviour, please, madam.'

'Goodness, Auntie - you haven't aged a day!' Gemma says, wrapping her arms about Marina's bird-like body.

Her aunt waves a hand in dismissal. 'Oh, if only. I'll be seventy next year, can you believe it? Now, let me look at this beautiful little girl.' Marina bends to cup Miya's face. 'Just adorable,' she breathes before ushering them both inside where the scent of lavender and lemons greets them.

Gemma takes in the faded elegance of Marina's cottage; the botanical prints on the walls, the embroidered cushions patterned with animals and birds. The hotchpotch of dried flowers and old china – things that would be banished from Gemma's own fashionable home, but which seem like priceless treasures in her aunt's domain.

'I expect you're both hungry after driving through lunch,' Marina says. 'We can eat in the garden if you like – it's warm enough.'

'That would be lovely,' Gemma beams.

Miya is busily peering into nooks and crannies, exclaiming at Marina's whimsical ornaments. 'I love it here, Mummy,' she whispers as they follow Marina into the kitchen, 'it's like a doll's house.'

Outside, the warmth has coaxed lilac and wisteria into early bud, their delicate scents adding to Gemma's delight as they make their way to a pergola groaning with clematis; beneath it, a wrought iron table laid with pale pink linen beckons.

Miya claps her hands. 'Oh! It's like a fairy tea party. Can we have cake and sandwiches?'

Gemma grimaces. 'Miya, what have I told you? It's rude to ask for things.'

'It's not rude,' Marina winks, 'it's enthusiasm. Now, you two sit here, while I fetch lunch.'

Beyond a low wall, the sea glitters in the distance. Gemma exhales, feels the tension leaving her body for the first time in months, and wishes she could spend all summer in this lush, wild garden, with its view of the sea.

*

On Good Friday morning, Gemma wakes early, pinned by Miya's left leg thrown sleepily across her midriff while they'd slept. A gap in curtains patterned with daisies reveals another bright day, perfect for exploring the beach.

Extracting herself gently so as not to wake her daughter, Gemma creeps out to the bathroom, then takes the steep, wonky staircase down.

'Morning, Auntie. And there's me being careful not to wake you!' Gemma says, finding Marina by the window watching a platoon of tiny birds ravage a hanging feeder stuffed with nuts and seeds.

'I'll make some tea,' Marina says, getting up and gliding towards the kitchen. 'Did you sleep well, Gemma?'

'Like a log. Miya's still out cold. I'll leave her a while – we've nothing to rush for. Oh, unless you have plans? I just thought with it being Good Friday, everything would be closed.'

Marina fills the kettle. 'You're right. Which is why I went shopping yesterday. We can take a picnic to the beach, if you like.'

'Perfect. Miya will love it. Here, Auntie, let me do that. Go and sit down, please. Finish your tea.'

A blissful hour floats past as the two of them chat idly, catching up on family news and enjoying the peace, except for the frenzy of birds outside the window. Miya wakes up bright-eyed and curious, keen to explore, and by noon the three of them are pitching a camp on the sandy bay.

'How come there aren't more people on a bank holiday?' Gemma asks, shielding her eyes from the midday sun.

Marina shrugs. 'There's nothing much to attract the crowds: no shops, or cafés, no amusements. If people want all that, they can find it a mile or two either side. But Wyncombe Bay? It's a hidden gem – and long may it last,' she says, gazing out to sea, a smile broad on her lips.

The mood is broken by a sudden yelp from Miya, startled at the sight of a small dead fish tangled in a nest of seaweed washed onto the shoreline.

'Well, come away then and leave it alone,' Gemma says, after Miya has amply expressed her revulsion.

They eat lunch from Tupperware boxes, topped off by more of Marina's homemade cake, then sit around on throws and cushions, marvelling at the extraordinary weather.

By four o'clock, with no sign of the sun abating, they walk home, sticky with salt, hair tangled by the wind.

'Mummy, can we move to the seaside?' Miya says as they decamp to Marina's garden.

'Sadly, no, sweet pea. We have to stay in London so that Daddy can go to work every day.'

Gemma looks up to find Marina's eyes searching her own.

Dusk has fallen and with it a chill. The doors and windows of the cottage are closed, Miya is tucked up for the night – exhausted from her day of beachcombing – and Gemma and Marina are halfway down a bottle of rosé wine.

Features softened by candlelight, Marina turns to face her niece. 'Is there anything troubling you, Gemma, darling? Only you've barely mentioned that handsome husband of yours since you arrived yesterday. Has something happened?'

Gemma exhales, aware that she's on the edge of a precipice now, knowing that once she steps off – *if* she steps off – there's no telling where she might land. She hesitates, then meets Marina's gaze.

'Oh, Auntie,' she swirls the wine in her glass, 'how long have you got?'

CHAPTER THIRTY-FIVE

Beth

With no plans for Easter Monday, Beth had fought the urge to stay in bed dozing and reading, instead forcing herself out into the glorious spring weather. Wearing comfortable flats for walking, she'd ended up at Crystal Palace, one of several Victorian parks within fifteen minutes of home.

Now, after a relaxed lap, in which she'd taken in the boating lake, the dinosaur zone and the vast lawned areas with their regal magnolia trees and rhododendron bushes, Beth sits inside the park's café and looks around at the eclectic mix of hipsters, housewives and yummy mummies with shouty toddlers. The boisterous buzz of conversation is transcended by the piercing yelps of two tots squabbling over a chocolate brownie. 'What did Mummy say?' the mother intones patiently. 'Mummy said it was *to share*, didn't she?'

Beth catches the young mum's eye and suppresses a smile, wondering if referring to oneself in the third person is a parental trait.

Her thoughts turn to her father's parting remark from yesterday: something about not digging too deep and leaving the past in the past. What exactly had he meant by that? Her relationship with her dad had always been so full of love and trust. Her mother – not so much: spikey and difficult were the words that came to mind.

Making a mental note to press her dad on it the next time she saw him, Beth drains the last of her coffee and heads back outside where golden sunshine shimmers through the newly clothed trees.

Suddenly, her step is frozen by the sight of the Binks twins on the narrow path ahead. Identical, except for the colour of their T-shirts, the brothers stand either side of a smiling red-haired little girl who is taking small, faltering steps on shiny new roller skates.

'That's it, Erin. Go on, girl. Wow! You're doing it!' One of the men is saying, a look of pride on his face.

Her heart galloping in her chest, Beth veers off the path and onto a grassy bank where she hides behind the broad trunk of a horse chestnut tree. At once, she's aware of her breath coming in ragged gasps and the sudden rhythmic pounding in her ears.

Immobilised by fear, she feels sweat bloom on her face and neck, while her palms and underarms prickle.

As the trio moves closer, Beth can hear the child's excited cries. 'Look, Daddy, the ice cream van. Can I have one, please? Can I?' she says, her upturned freckled face a picture of happiness.

''Course you can, princess,' says one of the men, 'you wait with Daddy, while your Uncle Kev gets us all a ninety-nine.' His grin is broad as he strides towards the ice cream van, hands thrust in his jeans' pockets looking for change.

So, Billy Binks is a father – and Kevin, a doting uncle.

With a shudder, Beth's eyes stray to Kevin's back, as he queues by the van, the taut muscles of his shoulders visible through his T-shirt, the tattoo of a coiled snake on the back of his neck.

Desperate to escape, Beth is plotting her exit route when she is struck by a sudden change in the light, like an eclipse blotting out the sun and leaving darkness in its place, lit only by the rosy glow of candles or a fire.

In the distance she can hear tuneless singing, a song she knows well – has always known. She wrinkles her nose; there it is again.

The smell of old fur that she has grown to loathe and fear. What the hell? What *is* it?

Beth waits, not trusting her legs to carry her.

It will pass. It always does, she tells herself, digging her nails into her palms.

CHAPTER THIRTY-SIX

Beth

Only a week has passed since Beth's last therapy session, but again Zara has made more subtle changes to the room.

The second Mondrian print has duly arrived and now hangs opposite its counterpart, a vase of purple irises adorns Zara's desk and a shiny new Anglepoise lamp sits on top of a metal filing cabinet.

'It looks nice in here,' Beth nods, taking a seat opposite her therapist, the familiar sense of apprehension fluttering in her stomach.

Zara smiles. 'So, Beth, how have you been since I last saw you?'

Beth sighs. 'Honestly? It's been a tough few days.'

'All right,' Zara says softly, her gaze unflinching, 'why don't you tell me about that.'

Beth takes a deep breath, and relays the story of seeing the Binks brothers in Crystal Palace Park. 'And just like the other times, it came out of the blue. One minute I was fine, walking around, enjoying the sunshine and the spring flowers. I'd even spent a very pleasant forty minutes by myself in the café and had coffee. But then I saw them – the twins – and straight away, I felt terrible… ill, really scared, you know? And that choking, rotten smell. Zara, I'm so sick of this. I just need to know *why*.'

Zara nods. 'I understand. It must be very frightening for you, Beth.' She writes something on her notepad. 'Okay, let's build upon the work we did last week. I want you to close your eyes, and picture yourself during the summer you were thirteen. Don't try too hard, just relax. Listen to my voice and breathe deeply for a count of five, four, three…'

*

June 1994

'I know something you don't know.' Beth taunts, looking to Laura for a reaction.

'I doubt that,' Laura says, affecting boredom.

Beth smirks. 'Oh, yes I do. And you'll go mad when you find out what it is.'

'Good mad or bad mad?' Laura asks, her curiosity getting the better of her.

'Oh, good mad, definitely.' Beth loosens a huge dandelion with a trowel, pulls gently and inspects its bulbous and hairy root. 'Wow! Look at this one, Laur,' she exclaims before tossing it into the rapidly filling plastic tub between them.

The girls had thought it a novelty at first; squatting in the dirt behind the leylandii, their gloved hands pulling weeds while they chattered out of earshot of their parents.

But an hour later, with the afternoon sun beating down on the backs of their necks, bored and thirsty, they yearn to lie on the swing seat with a cold drink, or go for a bike ride; either would be better than this.

'We'll still be here at flipping bedtime,' Beth grumbles, despairing at the overgrown borders.

'You heard Mum… "Extra pocket money must be earned, not given",' Laura says, mimicking Jeanette in a faux posh accent.

Beth straightens up, wipes the sweat from her brow. 'What do you want the extra cash for anyway?' she asks.

Laura shrugs. 'Just stuff. Clothes, make-up. I want to look decent on my birthday, don't I?'

Beth smirks. 'So that you can go out with your boyfriend, Kevin?'

Laura sighs. 'Maybe. I don't know yet. I might go out with someone else. He's not the only boy in town, you know. Anyway, I've had enough of Kevin. And his weird brother who just stares and never says anything.' Laura stabs her fork into the ground. 'What's this big secret, then?'

'Wouldn't you like to know?'

'Obviously, I just asked you, didn't I?' Laura sighs. 'We'll never get all these weeds done. Nobody walks up here anyway – it's just a dumping ground.' She wrinkles her nose, 'And it stinks.'

'It's just compost,' Beth says. 'Laura, it's brill. You're getting a party for your sixteenth. It's fancy dress, with a DJ and a bar and everything.'

Laura's face lights up. 'Seriously, they said that? Mum and Dad are giving me a party?'

'Yep. But it's meant to be a surprise so you'll have to pretend you guessed or something.'

'Wow, I can't wait! This is going to be the best birthday ever!' Laura shrieks, her eyes shining.

*

Beth comes to and is surprised by the tears pricking her eyelids.

'Only it wasn't. It wasn't the best birthday ever,' she says, her voice barely a whisper as she hugs herself. 'Something happened that night. To Laura? Or to me? God, Zara – I wish I could remember, but it's hopeless… trying to recall something I really don't want to.' She slumps in her seat, exhaustion washing over her. 'Help me, Zara. I need to fix this.'

'Beth, try to stay calm and positive. You're doing really well; in fact, you've made great progress. You couldn't remember any of this before we started the process.' Zara sits forward in her seat.

'Perhaps the next time we meet, we can go deeper. If you feel ready, of course. But there are associated risks.'

Beth shrugs. 'Such as?'

Zara hesitates. 'Well, if you were to uncover a traumatic experience from the past, there's a possibility that your mental health could get worse before it gets better. Worst case scenario, you could experience depression, anxiety, even psychotic episodes.'

Beth clenches and unclenches her suddenly clammy hands. Hoarse, nervous laughter escapes her. 'Great. Well, I already have two out of three. Perhaps I should go for the full set? Zara, you're really not selling this well.'

'I'm just trying to prepare you, Beth.' The timer bleeps, signalling the end of the session. Zara pushes her chair back. 'Please, give it some thought. Talk it over with your sister. It's brilliant that you have her support.'

'Pub,' Beth gasps, sliding into the passenger seat of Laura's car. 'I need a drink.'

Laura nods, alarm registering on her face before she pulls out into the traffic. 'Okay. Fox?' she asks, heading north on the main road.

'Anywhere that serves alcohol,' Beth whispers, staring out of the car window but seeing little.

Perhaps the next time we meet, we can go deeper. Zara had made it sound like hypnosis – a trance-like state.

But what if she spun out? Had some bizarre, violent reaction? *A psychotic episode,* Zara had suggested as much.

Idling at traffic lights, Beth can feel her sister looking at her.

'Love, are you okay? Please tell me what happened in there, you're shaking.'

Beth chews her lip. 'I'm all right, Laur… could do with a drink, though.'

Ten minutes later, they are swinging into the car park of The Fox & Hounds which is already buzzing.

'Let's sit over there, it's a bit quieter,' Laura says, scanning the packed bar and taking charge.

Relieved to find herself in such a wholesome and jovial atmosphere, Beth follows, and busies herself with people-watching while her sister goes to the bar, returning with two G and Ts.

'Cheers,' Laura says, adding 'I must say, I feel very decadent being in a pub on a Thursday night. Mike looked a bit jealous as I went flying out the door to pick you up.'

Beth drinks gratefully. 'Cheers. Thanks for coming with me. I know you've got enough on at home, what with the boys' homework and mealtimes.'

Laura shakes her head. 'Right now, you're my priority. I said I'd support you through this and I meant it. Now, spill.'

Beth finishes her gin and tonic and sets down the empty glass. 'I feel as though I'm on the brink of discovery. Something connected with your sixteenth birthday party. Not that I can remember that night… Honestly, not a thing… but all sorts of odd peripheral images are coming back to me. Daft, small things. Just now, in the session with Zara, I remembered us weeding in the dump behind the leylandii hedge for extra pocket money when I was teasing you because I knew you were having a party before you did. Can you believe that? Laura, my thoughts are so *random*. None of it makes sense. And yet I feel as though it's just a case of joining the dots.'

Laura places a steadying hand on Beth's. 'You'll get there. Although goodness knows why you remember us weeding the garden. So, what's next? What does your therapist think?'

Beth takes a deep breath. *We can go deeper.*

'You remember I told you that Zara has worked with other people suffering from PTSD? Well, she's qualified in age regression therapy. It's a kind of hypnosis that can help people to unlock memories. Laura, she could take me back to my childhood, as if

I were reliving it. Oof, it scares the hell out of me. What if I find out something I really can't handle? Something that tips me over the edge?'

'Then we face it together,' Laura says. 'Beth, you can do this. You have to do this.'

CHAPTER THIRTY-SEVEN

Gemma

They'd said a tearful goodbye under the lilac tree in Marina's front garden.

'Don't look so sad, Gemma, darling. You and Miya are welcome here anytime. And I mean that. I might not be around the corner, but I'm certainly closer than your mum in Malaga, so don't be a stranger,' she'd said, her voice cracking with emotion before hugging Miya and walking them both to the car.

Miya had waved until Marina's cottage was out of sight. 'I loved it at the seaside, Mummy. Can we go again in the summer?'

Gemma had brushed a tear away. 'Of course. You heard Auntie. Anytime.'

By the time she'd joined the London-bound motorway, the warmth and motion of the car had lulled Miya to sleep, leaving Gemma alone with her thoughts as they sped towards home.

She'd barely communicated with Guy in days; a *night night* text at Miya's bedtime every evening had been the extent of their contact. She'd pictured him, working through the weekend, dealing with international suppliers who paid little heed to the bank holidays, writing projections and proposals, then arriving home, laden with takeaway, before watching the ten o'clock news and crashing into bed. No wonder he was so ill tempered.

Gemma, on the other hand, had treasured long sandy walks with her aunt, Miya skipping ahead, peering into rock pools and crevices with a mixture of delight and disgust. Gemma had loved wearing the same jeans and fleece for days, and that she hadn't once opened her make-up bag. Neither had she paid any attention to her diet and exercise regime. None of it had mattered, hidden away in Marina's cosy cottage where she'd felt fifteen again. No wonder she'd slept a straight eight hours every night.

Nearing home, the sky has changed from wide and blue to a mottled grey, pinched between buildings. As if sensing their arrival, Miya opens her eyes and yawns.

'Are we home, Mummy?'

'Two more minutes, sweet pea,' Gemma says, glancing in the rear-view mirror.

'Will Daddy be home?'

'Not on a Tuesday, angel. He's at work. We'll see him tonight.'

'Hurray! I missed him,' Miya cries, wriggling in her booster seat.

'Me too, sweet pea,' Gemma lies, turning into Darwin drive and realising with a stab of guilt that she hasn't missed Guy at all.

*

'Who is this tanned little beach bunny?' Guy cries, wrestling Miya down and tickling her stomach as she shrieks with laughter.

Over her head, Gemma and Guy's eyes lock. Releasing his daughter, Guys sweeps Gemma into his arms, lays his cheek against hers, his breath warm in her ear.

'Oh, I missed you so much. Coming home to an empty house was horrible. Don't leave me again. Next time, we'll all go. I even considered coming down to surprise you, but then I realised that I don't have Marina's address.'

Gemma extracts herself. 'Oh, really? I'm sure it's on the computer. It must be, I always send her cards for Christmas and birthdays.'

Guy dumps his suit jacket in the hall and returns, grinning. 'Let's all go out to dinner. I don't want you cooking tonight, Gem.' He caresses her face. 'You look beautiful, rested. Coastal life agrees with you. Right, I'll get changed. I fancy a great big, cheesy Burger-Meister with sweet potato fries.'

'Yay!' Miya is pogoing on the spot. 'And chocolate brownies for dessert, Daddy.'

'Whatever you like, angel,' Guy calls, jogging upstairs.

Gemma chews her lip, shocked by the warmth of his welcome. Well, if Guy can make a renewed effort, so can she.

Half an hour later, they are in Guy's car bound for the nearest branch of Miya's favourite organic burger chain.

Gemma steals a look at Guy's profile. 'You look tired, darling,' she says softly, checking that Miya's headphones are in.

Guy nods resignedly. 'I know, can't seem to get on top of things lately.'

'Then let's cancel our plans for the weekend and hole up at home,' Gemma says, her heart thawing. 'We can take Miya to the park, have TV dinners and just be, rather than do. How does that sound?'

Guy groans with relief. 'Perfect. I might need to pull an all-nighter in the office before we get there, but it'll be worth it. Gem, I wasn't joking. I missed you so much – far more than I expected.' He pauses, his eyes flicking to Miya in the rear-view mirror. 'I've been a complete shit to live with for months and it has to stop. From now on, you and Miya come first.' He puts out his left hand and Gemma takes it, feels the warmth of his squeeze.

'Well, perhaps I need to be more supportive,' Gemma says, 'and a little less self-absorbed.'

Guy smiles. 'Don't be daft. You do everything for this family, Gem.' He raises his voice. 'Right, here we are. Now to find a parking space.'

Walking two blocks from the car with Miya swinging between them, Gemma's spirits lift.

It will be okay. It will all be okay. Clearly, in her absence Guy has had a wake-up call, an epiphany.

Under a striped awning, a queue straggles from the restaurant. Gemma braces herself for a barrage of unpleasantness, but Guy only laughs. 'Gosh. On a Tuesday night? They must be raking it in. Never mind – we'll enjoy our food all the more when we get it.'

Epiphany? More like a personality transplant, Gemma thinks, beaming at her husband and daughter.

Once seated a while, sipping drinks and practically drooling at the food being ferried past them, Guy sits up straighter. 'Bugger me,' he says, raising a hand in greeting to a family occupying a table near the back of the restaurant.

Gemma raises her eyebrows. 'Someone you know?'

'Yes, you know them, too – well, you've met them, anyway. That's Laura – Beth's sister – and Mike and the children.'

Unwilling to go tramping across the restaurant to interrupt their meal, Gemma's smile is tight. But Laura has seen Guy wave and is on her feet, squeezing between tables towards them.

'Laura! Hi! How are you? Long time no see,' Guy says, getting up and kissing Laura on each cheek. 'You've met the missus, haven't you?'

Laura smiles. 'Of course. Hi, Gemma, how are you? And is this Miya? My goodness, aren't you a poppet? You were a baby last time I saw you. Ooh, here's your food. The burgers are delish, by the way. Right, well I'll leave you to it.'

'Oh, how's Beth?' Gemma asks, remembering her manners.

A look of consternation crosses the other woman's face. 'Oh, you know. Good days and bad. Getting there, I think. I'll give her your love. Anyway, see you… Enjoy your dinner!' She blows a kiss and weaves back to her own table.

Gemma frowns. 'What did she mean by that? Is Beth okay, do you think?'

'No idea – you're closer to her than me these days. When did you last see her?' Guy takes a large bite of the burger, closing his eyes with exaggerated pleasure.

Gemma thinks back to her last conversation with Beth: it had been on the phone, over two weeks ago – the night Guy had come home late and morose. She'd been drinking and feeling sorry for herself and had unintentionally hogged the conversation, confiding in Beth about how difficult things were at home. Beth had seemed content to listen, finally mentioning that she'd restarted counselling and that her therapist had a theory about the panic attacks being flashbacks. But the conversation had ended there as Guy had arrived home. She'd meant to call Beth back the next day, but as usual, family life had overtaken her.

Good days and bad. Getting there, Laura had said. The kind of comments people make when someone is ill or depressed.

'Mummy, are you listening to me?' Miya says, her face upturned.

'Sorry, sweet pea. I was just thinking about Auntie Beth and how I must give her a call tomorrow.' Her eyes meet Guy's.

He nods. 'Good idea. I do hope she's all right.'

After putting Miya straight to bed, Guy had been in the mood to talk, making Gemma a herbal tea, settling her on the sofa and then gently taking her feet in his lap.

'You used to rub my feet when I was pregnant.' Gemma smiles, stifling a yawn.

'I did, didn't I? Can you remember how excited we were? Living in the flat in Crystal Palace, wondering how we'd ever cope when Miya came along?'

Gemma nods. 'Of course, I remember. Happy days.'

Guy's expression is tender. 'Well, maybe we need to bring that time back.'

'What, move back to Crystal Palace?' Gemma giggles, unsure where the conversation is heading.

'No, of course not. I mean,' Guy hesitates, drops his eyes for a second, 'perhaps we should try for another baby. A little playmate for Miya, another child to bring us closer.'

Gemma swallows hard. Only that morning, she'd woken early to the distant sound of the sea, Miya's hot sleeping body pressed against her, wondering how she could face Guy again and sad to be leaving the haven of her aunt's house. Yet here is Guy, selling her a bright new future. One that includes a new baby. Her heart contracts.

'Darling, is that what you really want? Because, Guy, I am fine with it being just the three of us,' Gemma says, stalling for time while allowing the idea to percolate.

'Would it be such a bad thing?'

'No, of course not. It's a lovely thought. I'm just… surprised, that's all.' Gemma gets up and stretches. 'We should go to bed. I know Miya's not back at school until Thursday, but you've got work as normal. Come on, we can talk about this another time.'

After finishing up in the bathroom and making a last check on Miya, Gemma finds Guy sleeping soundly. He stirs slightly as she gets into bed, murmurs that he loves her.

Gemma lies on her side, facing him, listening to his rhythmic breathing. She fingers a lock of his hair; it's looking long, rakish. She inches closer. 'I love you, too,' she whispers.

Would another child bring them closer? Guy seemed to think so. And perhaps it was time. Miya appeared to be shooting up before their eyes and the thought of a baby, tiny and innocent, stirred feelings long forgotten.

But could she really trust Guy? Tonight, his tender words melted her heart, but the last few months were a rollercoaster of bitter, violent rows and misunderstandings, as Gemma had constantly monitored her own behaviour, careful not to irritate or anger him.

In Sussex, she'd confided in her aunt, laying bare her marriage and its shortcomings. But perhaps if you scratched the surface, every couple had issues.

Gemma closes her eyes. She'd slept so deeply at Marina's house, carefree as a child and able to let go of her fears and insecurities.

But now, Guy's curveball has left her tense and wakeful. A baby: a desperate measure to heal a flagging marriage? Or simply the next step and the natural way to complete their family? Finally, Gemma falls asleep, waking only to Guy's six thirty alarm.

CHAPTER THIRTY-EIGHT

Beth

At Café Nine, a baby cries at the next table: an insistent low-grade grizzle that his mother has evidently tuned out, but which is making Beth grind her teeth. She is about to move when Gemma arrives, fresh faced and loose haired. She unwinds a scarf from her neck and leans to kiss Beth, releasing a delicate scent of roses.

'Hi, Gem, you smell gorgeous. And you look so well!' Beth says, struck by the glow her friend is emanating.

'Ah, thanks. Must be all that sea air at my aunt's. Miya and I had a wonderful time and it was great to see Marina.'

Beth's eyebrows shoot up. 'Oh, so you went, then? I know you were considering a break…' She trails off, remembering how Gemma had longed to escape Guy's suffocating and argumentative mood.

Gemma beams. 'I took your advice – and it was just what I needed.'

An apricot-haired waitress greets them and offers to take their order, her finger poised over a tablet.

After ordering their favourite poached eggs and avocado on rye with two flat whites, Beth studies Gemma, who is positively radiant. She's about to ask what's new when the baby at the next table lets out a wail, louder and more demanding this time.

Gemma turns to the child's mother. 'Oh, poor little chap. Is he teething? Look at his cute red cheeks.' Then there's an exchange of empathy and teething stories, leaving Beth smiling benignly into the middle distance while the two young mums collude about something she can never be part of. Beth is relieved when the mother begins gathering up the baby's things and prepares to leave.

'Adorable,' Gemma says, after the woman has gone.

'Gemma, if I didn't know you better, I'd say you sound broody,' Beth quips before she can stop herself.

Gemma smiles, her eyes downcast. 'Maybe I am. I mean, if we're going to have another child, we'll need to crack on. I'm not getting any younger and neither is Guy.'

'I'm sorry. I didn't think you'd—' Beth's words freeze on her lips. *Didn't think you'd use a baby to mend your marriage*, she finishes silently, remembering their last conversation. Gemma, drunk, alone, wondering when Guy would be home and what mood he'd be in when he arrived.

Gemma brushes the subject aside. 'It's just something I'm considering,' she says, 'and anyway, I want to hear about you, because to be honest, I'm worried.'

Beth's eyes widen. 'About me? I'm fine.'

When their food arrives, it's a temporary distraction. 'How do they always manage to poach the eggs to perfection in here?' Beth says, slicing a golden yolk with her knife and watching it leak onto its bed of green. 'I can never get them like this at home.'

Gemma frowns. 'Don't change the subject. Look, I feel awful that I cut you short on the phone. You were telling me about your therapist, how she'd mentioned that you might be experiencing flashbacks, but then Guy came home, and I practically hung up on you. Beth, I know something's up, because I saw Laura on Tuesday night and she hinted that you weren't well.'

Beth purses her lips. 'Laura shouldn't have said anything, she worries too much if you ask me.'

There's a short lull in the conversation while they eat in silence.

'So,' Gemma tries again, 'what's going on with you?'

Beth puffs out her cheeks, sets down her cutlery. 'You're right, Gem. I'm not great at the moment. It's the whole therapy thing. I seem to be going down a track I'm not sure I want to follow. Well, I do and I don't. It's just that—'

Gemma frowns. 'Beth, slow down. What track? Tell me properly, please. I'm worried about you, we both are. Guy and I think the world of you. You're like family to us. No wonder your sister's so worried.'

Touched by her friend's obvious concern, Beth explains Zara's suspicion that her panic attacks are in fact flashbacks to a traumatic event that had happened many years ago.

'And at first,' Beth explains, her voice low, 'I dismissed the idea but as time has gone on, the weird episodes have got worse and there's a horrible inevitability about them now. And a kind of pattern: a horrible smell, a feeling of total panic and of a weight pushing down on me. And the other day I got a sense of firelight or candles or something. Look, I know I sound barking mad. But I keep getting this feeling more and more as time goes on that it's all connected to an old boyfriend of Laura's and a party she had the summer I had glandular fever.' She stops speaking abruptly. 'Gemma, can you remember being thirteen?'

Gemma looks amused. 'Yes of course. Why do you ask?'

'Because I can't remember anything about that year. Seriously, it's just blank to me. I mean, Laura tells me things and sometimes they begin to trickle back to me; and Zara seems able to winkle memories out of me during our sessions, but other than that – nothing. It's as though I blanked that whole summer out.'

'God, Beth, I'm so sorry… This is awful. No wonder you're at such a low ebb. What are you going to do? I mean, what *can* you do?'

Beth inhales sharply. 'I'm considering a different type of therapy, something Zara mentioned, but I'm not sure I want to go there…' She shrugs, unwilling to drag Gemma into her private hell any further than she has already. 'Please don't worry, I'll be okay. Let's talk about something else. Tell me more about seeing your aunt. Did you go to the beach?'

And then there's a shift in mood as they swap recent news and compare the Easter holidays and Beth begins to feel lighter and more hopeful, to the point where she is disappointed when Gemma looks at her watch and reaches for her wallet.

'I'm sorry, hon, I've loved catching up, but I've got to go. I'm picking Miya up from dance class. Guy offered but he's working from home today and I wanted to give him a good run at it. Hey, do you want to come with me? Miya will be so pleased to see you. Then you can chill at ours for the rest of the day if you like.'

For a moment, Beth considers leaving with Gemma, fitting around her Saturday plans, and sharing a relaxed takeaway in the evening.

She shakes her head. 'No, but thanks anyway; another time.'

Gemma is on her feet, putting cash on the table and readying to leave. 'Okay. I have to run. But if you change your mind, just come straight over.' They hug goodbye, then Gemma is striding for the door, hair flying behind her.

*

Sunday morning dawns bright and clear. Standing at the window, drinking tea from her favourite mug, Beth watches people drifting into the park opposite for no other reason than to be outside. Two elderly ladies are shuffling in step, an ancient pug waddling between them, its tongue lolling pink as ham, its bobble eyes following the pigeons. Three teenagers balanced on skateboards roll past a couple who are holding hands and glancing shyly at each other.

Other people living their lives, while mine is buried in the past, Beth thinks, finishing her tea and heading to the shower in readiness for the day ahead.

*

Tim stands watching as Beth parks her car at the bottom of the drive. On the tarmac, moss shines brightly.

'I need to get out here and deal with that,' her father says, following Beth's gaze as she walks towards him.

'No, Dad. I don't want you out here, you could easily slip. I honestly think it's time to get a gardener. Laura and I will chip in. It'll smarten the place up a bit. What do you think?'

Tim shakes his head, his expression mournful. 'Why bother? Nobody comes now. Except you girls, of course.'

Beth exhales in exasperation. 'Well then, do it for us. Goodness, Dad – the path is treacherous, and everything is terribly overgrown. I'll talk to Laura when she gets here.'

'He's a stubborn old sod at the best of times,' Laura concedes later that afternoon, when they are in the kitchen, clearing up the lunch pots. 'And honestly, it is wearing thin. He won't consider selling up and moving somewhere smaller, but he won't let us get anyone in either. Meanwhile, this place is starting to look like some spooky old mansion.'

Beth giggles. 'Don't let him hear you say that.'

'Don't let me hear what?' Tim has stolen up on them, his carpet slippers complicit in his stealth.

Beth and Laura exchange glances. 'We're talking about the state of this house, Dad,' Laura hangs up the tea towel and fills the kettle.

Tim shakes his head. 'Why does everything have to be shiny, new and modern these days? It's so wasteful. There's nothing wrong with this house that a good clean and a lick of paint wouldn't fix and there'll be plenty of time for that after I've gone. As I told your sister earlier, nobody comes so it couldn't matter less.'

'If you say so.' Laura shoots Beth a look. 'Dad, can you watch the boys for a minute please? Beth, come outside, let's see if there's anything we can tackle ourselves next weekend. I'll get Michael to give us a hand.'

Beth and Laura walk into the garden, where the temperature is still pleasant although the sky has clouded over.

'Remember the swing seat,' Laura says, 'we hogged that thing every summer. Poor Mum and Dad didn't get a look in.'

Beth nods. 'I know, we loved it. Bits are coming back to me, you know, Laur… with the therapy, I mean.'

'Good. I'm glad it's helping. Right, what shall we do out here?' Laura says, changing the subject as they walk away from the house and stare out at the overgrown lawn and the tangle of weeds in flower borders long since gone to seed. 'Perhaps now the weather's better, you, Mike and I can get stuck in – do a bit of cutting back, mow the lawn, maybe even trim the hedge. What do you think?'

But Beth cannot answer. The sky has become a roiling charcoal, and the scent of the leylandii, mixed with a growing fusty smell, sucks the breath from her lungs. Far away, flames glow, and there's music; distant, happy, and mocking. Beth's chest hurts. Wheezing, she fights for breath as something pushes her down, down onto the hard earth—

'Jesus, Beth! What is it? Don't try to move. I've got you.' Laura's voice breaks through as Beth looks up to find herself lying in the shadow of the leylandii.

'Oh, Laura! It was here!' Beth cries, bile rising in her throat. 'Something happened… just here… in the garden.'

There's a narrowing of her vision, her sister's face receding as sparks dance before her eyes, before silence and blackness take her down.

CHAPTER THIRTY-NINE

Beth

As Beth comes round, she can see and feel Laura's panic, as if she is understanding the gravity of her sister's mental state for the first time.

'I'm calling an ambulance,' Laura cries, her face ashen.

Shaking, Beth gets to her feet. 'No, please don't. I'm okay, I'll be fine in a minute. Don't tell Dad, either. Please, Laur – it's important,' Beth implores. She leans on her sister for support and limps unsteadily towards the house, where the boys are playing with their grandfather, all three of them in high spirits and unaware of the turmoil unfolding in the garden.

Laura's eyes are huge with alarm. 'All right, we'll keep Dad out of this for now. But Beth, we have to do something. What if it happens while you're alone in the house, or on a packed tube? You could hit your head and die. We need to deal with it. And fast.'

There's a note of bitterness in Beth's laugh. 'What the hell do you think I'm doing, Laura? I *am* dealing with it. I've been dealing with this thing since you and I walked into that pub and saw Kevin and Billy Binks playing darts. Because that's when it all started and now it needs to finish. I'm exhausted.'

'I know. Look at you, you're rail thin and I can tell you're hardly sleeping by the shadows under your eyes. Beth, you need to go back to that counsellor and tell her you need some answers,' Laura says hotly, adding, 'and this time, I'm coming with you.'

'No. No way. It's brilliant that you pick me up afterwards and we talk things through, but this is something I need to do alone, Laura. I can't have you digging around in my head. This is my stuff and I'll sort it.'

Beth recalls Zara's words at their last session: *we can go deeper…*

'I'll call my therapist tomorrow morning, see if I can get an appointment before my usual Thursday evening slot. Nessa won't mind, everyone at work has been brilliant about me leaving half an hour early for the last few weeks.'

'Well make sure you do,' Laura answers, still pale from shock.

*

On Tuesday evening, Zara's greeting is warm. 'Hi Beth, it's good to see you. Come and sit down.' She lowers the blinds on the early evening sunshine, while Beth looks around the room, a shudder of apprehension catching her unaware. Zara has made more changes. The office style chairs have been swapped for faux leather bucket seats and a glass coffee table has appeared on which a bowl of colourful wrapped sweets sits.

'Gosh,' Beth says, making conversation. 'It's starting to look homely in here.'

Zara smiles. 'I recently renewed the lease, so I figured if I'm staying, I may as well make it more comfortable.'

Beth sits, notes the time: six fifteen. Will she remember this as the time when her life changed? When her world shifted on its axis as her past spilled open and leaked into her present?

'I'm nervous,' she says, rubbing her arms although the room is warm enough.

'I understand,' Zara answers, 'and we don't have to do this if you're not ready. But your asking for an urgent appointment suggests that you've had a breakthrough and that you're ready to fully undergo the regression process.' She laces her fingers, her eyes locking with Beth's. 'Remember how we talked about gaining the support of friends and family? Have you thought about how you might—'

'Oh, it's all organised,' Beth interrupts. 'I'm staying with my sister for a while; she's picking me up, too. Laura knows what I'm going through and has been incredibly supportive. Please, I want to do this now. I just want to move on with my life.'

'Then let's start. I want you to close your eyes and let all the tensions of the day float away. Breathe deeply… in… out… slow, calm breaths,' Zara's voice is little above a whisper. 'Now together and in complete safety, we're going to a place where you can explore lost memories. Give yourself permission to go deeper as you approach a staircase. There are thirty-nine steps – one for every year of your life. You are taking the stairs, down towards your younger self…'

Beth feels a warm and pleasant numbness spreading through her as Zara counts back, through her thirties, her twenties, her teens, until she is thirteen years old, it is June 1994 and Laura is celebrating her sixteenth birthday.

CHAPTER FORTY

Beth

18 June 1994

Jeanette is in full sail as she directs two women from the cake company, a DJ who calls himself Disco Davy and two young men from the glass hire company tasked with serving drinks.

She inspects the designated bar area: a row of white linen-covered trestles where glasses sparkle in the sunshine and a variety of soft drinks and low-alcohol beer and shandy bobs in ice-filled plastic drums.

'And categorically nothing stronger,' she says, bearing down on the barmen. 'These children are underage, including my daughters, so I will be holding you both accountable if there are any incidents.'

From her vantage point in the apple tree, Beth watches the young men snigger to each other as Jeanette turns her attention to the cake people before finally focussing on the DJ.

Feeling the bark digging into the back of her thighs, she tucks her hair behind her ears, all the better to eavesdrop on her mother's instructions to Disco Davy, who is nodding pleasantly and thumbing an impressive stack of twelve-inch records, headphones on one ear and off the other.

Her father wanders out, dressed as though he's going to work, his camera hanging from its strap around his neck. And in a way he is, Beth considers, seeing as he'll be capturing the evening.

Beth's attention is caught by an upstairs window being flung open as the sound of a hair dryer and Laura's Take That album pipes out.

Jeanette looks up at the open window and shakes her head. She steps back, pivots around.

'Where is that child,' she says, shielding her eyes from the sun, before spotting Beth's left leg dangling from the tree.

'Come down from there! Shouldn't you be getting ready by now? Have you had a shower? I don't want you showing me up tonight or ruining things for your sister.'

With a groan Beth jumps down. 'Mum, why would I do that? Anyway, I showered this morning and I've done nothing to get dirty since.' She pouts. 'It's so unfair, Laura gets to be Madonna and look really cool while I'm flipping Snow White! Mum, my costume smells funny – like everything else in that bloody costume hire shop. Do I have to wear it?'

'Language!' Jeanette snaps. 'I'll have you know that outfit cost me a fortune – and don't spill anything on it, or it'll be another ten pounds on top. Now stop complaining and go and get ready.'

Beth mooches inside, through the kitchen which is groaning with cling film-wrapped food, and into the hallway where helium-filled balloons bob on weights, before taking the stairs two at a time.

As she passes Laura's room, she hears her singing along to her music, accompanied by the hiss of an aerosol. Beth smiles as she pictures her sister spraying her hair into an elaborate mane, Madonna style.

Beth's room has taken on the smell of stale perfume that clings to the detested outfit, now hanging on the back of her door.

She pulls it over her head with a grimace, intending to wait until the adults are drunk, then change back into jeans and T-shirt, like any normal thirteen-year-old. Jesus, she'll be a laughing stock in this!

From the garden, there's a blast of dance music, then the searing whine of the DJ's mic. 'One-two. Two-two,' he breathes nonsensically.

Beth goes to her underwear drawer and carefully takes out several metres of white ribbon. Grinning she runs downstairs as fast as the floaty satin dress will allow.

'Dad, look at this,' she says, holding up the ribbon for Tim to inspect.

'Very pretty, darling. What's it for?'

'I'm going to decorate the trees, put bows on them. I saw it in a magazine. Do you think Laura will like it?'

'I think she'll love it, darling. Better be quick though, people will be arriving soon,' her father says, tapping his watch.

As dusk falls, Beth's eyes roam the scene, excited. Fairy lights decorate Jeanette's shrubbery and the trees now flutter with white ribbon. Someone has draped a banner with the words 'Happy Birthday, Sweet Sixteen' across the boughs of a wisteria. Delighted, she studies the crowd. A mishmash of zany wigs and outfits – a shimmering sea of nylon and satin – glow in the fading light. Half the teenagers in the street have turned up, most in fancy dress, sticking together in little cliques, too self-conscious to strike out and talk to their lesser-known peers. Some of the older children are smoking, cigarettes held discreetly at thigh level, while they suck on bottles filled with brightly coloured liquid. Beth's eyes widen. Alcopops… Mum will have a fit!

She observes a group of Laura's school friends as they pout and swish long, sun-lightened hair. Some younger children charge around, screeching and dancing in a ring, not yet infected by the awkwardness of their teenage siblings.

The adults congregate in the kitchen, pretending to supervise their offspring – a vocation soon ditched as the wine and spirits begin to flow. Even Tim, photography duties dispatched for now, is among them, throwing back gin and tonic, shuffling without rhythm to dance tunes he's heard on the car radio.

In peach chiffon, hair in a precarious up-do, Jeanette sweeps round, offering snacks from large platters and topping up glasses, her face flushed and shiny.

'Blimey, even Mum's having a good time,' Beth tells Katie Mead from number seventeen, as they peer into the crowded kitchen.

'My dad's drunk,' Katie says. 'I can always tell. His eyes go all funny. Like this,' she says, crossing her eyes comically so that Beth hoots with laughter.

Guy Ward slouches over, a livid scar drawn on his left cheek, a scarlet waistcoat open over one of his father's white shirts and a pair of outgrown school trousers shredded at the knees. 'What are you two giggling at?'

'You make a brilliant scarecrow, Guy,' Beth says, winking at Katie.

'Fuck off,' Guy says. 'Any moron can see I'm a pirate. Come on, let's find Laura. I can't stand here watching my old man dance like some total saddo. Why are adults so tragic?'

Beth shrugs. 'Don't know— hey, watch it!' She fends off a tall, slightly built boy wearing regular street clothes except for a toy policeman's helmet, who has smacked squarely into her and is now grinning sheepishly.

Beth looks up into the hollow-cheeked face of one of the Binks twins. 'Oh! Which one are you? I didn't know you'd been invited.'

'It's Billy. We weren't,' he says, looking over Beth's shoulder, presumably scanning for his brother. 'Well, not officially. Don't tell your parents, right?' Billy stalks off towards an older group, his denim-clad legs reminding Beth of pipe cleaners.

Guy sneers. 'What are those dickheads doing here? Just look at them – assuming that's the other one in the wolf's head.'

Beth follows Guy's gaze. 'Wow. He didn't get *that* in the fancy dress shop!' she breathes, awestruck by the matted lupine head that reminds her of a pantomime she'd seen when she and Laura were little.

Katie nods and purses her lips. 'They look like Bros, don't you think, Beth?'

'Christ, not you as well, Katie,' Guy tuts, adding, 'Look, don't say anything, but I need to nip home for a minute.'

Beth folds her arms, a knowing smile on her face. 'He means he needs the toilet.' She and Katie burst out laughing.

'Shut up. If you must know, I'm going to raid my old man's booze cabinet. Get us a proper drink.'

Then Beth and Katie watch Guy make his way past the growing throng of dancers and slip out of the back gate.

'C'mon, let's find my sister,' Beth says, linking her arm through Katie's and leading her to where Laura stands surrounded by admiring boys. She tosses artfully teased hair, licking her glossed lips and flashing heavily kohled eyes as they fawn around her, twitching and jerking in time to the music. The twins hover, edging their way into the circle.

Laura, laughing at something Beth cannot hear, allows herself to be pulled from her admirers. Beth nudges Katie, who stares in fascination. 'Kevin fancies Laura. Don't tell anyone, but she's been out with him twice already.'

The girls watch as Kevin removes the animal head and kisses Laura on the lips. She kisses him back, then pulls away, her eyes full of mischief.

Beth bowls up to Kevin. 'Thought that was you,' she says, pausing long enough for him to translate Snow White into Beth Harding.

'Wotcha, Beth. Feel this,' Binks says, surprising her by thrusting the wolf head into her hands.

'Ooh, it's heavy, isn't it? Like it's stuffed with sawdust. Where did you get it?'

Laura rolls her eyes. 'Ignore Beth.'

'Nicked it,' Kevin answers, with unmistakeable pride. 'From a junkshop in Crystal Palace. It was hanging up outside – so I took it.'

Beth shudders and fans a hand in front of her nose. 'And I thought my outfit smelled bad. That's disgusting. You don't know where it's been.'

Kevin's laughter is hoarse. 'No, but I know where it's going,' he says, trailing a hand up Laura's thigh.

'Get off!' She turns away, looking simultaneously pleased and embarrassed by Kevin's attentions. Just then, the music morphs into INXS as 'Suicide Blonde' blasts into the night sky.

'Oh, I *love* this. Come on, let's dance,' Laura says, grabbing Beth's hand and motioning for the others to follow.

And then Beth is dancing; a summer breeze stirs the skirt of her filmy dress, and she mimics her sister, gyrating wildly and singing along. And it feels as though the whole party has converged on one record as kids of all ages thrash around, outdoing each other, while from the corner of her eye, Beth sees Guy return, concealing something beneath his waistcoat. She gives him a thumbs up, but he doesn't acknowledge her, just skulks by the apple tree, his contraband out of sight.

When the song ends and melds into the next, most people stay where they are, caught up in the music. But Beth, Laura, Katie and the Binks brothers drift towards the bar area, grabbing bottles of low-alcohol beer.

'She'll have coke,' Laura tells the barman, placing a hand on Beth's shoulder and ignoring her protests.

Guy sidles over. 'Anyone fancy a *proper* drink?' he says, opening his waistcoat to reveal a full-sized bottle of vodka.

They back away from the bar – even Kevin and Billy are suddenly paying attention.

'Where'd you get that?' Kevin sneers.

'From home,' Guy answers, with a note of triumph.

Laura's eyes widen. 'Your dad will go batshit.'

Guy squares his shoulders. 'And?'

'So fucking what?' Kevin says. 'Me and Billy drink vodka all the time. Don't we, mate.'

Billy nods. 'Yeah.'

Laura groans and covers her eyes. 'Oh, no. Here comes Mum. Guy, hide that stuff, will you?'

'Bollocks,' Kevin mutters, putting the wolf's head back on.

They watch Jeanette stagger across the lawn, kitten heels digging into the grass. She stops a few metres short, calls out and asks if they're having fun. Then she peers in the direction of the twins.

'I don't think I know everyone, do I?'

'You do, Mum,' Laura says, thinking on her feet. 'It's Seb and Jason from sixth form.'

Mollified, Jeanette staggers back towards the house with a wave.

'Phew. That was close,' Laura says, her eyes shining. 'Now let's get wasted.'

CHAPTER FORTY-ONE

Beth

18 June 1994

In the darkest recesses of the garden, Beth catches the familiar scent of the leylandii hedge as the teenagers gather round their new leader, Guy: he who holds the bottle. Tonight, as well as the nearby glow from the house, there's just enough moonlight for the six of them to make out each other's silhouettes.

'Ladies first, and anyway, it's your birthday,' Guy says, passing the vodka to Laura.

Grinning, she unscrews the cap, then tips her head back and drinks as the others wait. 'Whoa! That was great,' she says, full of bravado.

Beth takes the bottle from her sister, holds it tentatively to her lips and takes a swig, aware that five pairs of eyes are watching her.

She chokes. 'Ooh, it's horrid. How can people drink that stuff?' She splutters over the grass and wonders if she'll be sick.

The boys laugh and jeer. But Laura snatches the bottle away crossly. 'That'll teach you. Katie, want some?'

Beth expects Katie to pass following her own salutary lesson; instead, at only a year older, Katie drinks with gusto, smacking her lips in appreciation.

It is Guy's turn next. He wipes the bottle with the cuff of his shirt.

'Come on – we haven't got all night,' Kevin moans, setting the wolf's head down beside the compost heap, its glass eyes glinting in the moonlight.

He and Billy drink last. 'Nice one, cheers for that,' Billy says.

'Yeah, but it's fuck all between six of us,' Kevin remarks, wiping his mouth with the back of his hand.

'Oh, I'm sorry I only managed to steal the one bottle,' Guy says, his tone loaded with sarcasm. 'Tell you what, why don't you two go back to the party and we'll finish the rest.'

Kevin takes a step towards Guy, speaks inches from his face. 'So now you're the big man because you nicked a bottle of vodka? Well, so what? Me and Billy have nicked *cars*, for fuck's sake. Now piss off, you virgin mummy's boy.' He looks around for approval, but nobody laughs or joins in with his name-calling.

Embarrassed, Kevin reaches for Laura and starts kissing her. Beth watches her sister, seemingly eager at first, but then she is pushing him away, telling him to stop. 'Not in front of everyone,' Laura cries, shaking herself free. But Kevin catches her roughly by her arms and pulls her back.

Guy steps forward. 'Piss off, creep. You heard her.' He's got the bottle again and is swigging sporadically.

'My turn,' Katie says, taking it from him.

'Look, stop being a dork,' Laura says to nobody in particular, striding away and turning her back on everyone.

'Are you talking to *me*?' Kevin stands rigid, legs apart, balanced on the balls of his feet. 'There's a word for girls like you, you know. Prick tease!'

'That's two words,' Laura says haughtily, a hand on her hip.

'Well, try *fucking bitch*, then,' Kevin spits back at her.

Laura yawns. 'Also two. Come on, let's go back to the party. It's my birthday after all.'

Kevin starts after her. 'You wanna watch yourself, bitch. I ought to fucking teach you a lesson,' he shouts, throwing up his hands before turning back to Guy and snarling a few angry insults in his direction.

Beth hurries after her sister, leaving the two boys squaring up to each other. Disco Davy is playing an Abba medley, and everyone is up and dancing; even some of the parents have left the safe haven of the kitchen and are jigging around with their children.

'What about Katie?' Beth mouths over the music.

'What? Oh, she'll catch us up. Boys, eh? They're all tossers. Come on – dance with your big sister!' Laura weaves through the dancers and preens in the centre, revelling in a burst of spontaneous applause and shouts of 'Happy Birthday'.

When the music changes, Beth drifts away from the dancers and is contemplating changing into her jeans when a neighbour's son whom she knows only as Spud jogs up to her, his expression grave.

'Beth, Guy was looking for you. It's Katie, come quick! She needs you. She's being sick.'

Beth makes a face. 'Well, what am *I* supposed to do about it? Can't Guy help her?'

Spud spreads his hands. 'He went home – said he can't stand puke… Oh, and he said not to tell anyone, or you'll all be in deep shit about the vodka.'

Beth scoffs. '*He* will be. He was the one who nicked it. Bloody hell, Spud. All right. Go and get Laura, will you… tell her to meet me behind the hedge.'

Beth swears under her breath as she plods down the garden, wondering why the others had left Katie in the first place. Now she really wishes she'd changed. Supposing Katie pukes on the Snow White costume. Her mother will have a fit.

'Katie,' she calls softly, feeling her way in the dark, 'it's me, Beth.' Silence. 'Katie!' she tries again, apprehension setting in. *Oh, God. Please don't let Katie have passed out.* She'd read in a grownups' magazine once about a pop star who'd choked on his own vomit. Could there be a more disgusting way to die?

'Katie. Where are you?'

Beth is tucked behind the leylandii now, suddenly conscious of every rustle and crack beneath her feet.

From behind her, there's a sudden impact, someone slamming into her, an arm sliding across her chest as she is dragged backwards and toppled down onto the dew-soaked ground. She opens her mouth to cry out, but only a hoarse moan escapes her. This is not a game, somebody has knocked her down and is on top of her, their body straddling hers. Realising that her eyes are closed, Beth opens them and stares into the glass eye of a wolf. Her nostrils begin to burn with its stale mustiness; she feels its matted fur rough against her cheek and throat as she turns her face away, still unable to scream.

'Stop it! Please. Leave me alone, you're hurting me.' Her voice is barely a whisper as she feels her dress being pulled up to her waist. A fleeting thought – her mum will be furious if the dress is ruined – and then hands are pulling at her underwear, driving her legs apart, as she begins to thrash and kick. This cannot be happening and yet it feels real enough. There's a hot, searing pain; a ripping feeling that seems to slice through her thighs and into her stomach.

'It hurts, please don't,' she whimpers, her voice that of a little girl crying. She is limp now, the breath sucked from her by the weight on top, the wolf's head pressing against her throat, making her gag.

And then it's over. Released, Beth feels the draft of cool air where her dress and knickers should be.

A sob followed by a thin wail leaves her. Why ever would Kevin do such a horrible thing to her? What exactly had he done? She puts a hand to her underwear, finds it torn and askew.

'Katie?' she croaks as though her friend might suddenly appear and come to her aid. 'Laura? Laur… help me…' Beth moans. She straightens her clothing and tries to stand, but her legs won't work and she sinks down and lays weeping softly, trying to gather enough strength to move – to make her way back to safety. After a few minutes, still shaking violently, she manages to get to her feet. There's a new sensation as a damp warmth travels between her thighs. A fresh horror dawns. Has she actually wet herself... wearing the dress?

The music has stopped, a squeal reverberates from Disco Davy's PA system. Beth picks out the words 'Join me in wishing Laura a happy sixteenth birthday.' It's a breathy burble as though the mic is inside his mouth.

Limping towards the safety of light and people, Beth sees her mother – her face suffused with pride – as she carries the cake, ablaze with candles, towards Laura. Her father stands by, camera poised, the pop of his flashgun dazzling the rapt crowd as 'Happy Birthday' reaches its tuneless crescendo. Laura beams with happiness, relishing her moment in the limelight, her spat with Kevin Binks clearly forgotten as people clap and gather round her, shuffling forward in anticipation of a slab of rich cake. For a moment, it occurs to Beth that Laura will be missing her, that she must paste on a smile, stand beside her sister, and eat a piece of the expensive cake her mother ordered.

Beth watches her father, longs to feel safe in his arms, but he's holding the camera, getting Laura to turn this way and that, while Jeanette fusses round her, hugging her and posing for photographs.

Her mother's words that afternoon come back to her: *I don't want you showing me up tonight or ruining things for your sister.*

Wincing with every step, Beth creeps behind the swell of revellers, and in through the back door, blinking under the glare of the kitchen lights. It's a relief that nobody is there, until her mother's voice startles her from behind.

'Look at the bloody state of you!' Jeanette barks, as she marches into the kitchen and picks up a stack of paper napkins. 'What did I say about getting that dress dirty? For heaven's sake, Beth.

How on earth did it get like that? Have you been poking around that compost heap?'

'No Mum, I haven't… Something just—'

'Get upstairs and change. *Now*, madam. You can have your cake when you've smartened yourself up.' Jeanette's eyes blaze, one arm thrust in the direction of the stairs.

Beth moves past her, runs straight to the bathroom, where she is sick twice in quick succession. Then, teeth chattering, she discards the satin dress and runs a bath before lowering herself into the water and sponging the blood from her thighs.

Lying in the steamy warmth, she can hear laughter and shouts of *goodnight* as the party plays out its conclusion. And then the house is quiet except for the telltale sounds of clearing up in the kitchen.

Exhausted, Beth climbs out of the bath, goes to her room, puts on pink pyjamas and sits on the edge of her bed. Nobody is looking for her. Her parents have miraculously sobered up and are at work scraping plates, washing up and collecting rubbish. She can hear Laura's excited yelps as she relives her highlights whilst pretending to help.

Beth goes to the window and peers into the darkness. The hedge looms, black and menacing. Tonight it is a different place to the one where only two weeks earlier she and Laura had pulled weeds for extra pocket money. Tonight it is a place stalked by wolves – not *real* wolves, but by a mean, hateful boy who viciously attacked her. And that *thing*… the thing he did to her, is something she cannot name, yet she knows with complete certainty that it is vile, wicked and forbidden.

Beth gets into bed and turns out the light, her eyes tight shut. 'It was only a game,' she whispers to comfort herself, 'just a mean, horrid game.'

CHAPTER FORTY-TWO

Beth

Beth had barely remembered her sister picking her up and driving her home to Beckenham, where she'd holed up for forty-eight hours, drifting in and out of fitful sleep in Laura's guest room.

As though inheriting a third child, Laura had taken care of everything, contacting Nessa at Beth's office, and telling her that she needed time off due to severe emotional trauma. Then she'd convinced the boys to stay out of Beth's way while their auntie recovered from a nasty virus. It was an easy cover story and Jack and Alfie picked flowers from the garden and made get well soon cards, which they slid under the door.

That first night, Beth and Laura had huddled together, drinking wine and tea, while emotion gripped them in waves: shock, disbelief, anger and on Laura's part, guilt.

'I can't believe that this happened to you. How could I not notice? What a self-obsessed little cow I must have been – and what a rubbish big sister,' she'd sobbed, clutching Beth's hands. 'And what about our parents? Where the hell were they in all this?'

Unable to cry another tear, Beth had entered a numb phase next. 'It's not your fault, Laur. I didn't tell anyone. I didn't even have the words then. I was going to tell Mum right after it happened, to try and explain, but she went ballistic about the costume and sent me upstairs to change. I didn't want to spoil your night. You looked so happy, so beautiful.'

Laura had wrung her hands. 'But what about the next day? Or the day after that?' Suddenly her eyes had widened. 'Christ, you were ill, weren't you? On the Monday morning after the party, I remember walking to school on my own… you missed the whole of the last week of term. Yes, that was the start of it: you were in bed with glandular fever for most of the holidays. I remember feeling so sorry for you, but even more terrified of getting it myself.'

Beth had nodded. 'Yes. I remember it now. I remember everything as though it happened last week. Mum running cool baths and making me lie in them for ages, just to get my temperature down; puking endlessly – the only thing I could manage was tinned peaches for some bizarre reason; and fading in and out of sleep for days, weeks, even. Being attacked at the party became part of that… one horrible, unending nightmare, and it didn't feel real. Laura, I thought I'd dreamt it all.'

*

Beth shakes the duvet and carefully smooths it over the guest bed. Then she throws the window wide open and goes for a shower, borrowing Laura's citrus body wash and apple shampoo.

Neither Beth nor Laura have talked about the future. Nor about her attacker or about justice or retribution. Well, today is the day. Because three days spent weeping, grieving for the tragic abuse of her thirteen-year-old self, is enough. Now Beth feels anger.

So, galvanised by a quiet and reassuring rage, Beth puts on the same jeans she's been wearing for days and a borrowed T-shirt of Laura's and goes in search of her sister.

Downstairs, Laura sits at the kitchen table, a ring binder of household bills open in front of her. 'Good morning,' she says gently. 'Did you manage to sleep much?'

Beth nods. 'I did. How are you?'

'I'm fine. Michael's on the school run so it's just us. Are you sure you're okay? I'll make you some tea. Can you manage some breakfast today?'

'Tea would be great, Laur. Then I'll get out of your hair. I've got things to sort.'

Frowning, Laura fills the kettle and takes a clean mug from the dishwasher. 'Okay, but why the rush? Beth, I don't want you to be by yourself for a while yet. You've just had a terrible shock and relived a highly traumatic experience. I need to look after you.'

'Laura, you don't. I have to deal with things in my own way. And anyway, I'm going to keep seeing Zara – it was kind of conditional – so you needn't worry that I'll shut myself away.' She tucks still-damp hair behind her ears. 'Look, we both know who did this, yet neither of us have even mentioned Binks's name. Kevin Binks raped me. I was thirteen years old. It doesn't get much worse than that. But I survived it then, and I will now. Only now I want him to pay for what he did.'

Laura hands Beth a mug of tea and paces to the window. 'Beth, you don't know that it was Kevin,' she says, her back still turned. 'There were as many boys as girls there that night… half the neighbourhood rocked up.'

'Of course it was him! You'd have been in no doubt if it was you, having that stinking wolf's head scraping round your face and chest. He did this, Laura. Jesus! I can't believe you're defending him.'

Laura turns to face her sister. 'I'm not defending the vile animal who attacked you, but we need to be sure we've got the right guy before we start accusing anyone.'

'It had to be Binks,' Beth says, setting her tea down harder than intended and causing it to spill. 'Otherwise, how do you explain months of me freaking out whenever I saw him? It was the PTSD that led to my finding out.'

'But it could be just an association, because he was there that night, drinking and gobbing off, and wearing that vile thing on his head. It doesn't mean he was the one.'

Some of Beth's certainty ebbs away. Binks was a convicted predator – had actually done time for *a serious sex offence*. She'd researched and read up on him online, with her own eyes. And yet, a niggle of doubt stops her from driving to the nearest police station.

Beth balls up her fists in frustration. Laura is right. If she's to accuse Kevin Binks, or anyone else for that matter, she'll need proof – if not to bring a case against him, then for her own certainty and satisfaction. And given that her attack had taken place more than two decades earlier, real evidence will be hard to come by.

A new thought pops into her head. 'What about Billy – do you think he was capable?'

Laura scoffs. 'Billy couldn't knock the skin off a rice pudding. He was completely in his brother's shadow. He liked you, anyway, Beth, he'd never have—'

'When you say *liked me*, liked me *how,* Laura? What if Billy—'

'Beth, it wasn't Billy, okay? Please try and stay calm. You're doing brilliantly.' Laura's eyes widen, her mouth falls open. She grabs her sister's wrists. 'Beth, I've just had a brilliant idea…'

CHAPTER FORTY-THREE

Gemma

Gemma opens the car door and gropes under the passenger seat. Nothing. In the last two weeks alone, she's retrieved a handful of Haribo Starmix, a sparkly hair clip and her Berry Burst lip liner. 'There goes that theory,' she mutters straightening up.

She'd been so sure she'd find her birth control pills there. Guy is always on her case to zip up her handbag to prevent the contents flying out while she's driving, after tossing it on the passenger seat as is her way.

She locks the car, goes inside and checks the places she could have put them while distracted, rifling the bits-and-bobs drawer in the kitchen, and the hidden shelf on the hall consul table, before jogging upstairs and checking her bathroom cabinet and dressing table for the second time.

Gemma frowns, thinks back to taking her pill at nine o'clock yesterday, straight after the school run. She picks up her bag again, checks the lining for holes. Has she really dropped them in the street, at the school gates or in the supermarket? Feeling idiotic, she goes to the utility room and puts a wash on, glancing at the time. Half past ten. There is no time to phone her GP and sit waiting on hold to arrange a replacement pack. She cannot be late for her training session with Caleb and endure a forfeit of twenty extra squats. Instead, she'll swing by the surgery on her way home. Because the last thing Gemma needs is to skip a pill and increase the risk of getting pregnant. Especially now she's made her decision.

It's the perfect day for training outdoors. The temperature is a comfortable fifteen degrees, there's no threat of rain and only a gentle breeze to run against. Gemma parks up in her usual place and scans the area for Caleb's car.

When there's no sign, she checks the time on her mobile phone and finds it is bang-on eleven o'clock. By eleven fifteen, concerned, she sends Caleb a text, expecting an apology, or an expletive or two about the traffic, but her phone remains ominously silent.

At eleven thirty, puzzled as well as irritated, Gemma calls Caleb's mobile and gets his voicemail. It seems odd to her, given he's never been a minute late before, let alone blown her out altogether.

Deciding that something must have come up, Gemma is soon back in the traffic and bound for the doctors' surgery, hoping that a personal visit will shortcut the process of replacing her birth control pills.

A little later, nibbling on avocado on toast for lunch, Gemma muses on her day. So far, she's managed to lose a packet of contraceptive pills and her personal trainer in one morning. *Way to go, Gemma.*

To her disappointment, when she'd called at the medical centre, the in-house dispensary had been unable to provide Gemma's pill, promising to phone later and let her know when she could collect a supply.

She finishes eating, goes to the study and opens her laptop. Twenty-seven new emails soon download – twenty-six of them trying to flog her stuff she doesn't need or want and one from Guy, asking her to iron his salmon pink shirt for a short interview on BBC 2's *Business Day* tomorrow. There is nothing from Caleb, which makes total sense as they usually communicate by text. She checks her phone again and with a sense of déjà vu, finds a message from Guy, reiterating his need for the pink shirt, and another from a tanning salon she's never even heard of – and still not a word from Caleb.

A pang of unease stirs. Gemma shakes it off, goes to the utility room and digs Guy's shirt out of the ironing pile. Having set herself up, she works steadily through the stack, finishing just in time to collect Miya from school.

She's at the gates, listening to Katya rhapsodise about a new hairdresser's in the high street, when her phone lights up.

'I have to go, it's the surgery about a prescription I need urgently. See you in the morning, love. Bye.' Gemma blows the other mums a kiss and shepherds Miya to the car, her concentration divided between belting her daughter into her booster seat and speaking to the dispensary.

Gemma and Miya are in the kitchen when Guy arrives home.

'Daddy!' Miya is on her feet, ready to ambush him at the door. Gemma follows, enjoying her daughter's joy at seeing her dad.

'Hello, stinker,' Guy says, swinging Miya off the ground, 'have you been good for Mummy today?'

Miya nods. 'Always.'

'Wonder if Mummy agrees.' Guy kisses Gemma's cheek then dumps his suit jacket in the hall before herding the girls back into the kitchen.

'How was your day, darling?' Gemma asks. 'I got your message by the way; your pink shirt is hanging in your wardrobe. Well done for getting the interview. Is that down to you or the PR agency?'

'Credit where it's due, the agency – which is what I pay them for, after all,' Guy says, going straight to the fridge. 'What are we eating? How was your day, hon?'

'Shop-bought quiche and salad,' Gemma says. She hesitates. 'I've had a funny day really.' She glances at Miya, lowers her voice. 'Guy, I don't suppose you've seen my contraceptive pills, have you? Only I've looked everywhere.'

He gives her an awkward little shrug. 'Let's talk about it once Miya's in bed.'

Gemma frowns. What an odd response; has he, or hasn't he?

'Okay,' she says, turning on the oven for the quiche. 'That's not the only thing I've lost – and this is just plain weird. I turned up for training today, only Caleb was a no-show. I know things crop up sometimes, but you'd think he'd ring me or at least get a message to me somehow.'

Guy's face is unreadable. 'I thought he was a bit flaky when I met him.' He changes the subject. 'How long until supper?'

By eight thirty, Miya is tucked up in bed, dinner has been eaten and cleared away and Gemma and Guy are sharing a drink in the sitting room.

Sensing an agenda, Gemma tucks her feet under herself in an attempt to look more relaxed than she feels. 'So, hon – have you seen my pills around? I must have dropped them.'

Guy takes a sip of wine, before searching her eyes. 'Gemma, you don't need them. You can stop filling yourself with toxic chemicals now.'

Alarm bells ring in Gemma's head. 'Why… why do you say that?'

'Because it's true.'

'Guy, what have you done with my pills?' Gemma says, suffused by a sudden queasiness.

'I've put them where they belong, Gemma. Out with the rubbish.'

'You wouldn't do that, surely.'

'Darling, now that we're trying for a baby, the sooner you get off that shit, the better.'

Gemma's thoughts race. The alarm bell has become a siren.

She eyes her husband with incredulity. Never in her worst nightmares could Gemma have imagined Guy stooping to this level of control freakery and manipulation. Was he losing his mind?

She gets to her feet, overwhelmed by a sudden and desperate urge to escape. 'Back in a moment. I'll just check on Miya.'

Guy's voice is a growl. 'Miya's fine. Sit down. You seem worried. Can't you see, I've done us both a favour? God knows what those things do to a woman's long-term fertility. What with that and all the bloody hormones in the food we eat. You can't be too careful.'

Gemma clenches her hands unconsciously.

'Relax. I don't know why you're so upset,' Guy says, his eyes flicking to Gemma's balled-up fists.

Defiance creeps into her voice. 'Because you had no right. Surely you can see that it's my choice, whether to take the pill or not. Not yours or anyone else's, Guy. *My* choice, *my* body,' she adds hotly.

'Christ, you sound like one of those tragic feminists,' he sneers. 'You'll be shaving your head next and wearing dungarees.'

Gemma gasps. 'How dare you speak about women like that. What's got into you?'

'I could ask you the same thing, Gemma. One minute we're having a baby, the next you're getting hysterical over a packet of pills.' He drains his glass, his eyes glittering darkly.

'But that's just it, isn't it? We've had one discussion about having another child, and I said I'd think about it. Well, I have, and it doesn't feel like the right time. I'm not ready, Guy.'

'Not ready?' His laughter is cold. 'What the fuck else have you got going on that's so important? Not even that dickhead of a personal trainer now, it seems.'

Gemma feels her knees liquify. 'Guy, what have you done? You know something about Caleb, don't you?'

'I know you two fancy the pants off each other,' he snarls, his face contorted with anger.

'That's not fair and it's not true. We train once a week and that's it.'

'Oh, really? So, why put kisses on texts?'

Tears spring into Gemma's eyes. 'Once! And it was automatic. I put kisses on all my texts. Oh my God, I don't believe this. You've been spying on me – checking my phone? Guy, that's shameful… a new low, even for you.'

Gemma watches as Guy's knuckles turn white. 'What the fuck does that mean, exactly?' he says through clenched teeth.

Gemma moves towards the door, but Guy is on his feet, blocking her path. 'I asked you a question,' he says, his eyes black and hollow.

'I really have to check on Miya.' She dodges out of Guy's way and crosses to the hallway, but he steers her into the kitchen and shuts the door.

'This discussion is over when I say it is.'

Gemma swallows hard. 'Fine. Let's talk. What have you done with Caleb?'

Guy's laughter is soft and mocking. 'Don't worry about lover boy. I just warned him off, that's all. No more training sessions, no more cute texts. You won't be hearing from him again.'

Gemma clenches her jaw. How dare Guy go around threatening people, like some two-bit gangster?

She squares her shoulders. 'Guy, we can't go on like this. I'm exhausted from walking on eggshells, wondering if I've upset you and what mood you'll be in. Last week you apologised and admitted you've been a nightmare. But now I find out that you've spied on me, sacked my personal trainer and thrown my birth control pills in the bin! This is not normal behaviour. Married people don't do this to each other.'

'You're making me out to be a monster,' Guy hisses.

'And you've been acting like one for months! Just because I never mentioned the dress you cut up and threw away, or the fact that you stamped my hand onto broken glass, doesn't mean it's okay!' Gemma holds her breath, fear coursing through her, fighting the urge to run.

She's trapped now, between Guy and the kitchen island. And she knows, somehow, anticipates what is coming next. There's a horrible inevitability as his eyes, black and thunderous, bore into her own, just before he shoves her with both hands. There's a sickening crack as Gemma's coccyx connects with the marble counter and a strangled scream escapes her as winded, she crumples to the floor.

Without another word, Guy stalks from the room – as though *he* is the injured party – and she can hear his footfall first on the stairs and then moving in the direction of the spare room.

Shaking violently, Gemma gets into bed, wishing the door had a lock on it. Tentatively, she touches the small of her back where an angry welt is forming. Lying on her side, she is rigid with tension, her thoughts spinning.

Guy had wanted them to have another child together – telling her that he'd change his ways and make her and Miya his priority. Yet days later, his mood is darker than ever. Learning that he has checked her texts, sacked her trainer and thrown away her pills has shocked Gemma to the core. Now, for the second time, he has lost his temper and inflicted physical pain on her. What next? A vicious punch, or a brutal kick? His hands around her neck…?

Somehow, they have crossed a line. There is no way back now. Tomorrow she will arrange a sleepover for Miya. Katya will be open to that; Miya and Sophia adore each other. Then she will marshal her courage and tell Guy that they are over.

It's almost one in the morning and the house is silent. Gemma wonders if Guy is asleep or still seething with rage. Craving sleep and knowing that it will never come to her in this state, she creeps to the bathroom and bolts the door before reaching for her pills and taking half a Zammertil, too exhausted to dwell on why there are so few left in the packet.

Whatever the future holds, it must be better than this, her last conscious thought before slipping into a deep, dreamless sleep.

CHAPTER FORTY-FOUR

Gemma

On Friday morning, Gemma wakes to Miya bouncing on the bed, already in her school uniform. 'Mummy, can you do my hair, please?' She cups Gemma's face. 'Mummy! Come *on*. I'm going to be late.'

'What?' Gemma is confused. There's cotton wool in her mouth and her legs are leaden. 'Coming, sweet pea,' she says, sitting up carefully. She lowers her voice. 'Where's Daddy?'

'He's gone to work. We had Coco Pops and juice together.' Miya continues to babble about the minutia of breakfast with her father as Gemma struggles to come round.

'Okay. Miya, just give Mummy a minute, will you. You can watch TV if you like.'

Perking up at the idea of some pre-school cartoons, Miya trots downstairs while Gemma heads to the bathroom.

Shocked by the sight of the pale and puffy-eyed woman in the mirror, Gemma's fingertips trace the vivid purple bruise on the small of her back. She remembers Guy's rage, the way he'd lost all control. Then she'd taken half a Zammertil, just to blur the pain and allow her to sleep.

Realising there's no time to shower, Gemma splashes her face, cleans her teeth and spritzes on a rose-scented body spray before pulling on yesterday's jeans and a grey hoodie.

Descending the stairs, she hears Miya giggling at cartoons.

'Come on, sweet pea. Ponytail or plaits today?' Gemma calls, zapping the kettle on and spooning instant coffee into a mug.

Plaits and caffeine despatched, Gemma steers her daughter into the car, buckles her booster seat and they set off for school, arriving with two minutes to spare.

'Katya!' Gemma calls, catching her friend's eye as Miya hurries to catch up with Sophia.

'Hi, Gemma. How's it going?' Katya's eyes sweep over Gemma's dishevelled appearance. 'Are you okay, you look a little… tired.'

Gemma shrugs. 'I overslept.' She rakes a hand through her unbrushed hair. 'Look, I have a big favour to ask. Something's come to a head with Guy and I need to keep Miya away while we talk properly. I wonder… would you be able to have—'

'Just say when,' Katya jumps in, seeming to understand at once. 'How about a sleepover tonight? The girls will love it.'

'Are you sure? That's incredibly kind, thank you,' Gemma feels a lump come to her throat. 'I'll drop Miya's overnight bag round this afternoon, shall I?'

Katya nods and holds her gaze. 'Gemma, I'm here if you need me. Just text me and I'll—'

'Thanks, but he's been checking my phone,' Gemma says, her voice cracking with emotion.

Katya grips her forearm. 'Then we use a code. Send a message asking what perfume I use, and I'll know you need help.'

'Bless you. Thanks, that means everything. How did you know?'

'I guessed. He's a powerful man – in every sense. And recently, you've looked so tired and stressed.'

Gemma hugs Katya; a blend of hope, gratitude and panic stirs. 'Thanks, you're very kind,' she whispers, before striding back to the car and driving to the medical centre for the second time in twenty-four hours.

*

At the surgery, Gemma bypasses reception and goes straight to the dispensary hatch, grateful that the queue consists of only one elderly woman. They exchange awkward smiles and then it is Gemma's turn.

'Hi, I'm here to pick up a prescription. The name's Mrs Ward – can you check, please?' She steps back, her eyes flicking to the notice board which is littered by fliers offering advice and helplines for everything ranging from stopping smoking to domestic abuse. The words leap out at her. Domestic abuse: is that her problem now? Has she somehow recently become a victim?

The face reappears at the window, smiling and efficient. 'Here you are, my love. Do you pay for your medication?'

Gemma nods and gets out her debit card, before doing a double take. 'Sorry – I'm in a complete daze today. It's my pill so there's nothing to pay.' Her smile is sheepish as she returns her card to her purse.

There's a beat's delay while the other woman reads the printed slip attached to the bulging paper bag. 'Hang on... yes, there are two items, as requested: you've got your pill and another three-month supply of Zammertil. Okay?'

Gemma frowns and leans towards the window. A young man is queuing behind her now, so close she can smell his aftershave. 'I... there must be a mistake, I haven't asked for the Zammertil—'

'One moment,' the dispensing assistant moves out of sight and is back seconds later. 'We received an email from you last weekend. The message said you'd be in to pick it up on Saturday morning? Only you're here now, so...' She trails off, dusts something from her jacket lapel.

Gemma can detect a hint of impatience in the woman's voice now, and the young man behind her sighs loudly.

'Oh... yes, of course,' she says with a giddy little laugh. 'I'd forgotten all about it. Sorry – my fault.' She steps out of the queue and leaves, feeling her cheeks redden as she makes her way to the car where she tears open the paper bag and examines the contents: a three-month supply of Zammertil, in addition to the contraceptive pill that she had asked for. Gemma switches on the ignition, a leaden weight in the pit of her stomach.

What email? She has sent no such email – although in the past she's requested medication online, rather than phoning or making a personal appearance at the surgery. Eager to get home, she puts her foot down and is soon parking up at Darwin Drive.

Once inside, she goes to the study, grabs her laptop and carries it to the kitchen. While it's booting up, she makes herself a strong cup of coffee, even though her heart is already racing in her chest and she's aware that caffeine is probably the last thing she needs.

'C'mon, please… *bloody updates*,' Gemma mutters, watching the buffer ball whir on her screen. Then she's in, her email browser is open and she's going straight to her Sent box, where naturally there's no sign of any email to the surgery, asking for Zammertil or anything else. Because Gemma *knows* with total certainty that she has not sent any such message.

But *Guy* on the other hand… His behaviour has become so strange, so erratic. What if he had emailed the surgery to gain a supply of Zammertil, using her computer?

Gemma stares blankly at the screen. What on earth would Guy want with them? What possible benefit could there be to him? That there is nothing in Gemma's Sent folder says little. Guy would be savvy enough to delete any emails sent from her personal email address. But would he think to empty her trash folder as well?

Gemma clicks on the little dustbin symbol that she rarely empties, wading through dozens of sales emails, deleted, unwanted and unread. She tries sorting them by recipient. *Bingo*.

Dated from last Saturday, almost a week ago: an email asking for a further supply of Zammertil, with the sign off *Kind regards, Gemma Ward*.

Gemma feels a cold finger trail down her spine. She has never signed an email with kind regards in her entire life – so formal!

She looks at the time of the email: eleven forty-two. She'd been out then, having dropped Miya off at dance class before stopping off in Lordship Lane at the artisan bread shop, then going on to meet Beth at Café Nine, giving Guy ample opportunity to use her laptop.

She sets down her coffee mug and takes the stairs two at a time.

She opens her bathroom cabinet and removes the pack of Zammertil, staring dumbly at the depleted supply, when she *knows* that she has only taken a handful in as many weeks.

What the hell is going on? Is Guy taking them and hiding them somewhere? And if he is, why? To confuse her perhaps – make her think she's taken more than she has? Or is there a darker reason? Is he saving them up to drug her at some point – to make her sleepy and compliant?

With a snaking sense of fear and apprehension, Gemma goes downstairs and texts Guy, determined that their conversation will not get hijacked by drinks with colleagues – a Friday night liability that can crop up unannounced.

She keeps her message light and mysterious. Let him think he is coming home to an apology or a reconciliation; Gemma's mind is made up.

It's seven twenty when Guy's car pulls onto the drive.

Gemma glances in the hall mirror and whispers to her reflection. *Keep it together, Gemma. You can do this.*

Their greeting is mutually cool as she pours them both a drink.

'How was your day?' she asks, handing him a glass of wine.

'Trying,' Guy sighs, flopping down on the kitchen sofa. 'Where did you say Miya is?'

'She's having a sleepover with Sophia. I asked Katya to have her and she was happy to. It gives us chance to talk properly.'

'Oh great, so you've been hobnobbing at the school gates, telling everyone our business. That's just perfect.'

She can see Guy wilting. He looks tired, dejected. Her fingers stray to the bruise just above her coccyx, the memory of last night hardening her resolve.

'I'm surprised you even know where our daughter is, the state you were in this morning. I tried three times to wake you, but you were bombed out on pills. How many did you take this time? Or have you stopped keeping track all together?'

It's a verbal slap in the face, but the perfect reminder of what she must do.

Gemma smiles serenely, determined not to be baited.

'I was upset after our conversation – and the way you… pushed me. But I only took half a tablet. And anyway, I was fine once I got going. Guy, we have to talk. We can't run away from this any longer.'

'Run away from what, exactly?' Guy says, sounding bored.

'Please, don't make this harder. We both know that things aren't working. Living like this is making both our lives utterly miserable. You're constantly stressed and disappointed in me and I'm walking on eggshells every day, wondering what mood you'll be in. We have to stop this, before we destroy each other, and Miya.'

'You're right. I need to dial it down… start trusting you again. Now that Caleb is out of our lives and—'

'Caleb was never *in* our lives.' Gemma struggles to keep the exasperation out of her voice. 'Nothing happened. I think you know that. It's just an excuse. You're so hyper-critical of everything I do, watching my every move. And all this anger… I have no idea where it's coming from.' Gemma sighs. 'Guy, it's too late for either of us to change. We need to separate and try living apart for a while.'

Guy shakes his head as though he's misheard. 'Let me get this straight. You think we should split up? Gemma, don't be absurd.

Why on earth would we do that? We have a child for Christ's sake. We made vows to each other.'

Tactical. Taking the moral high ground. Gemma takes a deep breath. 'Guy, it won't work. I'm not open to emotional blackmail. I'm leaving you. It's all decided.'

Her heart sinks: it's a lie. Nothing is decided. Her only option is to drive to her aunt's house in Sussex, which is far from ideal given Miya's schooling. On the other hand, it is the perfect bolt hole, seeing that Guy has no clue where Marina lives. Once there, she can let the dust settle, plot her next move and find herself a good solicitor.

He is staring at her now, his eyes black and brooding. He drains his wine glass, fills it again without offering Gemma any. Then he is on his feet, pacing, agitated. He spins round to face her.

'All right. Go. Whenever you want. Only don't think for a minute you're taking my daughter with you.' His expression is triumphant, as though he's about to play a trump card.

'Guy, don't be ridiculous. I'm her mother. Miya will live with me and you'll see her whenever you want. That's what couples do when they separate. There's not a court in the land who'll sanction Miya living with you. Just look at your work schedule.'

'I beg to differ,' Guy says primly, as though already pleading his case. 'No *court*,' he adds with relish, 'would allow a child to live with her drug addict, alcoholic mother, so I think you'll find things will fall very much in my favour.'

'Oh my God! But you know it's not true. Why would anyone believe you?'

'Why wouldn't they? You're addicted to tranquilisers and you drink at least a bottle of wine every night. Other people can corroborate that.'

Gemma is stung. How can he sink so low? Has he lost his mind?

'*Corroborate*? Listen to yourself, Guy. It's all nonsense.'

He is smirking now, enjoying himself. 'My mother... Beth... they know about your little problem, let's ask them, shall we? Oh, and I'm sure your GP will confirm that you're taking an ever-increasing dose of Zammertil. Gemma, it's your word against mine, isn't it?'

Gemma swallows the lump in her throat, realising that he's been covering the bases against her leaving – possibly for months. She straightens up and holds his gaze. 'Actually, I know all about your little stunt at the medical centre, emailing them and asking for a repeat prescription. I was there today, picking up more contraceptive pills after you threw mine away. You can imagine how shocked I was when they handed me a large supply of Zammertil.' She shakes her head. 'I can't believe you'd go to so much trouble just to make me look like a bad mother. You're twisted, Guy, you know that?'

Gemma braces herself for Guy's reaction, but he only laughs, a dry, bitter bark. 'So what? You think you've got the upper hand? You forget who I am, Gemma. A pillar of the community, a significant and highly regarded employer – always on TV, promoting ethical practice and sustainability. *You*, on the other hand, would only epitomise the gold-digging, soon-to-be ex-wife, spoilt, selfish and lazy. Are you with me, Gemma? Has the penny dropped for you yet?'

Gemma takes a step back. 'I'm not listening to this! I'm leaving you, Guy. Accept it.'

She marches from the kitchen, grabs her bag from the bottom of the stairs and opens the console table drawer where her car keys live. But Guy is behind her, slamming her fingers in the drawer with such force that she screams in pain.

Then he pockets both sets of car keys, and calmly returns to the kitchen while Gemma sits on the bottom stair, rubbing her red, throbbing hand and fighting the urge to throw up.

'Christ, Guy – my hand! Not again. How could you be—' Tears of pain, frustration and fear are coursing down Gemma's cheeks now. She has gone about this all wrong. If she's to escape with her health and sanity, she'll need the element of surprise – and some serious, fail-safe planning. What had she expected? That Guy would cheerfully pack a holdall and move into a hotel for the weekend?

He reappears, his anger already dissipating, as if hurting her has provided him with some release.

He squats on the stairs beside her. 'Gemma, I'm sorry. I didn't mean to do that, but you left me no choice. Come on, let me take a look at that hand – check there's nothing broken.'

Gemma wants to rage and scream at him. Instead, she plays along, biding her time. Shakily, she gets to her feet and follows Guy into the kitchen.

CHAPTER FORTY-FIVE

Beth

Parked outside her father's house, Beth tries to still the shaking of her hands and knees.

Going through the photographs from that night had been Laura's idea. She'd remembered their dad proudly capturing her sixteenth birthday, snapping everyone in fancy dress as they'd arrived, nervous and excited, and then again, much later, at the cutting of the cake while everyone sang 'Happy Birthday'.

'At the very least,' Laura had reasoned, 'the photos will remind us who was there, and their whereabouts. Who knows what they'll throw up, but it's worth a punt, surely?'

Her sister had wanted to be there, of course. But Beth's resolve had been firm. 'No, Laur. I want to do this by myself. I'll tell Dad I'm making an album from our childhood or something. He mustn't know any of this. Not yet. It'll all come out in the end but let's not upset him now – there's no point.'

Reluctantly, Laura had walked Beth to her car and hugged her. 'I can be there in ten minutes flat if it all gets too much. Promise you'll ring me,' she'd said earnestly.

'Don't worry about me. I want to do this. I have to know… It's the final piece of the puzzle before deciding whether to go to the police or not. I'll ring you later from home.'

Feeling oddly calm, Beth had driven the ten minutes to her father's house and parked in the same spot where she had every Sunday since her mother's passing.

Now, she looks up at the house: the house that she and Laura were born in. The house where they had laughed and cried, and run riot in the garden, and ridden bikes and scooters and scraped their knees. Where there'd been arguments and tantrums and promises made and broken. Just a normal family, living their ordinary suburban life. Except that something extraordinary had happened there once. Something ugly, dark and wicked, but forgotten – or hidden?

She looks up at the house, with its too-long lawn, its flower beds in need of weeding, its maroon front door, dulled by age to a muddy brown.

Nothing and everything has changed. Saliva pools in Beth's mouth. Swallowing her apprehension, she opens the car door and walks up the path.

Before Beth can ring the bell, the front door opens.

'Well, this is a nice surprise, darling. But it's Friday – why aren't you at work?' Tim says, his cardigan hanging loose on his shoulders, his slacks held up by the brown leather belt he often wears.

'Hello, Dad. I'm owed some holiday,' Beth says vaguely, following him into the gloom of the hallway and giving him a hug.

After they've exhausted the ritual of making and drinking tea together, Beth goes to the sitting room window, unable to look at her father while she lies to him.

'Dad, the reason for popping round,' she begins, 'Laura and I were thinking about making an album from when we were kids. I know you've got hundreds of photos upstairs. Do you think I could have a look, pick out a few from our teens?'

'Of course, but they're not in any order. There are work shoots and family photos all mixed up in one trunk. They need sorting out, but I never seem to get round to it.'

Beth's breeziness sounds forced, even to her own ears. 'Oh, that's no bother, Dad. It'll be fun to go through them. Are they still in the loft?'

Tim nods, his eyes dull and faraway. 'It's very dusty up there; are you sure you want to go up?'

But Beth is on her feet and taking the stairs before she can change her mind.

Going straight to the airing cupboard, she looks for the pole with a hook on one end for opening the loft hatch, and for pulling down its stiff and creaking aluminium ladder. With the steps in place, Beth tests her weight, then gingerly climbs up into the loft's dark mouth. She feels for the light switch; it casts a sickly glow under the rafters. A dry stench of dust and something else more pungent – mouse droppings, perhaps – fills her nostrils. With a shudder, she looks around at the odd collection of abandoned, unwanted things: a standard lamp half covered by a dust sheet, like a wilting spirit silently observing. Long forgotten tea-chests, a bank of cardboard boxes marked 'Accounts' and 'Work', bits of broken furniture never to be repaired and, just visible beneath a rolled-up rug she remembers spilling Ribena on, her father's brown trunk.

A soft thud makes Beth jump and gasp as a bird grazes the filthy window. 'Jesus, this place is creepy,' she says aloud, thinking how small and foolish her voice sounds.

Is she really going to squat here, in the middle of all this grime, and go through decades of old photographs, digging through her family's past – and possibly rewriting its history?

She takes a deep breath, then drags the ruined rug off the trunk, stirring a choking cloud of dust. She coughs hard, closes her eyes, wondering if she really has lost the plot.

The trunk has a lock on it. Beth's heart sinks. Oh, please – just let her get in and get out. The idea of being stuck in the attic a moment longer than necessary makes her knees weak.

To her relief, the trunk opens easily, its spring-loaded catch flying open to reveal a combination of loose and wrapped photographs. Remembering her father's Job Bags system, she feels a twinge of optimism at the sight of several large brown envelopes faded with age, their contents listed in marker pen. She rifles through a dozen: Wright, portraits; Kinsey, christening; Archer, wedding – and so on. A two-word summation of events once deemed significant – a moment in time, yet still remembered. Then she's fingering a parcel of prints, wrapped in pale tissue that might have been pink once, tied with ribbon – and she knows, just *knows*, that the contents are personal and sacred, a family occasion, perhaps intended for a photo album once.

Hands shaking, Beth unwraps the bundle. There, on the top of the pile, a 10x8 portrait of Laura. Pin up for the night: eyes shining with happiness and anticipation, a dazzling smile on scarlet lips, blonde hair in loosely pinned curls, approximating her idol, Madonna.

An icy draft travels up Beth's spine as her sister's words come back to her. *Who knows what they'll throw up?*

For a moment, Beth is still, immobilised by the fear of what might be.

Get a grip. Look at them. Look!

She studies the prints of various sizes, each capturing a unique moment in time, and feels a wave of warm familiarity wash over her. A nostalgic roll-call of the neighbourhood children and teenagers, friends and schoolmates – her sister, her parents and their friends. All assembled for a night of exuberant celebration.

Only a week ago, she'd been unable to remember Laura's party at all. Now, she remembers the names of most of the guests. She pauses at a rare photograph of her father – someone must have turned the camera on him, perhaps at his own request – looking suave, in a mint green polo shirt and cream chinos, glass in hand. And there's Jeanette, resplendent in peach chiffon, her hair swept up dramatically, her cheeks rosy from alcohol.

And then, with an odd detachment, Beth is gazing at an image of herself in the despised Snow White costume. It had felt like a punishment, an act of spite at the time, childish and ridiculous, given that half the other kids had gone as pop stars, but now Beth can see how sweet and endearing she'd looked – and younger than her thirteen years.

She is halfway down the pile now, and still there's not a ghost of the Binks twins. Perhaps they had deliberately avoided being anywhere near the camera, knowing that they were not invited. More likely, they had skulked in corners and scorned the attention sought by the other kids.

Beth spots Katie Mead, posing under a darkening sky, in green tights and pixie boots, with ribbons in her hair – what had she come as? Something to do with *A Midsummer Night's Dream*, perhaps? She smiles to see Guy Ward, arms folded and scowling – an unconvincing pirate in a too-white shirt and scarlet waistcoat, a pair of old school trousers cut artfully into rags.

She breathes in sharply, double takes at a snap of Laura, posing coquettishly, one hand on a jutting hip, the other blowing a kiss, while over her shoulder, huddled in the background is the fuzzy image of the Binks twins. Both in their regular street clothes, the wolf's head abandoned by this late hour. They appear to be watching Laura intently as she poses for the camera. Half a dozen other photographs appear to run on from this timeline. There is no sign of Beth in any of them. She steels herself to keep going, sensing the party is nearing its climax.

An involuntary cry escapes her lips as she comes to a dozen frames of her mother carrying the cake, their timeline so close that end-to-end they could almost be a moving image. Laura, posing again, glowing by the light of her birthday candles with Jeanette fussing round her; a princess surrounded by her subjects – the Binks brothers visible among them – all singing and clapping. Kevin, thumb and index finger in his mouth, whistling his approval.

Feeling a dull throb in her stomach, Beth closes her eyes – and can almost hear the tuneless but rousing chorus of *Happy Birthday to You* as everyone gathers.

Everyone except Beth and her attacker. A boy – or a man – in a rough, stinking, moth-eaten wolf's head.

A handful of photographs remain now. She is playing poker with each print; win or lose on the turn of a card. She gasps, her breath becoming ragged, a swirl of nausea rising in her gut.

Beth drops the image she is holding, as though scalded. It depicts the same scene, happy, smiling faces but with one addition. Barely in shot, on the far right of the frame, Guy Ward has joined the well-wishers, hair askew, face unsmiling. But it is the look in his eyes that leaves Beth feeling winded, unable to exhale; his expression, bleak and unseeing, as though he's in another world, and tucked under one arm, just visible, is the wolf's head.

CHAPTER FORTY-SIX

Beth

'Dad, I've got to go, something's just…' Beth wheezes, bolting from her father's front door, sucking air into her lungs and shaking so violently that she drops her handbag on the path. Then she's scrabbling among the weeds, scraping the contents together before staggering to the car.

Once behind the wheel, she breaks down in wracking sobs, barely able to see as she jerks the car around the block and pulls over, away from the prying eyes of her dad's neighbours.

What the hell? All bets are off. She'd expected to find something vile and brutal in her past – and had recently been mentally preparing for it. But *this*?

How the hell is she supposed to deal with knowing she'd been viciously raped at thirteen years old – a mere child – by someone she'd called a friend *all her life*.

On some unconscious level, she'd always known that she was different to other people, that something bleak and unseemly lurked in her distant past; that she'd been burying the truth, banishing it – into a swirling fog of fever and sickness. But that the nameless event had involved a close friend?

Well, there will be no burying anything now.

She will tell. First, she will tell Laura and then she will tell Gemma. Oh, God, Gemma with her picture-perfect life… It could destroy her. But it could save her, too. Only recently she'd alluded to the change in Guy's behaviour: a new watchfulness; his outbursts of temper.

Beth drives through the streets in a blur of tears, arriving home to find a staleness in the flat after it has stood empty for several days. She opens the windows, puts the kettle on and makes herself a mug of black coffee as there is no fresh milk.

Then, in a trance-like state, she perches stiffly on the edge of the sofa and calls her sister, knowing she is dropping a bomb.

At once, the words begin to spill out, quietly, mechanically, her voice hoarse and congested, Beth's heart breaking for a second time as she pictures Laura, struggling to comprehend the news.

'No, Beth, that's not right. It *can't* have been Guy. He's a friend… a *family* friend. We grew up together… he was practically the middle child in our house – our brother. Christ, I feel physically sick.' There's a short, stunned silence before Laura gasps, before blurting out her epiphany – a light bulb moment that makes total sense. 'Oh, God. Is that why he was sent away? Remember how Guy went off to finish his exams at that private school in Surrey? Was it because—?'

'Laura, don't… I can't think about that now,' Beth says, shutting her down. 'Look, you need to go – you'll be picking up the boys from school soon. Please don't worry about me. Believe it or not, I'm okay… Well, not *okay*, obviously, but I feel surprisingly together considering. I'll speak to you later. Love you.'

The coffee mug, still half full, has cooled in Beth's hands. How long has she been sitting there, frozen by shock and indecision?

It is Friday – she pictures her colleagues, frantically finishing up tasks, backing up work and logging out of laptops, before heading to the Bricklayers Arms and queuing at the bar, eager to taste that first refreshing round of drinks.

She wonders whether Kevin Binks will be there? Unlikely, given that he'd been shop-fitting only a few doors away when she'd seen him in the Brickie, and the job had since come to an end. Beth recalls him lining up at the dartboard, full of testosterone-fuelled banter – and then, genuine surprise at seeing a face from the past as she'd emerged from the ladies' room, almost slamming into him. Had he noticed her trembling pallor? Well, how misplaced *that* fear had been! Not Kevin-the-wolf, after all.

Because the wolf wears city clothing: well-cut suits for work, and designer jeans with fine linen shirts and cashmere sweaters for home. The large, luxurious home he shares with his beautiful wife and cute daughter…

Skin prickling with revulsion, Beth gets up, dumps the cup in the kitchen sink then goes for a long hot shower, scrubbing her body until it's a livid pink.

Saturday morning brings a sense of detached numbness. There'd been a brief moment when Beth had first woken up to the song of a robin on her windowsill, when she hadn't remembered. A fleeting, cosy, Saturday morning lie-in mood, as she'd stretched out and rolled over, snug under the duvet. Then the truth had hit her like a speeding truck and she'd sat up sharply in a rush of vertigo.

Today she will speak to her father: find out what, if anything, he remembers from the party.

Last night, three times she'd taken out her mobile, her thumb hovering over his number, but something had prevented her from calling. She'd already sent her sister spiralling into shock, anger and sadness. Could she really do that to her seventy-nine-year-old dad, with his failing health and melancholy? It could tip him over the edge, causing him to have a stroke or heart failure. Pushing her father's reaction to the back of her mind, Beth's thoughts turn to Gemma.

How the hell is she supposed to tell her kind, loving and decent friend that she is married to a rapist?

That she has *a child* with a brutal attacker?

Beth's heart spasms when she pictures Gemma and Miya; their happy, trusting faces.

Well, hold that thought. Because as hard as it will be to break the news that Gemma is married to a monster, not telling her is unthinkable. What kind of a friend would she be if she lets Gemma stay with an evil, manipulative bastard?

So, Beth will tell.

She will tell Gemma.

She will tell her father.

And she will tell the police.

CHAPTER FORTY-SEVEN

Gemma

On the morning after their fight, Gemma had woken up to a bruised hand and a steely resolve. She will leave Guy – but tactically, strategically and when he least expects it, the element of surprise giving her a slim and much needed advantage.

And in the meantime, as far as Guy is concerned, Gemma will pull out all the stops to be the perfect wife, mother and hostess, while biding her time and plotting her escape.

By mid-morning, with a renewed determination, Gemma is using Guy's car to drive Miya to her Saturday dance class, wincing every time she changes gear – her bruised hand a pertinent reminder of why she's planning her escape.

She glances at Miya in the rear-view mirror, singing along with the radio, oblivious to her mother's inner turmoil.

Guy had frightened her last night. His threats to take Miya away had been vicious and calculated – an obvious attempt at blackmailing Gemma into staying with him. Which – as horrific as it seemed – made her realise that he was desperate to fight for her. To keep the family together, under his roof – and under his control. Otherwise, why not just agree to a trial separation and to living apart like millions of other estranged couples? No, Gemma reasoned, Guy's extreme reaction came from a place of twisted desperation. Hence throwing away her contraceptive pills and firing her personal trainer, both perceived threats to their future happiness as a family. And as for his little stunt with the Zammertil, it beggared belief that he'd go to so much effort to make her look bad.

Well, let Guy think he has her where he wants her for now.

Gemma smiles at Miya in the rear-view mirror. 'Sweet pea, shall we do something nice for Daddy later? He works so hard – that's why he gets tired and grumpy. Shall we bake him a cake?'

Miya squeals. 'Ooh, yes! Can we make cupcakes with glitter icing? They're my absolute favourite, Mummy.'

Miya's enthusiasm is infectious. 'Yes, why not. We can bake while Daddy's out getting my car serviced.' Another thought occurs: perhaps she'll get all dressed up, book dinner and drinks somewhere locally and act flirty and feminine to mollify Guy. After all, she has an open-ended offer of babysitting courtesy of her neighbour Lucille Goff, which she's yet to take up and can easily sort by knocking on Lucille's door this afternoon.

Pleased with her plan, Gemma swings into a newly located space outside the community centre, where a handful of little girls are skipping and pirouetting around the entrance of the Tinkerbell's aged five to eight class.

'Okay, angel. See you in an hour – have fun.' Gemma kisses her daughter and walks back to the car. On a whim, rather than driving home for the short window Miya's class affords her, she buys a Pay and Display parking ticket and walks two blocks to a nail salon she's passed many times but never ventured into.

In the window, a neon sign flashes above a display of gaudy fake nails and a golden cat waves its paw, beckoning Gemma inside where the telltale smell of acrylic hits her. She glances down an aisle of four young women of East Asian appearance. The technician closest to the door doubles as receptionist. Her eyes smile behind the mask she's wearing.

Gemma smiles back. 'Hi, I don't have an appointment, but can anyone sort these out for me, please?' She splays her fingers, realising how much she's neglected herself since her trip to Marina's. Well, it has to stop. Being groomed and elegant will form a vital part of her Oscar-winning performance as the perfect wife.

The young woman lowers her mask. 'Ooh, that look nasty, girl,' she says, staring at Gemma's swollen hand.

'It looks worse than it is – I trapped it in the car door yesterday…' She rolls her eyes and laughs. 'I'm *so* clumsy.'

The technician frowns, then nods once. 'Okay, I do gel nails in ten minutes, take a seat please.'

Fifty minutes later, Gemma steps out onto the street, admiring her glossy new manicure, before walking briskly back to the community centre where a dozen little girls, all smiles and flushed cheeks, are spilling into the sunshine.

Once home, Miya jumps out of the car, dance class already forgotten in favour of an afternoon spent elbow deep in flour, butter and sugar.

'What time will Daddy be home?' she says, watching Gemma crack eggs into a bowl.

'I'm not sure, sweet pea. It depends how long the garage takes to service my car. Five o'clock, maybe?' Gemma hands Miya a small whisk. 'Now remember to add the eggs slowly or the batter will curdle – and try not to get it everywhere, please.'

At three thirty, with Miya's cupcakes cooling on the island, and Lucille Goff cued up for babysitting at seven o'clock, Gemma phones Guy to get an ETA. Her call goes straight to voicemail so she leaves a message, realising that he's probably driving, given that the specialist Range Rover garage is in Sevenoaks, at least an hour away.

Later, she's about to call a second time when Guy arrives.

'Daddy!' Miya squeals, hugging him at the front door and gabbing excitedly about the cakes she's made.

'Got your message,' Guy says, once Miya has backed off and he's able to get through the door properly. 'I'm surprised you want to go out tonight,' he says, sounding guarded.

Gemma smiles. 'Darling, I want to put last night behind us. Think of it as a making-up dinner. It's ages since we got glammed up and went on a date. Anyway, it's all organised. Lucille's coming to babysit at seven, the cab will arrive at seven fifteen and our table at the Belfry Bar & Grill is booked for eight. I thought we could have a glass of champagne in the bar first,' Gemma says, her smile warm and intimate. They are standing close together now, Guy's eyes searching hers.

'Well, you seem to have thought of everything, Mrs Ward,' he says eventually, giving Gemma his most charming smile before changing the subject. 'So, your car is all sorted. I even had it cleaned.'

'Thanks, darling, that's great,' Gemma says. 'Right, we've got an hour if you want to change. I'm all showered and made up, just need to slip on a decent dress and heels.'

Guy's expression softens. 'Gemma, I'm sorry about last night,' he lowers his voice, 'I just snapped... Your poor hand.' He notices her new manicure. 'That looks pretty... like the rest of you,' he says, gently kissing her swollen knuckles before going off to change.

CHAPTER FORTY-EIGHT

Beth

On Sunday morning, Beth is awake, showered and dressed by eight thirty, aghast at how calm she now feels. Saturday on the other hand, had been a blurred patchwork of agitation and anger, sadness and self-pity – and several hours spent in a listless and trance-like state.

Again, she'd put off calling her dad, picturing his face, shocked and confused when – *if* – she broke the news of her attack to him.

Now, she couldn't help but wonder whether he even needed to know. What was the point of telling him? What good could possibly come of him knowing that his youngest daughter had been a victim of rape?

Laura already knew. Gemma, she was working up to. The police… that was a whole other mountain to climb and she wasn't even at the foot of the hill yet. But her father…?

Realising that she doesn't trust herself not to blurt out the truth – not to mention her unwillingness to return to the crime scene – Beth waits until nine o'clock before phoning Tim to say she's unwell.

'It's not serious, Dad. Just a throaty thing but I'd hate you to catch it, so I'm chilling at home today,' she lies, hanging up soon afterwards for fear of giving herself away.

With the sun already streaming through her windows and the day ahead an empty space, Beth contemplates getting out of the flat. In the little park across the road, the dog walkers and regular joggers are already out enjoying the warm temperature.

Her empty stomach rumbles. Last night, she'd collected takeaway from her local Indian restaurant with the vague notion that whatever else happened she needed to keep body and soul together, even buying a bottle of Indian beer to wash it down. But she'd hardly touched the chicken jalfrezi she usually devoured and even her favourite naan and cauliflower bhaji had failed to tempt her.

Grabbing a light jacket and her purse, Beth cuts through the park, nodding to some of the dog walkers as she strides in the direction of the high street.

Once inside the supermarket, the smell of warm bread rising in the industrial-sized ovens and sticky pastries bagged up and ready to go leaves her salivating. Hunger: it's a relief to feel something ordinary and normal. She fills her basket from the fresh bake aisle, buys milk and orange juice and even a tabloid newspaper that has a popular actress on the cover, claiming her marriage is over, and walks home at a brisk pace.

Soon Beth is enjoying a good breakfast, feeling more human again and contemplating going further afield.

It suddenly occurs to her that Laura might turn up at their dad's house – neither of them had mentioned their usual Sunday visit the last time they'd spoken.

Remembering how shocked and broken her sister had sounded, she reaches for her mobile and pastes on a bright smile, hoping it will transmit through her voice.

Laura answers on the second ring, sounding breathless. 'Beth? Are you all right? What's happened?'

'I'm fine Laur, really,' Beth soothes. 'I slept okay – well, on and off. I've been out and bought breakfast, eaten my own body weight in croissants and now I'm just deciding where to go for a walk.'

'Hmm, you don't fool me. I know you're just trying to sound upbeat so that I won't worry about you so much. What about Dad? Are you going today?'

Beth inhales sharply. 'That's why I'm calling. I can't face him yet – or going to the house… Laur, I'm still wondering how the hell I'm going to tell him – *if* I'm going to tell him.'

'I understand,' Laura says. 'Look, I'll pop over there, put a wash on and check the fridge for dodgy food and make him some lunch. What shall I tell him?'

'Dad thinks I've got a throat virus so if he asks, stick to that.'

There's a pause on the line. 'Beth, have you thought any more about going to the police? I could kill Guy for what he did. He can't just get away with this.'

Beth scoffs. 'Oh, don't worry, he won't get away with anything, Laura. But I need to speak to Gemma before I go reporting him. I mean, it's over twenty-five years ago. I need to think about how I'm going to approach this so that the police will even give me the time of day. I can't just rock up at the local nick and say, *Oh, hi, officer. I've just remembered I was raped in 1994*, can I?'

'No, of course not…' Laura sighs. 'Look, just remember that I'm on your side and will do anything it takes to support you.'

'I know – and I love you for that,' Beth says, the words catching in her throat.

After squaring things with her sister, she'd settled on a walk in Dulwich Park: only three miles away and a pretty drive to boot.

Now, sunglasses and trainers on, Beth takes a deep breath, grabs her bag and car keys, and sets out, proud of herself for making an effort.

CHAPTER FORTY-NINE

Gemma

'Breakfast in bed, m'lady,' Guy sets down the tray and bows with a flourish.

Gemma rubs her eyes, pushes herself up against the pillows. 'Hey, thank you… What's all this? How long have you been up?'

'Oh, long enough to pick up fresh croissants,' Guy says. 'Miya's awake but she's still in bed, playing with her tablet, so we get a reprieve this morning.' He opens the curtains, letting the spring sunshine stream in. 'Another glorious day. It's like summer came early this year. What shall we do today?'

Gemma sips her coffee, tears off a piece of the still warm croissant. 'I don't mind. How about a walk in Dulwich Park? Or I can cook Sunday roast – invite some people, maybe Beth and a couple of the neighbours if they're free?'

Guy groans. 'Another time. I'm loving being in this cocoon, just the three of us, and I'll be back in the office this time tomorrow.'

Gemma nods. 'Just us it is then, sounds perfect. Hey! Good morning, sweet pea,' she says, opening her arms as her daughter barges in and climbs on the bed.

'Miya, let Mummy finish her coffee in peace,' Guy says, with a note of mock sternness. 'Come on, let's go downstairs, give her some space.' He turns back to Gemma. 'You shower and dress when you're ready, I'll keep madam amused for a while.'

Astonished by Guy's apparent transformation from bullying control freak to husband of the year, Gemma listens to the two of them giggling and chatting about nonsense as she revels in the unexpected luxury of some time to herself.

In the park, lured by sunshine, people litter the lawns in droves.

'It's so crowded today,' Gemma says, narrowly avoiding a child on a scooter as he almost rams her legs, to the indifference of his parents.

Guy spins on his heel, his face dark. 'Careful!'

Miya dawdles between them, holding Guy's hand and singing to herself, until the lake comes into view and her pace quickens. 'Can we see the ducks, please?'

'Of course, you can, sweetheart,' Guy says.

But when they get there the area is so rammed with people and their dogs, and mum's towing toddlers in pushchairs, all wanting to get close to the newly hatched ducklings, that Guy becomes irritable.

He wrinkles his nose. 'Whiffs a bit,' he says, picking up the scent of pond weed and the oily droppings of the Canada geese. 'Shall we get ice creams instead?'

'Aww, Daddy, we've only just got here,' Miya whines. 'I want to get closer to the babies, they're so sweet.'

Gemma shrugs. 'Why don't you head for the café, find us a table in the garden and we'll join you in ten or fifteen minutes – give Miya more time here.'

'Okay, no rush, darling, see you shortly,' Guy says, pecking Gemma on the cheek and making a hasty retreat.

She waits a while, enjoying Miya's pleasure and her obvious tenderness for animals, as she stops to pet a pair of small dogs waddling past.

'Can we have a dog? Please, Mummy – one just like that,' she says, after fussing a golden cockapoo who licks her hands while she laughs with delight.

Gemma stops to admire the unbelievable cuteness of the dog and wonders if a pet might provide a welcome distraction for Miya in their new life without her father. 'Maybe. Let's talk about it at home, shall we?' she says, taking Miya's hand and leading her in the direction of the tearoom.

But Miya begins waving to someone and calling out. 'There's Auntie Beth! Look, Mummy, there she is,' she cries, tugging Gemma's hand and pulling her in Beth's direction.

Waving, Gemma quickens her pace, but to her surprise, Beth, who had been moving towards them, stops abruptly and changes direction, her face half hidden by sunglasses.

Gemma frowns and waves again. Perhaps Beth hasn't seen her. She calls her name, which only sends Beth practically running in the opposite direction.

'Where's she going?' Miya says, her face rumpled with hurt.

'I don't think she saw us, sweet pea. Never mind. I'll give her a call later. Come on, let's go find Daddy and get some ice cream – I'll race you there!'

Guy sits alone, scrolling through his phone, a trio of cold drinks on the table in front of him.

'I got Coke and Fanta,' he says, adding. 'I'll get us three cornets now you're here. Back in a mo.'

Watching Miya sip fizzy orange through a straw, Gemma considers Beth's hasty getaway. Why on earth had she changed direction like that? It was so clear that Beth had seen and then avoided her, but why?

'Here you go,' Guy says, handing out two ninety-nines before licking a creamy dribble off his thumb. 'Oh, look at the state of me!' Then he notices Gemma's expression. 'Are you all right, hon? You seem a bit worried.'

Gemma frowns. 'Yes, I'm fine. We saw Beth a moment ago and she so obviously avoided us. It was weird.'

'She ran away, Daddy,' Miya interjects, her eyes wide.

'Did she now? Well, that was a funny thing to do, wasn't it?' Guy says, making a goofy face for Miya's benefit.

'Yeah, she definitely saw us,' Gemma says, looking pensive.

Guy shrugs. 'She can't have. Why on earth would she avoid you? Gem, you know what she's like, probably miles away and thinking about work tomorrow.'

'Maybe,' Gemma nods, far from convinced.

CHAPTER FIFTY

Gemma

On Monday morning Gemma opens her eyes five minutes before the alarm sounds. She turns to Guy, his face half buried in the pillow, squiggles of grey hair visible in his dark nest of curls.

Something had shifted in him during the last forty-eight hours. Friday night had been truly grim and she'd seen flashes of real hatred in Guy's eyes and a coldness she'd never thought him capable of. Yet somehow, to all outward appearance, they'd found their way back to each other and their weekend had been full of laughter and tenderness.

'Oh, make it stop,' Guy groans at the sound of the alarm buzzing. He sits up. 'Morning, gorgeous. Did you sleep well?' He lifts a stray lock of hair from Gemma's face and smiles. 'Shall we just cancel Monday and stay here all day?'

There's a thud of footfall from Miya's room followed by the sound of curtains being dragged across a pole.

Gemma smiles. 'Maybe not. Sounds like we won't even get our quiet coffee together this morning.' She gets up, slides on a robe and goes to the bathroom.

Downstairs, the usual pre-work and school routine ensues as the three of them march through breakfast, showering and dressing before there are hugs and kisses in the hallway and shouts of 'Be careful' and 'Have a great day'.

On the school run, Miya returns to the subject of getting a puppy. 'I'm going to call him Harvey... that's a brilliant dog's name, isn't it?'

'Yes, sweet pea – but nothing's been decided yet. We need to discuss it properly with Daddy.'

'Oh, he won't mind, will he? He'll be at work, so you'll be looking after Harvey, won't you, Mummy?'

Gemma laughs. Out of the mouths of babes. 'Wait and see,' she says vaguely, concentrating on the traffic. But Miya has got the bit between her teeth.

'Mummy... Mum! We *have* to get a dog. I'm the only person in my class who hasn't got any pets. Even Sophia's got Snowflake the rabbit... It's not fair.'

'I said later, okay?' Gemma double parks, hazard lights flashing as she unloads Miya from the back seat. 'Look, there's Sophia. Love you, have fun.' She bends to kiss her daughter and waves at Katya.

'Hi! Can't stop – got a plumber due at the house,' Gemma lies, heading straight back to the car, aware that the last time she and Katya had talked, Miya had gone for a sleepover and her friend had been on standby in case of any domestic emergencies.

From now on, she needs to keep her powder dry and that includes no more confiding in other mums.

She flexes her left hand and reminds herself that no amount of breakfast in bed, compliments and affection can compensate for Guy's recent aggressive – no, *violent* – behaviour. She makes a mental note to text Katya from home, explaining that she and Guy are back on track, before joining the traffic bound for home.

In six hours, she'll be back at the school gates but until then, Gemma's time is her own. Feeling strong in her resolve, she imagines a punishing gym workout, followed by a dip in the club's pool. Then maybe tomorrow, she'll go for a 5k run. She'll need to keep active, now that Caleb won't be putting her through her paces anymore.

She catches her breath. Poor Caleb; fired by Guy – God alone knows how that conversation had played out. Turning into Darwin Drive, Gemma pushes him from her mind and waves to Lucille Goff who's carrying cardboard to the recycling bin.

Once inside, she's soon sitting up at the kitchen island, enjoying a fresh coffee and a moment's peace when a text arrives from Beth.

Gemma. Sorry for avoiding you yesterday but I need to see you urgently. Are you free at noon today?

Gemma frowns. It's unlike Beth to send such an abrupt message, with no 'hope you're well', no kisses, no smiley faces. Bristling slightly at what sounds more like an order than a request, her answer is equally brief.

Was going to gym but can meet if urgent. Are you okay? Come to mine.

Beth's reply pings back presently. *Not at yours. Meet me in the park where you train with Caleb. Car park at 12.00. Gemma, DO NOT TELL GUY. Be careful. Bx*

Gemma texts back, saying she'll be there, a sinking feeling in her gut. What on earth has happened? Why the cloak and dagger routine? Whatever Beth's news, her instincts tell her that it will not be cause for celebration.

She checks the time: ten forty. With a growing unease, Gemma finishes her coffee and potters through a few chores before setting off to meet her friend.

CHAPTER FIFTY-ONE

Beth

At noon, in the recreation ground's car park, Beth watches for Gemma's car, rigid with apprehension. She's only been there three or four minutes when the white Range Rover rumbles into view. Gemma parks, steps down onto the tarmac and straightens her jacket. Seeing Beth, she waves, her eyes crinkling as she smiles.

Sweating, Beth feels her heart racing as she walks towards her friend; a friend who may not be one after she has said all she needs to. She embraces Gemma, inhaling her delicate perfume, then steps back, searching her face.

'Thanks for meeting me at short notice. I had to see you. Gemma, I wish there were some other—'

Gemma shakes her head, confusion on her face. 'Beth, why all the secrecy? I can't believe you ran from Miya and me yesterday. It upset her, actually. I pretended you hadn't seen us, but I know you did. What's going on?'

Beth scans the immediate area. A handful of people are jogging, a woman with a pushchair is pointing out trees and flowers to an apple-cheeked toddler and a man in his seventies is walking a rotund, elderly Labrador. She spots an unoccupied bench.

'Let's sit over there,' Beth says, ignoring Gemma's obvious confusion.

As they approach the weathered seat, Beth hears the ping of a text from Gemma's phone. She takes it out, looks at the screen.

'It's Guy, just telling me he can't wait to get home this evening,' Gemma says, a slight flush creeping into her cheeks.

Beth's heart sinks… This is going to be even harder than she'd imagined.

'Gemma, please – could you do me a favour? Just turn your phone off for a moment. And don't tell him you're here. It's important!' She finishes, her tone shrill.

Gemma frowns. 'I'm listening, okay?'

Beth balls up her fists, takes a deep breath, exhales slowly. 'God, I've been dreading this. Gemma, you know that I've been seeing a therapist… Zara, I told you about her… and how she believed that I was experiencing flashbacks linked to some traumatic event in my childhood? Something awful that I'd buried… sort of a suppressed memory.'

Gemma is nodding, concern in her eyes.

'Okay, well, last Tuesday, I had a special therapy session, a kind of hypnosis really… and Zara took me back to when I was thirteen and the summer of Laura's sixteenth birthday party.'

Gemma frowns and nibbles her thumbnail. 'Beth, I'm so sorry. If I'd realised, I could have gone with you. I wish you'd told me. Guy and I could have been there for you, supported you more.' Her eyes are brimming with kindness now, any irritation at being summoned at short notice forgotten.

How long before Gemma's concern is replaced by fury and disbelief?

Beth shakes her head, steels herself to keep on track. 'No. Not Guy. He can *never* be there for me. Gemma, I'm really sorry… if there was any other way—'

'Okay, you're scaring me now,' Gemma says. 'Just tell me, please!'

Beth takes a ragged breath. 'The year I was thirteen, I was raped. It was during my sister's sixteenth birthday party – all the local kids were there, school friends, neighbours… Gemma, I believe it was Guy who attacked me.'

Beth watches Gemma's face: poised, impassive for a second – as though she's hanging on for the punchline of a joke – before waves of emotion break over her. Confusion, sadness, disbelief – then anger as the words hit home.

'No! No, you're wrong! Beth, that's truly awful… such a terrible thing to happen – to anyone. Devastating, in fact, but that wasn't Guy. How ridiculous! How could you even *think* that?' Gemma gets to her feet, turns away and plunges her hands into her jacket pockets. She turns back to face Beth. 'That's a terrible thing to say. I mean, what the—'

'Obviously, you're shocked and angry – anybody would be – but you need to know. Gemma, your husband raped me when he was fifteen years old. Christ – why the hell would I lie about a thing like that?'

Gemma's eyes blaze. 'Because you're not well. Beth, I've seen you change. I've watched you go downhill for months. It's not your fault… clearly this… *therapist*,' Gemma mimes air quotes, 'has a lot to answer for. Putting crazy, ridiculous ideas in your head. It's shameful!'

'Do you think I would lie? About being raped?'

Gemma's cheeks are flushed now; tears shine in her eyes. 'No! Of course, I don't think that. But I can tell you now, with complete certainty, whoever did that terrible thing to you, it wasn't my husband. It wasn't Miya's father. Beth, you've been friends since primary school, how could you think…' She pulls a crumpled tissue from her pocket and blots her eyes.

Beth stands her ground despite her friend's evident pain. 'Gemma, I totally get why you're upset. Nobody wants to find out that they're married to a monster, but I have proof. There are photos from that night – I brought them, they're in the car. They clearly show—'

'Show *what*?' Gemma wheels round to face her. 'Kids at a party? I don't know what you think you can prove, but you're wrong. Guy would *never* do such a thing – at any age! I mean, he's not perfect and he can be a bully, I know that better than anyone, but raping a child?'

Beth blinks back the tears that have sprung into her eyes. 'But you've no idea what's in his past – people keep all sorts of bizarre secrets. Gemma, it was him. It all came back to me during the regression therapy, where, when and how. I just needed to know who was under the wolf's head – and I found out from the photos. They prove that—'

But Gemma has clamped her hands over her ears and is striding towards the car. 'Wolf's head?' she calls over her shoulder. 'Just listen to yourself. How dare you? I thought we were friends. But until you're ready to apologise – and to get some proper help for your problem, just stay away from us.'

'Gemma, wait! Can't we talk about it?' Beth hurries after her. 'I'm trying to protect you and Miya.'

But Gemma gets into her car, revs the engine hard and pulls away in a squeal of tyres.

Beth trudges slowly to her own car, a niggle of doubt worming into her head. What if she has just alienated her best friend and it's all a mistake? What if it wasn't Guy at all?

A few days ago, before the regression therapy, she'd been sure that Kevin Binks was responsible for her inexplicable terror, without even knowing that she'd been attacked. What if her newly uncovered *memories* aren't memories at all, but dreams or images triggered by a film she'd seen or a book she'd once read?

Beth unlocks the car and feels the spit of rain as a black cloud slides into view. It seems like a metaphor for her misery.

Sitting at the wheel, watching the rain make patterns on her windscreen, Beth thinks back to that night. During the hypnosis, she'd seen it all, everything that had happened, as clearly as if she'd been watching a film, reliving the terror and anguish of her attack. Now though, she feels an odd detachment, as though watching a young actress going through her paces. What if Gemma has a point and the memories she 'unlocked' were false?

She starts the engine and pulls slowly out of the car park. She's been on the road for five minutes when she realises: she has subconsciously taken the road to her father's house.

CHAPTER FIFTY-TWO

Gemma

It's one fifteen by the time Gemma arrives home. She is so shaken by Beth's revelation that she'd almost hit a white van as it stopped on amber at the traffic lights near the top of her road. The squeal of her own tyres had been an alarm call. The last thing she needed was an accident – her car had only been in the garage two days earlier. Thank goodness Miya had not been with her.

Screw Beth for her vicious – no, *deluded* allegations. For months, at times, Beth seemed remote and preoccupied. Well, now she's truly lost the plot!

Too wired to eat, Gemma heads upstairs to change into her running gear and is soon pounding the pavements near home harder and faster than ever before. How *dare* Beth put such horrible thoughts into her head? Of course, there was no truth in the things she'd said. None whatsoever. They were simply another manifestation of the depression and anxiety which had been getting steadily worse all year.

Gemma breathes deeply, aware of the stitch forming in her side. She slows her pace, her anger beginning to ebb away, her mind slipping into rhythmic analysis as a conversation starts up in her head…

No way is Guy capable of raping a woman.
Ahh, but he is capable of inflicting physical pain.

Yes, but rape is in another league entirely. Surely, he would never…

But Guy has a temper. And a mean streak. He likes to be in control.

But raping a child? That's not being in control, that's losing it entirely… No way is he capable of such cruelty, such sick abuse…

Round and round Gemma's thoughts go, until she arrives home, hair dripping with sweat, a sick feeling in the pit of her stomach.

Guy returns from work in a sober mood, teasing and play-wrestling with Miya, but his response to Gemma's questions about his day are cryptic.

'What can I say? A bog-standard Monday and far less exciting than yours, I suspect,' he says, watching Gemma lay the table for supper.

She turns away. If only he knew! Her day *had* been interesting, but not in a way she can share or give any further consideration to. The whole conversation in the park with Beth seems nightmarish and surreal now.

After leaving Beth, Gemma had checked her phone at regular intervals, half expecting an apology – if not a total retraction of what she'd said. Instead, at around four thirty, a message arrived saying Beth had spoken to her father and she was even more convinced! The whole sorry business beggared belief.

She studies Guy, Miya under his arm, pretending to drop her as she shrieks and giggles with delight. 'Come on then, stinker. Bedtime for you, so that Mummy and I can have our dinner in peace.'

Miya scowls and protests mildly before kissing Gemma good-night and allowing herself to be led away.

Unsmiling, Guy reappears and sits down at the table.

'I swear that Miya's bedtime story with you is the highlight of her day,' Gemma says, spooning wild mushroom risotto onto plates.

'She's a daddy's girl, all right,' Guy says, pouring white wine into two glasses. 'Thanks, Gem. This looks good.' He tastes the risotto, nods in approval. 'Wow, delicious. You're amazing, you know that?'

Gemma gives a little shrug. 'Risotto's not difficult, but I guess all the stirring takes a bit of patience.'

'And time,' Guy says, taking a sip of wine. 'So, it's amazing, really, that you've managed to put anything decent on the table tonight.'

Gemma's heart leaps into her throat. 'I'm sorry, hon?'

Guy inclines his head and chews thoughtfully. 'Actually, on reflection, it's a little salty, but I expect your mind has been elsewhere.'

Gemma's pulse is racing now. She opens her mouth to speak, but Guy continues, his tone icy. 'How *is* Caleb these days, after my little chat with him?'

There's a crash as Gemma drops her cutlery. 'I don't know what you mean. I haven't heard from him,' she manages, her voice hoarse.

'Ah, okay,' Guy nods slowly, his mouth a downturned crescent. 'So, the running kit in the laundry bin and the drive to the recreation ground, that wasn't an impromptu training session then?'

Gemma's eyes widen. *How does he know her movements for the day?* She feels the heat rising in her face and neck. 'No! Guy, I haven't seen Caleb, I can assure you. And yes, I did go for a run, but it was around the streets, locally – the same circuit I do on Saturday mornings sometimes. Guy, I can't imagine why—'

'Do you take me for a complete moron? You drove to the park today at around noon, so please don't bother to deny it, Gemma. There's really no point.' He pushes his plate aside, dabs his lips on a carefully pressed napkin. 'Well?'

Gemma shakes her head, a queasiness washing over her. She lifts her glass and gulps some wine.

'That's it, Gemma – have a drink. Here, knock yourself out.' He overfills her glass so that wine flows over the rim and onto the table, adding, 'I'll run upstairs and get your pills for you as well, shall I?'

Tears of utter panic spring into Gemma's eyes. 'Guy, I promise you. I've had a very boring day. Apart from driving Miya to and from school and the street run I've just told you about, it has been totally uneventful.'

A pained look passes over his face. 'There's no point in lying to me, Gemma, you only insult my intelligence.' Guy takes her left hand in his and squeezes it so hard that it throbs. 'I put a tracker on your car – well, obviously, not *me* personally.' His eyes glitter dangerously. 'The garage fitted it on Saturday. Gem, I had no choice. After your little threat last week about leaving home and taking Miya with you, I couldn't take any chances. You do understand, don't you?'

A sob escapes Gemma, as much from fear and frustration as from the pain in her still-tender hand. 'No! I *don't* understand, Guy. I thought we'd sorted everything. We had such a gorgeous weekend together. It was meant to be a fresh start. I can't believe you put a tracker on my car. Why would you spy on me?'

'Why would *you* lie to me?' Guy growls, releasing her hand.

'I'm not lying, I promise! I haven't seen Caleb – today or any day – you sacked him, remember? As you're so bothered, I met Beth in the park, we just went for a walk…' She stops herself babbling on, wary of tripping herself up.

Beth's words echo in her mind. *It was Guy who attacked me.*

Guy grimaces. 'You met in the park? How very teenage of you. Why didn't you meet for coffee or something?'

Gemma grabs a tissue and wipes her eyes. She squares her shoulders. 'No reason. Beth has taken a few days off work and she fancied some fresh air. She's thinking about getting back with Alex and wanted to talk it through,' she says, giving the first excuse for a girly chat that has come into her head.

Guy scoffs. 'Ha! That fool. Alex is pathetic. Beth was right to dump him. She needs somebody who's a bit more dynamic if you ask me.'

Gemma tries to smile and grabs the lifeline with both hands, pandering to his ego, and secure in the knowledge that nothing makes her husband happier than being right.

'That's pretty much what I said. I mean, it's her decision, but if he wasn't right for her then, why would they be any better suited now?'

'So how did Beth take that?' Guy asks, with genuine interest.

Gemma shrugs. 'Oh, she knows what he's like. She's just flattered because he still loves her.'

Guy brushes his fingertips along one damp cheekbone. 'As I still love you, Gemma. Which is the reason for the tracker on your car. It means that no matter where you are, I'll find you.'

He gets up and goes to the fridge. 'Did you make a dessert?' he asks pleasantly.

Doors – *options* – had seemed to slam around her then.

She'd already tried asking Guy for a trial separation in an adult, respectful way. But his response had been to threaten her with taking Miya away by resorting to bogus claims of made-up drug and alcohol addiction.

Plan B had been to bide her time; play the devoted wife, lull him into thinking things were cool between them and then, once she had all her ducks in a row, to simply disappear.

Now, with Guy watching her every move, monitoring her phone calls and tracking her car journeys, even Plan B seems insurmountable, begging the question: what exactly is left for her?

CHAPTER FIFTY-THREE

Beth

What had she expected? That they'd hug it out and Gemma would thank her for pointing out she was married to a monster?

Feeling she'd little more to lose, Beth had driven to her father's house, circling the block three times before parking up outside Mrs Mahoney's semi and rehearsing what on earth she would say to her seventy-nine-year-old dad.

She gets out of the car and walks up her father's path, hesitates before ringing the doorbell, nausea cramping her stomach. This has to be done. If there were any other way…

Tim's expression is a blend of joy and suspicion. Understandable, given that only the day before Beth had cancelled her regular Sunday visit home, claiming to feel unwell.

'Darling! Well, this is a nice surprise. Feeling better?'

'I'm fine, Dad. I should have phoned first, can I come in? I need to speak to you about something.'

Does she imagine the slight wariness in Tim's eyes as he waves her through to the kitchen?

Beth attempts a smile. 'I'll make us some tea, shall I?' Without waiting for an answer, she fills the kettle and drops teabags into mugs.

'I must say I'm surprised to see you,' Tim says, cleaning his glasses on the nearest tea towel. 'How's work going?'

'Oh, I'm taking some time off – I've got stuff to sort out. And then I might look for another job, or even go away for a bit. I don't know yet.'

She pours boiling water into the mugs and finds milk in the fridge that is just on date.

'Beth, come and sit down. Let's enjoy the afternoon sun after the showers we had earlier,' Tim says, gesturing for Beth to follow him into the sitting room. The otherwise drab room is a blaze of gold, which only highlights the thick dust and filthy windows.

Shielding her eyes from the sun's glare, Beth sits opposite her father, perching stiffly on the edge of her seat.

'Dad. This isn't really a social call. There's something I need to ask you… and I need you to be completely honest with me.'

Tim's eyes are hooded now; he nods. 'Of course.'

And slowly, in simple language, Beth takes her father back to Laura's sixteenth birthday party, reminding him of the guests in fancy dress, the DJ that had kept the atmosphere fizzing, the decorations, the staffed bar and the lavish cake.

Tim listens without interrupting, a faraway look in his eyes, the ghost of a smile on his lips whenever Beth mentions Jeanette.

'Dad,' Beth finishes softly, 'I'm so sorry to tell you this… I know it's going to be a massive shock… but I believe I was assaulted by Guy Ward that night. It happened behind the leylandii hedge, just before the party broke up.'

Assaulted. Beth has chosen the word carefully – an outright avoidance of the term rape – for who can stand to hear that of their child?

Tears leak from the corner of Tim's eyes. When he speaks his voice is barely a whisper. 'I've often wondered if this day would come.'

His words hit her like a slap. Beth shakes her head in confusion. '*What*? What do you mean?'

Tim gazes ahead, his hands pleating the fabric of his trousers.

'Dad! Tell me. Did you know about this?' She watches him as his lips move wordlessly.

His eyes are glassy, avoiding hers. She stands up, begins to pace, then turns to look at him, her eyes blazing. 'Dad? Talk to me!' Beth shouts. 'What do you mean, you *wondered if this day would come?*'

'I had my suspicions at the time…'

Beth grips a side table for balance as the room seems to spin. She sits down again, inhales deeply and presses on.

'Dad, for God's sake! Just tell me what you know about that night. I *need* to know. Do you understand?'

Tim fishes a handkerchief from his trouser pocket and dabs his eyes. 'There were signs – call it a sixth sense. But I started to wonder after a conversation with Alastair, Guy's father. You won't remember this, but the Wards went away that summer – they took a cottage by the sea – it was all very sudden. Before they left, after too much whisky, Alastair confided to me that there'd been an *incident* involving Guy – something he'd admitted to himself – concerning a girl. Oh, I never knew the details, only that it was something shameful and regrettable… completely out of character. The next thing we knew, the holidays were over and Guy had gone away to school in Surrey.'

'So, they sent him away,' Beth whispers, remembering how Guy had suddenly disappeared from their lives, reappearing two years later, no longer a boy but a promising young man about town.

Their eyes meet. 'Dad, why didn't you and Mum protect me? How could you do nothing? If you knew all along, why the hell wasn't he punished?'

'I told you, I didn't *know* anything, but I always wondered. And don't blame your mother. She hadn't a clue about any of this. It was kept between the men. Least said, soonest mended. It would have been far worse to stir things up. Imagine the scandal, the disruption… for both our families.'

Beth scoffs. 'Of course! How awful for you, Dad. So glad you and Alastair had your blushes spared at the golf club,' she says, her words heavy with sarcasm.

He shakes his head sadly, narrows his eyes, remembering. 'Two days after Laura's birthday, you were ill. You woke up on the Monday morning, your little face white as a sheet and round as a bowling ball. And that was it: you didn't get out of bed for a month. We called the doctor, of course, but there's no treatment for glandular fever, just rest, fluids, TLC. Your mother nursed you around the clock, watching over you as you faded in and out of sleep, delirious for days on end.'

Beth's heart contracts. 'Mum did all that for me?'

'Of course. Don't sound so surprised. Your mother's bark was always worse than her bite.'

'None of this explains why you did nothing,' Beth's voice is barely above a whisper as tears course down her cheeks.

Tim sighs and wipes his own eyes. 'By the time you recovered, you seemed bright and happy – your old self again, eager to be back at school. Guy had been removed and posed no threat. So, I'm afraid I took the view that raking up something that might not even have happened would have done more harm than good. I know now that I made the wrong call.'

Beth gets to her feet. 'Dad, I'm taking this to the police, and you can't stop me.'

'I won't even try,' Tim says, his expression resigned. 'What happened to you was terrible. I let you down then, but now I'll support you in any way I can. And I'm sorry. I should have been braver and dug deeper.'

'Yes, Dad, you should have! Do you have any idea how much I looked up to you – relied on you? Mum and me... well, that was always difficult, for some reason I annoyed her just by being in the same house. But *you*? We had a special bond... you were my hero.'

Beth sinks onto the sofa, her tears still flowing freely.

'I mean it, Beth. I'm deeply sorry,' Tim rasps. 'I'll talk to the police… tell them what I've just told you – if that's what you want.'

Beth wipes her eyes and stares back at him. 'What I *want*…? I have no idea. Look, I have to go. Take care of yourself, Dad.'

She grabs her handbag, and stumbles out of her father's house, not knowing when or if she'll be back.

CHAPTER FIFTY-FOUR

Beth

Beth paces the flat, her mind accelerating into overdrive. That her father had had his suspicions all along had shocked her to the core. How could he have done nothing to get justice for his thirteen-year-old daughter? It was unthinkable that the man who had always been her hero had tacitly colluded with the enemy.

And as for Guy... He must have thought that all his Christmases had come at once when Beth had failed to report the attack – thanks to being rendered semi-conscious by illness for the rest of the holidays.

If only her mother had listened to her that night – instead of sending her to bed as she'd staggered inside, dazed and bleeding. If only she hadn't been sick, too exhausted to think straight for weeks afterwards. If only her father had asked questions, instead of ignoring the signs.

If. Only.

But it isn't too late. Beth *will* seek justice. She will bring down Guy Ward, wipe the smug grin off his face and knock him off his pedestal – show the world *exactly* what kind of man he really is.

She glances at her watch. At three twenty it is smack in the middle of the school run. She pictures her sister, swearing under her breath as she tries to park outside Jack and Alfie's school as they stream out all smiles, hair mussed and starving hungry.

She will call Laura this evening, update her on one of the weirdest days of her life, after giving her time to despatch her sons' meals, baths and bedtimes.

Beth catches her breath as her thoughts turn to Gemma. She'd gambled on their friendship and lost. Gemma had been shocked and outraged, unable to believe that her dream husband harboured dark secrets. She'd been so stunned in fact, that Beth had briefly wondered if she'd made a mistake.

But now, after speaking to Tim, there's no room in Beth's head for doubt. The photographs of Guy holding the vile wolf's head directly after her attack had taken place, coupled with the knowledge that Guy had confessed to some shameful act to his father – and one serious enough to result in him being banished for two years – is all the proof Beth needs.

But will the police see it her way? How can she even begin to get justice for something that happened twenty-five years ago? After all, memories and theories are not evidence but merely hearsay.

Will her father stand up to being questioned by the authorities? Will Zara be called upon to validate regression therapy as a means of tapping into a person's forgotten past? From where Beth is sitting, the road ahead looks steep, winding and bumpy.

On a whim, she grabs her mobile and messages Gemma.

Hi Gemma, so sorry for shocking you today. I understand totally why you are hurt and angry. Spoke to Dad after I left you and learnt things that make me even more convinced that it was Guy who attacked me. Please, Gemma, be careful. I am here for you if you need to talk. Sorry things are this way. Your friend, Beth. X

Beth waits until eight o'clock and calls her sister's mobile.

Laura answers on the second ring. 'Hi, love, how are you doing?' she croons, as though speaking to an invalid.

'Weirdly fine,' Beth says. 'Well, not *fine*, obviously, but better than I've been for months. I feel released by knowing this stuff. For the first time in my life, I feel as though my eyes are wide open.'

'Maybe you're still in shock?' Laura says gently.

'No, not now. I was. But now I need Guy Ward to pay for what he did and to move on with my life; to start living, rather than existing.' She takes a deep breath. 'There's a reason I called. I've had quite a day.'

Beth can hear Laura's gasps over the line as she relays the conversation with Gemma in the park that afternoon. 'I don't know what I expected – it was never going to go well, was it? And now I've lost a friend. Worse than that, if Gemma tells Guy about the conversation, he could come after me.'

'Christ, Beth. I never even thought of that. Love, we have to go to the police – and soon.'

Beth steels herself, knowing she is about to drop another, bigger bomb. 'I'm afraid there's more. I went round to Dad's after meeting Gemma. Laura, he knows.'

There's a long pause on the line. Beth can picture her pensive expression. 'What do you mean, he knows?' Laura says eventually.

'He got upset and tearful. He said he'd always suspected.'

'*How*? Why did he?' Laura wails, 'Surely not… not our dad?'

'Guy's father Alastair told him something soon after it happened. The whole family took a cottage for the summer holidays, and then Guy was sent away to school in Surrey. Don't you remember? Nobody talked about it, he just disappeared.'

'Yes,' Laura whispers. 'So, why the hell didn't Dad do anything?'

'He… he didn't want to put me through all the potential trauma after I'd already been ill. He seemed ashamed… I've never seen him like that before. Laura, I'm not sure I can face him again.

Something broke today, you know? Dad was always my hero, but now—'

'You might feel differently once the shock has worn off a bit. Beth, I'm so sorry, for *all* of it – but mostly for being a shit sister.' Laura sniffs.

'We've been through all this. You didn't know… *I* didn't know. There's only one person to blame and that's Guy Ward. I'm taking him down, Laura. My mind is made up.'

*

On Tuesday morning after a surprisingly good sleep, rested, lucid and aware that Nessa's tolerance and goodwill must surely be at breaking point by now, Beth had telephoned her boss.

'Beth! What the hell is going on? I've been so worried about you after your sister emailed me last week. How's it going? When are you coming back?'

Beth had sighed deeply. 'Look Nessa, I'm really grateful for the time off and I'll tell you everything – but I need the rest of this week off. Unpaid leave, whatever… I'm sorry. Trust me. It's important.'

'Okay, well… keep me posted. But, Beth, I can't just keep your job open indefinitely, we're majorly busy here. Good luck with whatever you're dealing with,' Nessa had said, sounding resigned.

*

Galvanised by her father's version of events, the photographic evidence from his attic and her own – now vivid – recollections from the party and her attack, Beth spends the next two days creating a case file on her laptop. Keeping her notes methodical, factual and as devoid of emotion and speculation as possible, she creates a detailed timeline of events and lists as many partygoers as she can remember. Setting everything out in black and white gives her a sense of order and progress and after two days, Beth has created a weighty document and is pleased with her work.

Meanwhile Laura fusses like a mother hen, ringing or texting twice a day, keeping watch, her loving presence reassuring.

Gemma on the other hand is conspicuous by her silence. By Wednesday morning, a niggling doubt had snaked its way into Beth's mind about Gemma's own safety. Beth phoned twice within a couple of hours, but her calls clicked straight through to voicemail. Beth thought back to recent conversations with Gemma; how she'd alluded to the conflict at home, complaining about Guy's mood swings and obsessive, sometimes cruel, behaviour.

How safe was Gemma, really? Supposing – God forbid – she confronted him about her own allegations of rape. How would Guy react and what desperate measures would he take next?

Beth forced herself to push her concerns to the back of her mind; to focus on her own case.

By Thursday lunchtime, finally convinced that her seventeen-page document is comprehensive enough to pique the interest of local police detectives, Beth breaks for lunch.

She stretches her arms over her head and arches her back, realising that for the last two and a half days, she's done nothing but hunch over her laptop. Famished, she fixes herself a plate of cheese on toast and carries it to the sofa, the aroma of the cheddar making her mouth water. She's poised to take a bite when her mobile rings and Laura's name lights up the screen.

Tempted to ignore it but caving on the third ring, Beth puts her plate aside.

'Hi, Laura, how are you?'

'Turn the TV on. ITV local news – quick!'

Beth grabs the remote and lands on channel three, in time to catch the end of a news item about a missing person in East Sussex.

'What? What am I looking at?' Beth asks, nonplussed.

'I... I'm going online in a minute to google it... but Beth, I think it's Gemma Ward. Her car was found at Beachy Head this morning. The report said she'd last been seen early on Wednesday morning, and that her husband had raised the alarm last night when he couldn't reach her. The news said "police are treating the woman's disappearance as suspicious", and that CCTV cameras had picked up a small child inside the vehicle.'

Beth drops the phone as though scalded. *Suspicious*: what did that even mean? No, this cannot be happening. What on earth would Gemma be doing at Beachy Head with Miya? And yes, it was a suicide haunt, but it was ridiculous to think that Gemma would take Miya there, and...

Beth picks the phone up off the sofa. 'You still there, Laura?'

'Yes. Look, that's all I know. I'm going online now, see if I can find out anything else. Love, I don't know what to say... I'm so sorry... I'll call you later.'

Then Beth is tapping the keys of her laptop, her heart racing. She shudders as a cold numbness creeps through her body.

Police are treating the woman's disappearance as suspicious.

Wild scenarios begin to crowd Beth's head: Gemma, confronting Guy, asking him outright if he'd raped Beth all those years ago. Guy, cornered, lashing out, full of rage and denial, before dragging his family off to the coast.

Unless... Beth feels a stabbing pain in her chest... Gemma had driven to Beachy Head of her own free will, taking Miya with her, with the intention of ending their lives.

Beth's fingers fly over the keyboard, the headlines rolling up before her eyes; consistent, almost identical, each news hub regurgitating the story direct from the wire.

More chilling is the photo that accompanies the media links: a white Range Rover, spattered by mud, one rear door left open, a child's car seat visible, and beside it, a discarded small pink wellington.

'No!' A sob escapes Beth as she recognises one of Miya's favourite wellies. The vehicle's registration number has been pixelated but she already knows that she is looking at Gemma's car.

She clicks the link and starts to read, tears blurring the type.

There is growing concern today for the wife and daughter of wealthy entrepreneur and media pundit, Guy Ward. Mrs Gemma Ward (34) and the couple's six-year-old daughter were last seen at 06.00 hrs on Wednesday morning as Mr Ward left for work. The businessman raised the alarm on Wednesday night when he had failed to contact his wife, and her car (a white Range Rover) had been tracked to Beachy Head on the East Sussex coast. No sightings of Mrs Ward or her daughter have yet been reported and a spokesman for Sussex Police commented that they are treating Mrs Ward and her daughter's disappearance as suspicious, given the location of the abandoned vehicle...

Unable to read another word, Beth slams her laptop shut, staggers to the bathroom on marshmallow legs and splashes her face with cold water.

When will this nightmare end? How could Gemma do such a thing?

She pictures her friend's face at their last meeting, before she'd hurried away, hurt and angry, tears welling in her eyes.

Beth studies her reflection, guilt washing over her in a cold, damp wave. Is she responsible for this? Had Gemma been so devastated by her accusation that she'd driven for over two hours to a beauty spot tragically best-known for being a jumpers' point? She pictures Gemma, weeping and desperate as she leads a struggling and protesting Miya towards the cliff's edge—

Beth lurches over the toilet bowl and succumbs to the bile rising in her throat.

CHAPTER FIFTY-FIVE

Gemma

Gemma had stumbled her way through Tuesday, unable to eat, sleep or focus on anything for the utter panic jangling inside her head.

In the space of a few hours, her whole world had imploded.

At first, Beth's story had seemed far-fetched, incredible – born entirely out of her depression and anxiety, not to mention time spent with a fanciful therapist who clearly had an overactive imagination! And the saddest thing was, Beth really believed it. Gemma had seen it in her friend's eyes; fear, sadness – and a genuine regret as she'd broken the news in all its grim detail.

But that evening, Guy had dropped a bomb of his own: the revelation that he'd put a tracker on her car. His threat, *no matter where you are, I'll find you,* had chilled her to the bone.

And in that moment, Gemma had felt any last fragment of hope for her marriage get swept away like a leaf in a storm drain.

Guiltily, she'd pictured Beth then, pale and drawn, looking thin and angst-ridden as she'd screwed up all her courage to tell Gemma that she was married to a rapist. Rejecting the idea had been knee-jerk: how could Beth's allegation possibly be true? Guy could be a bully, manipulative and coercive – and recently, even physically violent. But a rapist?

And yet something about the coldness with which he'd uttered the words, before peering calmly into the fridge and demanding dessert, as if they'd been discussing some trivial domestic matter already forgotten, had made Gemma realise that she was married to a stranger. Somebody she barely recognised.

Somehow, Gemma had managed to get through Tuesday evening, careful not to irritate Guy by sticking to neutral topics of conversation like Miya's school, his work and vague plans for a weekend she doubts they'll see together.

'Oh, I almost forgot to tell you,' Guy had announced as he'd settled down to watch the ten o'clock news with Gemma beside him, 'I'll be leaving at six o'clock tomorrow morning. I've got a breakfast meeting with a potential investor then I'll be going straight into a board meeting until lunchtime.'

Gemma had placed a hand over his then. 'Bless you, Guy. You work much too hard,' she'd said, with a convincing tenderness she did not feel.

*

On Wednesday morning, Guy had left for work early, reminding her about his schedule.

'Darling, my mobile will be off until lunchtime so if you need me urgently give Martha a call and she'll hook me out of the board meeting, okay? Love you, Gem. Bye.'

Still in her robe, Gemma had kissed Guy at the front door. 'Love you, too. Drive safely,' she'd called. 'I'm sorry, don't hate me,' she'd whispered, waving until he'd turned out of Darwin Drive.

Next, she'd made herself a strong coffee before going to her laptop and emailing the school, explaining that Miya had the first signs of chickenpox and wouldn't be in for a few days.

Then she'd paced listlessly from room to room, eyes sweeping and fingertips caressing the fabric of her beautiful house – the *home* she and Guy had created together, its trappings of wealth and success now just the shiny veneer of a life no longer tenable.

Hearing her daughter's footfall overhead, she hugs Miya good morning, breathing in her warm caramel smell, and trying to quell the panic rising inside.

'Ow! Mummy, you're squeezing me too tight.' Miya complains, wriggling out of her grasp. 'Where's Daddy?'

'He's already left, sweet pea. He needed an early start today,' Gemma says, turning away so that Miya can't see the tears that have sprung into her eyes. 'Anyway, I've got some exciting news,' she adds brightly, 'you and I are going on a girls' adventure. We're taking a little road trip.'

Miya's eyes widen. 'But what about school?

'All good. I just sent them an email and they said it was fine.' It is a half-truth and will have to suffice.

'Yay!' Miya, jiggles from foot to foot, her questions tumbling over each other. *Are they going to the seaside? Will they see Aunt Marina? Will it be sunny? Can she take her iPad?*

'Wait and see – it's a surprise,' is all Gemma can manage through the plum-sized lump in her throat.

An hour later, they are in the car and bound for the A23.

'Mummy, where are we?' Miya says, fidgeting in her booster seat and gazing at the horizon. 'Ooh, look! I can see the sea!'

Gemma regards her daughter in the rear-view mirror. 'Yes. We're nearly there, sweet pea. You've been asleep for ages.'

'Nearly *where*?'

'Oh, somewhere exciting. I told you, we're having an adventure.'

That Miya had slept since the Purley Way had been a huge relief. Fielding her daughter's questions, thinking about Guy's reaction when he discovered they'd gone *and* driving safely for over two hours had seemed insurmountable, but somehow, Gemma had kept it together, her big comfortable car gobbling up the miles while the sky grew bluer and brighter as they advanced towards the south coast.

Ahead, it looks as though the edge of the world is rising to meet them as the sea sparkles beyond.

And it might as well be.

Gemma looks back at Miya again, her beautiful, innocent face alive with excitement in anticipation of their big adventure.

Gemma's eyes burn with unshed tears as she approaches the Beachy Head car park. If there were any other way... *any* alternative to this.

But Guy had left her none. He'd made her a virtual prisoner, casting himself as her jailer; a man she no longer loved, a man she was afraid of. Why couldn't he just accept that their marriage was over, but that they could continue to live apart as loving, responsible parents?

Knowing that Guy will track her car to this very spot, Gemma pictures his face, hollow with confusion, pain and, later, grief.

'Are we going to the beach, Mummy?' Miya sings from the back seat.

'In a way,' Gemma chokes on her words. Guy has left her no choice. It has to end this way.

Scanning the almost deserted car park, Gemma waits for a couple in their fifties to load an arthritic German shepherd into a dusty hatchback and drive away. Only one other vehicle remains.

'Come on, sweet pea, let's walk along the cliff tops – blow some cobwebs away.' Gemma unbuckles Miya from her seat and helps her down from the car.

'*Then* can we go on the beach?' Miya implores, adding, 'Oh, my welly got caught. Wait, Mummy!'

Not trusting herself to speak, Gemma drags Miya by the hand, barely registering the snagged wellington boot and ignoring her daughter's protests.

Vision blurred by tears, Gemma steers Miya to the chalky ledge as the wind sails around them and seagulls wheel overhead.

'Wow! We're on the top of the world,' Miya says, screwing her face up against the wind and sun.

'Or the bottom,' Gemma whispers, tightening her grip on Miya's hand. She looks down, hypnotised by the pull of the cold grey sea as it exhales its lacy foam onto the shingle below.

'Too close, Mummy – we're too close,' Miya cries.

CHAPTER FIFTY-SIX

Gemma

'Yes, much too close,' a voice echoes, 'it's easy to slip and fall.' A weathered hand tugs at Gemma's arm and gently pulls her back.

She turns to meet Marina's china-blue eyes. 'Auntie. God, am I pleased to see you. Is the coast clear?'

'There's not a soul around,' Marina says, stepping back from the edge and smiling at Miya, who beams happily.

'Hello, Auntie! How did you know we're having an adventure today?'

'Oh, I know lots of things. Come on, let's go to my house.' They walk briskly to the car park, peeling off to the far end where Marina's red Polo waits. She winks at Miya. 'Now poppet, we're going to play a game. Do you think you can hide for me?' Miya scrambles into the back seat, and lays flat, while Marina pulls a travel rug over her great niece. She turns to Gemma. 'Don't worry, my love. I'm only ten minutes from here and I'll drive very carefully. Right, all set?'

Gemma takes a deep breath. 'Not really… let's go before I lose my nerve.'

Tears of sadness mixed with relief roll down her cheeks as Marina slowly drives past Gemma's gleaming Range Rover – now a symbol of her old life – one rear door left ajar as if abandoned in a hurry.

'I've left him, Auntie,' she whispers, taking a tissue from her handbag and wiping her eyes.

'Oh dear, Gemma, love. I thought as much when you rang this morning and asked me to pick you up here. I must say, hiding Miya in the back sounded a bit dramatic, you had me terribly worried.'

'Miya was asleep – I couldn't explain in case she woke up. Auntie, I didn't plan any of this, I just saw an opportunity and grabbed it.' She turns to check on Miya, curled up beneath the blanket, a swatch of silky hair peeking from the plaid.

Gemma blows her nose and straightens her back. 'I'll tell you everything as soon as my baby is out of earshot…'

CHAPTER FIFTY-SEVEN

Beth

On Thursday evening, only hours after the news of Gemma and Miya's disappearance had broken, Laura had appeared at Beth's door.

'Laura, just go away,' she'd said into the entry phone, 'I'm poisonous. You don't want to be anywhere near me.'

But Laura had stood her ground, looking straight into the monitor, her expression determined. 'Let me in, Beth. Or I'll just stand here and annoy you, like this…' She'd kept her finger on the buzzer then until Beth had relented and let her in.

'What do you want?' Beth's voice had been a hoarse whisper then, all fight gone, her throat raw from weeping.

'Beth, I know what you're thinking, but this isn't your fault.'

'Oh, trust me. This one's on me. I might as well have gone round to their house and shot the pair of them,' Beth had snarled bitterly, before reminding Laura about her meeting with Gemma in the park and bursting into fresh sobs.

'Beth, stop it. Really! You're not to blame for this. Yes, you told Gemma the truth about her shit of a husband, but you did it to protect her. How on earth could you know that she'd react like this? I mean, it's so *radical*. Why didn't she just leave him? Thousands of marriages break up every day and people move on… get past it. There'll be all sorts of reasons why she felt so trapped and desperate. Beth, you've got to believe that.'

'Yeah, but none as powerful as finding out her husband was a rapist. Laura, just go, will you? Mike and the boys need you more than I do right now. I'm not fit for company but thanks for caring. I know you mean well.'

Then Beth had hidden away in the flat, half expecting and totally dreading that Guy himself would get in touch, insane with grief, but no such call came.

And every time Beth contemplated leaving the house, to go for a walk or to buy food in her local high street, she pictured Gemma and Miya, hand in hand, jumping to their deaths, blonde hair flying, their cries snatched by the wind.

*

By Saturday afternoon, a degree of self-preservation has set in. Realising that there isn't so much as a dribble of milk or a biscuit left in the house, Beth showers, puts on clean jeans and an old hoodie and walks to the local shops. But it's too soon: every pretty young mother and daughter duo reminds her of Gemma and Miya, and after a quick trawl of her local Tesco spent throwing basics into a basket, Beth scuttles home, wondering if she'll ever feel normal again or whether she has just swapped one terrifying nightmare for another.

Nevertheless, by Saturday evening, revived by a ready meal eaten in front of the TV and two glasses of warming merlot, her thoughts return to Guy Ward – specifically to destroying him. Because despite all that has happened in the last week, Beth knows that for her own sanity, she must finish what she's started.

She goes into the kitchen, noticing how stale and grubby it has become, and vows to clean up the following morning. Then she washes the few bits of crockery she's used, guiltily pours herself a third glass of wine and returns to the sofa.

She picks up the substantial case file she has created and scans its pages. Can she really press on with trying to make a case against

Guy Ward for something that happened twenty-five years ago? Isn't losing his wife and daughter punishment enough?

The memory of that night flickers like Super 8 film, jagged and stuttering. The roughness of the wolf's head, coarse against her cheek and throat; the searing pain in a place that had never been touched before, let alone viciously ripped open. The sound of other people having fun, the whine of the DJ's mic. Beth's shame and confusion as she'd crept away when it was all over—

The ringing of a phone sends her crashing back to the present. She picks up her mobile, doesn't recognise the number and wonders who can possibly be calling at ten twenty on a Saturday night.

Convinced it will be a wrong number, or – God help the caller – an overseas salesman or scam artist, she presses receive. 'Yes?'

There's only silence at first, the sound of someone breathing.

'Hello?' Beth barks, her irritation evident.

'Beth. It's Gemma.'

Beth's heart leaps into her mouth. '*What*? Who… who is this?' Who the hell would call and pull such a disgusting stunt?

'It's me, Gemma,' comes the voice, louder this time.

'No!' she pulls the phone back, re-examines the number. It's a landline with an area code she does not recognise.

'Beth, please. It's me, honestly. Just listen to me,' the voice is saying, 'and I'll prove it. Miya's middle name is Rose – she's fine by the way, and fast asleep – and her favourite colour is—'

'Gemma? Where are you? What the—' Beth's heart is racing so fast she can barely catch her breath.

'I'm really sorry I pretended to—'

'But where are you?' Beth asks finding her voice. 'Are you both safe? Gemma, I thought you and Miya were dead. God, I…' Tears spill down her cheeks.

'That was the general idea, I'm afraid. But I'm okay – and at my aunt's in Sussex. I'm so sorry, but it was the only way I could get away from Guy. Beth, I told him I was leaving him, and he put a tracker on my car. I didn't have time to warn you or make a proper plan. It must have been a terrible shock, hearing about us on the news like that. I'm sorry for scaring everyone.'

'It's okay.' Beth sniffs. 'You're alive – and Miya… That's all that matters now.'

'No, it isn't,' Gemma says, defiantly. 'I believe you – about what happened, and I'll support you. You must go to the police. Tell them everything you can remember about that night and then I'll come forward and tell them all about Guy's bizarre and controlling behaviour during the last six months or so. Beth, he's been abusing me. Trying to convince me that I'm addicted to pills and alcohol; spying on me; once, he almost broke my hand. Look, I'll explain everything another time. But I'm going to lie low for now, let him think I've gone until after the police have arrested him.'

Beth clears her throat, sobering up fast. 'Gem, the police might not be interested in anything I have to say. They may not even believe me… it's been twenty-five years since—'

'Oh, I think my disappearance will fan the flames. Guy will stink like four-day-old fish once you've told them what you know. Then when he's in police custody, I'll come back, saying I had to flee for mine and Miya's safety.'

Beth blows her nose. 'Why didn't you tell me? Gemma, you could have confided in me. We could have helped each other. Jesus, sometimes I was even *jealous* of you… I thought you had everything.'

There's a pause at the other end of the line and an intake of breath. 'You were Guy's friend before you were mine,' Gemma says, her voice cracking with emotion. 'I thought you'd side with him.'

'I… I don't know what to say. I hate that he hurt you, Gemma. It disgusts me. Just thinking about Guy… What he did to me – and to you – he mustn't get away with this.'

'Oh, we'll make sure he doesn't,' Gemma says with conviction. 'Look, I should go. It's late. Keep this number – it's Marina's landline. Obviously, I can't use my mobile. Keep me posted, but please, Beth, don't tell a soul about any of this.'

'I won't, I promise,' Beth says, her heart soaring as she ends the call.

CHAPTER FIFTY-EIGHT

Beth

Five weeks later

Beth is at her desk, drafting a press release when the call comes to her mobile. It's a London landline – the area code tells her that much.

'Hello, Beth Harding speaking,' she answers, knowing it could be any one of dozens of work contacts.

'Beth, it's DS Alice Holbrook.' A pause, an intake of breath. 'I wanted to update you.'

Beth grips the handset tightly as the memory of walking into Lewisham Police Station with Laura floods in. It's been over a month, but it's still raw, visceral.

She scans the room; none of her colleagues are paying any attention to her call, engrossed in their own tasks.

'Hello, DS Holbrook. Has something happened?' Beth croaks as sweat prickles under her arms.

'We've managed to locate and interview some of the guests from the party that night, using the list you provided. We've already spoken to Katie Mead – now Katherine Cooper – and another potential witness, someone already known to us, a Mr Kevin Binks,' DS Holbrook says. The irony of Binks assisting the police is not lost on Beth.

She looks up to find Ray inching closer and clearly eaves-dropping. 'Can you hold on, please. I need to find somewhere more *private*,' she says pointedly, striding out to the hallway and descending the stairs. 'Sorry about that. Are you still there?' Beth is on the street now, straining to hear the detective above the traffic.

'Yes. Beth, both Mr Binks and Katherine Cooper have been helpful concerning the events of that night – and have certainly given us enough information to continue our investigation. Unfortunately, the fancy dress shop closed down years ago and the owner, a Mr George Wales, is now in a care home, which means we've drawn a blank on the dress. Regardless, it was a family business so we've spoken to Mr Wales' daughter and asked her to get in touch if anything comes to light.'

Beth doesn't know what to feel. At the very least she is touched and encouraged by Holbrook's commitment. 'Right, thank you. Is there anything I can do?'

'Not at this stage, but I wanted to reassure you that we are taking your allegation very seriously and still have a number of people to interview. It was incredibly brave of you to report what happened all those years ago, and I promise you, I'll do my best to see that Guy Ward is brought to trial. But Beth, I have to warn you, without forensic or physical evidence and given the timescale, it's a long shot.' She clears her throat. 'It's unfortunate that we don't have something more current to go on – or someone else who could come forward to corroborate Mr Ward's violent behaviour.'

Beth's thoughts turn to Gemma. 'Any more news about his poor wife and daughter?' she murmurs.

DS Holbrook hesitates. 'The investigation into the disappear-ance of Gemma and Miya is ongoing, although there are strong indications of murder– suicide. But without either body—' The detective stops speaking abruptly. 'I'm sorry, that must be very distressing to hear, Beth.'

'It is,' Beth whispers. Her head swims, knowing that Gemma is alive and well is proving a hard secret to keep. But knowing, too, that Gemma plans to emerge from hiding *after* Guy is at least in police custody is frustrating, given that Gemma herself could help to put him there *and* dismantle his reputation.

'Sounds like you need a miracle,' Beth says, edging towards the street entrance to her office and conscious that Nessa must be missing her by now.

'A miracle, or a confession,' DS Holbrook sighs. 'Beth, keep the faith. I am on this. Successful, wealthy men like Guy Ward think they're untouchable – well, let's see, shall we?'

A lump comes into Beth's throat as she thanks the young detective and starts up the stairs to the office. A confession, or a miracle. Could she really hope for either? She resolves to phone Gemma that evening.

Beth slumps on the sofa, the phone pressed to her ear. 'They think it was murder– suicide,' she says, her tone flat. Saying the words out loud makes her feel queasy. It's painful to think of any mother leaping to her death and taking her child with her.

Gemma's voice is faint across the line. 'Oh, God. It's the most horrendous and terrible thought – but you do understand, don't you, Beth? Why I had to just disappear? Guy would never have let me leave and I couldn't take any more.'

'Yes, I totally get it. But perhaps now the police are taking my attack seriously and interviewing other people, potential witnesses, maybe it's time for you to break cover. Gem, come with me... Tell the police what you've told me about the coercion and bullying, not to mention the physical violence. For God's sake, he put a tracker on your car! The police will know that by now – your Range Rover has almost certainly been impounded as evidence.'

'But what if I talk to them and he comes after me? Who will take care of Miya then? I can't risk leaving her in Guy's hands, I really can't.'

Beth stands and paces across her living room. 'It won't come to that. The police will protect you, I know it.' She picture's Miya's sweet face. 'How is she?'

'Confused, upset. She misses her daddy… talks about him every day – and about why she's been off school for over a month. I'm on the verge of cracking, Beth. As lovely as it is here at the seaside with Marina, I don't know how much longer I can stay holed up here like a prisoner.'

'It's Guy who should be in prison,' Beth says, darkly.

*

Beth marvels at her own capacity to keep functioning normally – whatever that means – to keep up a daily routine of going to work and meeting deadlines, of speaking to Laura most days, of going to the pub on Friday nights; a thin veneer of ordinariness she feels could be blown away like dust at any moment.

She thinks of her father, alone, in the cavernous house she grew up in – the same house where she'd been brutally raped – and wonders if she'll ever feel ready to forgive him. Laura, a reluctant emissary caught between them, had done her best to broker peace and, on Beth's part, forgiveness.

'Beth, I know you feel massively let down,' she'd begun the last time they had seen each other, 'but Dad adores you, always has, so he obviously thought he was doing the right thing in not dredging everything up. He probably thought you'd been through enough already, what with your illness and everything. Imagine being chucked into a round of police interviews and social workers. You were so young. And anyway, it's not as though Guy's dad gave much away – just a drunken account of an incident involving Guy and a girl. There was never any talk of it being you.'

Beth had pressed her lips into a thin line of disapproval. 'Nice try. You talk a good game, Laura. But it was Dad's job to protect me. End of. Maybe I'll feel differently one day, but right now, I'm not ready to move on.'

'Beth, please… think about it. He misses you and he's old. Imagine how you'll feel if he becomes ill. You don't need guilt on your plate, on top of everything else.'

Well, don't guilt trip me, then, Beth had mused, whilst conceding that her sister may indeed have a point.

*

The following Friday, as five o'clock approaches, Beth is tidying her desk and shutting down her computer in readiness to leave when her mobile phone rings.

'I'll catch you up,' she mouths to Claire who gives her a thumbs up and mimes raising a drink to her lips.

This time, Beth identifies the caller, having stored the number in her contacts.

'DS Holbrook. What can I do for you?'

'Beth, hi. We got our miracle.' She can hear the satisfaction and triumph in the detective's voice. 'Let's just say that something has emerged that's enough to arrest Guy Ward. And, if it goes the way I think it will, to charge him.'

'*Oh*! What's changed?' Beth sits down carefully on her office chair, suddenly giddy. She slumps low in her seat, letting her hair fall around her face, aware that Nessa is lurking close by, ready to leave for the pub.

'As I said, a miracle – certainly a breakthrough. Look, I'll tell you all about it, but not here and not like this. Please, trust me.'

Beth falls silent as she lets the words sink in. This is really happening. One of her oldest friends could soon be prosecuted for her rape.

'So, what happens next?' she whispers through the lump in her throat.

'We'll arrest him tomorrow morning, at eight o'clock,' Holbrook says, 'nice and public as the neighbours are getting the milk and the papers in,' she adds, a gleeful, facetious edge to her voice.

Beth skips her regular Friday night visit to the Brickie, unable to face small talk and work banter with her colleagues. Only Nessa knows what she has been going through – and even then, just the barest facts. It is simply too raw, too private. In addition to the privacy aspect, Beth can't bear for people's perceptions of her to change; for them to think of her as a victim. She's already spent thirty-nine years walking around the planet, making a life for herself, without wearing any kind of badge or label, and is determined for that not to change.

This is *Guy's* shameful, disgusting secret, not hers. Knowing – *processing* – what had happened to her at such a tender age is proving to be a release, as though she has permission to seek justice and retribution, then move beyond it and get on with her life.

She has committed to weekly counselling with Zara for the foreseeable future; not for digging around in a dark and terrifying past, but for learning how to live with the consequences on a realistic level in the future.

After making her excuses to Nessa, Beth goes straight home and phones Gemma, eager to share DS Holbrook's news.

'I'd like to see Guy's face when they drag him out of *my* house and drive him away in a squad car!' Gemma says with an uncharacteristic hardness.

'Then why don't you? Leave Miya with your aunt, borrow her car and drive up tonight. My sofa's comfy enough… Not that either of us will sleep a wink with this hanging over us.'

'Beth, how can I? I'm dead, aren't I? Christ knows what will happen when I appear safe and well – I'll probably get charged for wasting police time and for perverting the course of justice or something.'

'No. That won't happen. Stick to your guns, Gem. You had no choice but to leave as you were in an abusive relationship and you feared for your own and your daughter's safety. It will be okay. It will all be okay, trust me,' Beth says, recalling DS Holbrook's words.

CHAPTER FIFTY-NINE

Gemma and Beth

Gemma sits up carefully as her unfamiliar surroundings fall into place. She stretches, the stiffness between her shoulder blades testament to a night spent on Beth's sofa.

She can hear the bubbling of a rising kettle and the clatter of a teaspoon on china before Beth appears with coffee and a packet of digestives. Ignoring the biscuits, Gemma gratefully accepts the mug offered to her and takes a sip.

Daylight floods in as Beth opens the curtains. Hair askew and face pale, her smile is uncertain. 'Morning, Gem. Did you get any sleep at all?'

Gemma rubs her eyes. 'Yes, a bit. You?'

Beth shakes her head, motions for Gemma to make space beside her on the sofa. 'Not really… bit of a broken night. Still can't believe this is happening.'

Gemma inhales sharply. 'I know. One minute I feel sick and guilty as hell… all those years married to Guy – Miya's dad, for Christ's sake. I have to keep reminding myself how vile and crazy he's been acting for the last six months. And as for what he did to you—'

'Don't think about it. Are you sure you want to be there when the police pick him up?' Beth asks softly, draining the last of her coffee.

Gemma nods. 'Yes. I just want to get it over and done with.'

Beth reaches for her phone and checks the time. 'Right, we'd better get dressed and out of here. We need to be in place before eight o'clock.'

'Okay, pull over here – nobody uses this space,' Gemma says, indicating a narrow strip of paving at the entrance to Darwin Drive.

'All right.' Beth parks close to the kerb. She can see apprehension in Gemma's eyes, her chest rising and falling beneath her thin sweater. She takes Gemma's hand, grips it firmly. 'Look, we're okay. We've both been treated like shit by this man and we need to hang on tight to that. Here, put this on.' She hands Gemma an old baseball cap she hasn't worn for years. 'You need to tuck your hair right under… Yeah, that's good.'

Gemma scootches down in her seat, pulls the cap lower.

Then the women watch in silence as two marked vehicles pull up outside the Ward house at eight o'clock sharp, just as DS Holbrook had predicted. Five officers emerge and three of them stride up the driveway while two pass through a side gate – presumably to stop anyone leaving via the back exit.

Beth and Gemma's eyes meet briefly, round with shock and awe.

'Is this really happening?' Gemma says, her lower lip trembling. She looks around at the neatly manicured enclave that is Darwin Drive. Several of her former neighbours have come out of their houses and are openly gawping at the police entourage, agog as to what horrific tragedy has befallen the Ward household this time.

And then, despite being incognito, Beth and Gemma spring upright in their seats as Guy answers the door. They both gasp at his changed appearance. Frail and dishevelled, he is haggard and unshaven, pain and sleeplessness etched into the bones of his face. It's clear he's lost weight. *The grief diet*, Gemma thinks darkly.

They watch in silence as Guy staggers back, his expression shocked and bewildered, his shadowed eyes round with alarm as two male officers explain the reason for their visit. And they can't hear the words, but Guy is shaking his head and protesting, his hands raised either in submission, or to ward off the officers as handcuffs are snapped on and he is led towards one of the waiting vehicles.

The next few hours are a waiting game, with Gemma becoming spooked and agitated.

'We can do this, Gem. We've got each other's backs,' Beth says, amazed at how calm she feels. 'Remember why we're here. That man – your husband – raped a thirteen-year-old child. And don't even start me on the way he's treated you for months. We deserve better. *Miya* deserves better.'

'But what if I end up going to jail for faking my own suicide? What about Miya then?'

'Oh, Gemma, love; we've been through this. It won't come to that. Anyway, I trust DS Holbrook. I told you, she's had a breakthrough… some vital piece of evidence that could get him locked up. And you know, if he doesn't go to prison for what he's done, there'll be other routes we can go – starting with you bringing an injunction against him, to stop him going anywhere near you or Miya. We could even file a private prosecution… Oh, I don't know… But whatever way you look at it, Gemma, Guy's life is *over* – or it might as well be.'

It had turned four o'clock by the time Beth and Gemma had found the courage to walk into Lewisham Metropolitan Police Station.

There'd been a delay while DS Alice Holbrook was sent for; time spent drinking weak tea from cardboard cups in an airless room, watched by two male and one female officer, who'd clearly been briefed to keep them company but not to begin the interview without Holbrook.

And once it became evident that Gemma was indeed the missing East Sussex woman, a rapid chain of internal communication had ensued.

To her credit, Holbrook had played the whole thing down, claiming to understand Gemma's predicament at once. Then the women had been separated with Gemma taken to one incident room to report her abuse at Guy's hands, while Beth had been escorted to another where DS Holbrook waited, her eyes keen and alert.

*

Holbrook pats the thick file in front of her. 'We picked Ward up this morning. He's being interviewed as we speak,' she says. 'That was quite a stunt his wife pulled. Christ, she must have been desperate. Do you think Gemma will testify if we get to court? Of course, I will make sure she's protected in the meantime.'

Beth says nothing of witnessing Guy's arrest with her own eyes; instead she nods and confirms that Gemma is prepared to go to court. 'You mentioned you'd had a breakthrough… a miracle, you said. Can I ask what it was?'

DS Holbrook shoots a look at her junior officer, a fair-haired man with a cherubic face who looks barely out of his twenties and who, as yet, has said nothing other than to introduce himself.

'It was the dress.' It's a simple statement of fact, as though there'd been an inevitability about it.

'You mean—'

'Your fancy dress costume. The Snow White get-up. It's currently with forensics and there's a chance we'll find Ward's DNA on it.'

Beth inhales sharply. 'But… how? That's impossible… it was twenty-five years ago. I mean, I can't believe the dress even survived, let alone any…' *Blood and semen* are the words she cannot bring herself to use.

'You remember the fancy dress shop? As I explained, the owner is in a care home now, but Pauline Wales, his daughter, contacted us two days ago. She said that most of the costumes from her father's shop were still in her summerhouse at her home – that she couldn't bear to get rid of them for sentimental reasons. Beth, she's recovered the outfit you were wearing when the attack took place and it's currently being scrutinised by our forensic team for DNA. They'll be looking for blood, semen, skin cells; anything that can link that dress to Ward.'

'But it would have been washed and repaired. Nothing could survive... surely?'

'DNA can and does. A fabric like that would have been washed or dry-cleaned gently and at a low temperature. And as for the passage of time... Beth, cold cases going back decades are being solved all the time because of the technological advances we've made in recent years.'

Beth doesn't trust herself to speak. It all seems so unreal and farfetched.

'The thing is, we need to box clever,' Holbrook continues, glancing again at her colleague. She opens the file in front of her and takes out a 10x8 print of the Snow White costume; Beth winces at the sight of it.

'I believe seeing photos of the dress could trigger a confession,' Holbrook says, tapping the print with her index finger. 'Because as far as Ward's concerned, his wife and child are dead and as soon as the rumour mill cranks into life, following his arrest today, his reputation will be in shreds. There's a good chance he'll break down and confess everything – regardless of what we find on the dress.'

Beth exhales. 'Well... I don't know what to say... That's... incredible. May I have some water, please?' she says, as the room begins to spin.

CHAPTER SIXTY

Gemma

Three months later

At Darwin Drive, after parking her gleaming red Mini, Gemma pauses before entering her former home. Parched by the arid summer months, the front lawn is covered with browning petals from the magnolia tree, and the *For Sale* sign is listing perilously.

She steels herself to go inside, batting away the sense of loss she always feels on entering. Her regular visits 'home' – which Gemma always visualises in air quotes these days – have become as much a part of her routine as working at the small architect's practice three days a week, manning reception during Miya's school hours.

Starting upstairs, Gemma takes the tour, spritzing room fragrance as she goes, checking the carpets for dusty footprints, screwed-up tissues or any other debris dropped by potential buyers.

Today, satisfied that the house is picture perfect, Gemma strides through to the kitchen for a glass of water, only to be struck by a sole painting attached to the fridge by a magnet that says *Keep Calm and Carry On*. Miya's childish artwork depicts three figures: a tall man with dark curly hair and large black eyes, a woman, her yellow hair past her shoulders, and a child nestled between them, a half-moon grin on her round face. *My Family*, says the caption.

A lump rises in Gemma's throat. How had she missed this? She removes the painting and tenderly folds it into her handbag, before locking up and driving out of the close in the direction of her flat three streets away.

Finding a pleasant and cheaper home to rent that was still within Miya's school catchment had been a stroke of good luck and a huge relief. Gemma had been content with her ground floor flat, with its dated but cosy kitchen and French windows that opened onto a tiny patio garden. And it didn't matter that the rooms were small, or that she sometimes heard the music of her neighbour upstairs. She'd moved in a skeleton of furniture and personal effects for herself and Miya and made it their home, swapping space and grandeur for freedom and peace of mind.

Guy, meanwhile, had resolutely stayed put at home, denying the allegations of rape after his arrest and begging Gemma to come home to work things out following the shock revelation that she and Miya were alive and well and holed up in Sussex. But after two weeks of being doorstepped by journalists as he left for work every morning, and cold-shouldered by neighbours he'd called friends, Guy had finally conceded and moved out and was now sharing a flat in Kennington with a male colleague.

So now the beautiful house in Darwin Drive stood empty, a fact which didn't help its saleability at all.

The estate agent had been sheepish the last time Gemma had chased him about the lack of progress. 'Mrs Ward; it's not the house that's the problem, it's your husband – or rather, what the media is saying about him. I'm afraid people can be rather squeamish about such things. Perhaps after the trial, when things have settled down a bit – whatever the outcome – the right buyer will come forward. In the meantime, I can assure you we're doing our best.'

Gemma's sigh had been deep and heartfelt. 'All right. Drop the price then – do whatever you need to do. We all need to move on… I can't cope with the house hanging over us for much longer.'

*

After picking Miya up from school and feeding her fish fingers and spaghetti hoops (her current favourite), Gemma texts Beth and invites her over. At once, Beth replies her ETA of seven o'clock.

Gemma's eyes widen in delight as she opens the door. 'Hiya! How are you, love? Gosh, you look *well*,' Gemma exclaims, taking in Beth's glossy new haircut and colour.

'Aubergine,' Beth explains, pecking her friend on each cheek. 'Does it look all right? I wasn't sure.'

'You look like a pop star,' Miya says, reaching up to stroke Beth's shiny bob.

'Well, thank you!' Beth smiles and holds up an already chilled bottle of prosecco. 'Brought you this: we're celebrating.'

'Ooh, thanks! We are? What's the occasion?'

'Life!' Beth says, grabbing a tea towel and carefully twisting the cork until there's a muffled pop. 'New hair…' she pauses and winks at her friend, 'and new job. I got it! Head of PR for that children's charity I told you about.'

Gemma grabs Beth by the shoulders, shrieking her congratulations. 'I knew you would! Well done. Here's to new beginnings,' she says, her eyes glassy with emotion.

After Miya has gone to bed, they sit nestled on the sofa, finishing up the wine and snacking on crisps and carrot sticks.

'You've done well, Gemma,' Beth says, nodding her admiration. 'You've already made this place so homely for you and Miya. How's she doing?'

Gemma takes a ragged breath. 'She's okay. Clueless, of course. I've told her that Daddy's working away for a while. Not sure I can stretch that one much longer if Guy gets convicted after the trial…' Her eyes search Beth's. 'We both know it's a long shot… How will you cope if Guy doesn't go down?'

Beth shrugs. 'I'll be okay with it. Some might say Guy's been punished enough. He's lost everything: his wife and daughter, his beautiful home, his friends… I read online that even his business is in trouble.'

'It is. Which is why I want my share of the house and then a clean break. My divorce lawyer assures me that Guy won't contest any existing assets; there's Miya to think of, after all.'

'The weird thing is,' Beth says, her gaze distant, 'now I know the truth, I can deal with it… all of it. My new job, you living here, even making up with Dad… it all feels like a fresh start. Hey, did I tell you, Laura and I are meeting two landscape gardeners at Dad's tomorrow afternoon?' Beth drains her glass. 'There's something I need to do.'

EPILOGUE

Beth

It's one twenty by the time the branded van pulls up outside their father's home.

'I hope their gardening skills are better than their time keeping,' Laura remarks, moving towards the front door. Then Beth hears an exchange concerning where they've parked, the tools they've brought and using the side gate for access.

Beth turns to her father. 'Are you sure about this, Dad?'

Tim nods. 'Absolutely. Just cut the bloody thing down.'

'Right, shall we?' Beth says, shepherding her father into the garden as Laura appears through the side gate, two men in overalls in her wake, pointing out features of the vast and overgrown garden as they go.

'Smashing space – not often we get to work on a big old garden like this. No wonder it's gone to seed,' one of them is saying to Laura.

Beth steps forward, introduces herself and greets the men. 'And this is our father, Tim Harding. It's his home. So, as per my email then… you know what needs to be done. Whenever you're ready.'

The taller of the two men nods in Tim's direction. 'Leave it to us, sir. Soon get it looking respectable again.'

Then both men are hard at work, the whine of their power tools shattering the Saturday afternoon peace, as they saw, clip and mow their way through the dense, overgrown garden.

Lastly, they tackle the high hedge that wraps its way around the compost heap, and the sweet scent of leylandii – pine mixed with nutmeg – fills the air as great swathes of foliage come crashing down.

A LETTER FROM BEVERLEY

Dear reader,

I want to say a huge thank you for choosing to read *Close My Eyes*. If you enjoyed it and want to keep up to date with all my latest releases, just sign up at the following link. Your email address will never be shared, and you can unsubscribe at any time.

www.bookouture.com/beverley-harvey

Close My Eyes is my second psychological thriller and my fourth novel overall. For the location, I revisited my childhood home of Beckenham, a leafy south-east London suburb and the surrounding area. The idea of taking a seemingly gentle and happy upbringing like Beth's, and placing a dark, forgotten secret at the heart of it appealed to me. Likewise, the unravelling of what appeared to be the perfect marriage in Gemma's story – the old adage is true: no one knows what goes on behind closed doors.

I hope you loved *Close My Eyes*, and found yourself rooting for Beth and Gemma, and if you did, I would be very grateful if you could write a review. I'd love to hear what you think, and it makes such a difference helping new readers to discover one of my books for the first time.

I love hearing from my readers – you can get in touch on my Facebook page, through Twitter, Goodreads or my website.

Thanks,
Beverley Harvey

 Beverley Harvey Author

@BevHarvey_

beverleyharvey.co.uk

ACKNOWLEDGEMENTS

A big thank you to my patient and hardworking editor, Therese; thanks to Kim and Noelle, the best PR team in the business, as well as being successful authors in their own right; and another thank you to all at Team Bookouture – I am so grateful to you all.

Love and thanks to my family (and unofficial fan club) and a huge thank you to Mark: always positive, always encouraging. Last word goes to Brodie, my gorgeous terrier, who keeps me sane by just being there and who helps me problem-solve on our long muddy walks.

Printed in Great Britain
by Amazon